The Heirloom Girls

a novel

Chris Culler

ISBN: 0692635211
ISBN 13: 9780692635216
Library of Congress Control Number: 2016901898
Cullerful Imprint * Venice, California

The Heirloom Girls

Contents

To Douglas
With love and gratitude for our
"One Hundred Year Marriage."

And in memory of my grandmothers
Daisy Culler, Annabelle Culler, and Juanita Hyatt.
I'm beginning to understand.

"The best protection any woman can have is courage."

- Elizabeth Cady Stanton -

The Storm

Late afternoon

*H*urricane Sandy whirls across the Atlantic in a wide arching hook toward the eastern seaboard, a howling banshee blustering and punching against the shore. Scarlet leaves explode from the branches of a maple and swirl past the Stars-and-Stripes straining and tearing against its flagpole as if begging to be set free. Maya Jones doesn't park her father's Land Rover so much as slam its fender against the curb and jump out. Wind pummels her jacket. She tucks her head under her hoodie and runs toward the entrance of the Sea View Nursing Home. A rickety lawn chair slides across the handicap ramp and slams against the window where the pale worried faces of elderly men and women peer out. And just beyond, the dark sea swells high and ominous behind Rockaway Beach Promenade.

Maya darts inside with a mission. She is a Twenty-First Century American girl as myriad as the rainbow tattoo caressing the slope of her bare brown shoulder, a girl who cannot be categorized as white, black or Hispanic. She is the sort of girl who does not say, "someone should do something" but rather the kind who *will* do something, which is more than one can say of the mayor who has decreed the elderly should stay put and ride out the storm.

Inside on the third floor, Maddy Rosario grips her walker and imagines a girl riding a whale right out on Jamaica Bay. The Whale Rider reminds her of something important hidden within this room, but its location remains elusive, beyond the grasp of her 105-year-old memory.

Suddenly her great granddaughter bursts in, slips into the bathroom, and emerges holding a toothbrush and robe. Raindrops sparkle in her black curly hair.

"Grandma, where's your pajamas?"

"I sleep in the nude!"

"Not at Mom's house you won't!"

Although reduced to the physical embodiment of an asexual old woman, Maddy responds with a small smirk of defiance.

"We're packing in two minutes and going," Maya says, "So pick what's most important."

"I need one thing, one thing only." She holds her finger to her chin in a facsimile of The Thinker. "But oh, dear, I cannot recall…"

"What, Grandma, what?"

Maddy wheels her walker across the room and points to the ornately framed oil painting of a beautiful woman wearing a deep blue sumptuously velvet dress.

"That," she says, her finger zeroing in on the silvery brushstrokes of a crystal pendant dangling from a chain upon the woman's velveteen breast.

"The amulet?"

"Yes! But damn-it-all, I don't know where I put it!"

Wind shakes the building and windows rattle. Maya's heart thunders impatiently. How grim it must be, she thinks, when your brain becomes a sieve of forgotten thoughts.

"Oh, Grandma," she sighs. To her the amulet, this so-called family heirloom, isn't worth the futile expenditure of time it will take to search through the Indian artifacts, Afghan tapestries, Parisian deco and Venetian glassworks accumulated in her great grandmother's long life. As far as she sees it, no piece of jewelry, no matter how coveted and desired, can justify the long-standing rivalry that has existed among the women in her family.

"Let's at least take your mother's portrait."

Maya lifts the picture of the woman with celadon eyes, rumored by some to have been painted by John Singer Sargent.

"My dear mother," Maddy wistfully agrees, watching as she carries the precious oil painting toward the bed. The glistening representation of the pendant beams upon Maya at eye level. Refusing to be drawn to the amulet's mysterious beauty, she covers the jewel with the bright stripes of a Pendleton blanket, wraps the entire painting like a Szechuan dumpling, and slips it into a pillowcase.

"Okay, let's go." But her great grandmother is leaning over her walker, her gnarled hand reaching across a mirrored vanity. Speckled with age spots, the hand bypasses dusty French perfume bottles and framed sepia-toned photographs and with thin shaking fingers pulls open a tiny mahogany drawer. Maya joins her and together they peer inside at embroidered handkerchiefs and a single dried red rose.

A tree branch slams against the window and both women jump, automatically reaching for the other.

"Okay, that's it, time to go," Maya says, "I'll come back and find the heirloom later, Grandma." She snatches up the framed pictures – a young woman in a Victorian lace blouse, a World War I doughboy – and slips them into the pillowcase with the painting. "I promise."

From the thin wrinkled skin of her old worn face, Maddy's dark eyes shrewdly assess her sincerity. She nods, and when she does so her great granddaughter sees how it will be, how the jewel, this object of desire that has been in their family for generations, could very well be lost in the flotsam and jetsam of the storm.

Strong young arm hooked through skinny chicken bone one, they roll with the walker and pillowcase down the empty third floor corridor. Seawater puddles under abandoned wheelchairs and broken glass crunches underfoot. They step into the drafty elevator. Doors close with a troubling shake and they lunge down. Suddenly the elevator halts, unmoving, between floors. Maya hits the lobby button again. She slaps the red emergency one but there is no response, not a peep, and so she pounds all the buttons and still the elevator refuses to budge.

It dawns on Maya they could be trapped and she will have to stay calm for her grandmother's sake, but it is Maddy who is untroubled by their circumstance.

"*Don't worry, dear,*" she says, "*The doctor said Mother was an hysteric, but that was before the Whale Rider's gift changed everything.*"

1905
The "Hysterical Girl"

"The most common way people give up their power is by thinking they don't have any."

- Alice Walker -

Chapter 1

*F*or her own good, Madeline Gallacuty was confined to her room for six weeks and made to do nothing, think nothing, and eat soft, pale foods. The esteemed Dr. Thomas P. Wilson pronounced her a hysteric and her mother agreed, for Madeline was a nervous sort of girl consumed by wild passions and impulses. She cried over her needlepoint, complained of headache and other bodily pains, and exhibited no enthusiasm for the joys of domestic duty that made for a happy woman's life.

"Dear girl, you are experiencing puberty!" said the illustrious man of science, "The greatest event in a young lady's maturation to womanhood!"

Hefty arm encircling her slim seventeen year-old-waist, he told her she was suffering from cardiac inadequacy and chronic dyspepsia. As it was of utmost importance she conserve her limited resources for the full development of her uterus and ovaries, the wisest course of action *must* be The Cure. Curtail all activity. Receive no visitors. The doctor alone would monitor her progress daily.

And so it was that on the first week of The Cure, Madeline was to have no tea (too stimulating) or sweets (also too stimulating), and ordered to her bed. There were to be no more excursions to the library or talk of women's politics. No museums or attendances at public lectures. Made to drink milk and lie in partial darkness, she was instructed to read *The Twentieth Century Book For Every Woman* on how to Keep Thoughts High, for only by learning the art of Controlling the Thoughts could

9

she acquire The Girl's Treasure, which was A Beautiful Home Life, Her Husband's Affection, and Darling Children Of Her Own. No matter that she cried, paced, and pummeled the door, the household was ordered to ignore the young woman's entreaties, screams of temper and upended trays of food. It was a trying time for all.

"I demand complete obedience," the doctor told her on the third week of The Cure, and obedient she was out of some desperate hope of being released. Womanhood, it seemed, came with the price of Madeline's body being under the jurisdiction and rules of others.

Her will worn thin, she drank the dreaded milk with a goal to eradicate all that was fierce and furious within her. She struggled to understand in her heart the trueness of domestic tranquility. If she could become a giant uterus, perhaps the doctor would approve and declare her cured.

On the fourth week of The Cure, Madeline awoke from a fit of daytime dreaming to find the doctor seated upon her bed.

"You are a ripening fruit," he said, "A delicate budding rose. You must remember, young lady, that your body is produced by God in order for children to be born."

Sunlight filtered through the curtains and settled upon his hair, and she was struck by the sensation of lying beneath the raging cloud of a commanding male god. And yet the line of sweat beaded upon his temple was all too human, and his eyes wandered down her reclined figure.

"Wrong thoughts excite the blood vessels," he continued, "laying the foundation for disease of the reproductive organs. And so you must ask yourself, would you lose your capacity to be a good wife and mother by yielding to foolish temptation?"

Madeline knew not of what temptation he was speaking, although the doctor himself appeared highly agitated. He adjusted his posture. His pants appeared to constrict. He placed his damp hot hand upon her chest at precisely the instant the nurse entered with the glass of milk.

For once, Madeline was grateful for the despised beverage.

On the fifth week of The Cure, Madeline rose unsteadily to sit at the vanity and run a silver comb through her pale limp hair. As she did so she gazed upon an old photograph within a small oval frame. It was of her father's teenage half-sister who had mysteriously disappeared from their childhood home in New Zealand many years ago. She was of half Maori blood and severely dressed in Victorian lace, her posture that of a wounded creature. And yet the camera had captured a wild nucleus in her large sad eyes, as though she were looking beyond the photographer's lens directly into Madeline's very soul.

Afflicted by a familiar sensation of utter despondency, Madeline pulled her hair into a topknot and laconically searched inside one of the vanity's tiny drawers for a clasp. Instead she grasped what felt to be a small knickknack and withdrew an object folded within a piece of parchment. Unwrapped, the object fell into her palm:

It was a crystal pendant encircled by metallic filigree upon a silver chain, an ancient crafted piece of jewelry unlike anything she'd seen before. The paper into which it had been wrapped had words scrawled in a looping hand:

> *Know who you are.*
> *The Whale Rider*

How curious, she thought, and held the pendant up to the light. The crystal had a mysterious transparency and deep within the prism she glimpsed what appeared to be a metallic shard. Suddenly, as if from a mirror deep within, there appeared a fleeting reflection of her own face then just as swiftly her face was replaced by the visage another woman. The woman appeared clothed in the garments of a warrior, and then vanished to be replaced by the face of another woman, and another, one face rapidly superimposing over another until her aunt's dark eyes gazed out upon her before she too vanished into the crystalline depths and all the faces were gone.

Madeline's heart skipped and fluttered. She considered the doctor's diagnosis of cardiac inadequacy and yet she did not feebly creep back to bed. Instead she sat upon the window seat and turned the strange hallucinogenic pendant in her hand. Had it been an illusion? To whom had the pendant belonged? Not her mother. It originated from no shop she knew of. It was too ancient and unique, perhaps foreign, in design.

Then she remembered. She snatched up the photograph of her aunt and there it was below her aunt's white Victorian lace collar – the pendant.

Madeline slipped the chain over her head and with the crystal against her breast recalled how Papa had spoken of his boyhood in New Zealand as a distant dream. His older half-sister had been named Matilda by her white father, a sea captain whose Maori wife had died, leaving him with the little girl. The sea captain's second wife, Papa's mother, had also called her Matilda, and the girl had grown into a young woman who was sad and wild. She ran away, it was said, to "swim with the whales," leaving behind this one item for him to pass on as her legacy. And so the writing on the parchment was hers.

Know who you are.
The Whale Rider.

Madeline threw back the curtains and opened the window. Sunlight burst in and pierced the pendant's faceted prism at her breast. She breathed the fresh morning air and watched her father in his waistcoat leaving for the bank alongside other men carrying attachés, off to their business workdays. She saw her friend Hannah Amberfitch and her daughter Simone walking to the shirtwaist factory. Hannah's haggard face bore no resemblance to the picture of the Busy and Happy Mother in *The Twentieth Century Book for Every Woman*. Madeline thought of her own good fortune to have a proper home and education at Mrs. Sullivan's Finishing School, and fervently wished it for other girls who had been born with less but no less deserving of opportunity. And just as she was thinking about acquiring the means to improve the lives of Hannah and Simone, the nurse entered with the milk and oatmeal porridge, decried the dire consequences of too much stimuli, closed the curtains, and ordered her back to bed.

On the sixth and final week of The Cure, Madeline had a dream.

She was riding a fishing vessel alongside Dr. Thomas P. Wilson. A team of sports fishermen on board produced bait from their attachés. Permitted to fish at the rail beside them, Madeline felt a tug on her line and reeled in a large silver fish.

"I will dissect the fish and display its uterus," said the doctor.

She held the creature, cool and plump, and felt its vibrant life in her palm. Its gills gaped in the open air and she eased the hook from its mouth. The fish implored Madeline with its round, gelatinous eye.

She flung it back into the sea.

The sports fishermen howled with outrage and the doctor's howls were the loudest of all. And then the fish grew, and grew, becoming larger and larger still until it rose up into a giant whale and upon its back rode a naked woman with sun-darkened skin and hair flying wild.

Madeline awakened. Pendant swinging from her neck, she flung off her nightgown. She bathed at the sink bowl and dressed in a brown flared skirt with white cotton shirt and a high-stand collar. She slipped into a herringbone tweed jacket and placed upon her head the straw boater her mother despised.

There came the expected sound of a key in the lock, and in the looking glass she saw Dr. Thomas P. Wilson enter her room.

"I don't believe I heard you knock, Dr. Wilson," she said.

"What? What?" said the doctor, sounding less like an esteemed physician than a small barking dog.

"What? What?" she echoed then laughed with tickled, delighted joy. Her sick headache was gone and so were the sensations of uncertainty and foreboding. In the mirror she studied the crystal hanging from her neck and the boater upon her head. Hannah Amberfitch had such a hat. Hannah had spoken of a book called "The Woman's Bible" when they attended lectures together, but during the course of the doctor's Cure, Hannah was forbidden visitation. Deplorable, thought Madeline. She alone would decide who would visit. And who would not.

"It is time for you to leave my room, doctor," Madeline said to the esteemed Dr. Thomas P. Wilson.

"Young lady, you must return to your bed this instant!" the doctor replied.

"I have recovered," she replied, "I am in no more need of bed rest."

"No nervous disorder? No weakness of breath?" The man sounded sorely disappointed. "Surely you must feel pain in your feet. And what of dizziness? You *must* feel dizzy."

Madeline considered for a moment.

"No," she said, "Not dizzy. No pain." Deciding to soften him she added, "Your great Cure has worked miracles, doctor!"

She stepped past him before he could stop her, out, *out*, through her bedroom door. It was a delicious sensation to cross the threshold, dash along the hall and down the stairs. Behind her she heard her mother's cry of alarm, the doctor's threats.

Downstairs at the front vestibule, she opened wide the door to a Washington Square that never looked so thrilling with its carriages rumbling down the cobblestones and soaring leafy trees whipping in the wind and the sounds of the city, the wonderful noisy city, rising up to greet her in all its clashing inviting cacophony.

Chapter 2

*E*ven when autumn rain spattered the windowpane and blurred her striding form into a mottled impressionist painting, he could see she was a beauty. She wore a boater hat; pastel skirts billowed from a slim waist that bent like a willow in a breeze. Then one day she no longer came and he was afflicted with a brooding certainty she was forever gone. He wondered who she was, where she lived, and if she smelled of lavender. He was partial to lavender.

Jonathan Rosario was lonely for a woman who could soothe his heart and manage his home and bear him children. A beautiful woman upon whom he could rest his weary head after his long travels and who would say to him, "You wonderful man, you poor dear."

And then one day when rearranging the window display he looked up and found himself staring into her eyes. Up close, she was radiant. Skin porcelain white, cheeks flushed with exertion. She was alone, an apparition, he thought, wrought from his desire to see her again. Only when her breath formed a spot of moisture against the glass did he realize that she was real.

Suddenly a gust of wind blew her hat away and with no acknowledgment of having seen him, she ran off in pursuit.

Every fiber in his being told him that if he let her go he would never see her again, yet propriety forced him to stand rooted, watching behind glass. He observed how a draft from the hooves of a horse driven by a careless rider billowed and sprayed her skirts, nearly knocking her

15

down. She swayed, confused. She was in peril. He threw down his Mont Blanc pen and ran into the windy, noisy street, grasped her arm, and shouted angrily at the retreating horseman. Sweeping up her battered hat, he led her into the calm safety of his shop.

"Are you hurt?" he asked, although he could see she was simply unnerved, "Would you like a glass of water? Perhaps a little milk?"

"*No milk,*" she commanded.

Her voice was not as soft as he imagined it would be, and the realization of having at last seized her made him quickly withdraw his hand. Where was her mother? Her chaperone or companion?

He urged her to sit upon the velvet settee he was to deliver to Mrs. Hampton that day, and brought her water in a crystal goblet he had purchased in Murano. It was part of a set of six, and her hand shook so, he feared that she might drop it, but then he felt the quivering heat of her fingers brushing his, and gave no more thought to the goblet or any other object in the room. Her nervous breaths eased as she drank, and when she handed back the glass she smiled at him with an expression of genuine innocence.

"I was almost run over," she said, "and all for a silly hat. But I love this hat. It is not the sort of thing my mother approves of."

It was the hat of a rebel. Her blouse had a little bow tie that appeared mannish and odd, but while he considered women's fashions strange, he didn't dispute them. He suspected such a woman could be troublesome, but this wary observation quickly evaporated when he saw that her eyes were the pale celadon color of ancient bowls he had searched for through all of China.

"You have many lovely things," she said as she surveyed his merchandise, "My father would approve this shop. He owns a pair of authentic kangaroo dancing shoes."

"Yes?"

"From Australia."

"I see. Well, well!"

"This," she added, gesturing to a jewel that hung from a chain around her neck, "Is from New Zealand. It was his half-sister's and she has passed it on to me."

"Ah."

The gemstone glimmered with an unusual brilliance and he thought he saw something move within its prism, but as it rested upon her bosom he quickly looked away.

"I should like to own many of the things here," she said, "But must be frugal in my spending, for I aim to be an independent woman."

It was a forward thing to say but she did not appear aware of how it could be misconstrued.

"There is no need to purchase anything, Miss," he said. "Here, I'll wager you've never seen the likes of these miniatures."

Taking the keys from his waistcoat, he unlocked a desk drawer and produced a small wooden box. He removed the top of the box. Inside was a collection of shiny semi-precious stones carved into the shapes of animals no bigger than a thumbnail.

"How beautiful they are!"

On a daring impulse, he reached for her wrist and, feeling her quick pulse, turned her hand around to place a tiny green deer in her open palm.

"It's grazing on my lifeline," she giggled nervously.

"I purchased these from an old Pueblo woman," he said.

"You have been to the West?"

"Yes, indeed."

"I am going to the West someday," she declared.

"It is a dangerous place for a lady."

"I'm not afraid of danger. I am afraid of mediocrity."

It was a somewhat presumptuous remark for so seemingly gentle and sweet a girl, but then, she had most likely read the modern books and been to the lectures. He watched as she surveyed his shop more fully now, her eyes sweeping the room before returning to his and lingering. She is a vixen, he thought, a willful temptress, whether she knows it or not. Aware of his scrutiny, she lowered her eyes to the tiny stone deer on her palm then lifted it up higher to inspect. He too studied the carved ornament until the figurine lost focus and he saw instead the round pink hills of her lips. She did not smell of lavender, as he had imagined, but rather of something else. Milk perhaps.

"You may keep it, if you like."

"Oh, never! I couldn't separate him from the others."

"Then they are *all* yours," he announced magnanimously, and as she uttered appropriate expressions of surprise, hesitancy, and finally acceptance, he placed each little creature, one by one, into her open palms. There were eight in all, and he described each one as if telling a story to a child while turning them over in orderly succession: There was the garnet buffalo, the turquoise antelope, the agate horse, the yellow jackrabbit, the pink moose, the black bear and the green mountain lion.

"Do you see what you have done?" she said, "You have put them in a western scenario in which my thumbs are mountain ranges, and my heart lines rivers. You have unfurled a map of the southwest before me and now I need only travel there myself to experience it in reality."

"You have a restless imagination," he said, not certain if he meant it as compliment or judgment. She returned the tiny creatures to their box then lifted the pendant from her breast.

"And what do you think of this? As a procurer of unusual objects?"

Hesitating to stand close, he cautiously inspected the crystal jewel. A fleeting indecipherable visage moved inside, and he was struck with a feeling of sudden foreboding. He did not know if this was due to his strong attraction to the girl or the work of the strange stone into which he gazed, but he suddenly felt as though the status and stability of all things he knew was about to be upended.

"It is most unusual."

He said nothing more, for the object made him wary, he knew not why.

"I believe it has sent me a dream," said the girl with the celadon eyes. Then, as if he were in some way dismissed for his deficient answer, she abruptly thanked him for the gift and prepared to make her leave.

He placed his calling card inside the box holding the miniatures...

Rosario Imports — Jonathan Rosario

... and suggested she present the card to her father.

"I am Madeline Gallacuty," she said then added, "Come visit if you wish. We live in the brownstone with the mulberry tree on Washington Square across from the Arch."

The wind blew her skirt when she stepped into the street, affording him a glance of her stocking, and as she strode off with a spring in her gait that hastened to a buoyant trot, the hemline swung like the edges of an upside-down flower. A trolley obstructed his view. Then, in the distance, he saw her again, a flash of pale brown fabric, until her form vanished into the dappled colors of the busy afternoon street.

What a strange little woman she was! Frank and coy, hesitant and bold. He thought of how he would need to know her for the rest of his life simply to observe what she would do next.

Jonathan Rosario spent the afternoon in a state so agitated and exhilarated nothing would do but to walk the streets of the city. All about him there was motion and sound: The rumbling of the trains, the ferryboats tooting upon the river. Men sprinted jauntily by in silk derbies and ladies passed in groups with packages and impossible hats, though none chased theirs down in the street with the same abandon as Madeline had.

It was all Madeline, Madeline, Madeline, and the more he walked the more he heard her voice. "I am Madeline Gallacuty, Madeline Gallacuty, Madeline – " as though her name were skipping alongside him, moving faster with each stride, attaching itself to his very life force.

It was a most inconvenient time to fall in love. Tomorrow he would be on board a ship destined for Naples. There would be no canceling the voyage now; passage was already purchased.

Sunset cast its final brilliant light upon the front face of the buildings. Aggressive youths pushed onto the trolley. A matron hailed a carriage cab. And Jonathan Rosario's stride grew long with purpose.

Chapter 3

*I*t was a glorious October evening. The wind nestled into a gentle, sporadic stirring of the mulberry tree and the moon rose sharp and round in the clear, darkening sky. Gaslights flickered from within the brownstone. Jonathan could not believe his luck when it was she, the impetuous, outspoken girl transformed into a gracious lady in silk and scent, who answered the door.

"Oh," she said, "I had not expected you so soon."

She beckoned him into the foyer and floated off to retrieve her father. Buoyant masculine laughter emanated from the inner rooms of the house, and he could hear the clink of cutlery and serving dishes. To arrive unannounced at suppertime was most inappropriate, but her lingering scent, the echoing swish of her skirts, affirmed his goal, and he quieted his fretting. Madeline soon returned with a robust and portly man.

"An importer are you?" Mr. Gallacuty said in a voice turned raspy with drink and smoke, "Tell me, young man, have you traveled to the Australian continent?"

"No, Sir, I have not," Jonathan said, wishing with all his might that he had. Mr. Gallacuty eyed him, as if debating his dubious worth.

"But I encounter ships from Australia every time I am in the English ports," Jonathan added hastily, "And always speculate buying passage."

"Do so, man!" the older man said, and with a slap upon his back, heartily ushered Jonathan into the drawing room. "Australia and its sister country New Zealand are lands of great contrast and adventure. I once lived there as a very young boy. Auckland. My father was a sea captain, you understand, and while I may be a banker my heart is with the sea." Grasping Jonathan's arm, Mr. Gallacuty added in an urgent whisper, "Come hell or high water, I intend to return and make my home by the sea!"

This last part he added rebelliously, glancing toward his wife. The regal Mrs. Gallacuty was seated in the opulent parlor, a room gleaming with fine eighteenth century French pieces. She was in conversation with a muscular fellow in a striped shirt. The fellow was boasting about shooting buffalo while on holiday in the West.

"After a kill one becomes a barbarian," the fellow was saying to the hostess, "But it is good to be a barbarian, for then you know that you are at any rate a man."

Mr. Gallacuty introduced Jonathan to his wife and the other two men in the room.

"This upstanding fellow here is Mr. Ernest Wilkes, and this is the brilliant Doctor Thomas P. Wilson."

The introduction held a ring of sarcasm and Jonathan was seized with the distinct impression that he had stumbled upon a den of subtle adversaries playing a hostile game of conviviality.

"Mr. Rosario," Mrs. Gallacuty said, "Is that a Spanish name?"

"Yes, madam," Jonathan replied with a slight bow, "But my family are all citizens of this country, and for generations."

"I am so glad," Mrs. Gallacuty said, although she did not appear glad in the least.

"You *must* stay to dinner, Mr. Rosario," Madeline interrupted.

Before he could answer, Mrs. Gallacuty asked him how he came to know her husband.

"Why, he's the importer!" Mr. Gallacuty shouted, and poured himself more burgundy, "Maddy, have Felicity get him a glass."

"*I* shall get it," Madeline said.

"Allow me to present this to the woman of the house," Jonathan said, and produced from his valise a small package. Mrs. Gallacuty's distrustful frown disappeared in an instant and accepting the gift, she stuttered a word of thanks.

"How surprising!" she declared, "Bejeweled hair pins!"

"They are from Paris," Jonathan said.

"Well, Mr. Rosario, you must stay to dinner," the woman of the house said, "Horace dear, you didn't tell me you had invited a guest."

"Well," Mr. Gallacuty said, and looked to his daughter, who had returned with the wine, "I myself am fond of surprises."

They were shortly seated before a table of Irish linens and German china below a chandelier from Providence that Jonathan remembered having seen at the gas light exposition in Boston last year. The evening's menu included turkey with oyster sauce, which the younger fellow in the pinstriped shirt, maintaining that oysters were detrimental to a man's virility, hastily declined.

"What a man eats when he is twenty-five influences what he earns when he is fifty," Ernest Wilkes said. Jonathan laughed loudly until he realized no humor was intended.

"Ernest," Mrs. Gallacuty said, laying down her fork for emphasis, "You are a positive wealth of information."

"I recommend the new century diet for ladies," the doctor said as the contentious dinner proceeded, "As for the males, I leave such experimentation to the young Turks."

"It would behoove you to change your habits, Doctor," the earnest Ernest interjected, "I have it on good authority – "

"Authority is Ernie's specialty," Madeline announced. All caught her sarcasm; all but Ernest, who preened.

"Ernest is a fine fellow," the doctor said diplomatically, procuring a nod of approval from Mrs. Gallacuty and a noncommittal response from Mr. Gallacuty, who merely poured more wine. From across the table, Jonathan saw Madeline looking at him with expectation.

"I myself am a gourmet of all fine food and wines," Jonathan promptly said, accepting a bounteous helping of the oyster sauce and drinking down half his wine as through it were water. Madeline flashed him a smile of approval.

"More wine!" Mr. Gallacuty bellowed.

"Papa," Madeline said, interrupting Ernest Wilkes' lengthy description of the buffalo hunt, "I have decided to become an advocate of women's emancipation and nothing will stop me from fighting the fight from this day forward."

A sudden silence fell upon the dining table. Jonathan could see the girl was profoundly moved by her declaration. As her breast rose and fell the crystalline pendant she had shown him that afternoon rose and fell too with each exalted breath.

"You are a good girl," Mr. Gallacuty said. There was no mistaking that he was entirely besotted by his willful daughter. His wife, however, was not as easily charmed.

"Do not excite yourself, Madeline," said the mother.

The doctor cleared his throat loudly, a pronouncement that he was ready to take the girl in hand, if necessary. Madeline gazed at him, her eyes narrowing to slits of pure beaming heat that would surely blind the man if he dared contradict her. And he did dare.

"Dear girl," said the doctor in a burst of jocular pomposity, "I join with your mother in urging you to abandon your foolish notions and take up the domestic duties of wife and motherhood, for you must understand a woman's self sacrifice is surely the path for a prosperous happy life."

"Not mine, doctor," said she, "I would not volunteer to sacrifice myself to the endless tasks of wife and mothering as though it were a higher calling, when I believe self-development is a higher duty than self-sacrifice."

She seemed to be quoting a line from an erudite source, Jonathan knew not where, yet as a man of mercantile business with ladies of the home he'd learned to avoid serious arguments on any subject.

"What is this silliness," said Mrs. Gallacuty, and looked to her husband as though he was responsible, "And what is that hideous ornament you are wearing?"

All eyes focused on the pendant. Madeline held it up before the lamplight and Mr. Gallacuty gasped.

"Why, Madeline," said her father, "You are wearing the heirloom from my dear sister the Whale Rider!"

"I found it just yesterday inside the vanity drawer, Papa, and with it a note written in her hand."

"Horace," Mrs. Gallacuty said to her husband, but nothing more, for the man turned away from his wife to observe his daughter.

"It has always been a mystery to me, and so it was to my sister," said the father, "She acquired it from an old seaman and soon after she became The Whale Rider."

"Good lord," said the doctor, "An allegory."

"She was part Maori, my half-sister," Mr. Gallacuty said, "She walked into the sea, and some say, well – "

" – She became a Whale Rider. I see," said the doctor, with evident sarcasm.

"Think what you will," said the father, "You are a man of science, after all."

"A useless trinket," said the mother, "that excites her unnecessarily."

"It is nonetheless mine," their daughter said in a rising tone of tempestuous conviction, "Is it not, Papa?"

"Oh, yes, Madeline, it was indeed meant for you."

"Horace, really!"

The young fellow Ernest puffed himself up not unlike a toad preparing to devour a butterfly, and said, "Consider your weak constitution, Madeline."

"You needn't worry about me," replied the butterfly, "But do have some oyster sauce, Mr. Wilkes. Perhaps you will then stop killing buffalo."

"Come, Madeline, let's not bore the gentlemen with your gaudy trinket and selfish vocational interests," Mrs. Gallacuty said, "We must discourse on other subjects."

It was a spectacular insult from the older woman of the house, and it appeared to be par for the course, as father and daughter shared a swift glance of mutual understanding.

"I consider that a most wonderful suggestion, Mama," Madeline said and rose from the table, "Now that supper is concluded, perhaps we can hear of Mr. Rosario's travels."

"Nothing like tales of travel over a fine cigar," Mr. Gallacuty said and also stood. Jonathan followed his lead. The hostess remained seated, however, as did her other two guests. The lines of battle had been drawn into two camps: Those who followed the precocious woman child, and those who remained loyal to the reigning queen.

"I believe I have just the cigars, Sir," Jonathan said, and produced a handful of them from the inside pocket of his waistcoat. The doctor pushed back his chair and stood, all alliances forgotten.

"Is that a Havana?"

"Indeed sir it is," said the importer, and offered them round to the gentlemen. Ernest Wilkes declined with an upturned nose but the other men took them with avid thanks.

"You are a man of many gifts," said the matron of the house and still she did not rise. He had failed in befriending her, but some alliances had to be sacrificed for the greater good. Pleasing the mother,

Jonathan could see, meant alienating the daughter. He was amused to note this simple perception seemed beyond the understanding of Mr. Ernest Wilkes, who remained seated at table beside his despotic hostess.

The rest of the evening was spent in whimsical discussion on the benefits of travel, and Jonathan was pleased to see that Madeline chose to listen quietly on this issue, prompting further talk only when conversation appeared to be dragging.

"Do tell us more, Mr. Rosario," Madeline said, even though it had grown late in the evening and the doctor had already followed the example of the rejected Ernest who, having no fondness for brandy or cigars, left shortly after dinner without so much as a good-bye to the young lady of the house.

Mrs. Gallacuty had retired but her daughter took it upon herself to stay in the drawing room and sit at her father's feet. Jonathan could see that Mr. Gallacuty was pleased not only with the Havana, but with the way his daughter clipped and lighted it for him. It was a sight to behold, the little woman's tender, pretty lips puffing the cigar to life, and the indulgent father, laughing at his little pet. Jonathan felt a rush of disapproval until Madeline caught his eye over the flame of the match. It was a glance of naughty fun, of irrepressible delight.

"Papa," said she, "I do want to know more about the pendant and my aunt, the Maori woman. Is there more you might tell us?"

The man shook his head wearily, and Jonathan thought he saw something resembling discomfort cross the face of what had hitherto appeared to be that of a complacent, settled man. Now he saw yearning, sadness and confusion.

"I was but a boy and my sister Matilda was nearing womanhood when she befriended an old seaman from our father's ship. It was with some flourish the old seaman gave her the pendant. He said it had once been found on the European continent in the buried funeral boat of an ancient queen and that is was a tradition that it be given only to a girl coming into womanhood."

"A burial boat? What a mystery," said Madeline and then turned to Jonathan. "I like mysteries only when they can be solved, and think you are just the man to assist in solving this mystery, Mr. Rosario, for you are an expert authority in ancient objects from places far and away."

"Not so expert," he modestly replied, for he did not want to go the way of the rejected suitor Ernest Wilkes whom she'd accused of being an authority in all things.

"I have a pair of authentic kangaroo dancing shoes," Mr. Gallacuty said. His mysterious mood had lifted, for he was a man of flexible happy temperament, "And I aim to return to the Australian continent someday, perhaps on a merchant ship like my father's. Someday, yes. And so, Mr. Rosario," said the father, blowing cigar smoke over his lovely daughter's head of luxurious hair, "Tell us more of your travel expertise."

Riding on the inspiration of the bright round moon as it beamed its magic through the windows, Jonathan transported father and daughter to lands of golden pagodas and camel trains, ringing wind chimes and prayer chant warbling over rooftops burnished to cinnamon in the setting sun, to the clamor and incense of the Turkish bazaar, the throngs of Shanghai, and white hot Mediterranean beaches. He waxed and polished these scenes with all the fervent wooing of a lover until Madeline's eyes sparked and her cheeks glowed. The more he spoke and the more she queried, he found himself speaking exclusively to her, and as the moonlight passed on from the window and the fire in the grate began to ebb, he heard the clock in the hall chime twelve times too long and finally made his excuses to go.

Mr. Gallacuty murmured with a deep rumbling intake of breath and he saw now the man was sleeping. Rising, her skirts ruffling and unfolding, Madeline removed the ashen cigar from her father's fingertips and saw him to the moonlight-flooded vestibule.

"I am forced to go away for a time," he blurted, for there was no other way of saying it, "Two months at least."

She gazed at him with a dreamy expectancy he had not seen in her face before, and he saw with a swell of shock that this lovely creature, this defiant butterfly, was in love with him. Then she yawned, luxuriously, gorgeously, and swayed toward him until her hair was brushing his chest and he had to delicately right her. Perhaps she wasn't in love after all, he thought, but merely sleepwalking.

"I am sorry to see you go," she said with automatic poise, "Is it to Paris?"

"No, to Italy."

"The boot!"

"Yes, the boot," he said. To her, Italy was no more than a shape on a map in a schoolchild's geography class.

"Perhaps, when I am gone, you will take a moment sometime, just a minute or two on a given day, to think of me?"

He searched her eyes for an understanding that she would wait for him.

"Of course, Mr. Rosario. And can you do me a favor in return?"

"Anything, Miss Gallacuty," he said and meant it with all his heart. She lifted the gold chain and its pendant from around her neck, took his hand in hers, and placed it into his open palm.

"I would be most grateful if you might seek information on the value of this object. Not for sale, but for the purpose of understanding its mysterious properties and origin."

How could he refuse her? And yet he oddly feared the strange crystal, he knew not why.

"I am loath to part with it," she continued, "But I hope with your help to find serious enlightenment on its mysteries from the experts of European culture, of which I suspect you are in consort."

What could he say? He wrapped the chain around the crystal and slipped it inside a handkerchief. He then carefully placed her little trinket within his waistcoat pocket.

"I will consult with the glassmakers of Murano and the alchemists of Verona, and perhaps I can bring you significant particulars as to its origins."

"I will be in your debt, Mr. Rosario," said she.

"No debt is necessary," he replied.

He then took her proffered hand and held it as if it were the most delicate of roses and, leaning toward her, breathed in the disappointing scent of her father's tobacco lingering in her hair and bid her goodnight.

The next day Mama entered her bedroom and spied the stone animal figurines arranged upon the window seat.

"They are from Mr. Rosario," Madeline said with trepidation, for she knew her mother did not approve of the importer. Mrs. Gallacuty tightened her lips.

"You were rude to Ernest last night, and behaved in a most unbecoming, unfeminine manner. If you continue to act in such a way, you will lose your attractiveness and his attentions."

"I don't believe that pretending interest in Ernie's boorish talk about buffalo hunts makes me feminine, Mama. That's the old way of courtship. I'm a modern girl."

"Modern!" Mrs. Gallacuty scoffed, "Doctor Wilson would not approve. And this man – *Rosario* – is a foreigner," she said.

"He is American!"

"He does not look like an American. And besides, Madeline dear," Mama said, seating herself upon the upholstered chair beside the window seat, "You must remember what we have learned about the Law of Similarity."

"Oh no, Mama!"

"A robin mates with a robin, never an oriole."

"I am not a robin, and Mr. Rosario is not an oriole!"

"You must listen to me," her mother said in the soft, slow voice she reserved for these talks, "I must tell you the story of a sea captain who married an Indian girl. She seemed all that could be desired at the time they married, but sadly her race instincts were too strong, and it was but a short time before she died and their half-breed daughter relapsed completely into the savage ways of her people."

"You are speaking of Papa's sister," Madeline said.

"Half-sister," Mrs. Gallacuty said, "They shared no mother, certainly. And as *your* mother I urge you to take advantage of my counsel."

"But I think I am in love with him." Madeline said, regretting her impulsive declaration the moment it escaped her lips.

"How can you know this? You are succumbing again to your imaginings, and you know what that does to your nerves. Do you want me to call Dr. Wilson?"

There it was, spoken with all the confidence of a jailer threatening punishment. Mrs. Gallacuty rose and made for the door, "Be warned, you are not as modern as you think, and you should know that physical attraction is lessened by separation. By the time Mr. Rosario catches sight of those Parisian ladies, he will forget you."

"There are no Parisian ladies in Italy," Madeline replied.

"Ah, but there are ladies everywhere," Mrs. Gallacuty said, "And Mr. Rosario is a common man."

Chapter 4

*J*onathan Rosario set sail for Europe with a single image branded upon his brain: That of Madeline eyeing him over the flame of her father's cigar, an unmistakably alluring expression upon her face. In that moment the budding rose had revealed all the force of the larger bloom-to-come, and it was not without some misgivings that he saw an aspect of her character he found troublesome. He preferred a more malleable, docile woman, one like his mother, and while the spark in her eye had stirred him like no other, it propelled him upon hindsight to question the sincerity of her encouragement. He nonetheless found hope in the fact of her having given him the pendant alongside her expectation of its return.

Once the ship docked in Naples, Jonathan secured himself a room for the night then walked a familiar route to Viviola of the sumptuous hips, a spirited gypsy creature of the local marketplace who had once sold him his astrological fortune. He did not tell the gypsy woman about the astonishing accuracy of her last premonition that he would meet his true love by year's end, nor did he have any compunction about taking her to their favorite *ristorante* for calamari and enjoying her seductive charms the rest of the night. The next morning, his mouth and fingers redolent with the scent of calamari and Viviola, Jonathan left the gypsy's hideaway assuaged of all tormented desire for his tight American rosebud.

The train to Venice consumed a good portion of the following week, and by the time Jonathan settled into his tiny room off the piazza, he wanted nothing but sleep. He awoke at dawn to the peal of cathedral bells and after a breakfast of thick coffee and *ciabatta* joined the throng of businesses in the narrow walkways and turquoise waterways of the damp, medieval city. He bought five crystal chandeliers, strings of beaded necklaces at one tenth the price he would charge for them in New York, and a twelve piece set of rose-colored brandy snifters.

He had not forgotten his promise to Madeline regarding her girlish trinket and soon found his way to a remote glassblower's shop on the island of Murano.

Montevedio's was a tiny hovel. Eerie Gregorian chants echoed from the adjacent 6th century chapel where the air was filled with the haunted, ghostly presence of the many souls that had over the centuries lived, died and been buried in its graveyard. This was not the sort of atmosphere Jonathan cared for. He was an American in a hurry after all. But he'd assured Madeline he would show her piece of heirloom jewelry to the experts of Europe, and Montevedio came recommended in that category.

The interview did not start well. The old glassblower sat at a counter wearing an expression of disgust, and so to soften him Jonathan diplomatically purchased twelve boxes of assorted overpriced ornaments of the man's exquisitely crafted faerie spirits, dragonflies and winged creatures, though he doubted the average New Yorker would want to pay the hefty price he would have to charge to make a profit. He then requested the old man's opinion on the ancient crystal pendant he produced from the cloth inside his waistcoat. Montevedio took it in his worn, clawed hand and held it under the scrutiny of a large eyeglass. Then issued a strangled cry of surprise.

"What is this?" said the glassmaker in a soft, suspicious voice.

"Is it of value?"

"Value?" It seemed the word made the old man angry, "*Es du –* " and for a long moment he search for the word. "*Mundo – l'altro mundo.*"

The Gregorian chants rose in volume from the chapel next door.

"How so?"

With his thick magnifying glass the old man studied a slip of something dark and shiny within the crystalline form.

"*Es du* meteorite," he said, "*Elementes du* heavens. *Mire.*"

He pointed to the sliver of what appeared to be a flat iridescent gemstone shard inside the crystal.

"It is – space jewel – *al dentro du* crystal." The Venetian spoke with such certainty Jonathan dared not contradict, but still he did not understand.

"A space jewel – made by – humans?"

"No. Chain, human, but the stone, *millennia* – many years ago."

Then the old glassblower lifted his fierce milky blue-eyed gaze and Jonathan saw with a jolt the man was half-blind.

"*Es miraculoso!* " the old glassblower said.

The chanting, droning chapel voices sounded a passionate ode to centuries of humans ebbing and flowing through life and inevitable death, but Jonathan had had enough. The old man was deranged, that was all there was to it.

"Thank-you, Sir," he said, and held out his palm for the pendant, "I will make my leave."

But the old man clutched it in his fist and offered him many thousands of lire for it.

"Thank-you, no, it is not mine to sell."

"More, I will give you more!" The glassblower's voice rose.

"I am sorry, no. It is not for sale."

With reluctance the old man opened his palm. Jonathan snatched up the pendant and backed out of the shop, purchases in parcels under his arm. He hurried up the dusty walkway to catch the next *vaporetto* back to Venice and did not once look back at the glassblower's shop or the chapel and its graveyard.

The faster he walked, the faster the chanting voices faded from his ears.

He spent the following week in Florence and greater Tuscany attending estate sales, ingesting sumptuous wines and food, and doing his best to forget the ravings of the deranged old glassblower. In Umbria and Orvieto he purchased brightly colored ceramic dinnerware. In Bagnoregio he searched for an Etruscan artifact that was gone, taken by some other treasure hunter. It reminded him of another treasure back in Manhattan, and he wondered what he would tell her about the pendant and its presumed otherworldly properties. The glassblower's story would most certainly impress her, but the old coot was simply a madman. Space jewel, indeed!

The night before setting sail for America, Jonathan walked down a winding Naples corridor to a small jewelry store with a facade as rumpled and aged as the face of its proprietor. The jeweler was an Englishman and adventurer who in his recent travels to China had acquired many fine pieces: Water pearls, Tiger's Eye cufflinks, silver drop earrings with pendant bells, and a set of cloisonné hair ornaments in an exquisitely crafted jade box. Jonathan had not come for these, but rather for an item he had seen once before, something that had caught his eye but for which he had no use until now.

It was still there, a lady-like vision of slim white gold seated in a box of amber velvet, her shining band rising along a sloping shoulder to an arched neck of four pronged points holding a jewel of a diamond.

The English jeweler was pleased to sell him the ring. Jonathan smiled all the while, ring in his pocket, in anticipation of returning home at last to the lovely young lady he hoped with all his heart to make his own. His European purchases were itemized, packed and crated, his plans set in stone.

Then Jonathan remembered one more item of business that required a last bit of effort before his departure. He would seek a final opinion from this expert, an antiquarian jeweler after all, as to the mystery of this so-called family heirloom. The object had become a tiresome and irritating burden, and were it not for Madeline, he would have long ago chucked it into a Venice canal.

"Tell me, sir, if you don't mind," Jonathan said, "What think you of this?"

Handling the pendant with less care than before, he plopped it down upon the counter. The Englishman gave him a look of bemusement, as if expecting to find a piece of no value, but when he looked at the ancient jewel his face grew tense.

"How in heaven did you happen to acquire this treasure?"

"Treasure?" Jonathan joked, "Is that what it is?"

"You are in possession," said the Englishman, carefully taking the pendant in hand, "Of a most unique item."

"So I've been told, but other than being the inherited possession of a lady who happens to be my own object of desire, I see no use for it."

"Not for you, no," said the jeweler, "You are a man. But for the ladies, this *treasure* has notable significance."

"No doubt intended to be worn by the weaker sex," Jonathan said.

"Weaker sex, you say?" The man laughed. "Not for the little lady in possession this fine piece!"

"Oh? Does she become the Queen of England?"

"Interesting use of words, my friend. For if my suppositions are correct, and I am rarely wrong, I believe this was indeed once the possession of an ancient warrior queen, and I must say it is only by miraculous coincidence that you have found an Englishman in Italy to tell you its story."

"Another story," said Jonathan, "Pray don't tell me it is a space jewel, and I will believe you."

"But it is, dear fellow."

"A space jewel?" Jonathan smirked, but the wizened old Englishman made no effort to join him in mirth. Rather he leaned forward with his magnifying loupe to study the pendant more carefully.

"Most unique," said the jeweler, "The last place I saw one such space jewel was in Yorkshire, the city of York. You do know that York was formerly the ancient Roman city of Eboracum?"

In his young career as an antiques collector and seller, Jonathan had learned to indulge the authoritarian specialists of their field as they expounded on their knowledge. Invariably, the older the specialist, the more erudite he was on his subject, and so Jonathan steeled himself for the lecture that was to follow.

"Ah, yes, so I have heard."

"And are you not familiar with Eboracum's ancient Roman baths and the discoveries?"

"No, Sir."

"Well, you see, many unusual jewels from the Roman era were found in the baths, as that was where they were more often lost. Hair ornaments, necklaces, earrings and the like. Over two thousand years ago, before the birth of our lord Jesus Christ, the Romans conquered Britain. They brought with them their roads, buildings, baths and what have you, but the natives in Britain were fierce tribes from the time of the Iron Age – "

"This is most interesting, sir, but what has this to do with this lady's trinket here?"

"Trinket! Trinket, you say! This is the missing centerpiece to a necklace found on the skeletal remains of a buried queen known as Cartimandua!"

"I see."

The Englishman had turned red in the face and he was barking at him now.

"Queen Cartimandua! Of the Celtic Brigantes! An Iron Age tribe! She led her warriors in a battle against her husband Venutius, and she defied the Romans too!"

"Impressive." Jonathan searched for a means of changing the subject, but there was no stopping the Englishman now.

"Historical legend claims she had acquired a stone that had rained down from the heavens in a fiery ball upon the Earth. A meteorite. "

"Thus the term space jewel."

"It has been referred to as such. Meteorite stones were highly prized by ancient tribes. They pounded the metal into beads and turned the beads into jewelry. Some say that with one unique space jewel set within a piece of crystal – a piece identical to this very object – Queen Cartimandua of the Brigantes acquired tremendous power – "

"She became – " Jonathan searched for what he recalled from the carnival shows he had seen across the river in Jersey, " – a strong-woman? As in the carnival – "

The jeweler gave him an incredulous stare before finally regaining his speech.

"No, man! Do you Americans know nothing of ancient history? Carnival strongwoman, indeed! She changed history! She defied the Romans! She defied her husband!"

The last thing Jonathan wanted Madeline to have in her possession was a so-called space jewel that gave her the power to be defiant. As if reading his thoughts, the Englishman's expression turned crafty.

"And so, my friend," said the old jeweler, a slow smile spreading across his face, "You will ask for your lady's hand in marriage with the exquisite ring you have only just now purchased from me, only to later in time come to regret it."

"I beg your pardon?"

"Cartimandua's jewel is too powerful to be a possession of your little lady. It will destroy any hope of a happy marriage, sir. It was meant instead for a warrior queen."

"My beautiful Madeline is a queen to me."

"To you, certainly, but only to you, as well it should be. I could take the pendant off your hands. For a reasonable price, of course."

It was a tempting proposition. Not that he believed a hoot of the man's story. In fact, Jonathan suspected the cagey old Englishman had invented the business about its powerful attributes in order to get his hands on what was undoubtedly an object of worth.

"I am sorry, but it is not mine to sell to you or anyone."

The jeweler's face turned sour with thinly disguised disappointment. He then attempted a different tactic.

"How did an American girl happen upon such a piece of British history?"

He owed the man no explanation, but Jonathan recounted what Madeline's father told him: That his half-sister had acquired it from an old seaman who'd claimed it had been found at an ancient burial site.

"So the pieces fit!" shouted the jeweler, "It is the possession a Celtic queen!"

"Was," Jonathan corrected, "*Was.*"

The Englishman responded with a fierce glare.

"If you know what is good for you, you will turn it over to me. I will pay you at least. Anyone else would have you arrested."

"Arrested? I've done nothing wrong! You are the one who is suspect, sir, making threats to a tourist in your shop!"

Jonathan quickly took up the pendant and slipped it into the inside pocket of his waistcoat. The Englishman opened his mouth for a retort, seemed to think better of it, and adopted the appearance of regretful resignation.

"Very well. But you cannot say I did not warn you!"

"Yes, well. Good day."

Jonathan turned out of the shop without looking back, yet not without hearing one final word from the irate antiquarian jeweler.

"*If I were you,*" the Englishman shouted so loudly Jonathan could all but imagine blue veins protruding from his fiercely indignant white neck, "*I would propose with that ring to another lady! Or see to it that this one never regains possession of the Queen's jewel!*"

Later, when on his way to a final evening with gypsy Viviola of the sumptuous hips, Jonathan spotted two rough looking fellows following him. He dipped into the nearly deserted market place and found Viviola brooding at the *ciabatta* maker's booth. She acknowledged him with a soft smile and somber pronouncement.

"There is more to your fortune than I have told you, *mi amore.*" She placed her seductive fingers upon his arm and added, "I see a storm in your future."

A cold wind whipped across the square, and a tin of *bruschettas* tipped and spilled upon the counter. Jonathan assured her he had a seaworthy stomach and confidence in the ship's durability. He was nonetheless wary of the two ruffians who had followed him to the square, sent most likely by the English jeweler to steal away the heirloom. He knew had to stay true to the task to which he'd been entrusted, no matter how much he didn't care to return this strange and purportedly powerful jewel to Madeline.

And so he evaded the ruffians by slipping out through the back alleyways and returning not to his hotel but rather to Viviola's little room for the night, where they feasted on more calamari and each other.

On the windy day of his sea voyage he awoke at daybreak with a hangover from excessive lovemaking and grappa.

"Remember to be cautious my friend," Viviola said again as they parted ways, "I see a stormy union in your future."

Jonathan laughed her warning away, and by the time he arrived at the dock where the great steamer rocked in the rough unsettled sea, he thought no more of her prediction.

Chapter 5

*I*n the first week he was expected to return, Madeline waited by the window in her prettiest frock with the sash around her waist and her hair tied in a velvet Christmas ribbon. But Jonathan Rosario did not come.

From her perch she watched Hannah Amberfitch walk with her daughter to their employment at Triangle Shirtwaist and yearned in her loneliness to join them, a notion met with strong disapproval from her mother, not to mention the disdain of the doctor and Ernest Wilkes who, as factory manager, would never hire a young lady of means.

Older by more than a decade and certainly poorer, Hannah had been an unlikely acquaintance, but Madeline had begun speaking to her on strolls through Washington Square. It was through Hannah that she discovered the Suffragist Cause was not only about acquiring the vote but seizing the power to own one's own income instead of turning it over to husbands who squandered it on drink. Madeline seriously considered her friend's words, yet concluded Jonathan Rosario was not the sort of man who would deny his wife her properly earned means. Madeline was, after all, nearing eighteen, and this was the Age of Romance!

But on the third week of his nonappearance, her memory of Jonathan's face conjured not his smile but an impression of condescension, and the more she waited his return the more she suspected his adventures in the greater world to be superior to anything she could offer. Thoughts of the heirloom pendant she'd entrusted to him diffused into distant memories resurfaced only in dreams. Having worn it but once and for what seemed so very long ago, Madeline could not recall the sense of purpose with which she had been imbued when it had been in her possession.

Plagued by a sensation of loss, she walked through the snow in the park among ladies in furs and children bound-up in woolens, and it was there that she decided to forget about love and Jonathan Rosario. He was a swellhead, a conceited sophisticate, and so to get even, she would marry Ernie Wilkes who was, after all, a capitalist and a leader of men and belonged to the Rocky Hill Knights of Pythias Degree Team.

Ernest Wilkes made repeated visits to the Gallacuty home that was now filling with Yuletide decorations and the scent of mulberry, vanilla and spice. At each visit Madeline sat dutifully embroidering beside her mother. She concentrated hard on falling in love with Ernest who, despite his protruding ears and pinprick, beady eyes, had a fine physique. With a trim new beard hiding his weak chin and a mustache as thick as a shaving brush, he certainly appeared impressive.

"You cannot have a firm will without firm muscles," Ernest said, and Madeline had to agree this was true, for Ernie was undoubtedly firm about everything. She passed cookies in the shapes of sugar-encrusted wreaths and put on a face of devout interest when Ernest pontificated on the notion that, with humble study, she might be made worthy of him, a New Century Man. This appeared as near to a marriage proposal as Madeline had yet heard, and when her mother cast upon her a smile of triumph, she felt in league with her, as if both had been waiting long and hard to snare an animal at last seen moving closer to the trap.

On Christmas Eve night, Mrs. Gallacuty assured her daughter that a proposal was imminent. She commended her for having assiduously followed "Love's Golden Rule," which was to cultivate those qualities known to be womanly and lovable and to avoid all subjects and acts that were likely to arouse antagonism. Accepting her mother's praise, Madeline said nothing of her subversive distribution of emancipation flyers at Ernest's very factory, for this most certainly would not be deemed womanly or loveable by the man she aimed to capture.

"Ernest is a very smart man," Mrs. Gallacuty said. She had said this often, as if it were the only description of him that could come to mind. "He will propose when he is ready and certain that he is doing the correct thing. Everything you do must of course be done to convince him of this."

Madeline tried to appear thoughtful about this piece of advice. Mr. Gallacuty grunted and lighted his pipe. They were in the drawing room that blazed with the light of the fire in the grate and from the candles set precariously close to the Yuletide tree which glittered with ornaments of tinsel angels and walnut shells, acorns, rose hips and cranberries.

"Tomorrow he will be most vulnerable, you will see," Mama continued, "It will be Christmas Day, and he will be missing his family in Ohio, and when he attends our party he will be feeling lonely and sad. But then here he will be with his second family, and you, so lovely, so willing and perfect, he won't be able to resist."

"What a diabolical game," Papa said, and reached for his port, "Was I entrapped in a similar manner?"

"Pooh," Mrs. Gallacuty said, "You were a rabbit, but Ernest here, he is a lion."

"Papa is a lion," Madeline said and rose to embrace her father from behind his chair, crinkling his newspaper, "A gentle lion." He patted her hand and growled so like a pussycat it made her laugh. It also caused

Madeline to wonder why she wanted to marry at all; so cozy was she in her home, her quarrels with Mama nearly forgotten.

"Ernest is a very smart man," Mama said for the twelfth time that day, and father and daughter groaned in unison.

After Madeline had kissed her parents goodnight and had gone to bed, she felt a doubt pricking at her resolve and wondered if perhaps it wouldn't be better if her mother were to marry Ernest Wilkes instead.

Chapter 6

Christmas morning brought blankets of snow that coated the horse tracks and turned Greenwich Village into a landscape so clean and serene, it came very near to resembling a country town. There was a hush in the air; gifts were unwrapped in the warmth of indoors. Mama preened in her new silk hat with the ostrich feathers, Papa admired his silver manicure set, and Madeline modeled her green velvet muff trimmed in tassels and posies. There were kisses and hugs and exclamations of unbridled affection.

The kitchen filled practically to bursting with aromatic dishes for the mid-day meal. Party guests began arriving at twelve o'clock. Uncle Bradley brought port jelly for Papa, and Aunt Bess gave beautiful home-made pincushions to the ladies. Mrs. Heath cooked mince pies and the Smith brothers from the men's shop arrived with imported candies. The house was filled with the voices of guests and the delectable scent of roasting turkey and vegetable soup, plum puddings and cinnamon-crusted pies.

Madeline assisted the busy Mrs. Church with the setting of the buffet, while Mrs. Gallacuty received her guests with the spirited laughter of an anxious hostess. She had hung mistletoe and kissing bunches above every door, and waited anxiously for the arrival of her daughter's beau with all the giddy anticipation of a lovesick girl. Madeline tried not to think of how it would feel to be kissed by Ernie, and wished that Mama would kiss him instead.

Ernest arrived wearing a forest green waistcoat. He carried a book-sized gift under his arm that restricted his movements when he bowed to the ladies or engaged in hearty handshakes with the gentlemen. Madeline observed him from the kitchen door before she ventured to cross the room to his side, and was grateful for the obstacles along the way: the warm embrace from her music teacher Mrs. Brown, the quarrel between Bobby Lee and his sister Ella, a kindly pat on the head from Uncle Bradley, who reminded her he had known her since she was just so high.

Suddenly, unexpectedly and heart-wrenchingly, she found herself confronted by the apparition of Jonathan Rosario. He stood before her in the flesh, not a ghost, not a memory, and not the horrid snobbish swellhead she had chosen to reject, but rather the gentle dream, the dark-eyed rescuer. He greeted her with anxiety in his face and a stoop in his posture. For a moment all sound was muffled and they were the only two in the room.

"Miss Madeline Gallacuty," he said, as through he were savoring every syllable of her name, "I cannot begin to tell you how good it is to see your face."

"Mr. Rosario."

She was surprised at the chill in her voice, but when she heard it she felt it. She lifted her chin and let him take her limp unresponsive hand.

"We had terrible weather at sea," he stuttered, for her hand instantly withdrew from his.

"I forgot how long you would be gone," she said, "but do have some of Mrs. Church's marvelous cranberry muffins, and will you excuse me?"

She passed him by, wrenched by the hurt in his face yet glorying in it too. She then greeted Ernest with more lilting, laughing, delighted

enthusiasm than she had ever done before. With a smug grin of posses-
sive approval, Ernest surveyed the fitted bodice of her new pale green
silk dress.

"We are a perfect match," Ernest said, and held out his arms to
show her his jacket, which was the brighter green of a peacock feather's
eye and suited the peacock of a man himself.

"Yes," she said, seeing again how unsuitable, how stocky and awkward he was. "Do have some of Mrs. Church's marvelous cranberry
muffins."

And so she breezed by both men as Ernest said, "I should tell you,
after a kill one is a barbarian – " and from the hidden vantage of Mrs.
Brown's brocaded shoulder, she observed Jonathan stand with his head
tilted back from Ernest's heavy forward-thrust, and then Jonathan
politely turning to seek her out.

"I drink eight glasses of water a day, what do you say to that?" she
heard Ernie say. How could she snub Jonathan by marrying Ernest if
Ernest was a bore and fool?

"Mr. Rosario!" Madeline's father said as he passed into the room,
"And how were your China travels?"

"I was in Italy, Sir, not China, and unfortunately the voyage home
was long and fraught with peril."

"Peril, you say? It's those foreigners, can't trust them, can you."
Papa said.

Jonathan produced a slim package of cellophane from his pocket.

"Merry Christmas, Sir," he said.

Mr. Gallacuty took the package, held the cigar to his nose, and
breathed in with relish.

"You are a most capital fellow!"

"Do what you must do," Mama suddenly hissed in Madeline's ear,
and gestured with a rapid eye movement in Ernest's direction. Madeline

obediently made her way back to the buffet table and Ernest, who was proffering the book-shaped package to her father.

"Please accept this," Ernest said, "as a token of my sincerest admiration and concern, since I have come as of late to think of you not only as a friend, but a father too."

At that, Ernest turned to Madeline and gave her a wink. Jonathan caught the wink, stared at her in astonishment, and then looked away. Madeline stood silent, stupefied. Had Ernest proposed when he referred to Papa as *his father too*?

Mr. Gallacuty tore off the paper wrapping. Ernest had had the audacity to give her Papa the book, *The Virile Powers of Superb Manhood.*

"Well," Mr. Gallacuty said, "Madeline, dear, get me more wine, will you?"

Madeline stepped into the kitchen where her cousin Lucy Fleming was supervising the heating of a cornmeal sauce. Lucy was round with child.

"Oh, I'm so confused, Lucy," Madeline said, "It appears I will marry soon, and I don't know if I can stand the thought!"

Lucy stirred the sauce with her hand upon her belly and said nothing. Madeline seated herself upon a step stool and studied her cousin. Was she happy in her marriage to the stalwart and stern Philip Fleming, a man not unlike Ernest in many ways? Had she discovered some secret to marital pleasure?

"What does a woman do in marriage," Madeline said, "When she does not feel the attraction?"

"Well, Madeline dear," Lucy said, tapping the spoon against the rim of the pot, "Your highest duty in marriage is to suffer and be still. Just suffer and be still."

"Oh I see," Madeline said. She stood at the cask and poured more wine into the pitcher.

"You don't see," Lucy said, "But you will. And in the end it won't matter, really, for you will have a half dozen beautiful children whom you will love like life itself and who will delight your every living day."

At that moment, Lucy's Little Samuel came running in from the out of doors, lungs bellowing some injustice, his toy fire engine broken, his nose running and boots dripping melted snow upon the floor, and Madeline had to agree that yes, her cousin was right, she did not see.

Someone was playing the piano in the drawing room, and Dr. Wilson had just arrived, his waistcoat damp with snowflakes. Madeline hung back at the door, then felt a hand on her shoulder and turned to find herself in the embrace of none other than Ernest Wilkes.

"I've caught you under the mistletoe!" he shouted like the bully-boy he was, and kissed her wetly upon the side of her mouth. Amy Withers saw and tittered and whispered the news to Joyce Hall, but it was Jonathan who saw the most, for he stood nearby waiting her return and now he walked away, leaving her in the arms of the man who fancied himself her fiancé.

Madeline watched Jonathan leave and felt more regret and sadness then she had ever known possible, then Ernest kissed her again. She shoved the pitcher into his chest, saw with satisfaction the wine spill onto his lapel, and slapped him full on the cheek. Joyce Hall and Amy Withers gasped. Dr. Wilson turned to stare.

"How dare you?" she whispered furiously into his reddening face, and for once he was speechless with astonishment. The cad! The fool! What was he thinking, giving her father a book preaching abstinence! And whatever gave him the impertinent assumption that she, Madeline Gallacuty, was his to claim!

She ran down the hall, away from the piano playing where Mrs. Brown was singing *my true love gave to me*. She passed under another dreadful kissing bunch and ripped it down; she ran past the family portraits of Gallacutys and Flemings and babies in Christening linens, down to the dark end of the hall, to the lingering scent of her father's sweet tobacco.

There she beheld Jonathan, her *true love*, standing alone in the library, and she heard Mrs. Brown agree from the other end of the hall as she sang with all her heart the truth, which was *my true love… my true love…*

Mrs. Gallacuty strode out the front door to the walkway of her festive holiday home to greet her final guest and neighbor Old Mrs. Prentice. Mrs. Prentice was leaning upon the bony shoulder of Little Samuel, who was crying again, for the other children were hanging the old woman's cane upon the crooked branch of their Mr. Snowman and Mrs. Prentice was most displeased and letting it be known to the one in her most immediate grasp.

"Why, Mrs. Prentice, welcome, welcome!" Mrs. Gallacuty shouted with arms outstretched in greeting.

"These are the rudest children I have ever encountered in my eight decades of residence in this neighborhood!"

"Little Samuel, shame on you!" Mrs. Gallacuty said, taking hold of the elderly woman's arm and nearly slipping, for the walk had been made slick where others had tread, and her slippers were wrong for the out-of-doors. "Children, return Mrs. Prentice's cane this instant!"

In that moment, Mrs. Gallacuty happened to look up and see the lights to the library and the figure of her daughter standing near the window. The view into the library was blocked by a thick dark drape, obscuring the person to whom Madeline was speaking, but her darling daughter shined like a princess beneath the crystal lights, her posture picture perfect. Like a heroine in a novel, Mrs. Gallacuty thought with pride, for what she saw next was the moment of a mother's dreams:

The hand of a decidedly male individual presented Madeline with a small velveteen box. Beholding its contents, Madeline's hand went to her mouth, and she made some exclamation of great emotion to the man, who took the ring from the box and slipped it upon her finger.

It was wondrous! It was a culmination of many days and nights of scheming! Mrs. Gallacuty couldn't believe her good luck that she should be standing here to witness the very moment Ernest Wilkes proposed to her only daughter!

"Let's get on with it," Old Mrs. Prentice snapped, "You're slower than I and half as old, what is the matter with you?"

And then Mrs. Gallacuty saw. The horrible truth, the shameful reality, for when Ernest stepped out from behind the shadow of the curtain to embrace Madeline, he was not Ernest at all but that dreadful importer! And they kissed, oh how they kissed. It was magnetic attraction of the worst kind – passionate, unbridled, horrible, horrible and more horrible – and when Mrs. Gallacuty uttered a wounded cry of outrage, Mrs. Prentice followed her gaze and chuckled lasciviously.

"You'd best be getting your Madeline married mighty soon, my dear, for I've seen some kissing in my day, and I can tell you most certain those two are most seriously attached!"

Chapter 7

$\mathscr{B}$efore the commencement of the new year, it was announced
that Horace and Adelaide Gallacuty's lovely daughter
Madeline would be wed to the importer Jonathan Rosario at the First
Episcopal Church on the second day of February, 1906. Before this
propitious announcement there were of course efforts to stop the marriage, but they were ineffectual sallies handily defeated by the united
front that was now the betrothed couple. Ernest Wilkes promptly
retreated to the trenches of the factory he managed, where he lectured
vociferously to his seamstresses about traitors to God and Country.
Dr. Wilson concluded in his strategic analyses that Madeline's hysteria
would remain in remission so long as she stayed true to her role of wife
and mother. And finally Mrs. Gallacuty herself, the last bastion of resistance to the union, conceded defeat upon the persuasive insistence of
her husband, who rather liked the man with the Havana cigars.

Madeline had overnight grown serene. No longer in need of the
services of the brain doctor, her nervous fits dissipated. She also
accepted Jonathan's promise to return the pendant to her, replete with
a discourse on its properties, once they were properly wed. It was an
exciting prospect, and Madeline could only assume the heirloom to
be worth a great deal. Until the day he would tell her its mysterious
story, she would entrust the crystalline jewel to her future husband for
safekeeping, for whom better to see to its preservation than a man who
cherished such objects of desire?

The young bride and her husband were to begin married life on an adventurous Wild West excursion in search of Indian crafts and curios, a most unusual way to spend a honeymoon. The bride announced the journey plans were made in the interest of Mr. Rosario's import business, to which she named herself honorary partner. Between scheduled fittings at a bridal dressmaker and introductory teas at the home of her future parents-in-law, Madeline Gallacuty spoke excitedly of her new occupation, which would be not only that of wife, but advisor and buyer of imports.

Was she not a shopper herself, a New York consumer with impeccable taste?

The vision of herself as a lady importer was never far from Madeline's mind, yet she wisely refrained from talking of her business plans when in the company of her future father-in-law Leonardo Rosario, whose fierce eyebrows and dark commanding presence required her to play the role of demure daughter-in-law. Over tea and scones, Leonardo Rosario criticized her lithe frame as though she were an inferior side of beef, but seeing his son's happiness, pronounced her capable of fattening, a quality that had already been realized quite sufficiently in his wife. Doris Rosario was a round, pink and sweet-faced lady in ruffles and clearly subordinated to a husband who kept her as listless and silent as an overfed pet. And while Madeline obediently consumed an abundance of crumpets during the introductory tea, she silently vowed that she would not follow the sorry path of her mother-in-law.

Her own marriage by contrast would be a great romance between equals.

Jonathan Rosario and Madeline Gallacuty embarked upon their lifetime journey from inside a proper Anglican church where, before a blur of pews and faces, feather hats and scrambling children, they promised to have and to hold, through sickness and in health, from this day forward. With their vows sealed by the organ's soaring chords, they set sail into the world of society, properly and inexorably married.

Well-wishers grasped the couple's hands, and in a whirlwind of confetti rice and backslapping and cigar-swapping and mothers' tears, they traveled on to the station and the Chicago Limited.

Mr. Gallacuty approved the handsome paneling and leather seats of their sleeper while Madeline's trunks, hatbox, boot bag, cape and muff were stored in the baggage car. Mrs. Gallacuty proclaimed the washbasin's linen supply insufficient and counseled Madeline to see to a porter about it. Her daughter said that of course she would see to it. She was after all going to be a perfect wife and a proper supply of linens was only the beginning.

The conductor called for all to board and for those who were not holding tickets to leave. In the final rush of hastened good-byes, Madeline became teary. She kissed her father, the last to step off before the porter closed the door, the last face she saw through the window before the train glided into motion and rolled out of the station.

Jonathan followed Madeline down the rocking corridor to their compartment. After a flurried rearrangement of cloaks and cases, they collapsed into seats across from one another, alone for the first time as man and wife. To ease their discomfort, Jonathan pointed to the scenery passing by their window. Madeline looked out unseeing with a stunned and frozen smile, all the while carefully removing first the pin and then her hat and placing it on the seat beside her in a movement so feminine his heart caught in his throat. He felt bold and audacious when he reached for her hand.

"My wife," he said.

"My husband," she replied.

And then they both laughed as if they had staged some elaborate coup, for they were both strangers to one another after all, and no one knew it better than they.

Chapter 8

The porter called them to supper in the dining car at six o'clock that evening and for this Madeline was grateful, for she had not eaten on that day, her wedding day, too excited had she been to afford sustenance more than a passing glance. As they stumbled into the rollicking dining car, the scent of sauces and meats brought to her a sharp delicious hunger that signified more than a mere craving for food but also an anticipation of something wonderful. Jonathan would produce the pendant for her soon, she knew, and with it a proposition that they experience the world together as equals. She had been experiencing this sensation of imminent freedom since the train had begun lightly jarring her senses in a rock-a-by way, moving her onward to the new territory that would be the start of her first life adventure.

She had changed out of her wedding gown at the chapel hours ago but had the distinct impression of appearing like a new bride to anyone who glanced her way. The maitre d seated them at a linen-covered table set with simple china. Gently solicitous, Jonathan inquired as to what most appealed to her on the menu, saw to her missing butter knife, and directed her attention to the lighted church steeple among the passing scenery outside, now hidden among the darkness of the quickly descending night. When she looked to the window she saw her own face reflected back in amber from the lamp upon their table, and when she wasn't looking down at her hands or the place setting before her, she peered at Jonathan gazing upon her with all the frankness of a connoisseur appraising an exceptional object d' art.

His stare provoked her to shyness, and she felt constrained by the high-necked collar pressed against her throat. A silver-headed waiter poured burgundy wine in a crystal glass. Jonathan tasted it before allowing the wine to be served to her. Madeline sipped it carefully. She was no longer a child begging permission from her parents for a sip but instead a full grown woman, wife to Jonathan Rosario, a husband who would see to her temperance and protect her from wrongful gossip or assumption. Casting furtive glances at other tables, Madeline saw women, matrons and young, freely imbibing. She was safe in Jonathan's company, for he was a proper gentleman. Reassured by this, Madeline again sipped the wine. She felt a disorienting though not unpleasant flush, and no longer as shy as she had been moments before, raised her eyes to her husband.

"There are many advantages to marriage," Madeline said.

"Yes, indeed, indeed yes," Jonathan said. His fingers fanned across the cloth until his pinkie touched against her hand curled around the base of the glass. It electrified her.

"You are responsible for my welfare," Madeline continued.

"Your life is in my hands, and you can be certain that I will cherish it beyond my own," Jonathan said.

It was a fine speech. Kindly passengers at neighboring tables looked their way.

"And so," Madeline said, her voice so low Jonathan had to lean forward to hear it, "I could drink as much wine as Papa and you would see to it that I be properly put to bed."

Jonathan gave pause and a momentary look of disapproval crept into his eyes before it was overtaken by tender amusement.

"Of course," Jonathan said, "you are in safe hands with me."

Their mutton arrived. She ate voraciously, struggling to maintain a lady-like comportment yet wondering if she would always have to be a lady now that she was married. And yet with every sip of the fruity wine, a firm opinion rose to the foreground of her mind: She was going to be herself with Jonathan, more than a perfect lady, more than simply a wife. She was going to be free.

Over supper Jonathan spoke of his plan to expand his business, and to this she listened with an expression of such placid beauty, such innocent simplicity, he found himself inwardly smiling. She was an exceptional conquest; pliant, trusting, beautiful. She was an island of innocence upon which this night, their wedding night, he would bestow his worldly, manly love. He would be noble, tender, generous, just, and self-sacrificing with his passion for he could see for himself that she was already blushing with maidenly shame.

And yet as they ate their dinner, he found the evening evolving in a manner he had not anticipated. This he attributed to her justifiably nervous condition, which spawned odd conversational remarks.

"I think we should offer a few more modern items in the shop," she said, "That way, we might lure younger customers. Don't you agree?"

"But we are an antique shop," he said. Clearly his wife knew nothing about business and so he explained, "One must provide a reliable image to clientele, who expect consistency. Modern items would be out of place."

"Only to the old fuddy-duddies," she retorted. It was quite disturbing, really, to hear her so opinionated. "You see," she continued, "the shop is called Rosario *Imports*, not Rosario *Antiques*. Our sign promises new and different imports, not the same old things."

It was most audacious of her, and he struggled against feeling insulted, but insulted he was.

"I beg to differ with you, Madeline. I sell quality pieces that have withstood the test of time. I am not interested in passing fancies."

A faint fear crept into her eyes that he was gratified to see. He would have to keep her girlish whims at bay and impress upon her that he was lord and master of the business. If it hadn't been for their honeymoon, he would have left her in her rightful place, which was back home with his mother and father.

"I am sorry," she said, clearly aware she had gone too far, "You do know best."

She looked down in the most modest of ways and he instantly forgave her indiscretion.

Their glasses were replenished with more wine, and as they were he dared to linger his gaze upon those lips and those breasts swelling beneath the filigreed cameo brooch at her bosom.

"I shall be a true wife," she said, "My whole life and being will be given over to you. My soul, thought, and body."

At this she reddened. Jonathan smiled, touched by her romantic fervor. She continued, galvanized by the wine, her voice rising.

"I know you think me a silly child, but you will see that I am nothing like my mother."

"Don't worry yourself, Madeline, I see no similarities in the slightest."

"I want you to know I will be your partner in all things."

She grasped his hand, surprising him with the strength with which she clung. This was new to him, a wife so desperately clinging. He found himself hoping the benefits would out-weigh the sensation of burden. As if reading his mind, her grip loosened and her face turned soft and trusting again.

"Would you allow me, husband, to have a little more wine?"

He considered her state. Before he could draw any conclusion, her lashes fluttered shadows upon her cheeks and she said, "I am a little trembly about tonight."

How she wrenched his heart!

"You have nothing to fear from me," Jonathan said. He nevertheless poured her a hearty glass, half-hoping the delicate creature would be wise enough to sleep through the first night of what proper ladies regarded their greatest mortification.

She leaned freely against him during the rocking walk back to their Pullman. It was shocking behavior, made more prevalent by the occasional witness passing through the narrow corridor.

"Oh dear, I'm so dizzy, excuse me," Madeline said, thrusting herself against his chest as they made way for a large matron and her portly husband, who eyed the young couple with disapproval. Responsible for his wife's obvious inebriation, Jonathan took hold of her waist and nearly carried her, giggling and sighing, into their cabin. He locked the door, grateful for the privacy that had earlier discomfited them so. When he turned around ready to chide or subdue her, he saw that she was already seated prim and docile upon the bed the porter had prepared for them.

"I don't know what overcame me."

Jonathan sat beside her and took her hand in his.

"It is a case of nerves. And too – much – spirits," he said, playfully making a final tap with his finger upon her nose. She grasped his finger, brought it down to her lips and kissed it. It was a bold gesture done demurely, and it catapulted him into a flood of erotic sensation. Before he could think to stop, to go slow, his lips sought hers, kissing her deeply, island of innocence be damned. She responded with a cry of alarm and pulled away.

"Why did you do that?" she gasped with more surprise than loathing.

"Do what? Kiss you?"

"With your tongue," she said, wrinkling her brow.

Of course. His impulse had been thoughtless, founded on too long associations with low women and their ungoverned lusts.

"Forgive me," Jonathan said.

"Kiss me like that again."

"No, Madeline dear, you are too good a girl."

Madeline gazed down into her lap with an expression he mistook for shame. When she looked up at him again, he could see that she had been thinking, scheming in fact.

"Perhaps you would like to take off my brooch," she said.

It was an invitation he could not refuse. And yet as he complied with trembling fingers, the removal of the brooch led to his inevitable desire to see the displacement of other garments that had suddenly become irritating impediments to his final goal.

He was a man on a mission, and the urgency with which he ventured forth to his ultimate destination was tempered only with marginal success by his earlier, now seemingly distant self-promise to be noble in his passion. In an effort to slow his progress he placed the brooch in his pocket then removed his waistcoat, folding it carefully upon the washstand.

Madeline watched him with lidded eyes from which he could discern no notable emotion. Heartened by her inaction, he grasped her face in his hands and kissed her, parting her mouth until he felt her tongue pressing cautiously against his lower lip. He drove her back into the pillows then, and kissed her as fully as her heart desired until she clung to his arms and clawed her fingers down the length of his back and squirmed and whispered, "please," and "please" again until he stopped to check himself. He had gone too far once more, he feared, but pulling back he saw her eyes turned glassy with wine and her hands fluttering at her bodice.

"Please," said she, "I need to breathe. I must breathe."

"Take heart, darling," he said, "I will help you."

Never before had he seen so many buttons, and so small too and slippery with silk. As the train rollicked over the tracks, they escaped his eager awkward fingers, but with the utmost concentration and purpose he freed her at last. She kissed him gratefully with sighs of thrilling satisfaction and peeled her slender arms from the bodice's fitted, undoubtedly suffocating sleeves.

And yet there was more, and with this she did help him: A ribbon sash with hidden eye hooks beneath the pleats, the long skirt with more buttons still that clung against her hips as if refusing to relinquish their maiden to her now rightful owner, and finally, wonderfully, a white sleeveless camisole of lace and satin ribbon with yet another fastening of hooks.

Jonathan stopped to savor the moment. It was the final layer. The peachy hue of her rising-falling breasts lay but a gossamer ribbon's distance from his possession. She watched with eyes like smoke and uttered breathy gasps of mingled shock and approval as he unfastened each hook from its eye, one by one, parting the fabric of tissue to behold the mounding rosy gifts inside. It was better than he had imagined, had he but dared to imagine. And yet respecting her modesty, he did not gaze too long upon his treasure but rather pulled her to him in an embrace that crushed her lovely flesh against him.

She melted, she sighed; she unpinned her hair. He peeled off his shirt. She stared with childlike fascination at his naked chest then rose up upon her knees to kiss his neck.

"Madeline, sweet Madeline," he murmured, crushing her tangled hair in his hands.

The train jolted, flinging her conveniently down upon her back. He pulled the shade across the window, fleetingly wondering why he hadn't thought to do it before.

"Please," she said, reaching her arms up to him, her skin golden in the lamplight, "would you lie on top of me?"

"Certainly," Jonathan replied in a strangled voice.

Carefully, most carefully, lest he break his china doll, he complied. Her body stiffened and softened beneath him like a rising and falling tide until, after several repetitions of this, he came upon the appalling realization that she was writhing with desire.

"Hush, don't move," he said. The command in his voice froze her instantly.

"Don't move," he said again, and reaching down along the length of her waist slip, pulled it up, up, inch by inch. He unfastened her stockings from their suspenders, pulled her knickers down past her knees. She shuddered. She pulled the hem of her slip up over her hot face and waited, rigid, as he unbuttoned and pulled off his trousers. He laid atop her again, his skin against hers. She didn't move. He removed the slip from her face. Her eyes were shut tight, her face in a grimace of dread anticipation.

"Madeline dearest," he whispered, and kissed her softly upon her hot cheek. She opened her eyes to his and in their depths he saw simple terror. This was how it must be, he told himself as he stroked her inner thighs and parted them. She was indeed the perfect virgin.

The train shuddered as they picked up speed, their compartment lurching from side to side, but Jonathan was hurtling forward now, down into an abyss from which he would emerge an inescapable married man.

Chapter 9

hey had crossed the Mississippi and were traveling through a wide desert landscape without tree or flower or cloud, under a sky so brilliant it illuminated her deep down to the bone. Jonathan caught Madeline's hand as the train lumbered into Santa Fe. They had consummated their marriage in a most satisfying manner, and now she held her head high in anticipation of all this would mean. As a married woman her life would have more significance now, of this she was certain, and she would have a greater say in all things and ways of the world.

The porter opened the door, placed the step, and offered her his assistance. Setting foot upon the dusty platform, she was struck first by the stillness. There was no swaying beneath her feet, no iron wheels thumping against the rails, no wind. In the harsh brightness of mid-day, the town had no shadows, no trees, no colors even, if one discounted the beige of sand and adobe as color.

The Rosarios were transported to the Palace Hotel, a large square brick building at the lonely center of two crossroads at the edge of town. Madeline searched for cowboys along the way and saw only hard dirty men with stubbled faces and shifty eyes. She spotted an Indian, but he wasn't astride a pony or even wearing a headdress of feathers but rather slumped against a building in a stupor of half slumber. Madeline was sorely disappointed.

The softly lighted interior of the Palace Hotel was as ornate and eastern as the streets outside were barren and western. The wood-work was massive; doors and windows had fluted frames with plaster moldings shaped into decorative swirls. There was a Steinway near the reception desk with a red velvet cloth draped diagonally across its top and a vase of brilliant blooms that in fact were made of silk.

A German woman with a thin knot of white hair and small pale blue eyes showed them up to their respectable room and to the pristine bath down the hall. Dinner and breakfast were served punctually, Mrs. Schuler said, and evening entertainment could be had at the Beer Brewery, men only of course. Madeline felt a chill, and missing the lullaby rocking of the train, reached for her husband's arm.

"I won't be long," Jonathan was saying to her, freeing himself from her grasp, "Stay here and I will be back shortly."

"But where are you going?" Madeline cried, "May I come too?"

"I have business," he said.

"But I am your business partner!"

"We will converse on that later," he replied.

He kissed Madeline upon the head and left her to the unpacking. This was not how she thought he would behave, not after his romantic passion of the past several nights. He belonged to her now more than ever, as she to him, and so she did not comprehend his attitude of distance when before he had been so close, so completely and utterly hers.

Madeline poured herself a drink of water from the bedside pitcher then applied herself to the task at hand, seeing to her husband's shirts and trousers and linens first, hanging her wrinkled dresses last. She assembled her husband's laundry which, instructed by the firm Mrs. Schuler, was to be left in a cloth sack by the door for the house girl to pick up.

After all was in order, Madeline sat at the window overlooking the bleak, treeless street and realized to her regret that she was back in an all too familiar pose. She wondered how this came to be so soon in a married life that was to be a romantic union of equals, and yet felt certain that Jonathan had not intended for her to be unhappy. Rising from the chair, she reassured herself by unpacking his toiletries – his shaving brush and cream and razor, his comb – and it was during this task that she came upon the handkerchief with the solid shape of a brilliant stone inside.

The pendant. The Whale Rider's crystal, promised to her.

She laid the heirloom neatly upon a linen cloth beside the washbasin and saw her image pass through the glassine depths, revealing a section of her face, the spark of her eye, and then the faint flash of her reflection, now gone.

Carefully she took it up in her hands and set it upon the windowsill and watched it reflect the desert light but saw no more of her features inside. She thought of how Jonathan had promised to reveal the content of his consultations with the antiquarian jewelers of Europe after they were wed. Now they were, and still he had said nothing. She would know the reason for his reticence.

Shadows lengthened. Soon the pendant was cast in shadow and the sun was gone and the day darkened toward evening. What sort of business did Jonathan have, after all, and where did one conduct business in a dull western town such as this? There were no proper banks that she could see, no men in distinguished suits, no town hall or library, but rather ramshackle huts crouched close to the ground and the occasional lone Mexican man walking the street.

Madeline stood, took the pendant in hand, and clasped the chain around her neck. The crystal hung down upon the ruffled shirtfront of her breast. It felt right and proper there where it belonged; not among

Jonathan's shaving needs. The pendant was hers, after all. It was time she seized possession of it.

And where *was* Jonathan, her husband?

It was the stillest, most silent street she had ever encountered. She heard the barking of dogs in the warm clear air and from some distance away the beat of drums. She passed two children riding a goat, rows of adobe houses, and groups of unusual plants she had understood from the periodicals to be known as yucca. She saw a man standing in the doorway of a hut, his naked belly shockingly exposed between the flaps of his leather vest. Madeline hastened her step.

Soon she found herself in the more populated plaza. A ragged band of Indians played drums before a curio shop. She walked on. She saw an active throng of rough-looking men presumed to be cowboys, and broad-hatted teamsters standing before a six-bull wagon team. She paused before the window of a dry goods store to study a jumble of merchandise that included vats of pickles, rifles, and ladies' kid gloves.

Another turn in the street lured Madeline into a dark shop. Indian rugs and Mexican embroideries were displayed, but the old woman behind the counter could not be roused to smile, no matter what exclamations of delight Madeline uttered in praise of the merchandise. She returned to the darkening street.

The lanterns in the plaza were now lighted, casting a yellow glow upon the crowd. Madeline saw no ladies, and the rough laughter of the teamsters, the crack of their whip, caused her to jump in alarm.

She wrapped her shawl tightly about her and held the pendant against her chest. She wanted to return to the hotel now, but feared the dark street and the Mexican with the big belly. She searched the faces for her beloved Jonathan. Where was he? Why had he deserted her? What business was so important to warrant this abandonment?

Struggling to withhold tears of desperation, she paused before a gilded window proclaiming itself the Bank Exchange Hotel Bar. Glancing toward its interior, she saw a man who resembled, surely was, her husband. He was standing at the bar with a grouping of men who, upon shifting position, blocked her view. It was unconscionable! What was Jonathan, her Jonathan, doing in a bar? And how was she to reach him through the crush of the clearly all-male establishment?

There was a sign in the window of the Bank Hotel Exchange Bar:

DOORS OPEN TO LADIES IN MASKS

What a strange western custom! She recalled the masked balls among New York's sophisticates, but peering through the gilded lettering on the window, she saw no ladies and no masks. Madeline paced a step or two. She watched a fellow enter with all the as-you-please cockiness of one who could come and go as he wished. Insufferable! And to think she would have to depend upon a stranger to communicate her presence to her husband! Well, she would not be denied entrance. She need only find a mask and wear it into the bar, and thus be guiltless of any impropriety.

But where to find a mask?

And then she remembered. Tracing her steps back to the Indian curio shop, she found a somewhat appalling contraption of feathers, teeth and antler, useful perhaps for later anthropological study, but a mask nonetheless. Paying the somber woman behind the counter, who informed her she was purchasing a prized Pueblo deer head mask, Madeline envisioned her husband's praise for this unusual purchase. No one in New York had ever seen anything like this before! They wanted a mask, she would give them a mask!

She waited until returning to the entrance then, determined in her goal to procure her husband, held the mask before her face and entered the all-male establishment.

Chapter 10

$\mathcal{I}$t was one of the oddest sights Jonathan and his drinking companions had ever seen, and they all were greatly amused. A woman had entered the Bank Exchange Hotel Bar holding a sacred Pueblo deer mask before her face. Its horned antlers swayed high over her head and a row of pointed teeth and feathers disguised her face. She stumbled a little, the contraption undoubtedly distorting her view. Regaining her balance with the aid of the amused and courtly fellow with whom she collided, she proceeded on toward the bar with a most singular purpose. Many a man observed her attractive figure, which was slim and lithe but certainly belonging to a low, comely sort of creature who regularly put on such displays.

"The woman must be mad," Jonathan said to the trader Smithie. He then came upon the unsettling realization that the shawl the madwoman wore was shockingly familiar and that, even more unsettling, she wore upon her breast that damnable space jewel!

"Jonathan!" The madwoman said, "I have found you at last!"

Hoots of laughter trailing behind them, Jonathan grasped her arm and propelled her toward the door. It seemed she'd gone mad in the short space of an afternoon, and he could only surmise the crystalline pendant, that wretched piece of space trinket so coveted by the Europeans, had provoked her new behavior. She had clearly taken it from his toiletries when he'd secretly planned that she'd never see it again. It wasn't so much that he believed what the Englishman had

71

told him about the rebel queen and the power derived from a meteoric stone. No, he did not believe it. But the very notion of it, the very myth alone, distressed and angered him, and he would not have his wife entertain such ideas.

"What an adorable Western custom," Madeline was saying by the time they had reached the outdoors, "But I do think I would prefer a daintier mask next time. Tell me, what do the other ladies wear?"

Jonathan wrenched the mask from her hand.

"What in the world do you think you're doing?" he shouted.

"I wanted to reach you! I saw you at the window but you didn't see me!"

Her hair was disheveled and her eyes were pink. Even without the mask Jonathan perceived her as utterly mad.

"You could have asked a gentleman entering to draw me out."

"But I didn't want to draw attention to myself."

"Draw attention to yourself!" Jonathan choked on the words.

"Madeline dear," Jonathan said, and steered her away from watching eyes into the darker reaches of the street, "I was conducting business."

"Oh, certainly, and what sort of business is that, imbibing in a saloon?"

She emphasized the word "saloon," and he could see that she relished the western sound of it, as if she were play-acting a scene from a Wild West show.

"I acquire information on the latest Pueblo gatherings," he said with a tolerant sigh, "from those who are in the know."

"Well, you shouldn't shunt me off to do your laundry and sit alone," Madeline said in a haughty tone he did not like, "And you have kept my heirloom for yourself without telling me the reason for this unwarranted breech of trust."

Jonathan paused. If there ever was a time to exert his wise and superior power over her it was now. She had after all behaved abominably, and she had to learn that, as her benevolent and loving husband, his tolerance had its limitations.

"That pendant is not appropriate for a lady."

"Then I shan't be a lady," she said.

"That is enough!" Jonathan said, and threw the deer mask on the ground. Teeth and antlers shattered. He watched her eyes grow large then tearful. She must know now, he thought, that she had made a grievous mistake, for she had disappointed the single most important man in her life. He would forgive her of course, but he would have to be firm.

"I must request," Jonathan said with finality, "that you give the pendant back to me."

She gave him the sort of look he had once seen on the face of a cat, a large one from Bengal with massive claws.

"No I will not. It is mine."

"No, it is mine," Jonathan said, "I am your husband now, and by law all your possessions, including you, are mine."

She stared at him as though he were a monster. And that was when he knew. Knew he had made an irreparable mistake. He was now no longer the wise husband and she had ceased being the demure beauty he had first encountered in his shop. They were not the persons they had fallen in love with or the couple that had so passionately coupled over the course of their train journey. Their marriage was a tragic mistake.

"I hate you!" Madeline cried, and ran down the street, "I wish I were a man!"

I too wish you were a man, Jonathan thought as he followed her. *That way I might thrash you from head to toe.*

Jonathan and Madeline Rosario spoke little during the evening meal at Mrs. Schuler's, exhibiting only perfunctory interest in the conversation of the other hotel guests. An elderly gentleman with a walrus mustache of comical proportions who proclaimed himself one of President Teddy Roosevelt's infamous Rough Riders was more than happy to recount his adventures to the pale and pretty Mrs. Rosario, but she unfortunately did not profess the level of admiration that was due him. Another couple, older than the Rosarios but as loving and convivial with one another as perfectly mated leather gloves, happily recounted their day's adventures, eliciting a disparaging glance from the young Mrs. Rosario at her husband when they said they had been to see the Pueblo pottery makers.

The Rosarios at last left the table, provoking a collective sigh of relief from the others, who preferred partaking of the desert custard without the young couple's gloomy faces disrupting their enjoyment.

Up in their room, Jonathan and Madeline made silent preparation for their retirement. Madeline slipped out and spent an inordinate amount of time in the bathing room at the end of the hall. While Jonathan sat hunched in his suspenders at the writing desk pretending to be immersed in his business, Madeline crept back from the commode in her nightgown and slipped into bed. She was by all appearances asleep when Jonathan saw that she was still wearing the pendant, the crystal clutched in her fist as if fearing he would take it from her. He would if he could.

He turned out the light and crawled onto his half of the mattress, his body reluctantly rolling toward the sagging center where his wife lay. So furious was he, so consumed by his own smoldering rage, he did not notice this was the first night of his married life that he had failed to make love with her.

A wind rose up that night across the desert. It came battering through town, slammed at doors, pushed against windows. Madeline awoke with a cry of alarm. She clutched the heirlooom in her hand and lay there as Jonathan snored on unawares and shutters banged in the wind.

It was a demon, this wind. It hurled objects through the street and bellowed down the drafty hall, threatening, screeching. She lay in the vortex of its rage, and the pain in her head worsened. She began to shake with a deep fear she could not name or understand. She was in a wrong place, a strange place. She was the demon's victim, and she could only sob in terror. She wanted to go home to Papa and sleep in her own bed, not beside this stranger who claimed to own her and all she possessed.

"Tell me what is the matter, Madeline."

Awakened by her sobbing, Jonathan pressed her to name her ailment, but she was locked inside a terrible place in which her head succumbed to a relentless, increasing pressure.

"I'm sorry we fought," Jonathan was whispering, "Perhaps I frightened you, dear. I am sorry, it's all right now. It's all right," he said, stroking her hair.

His caring meant nothing to her. His voice was but a distant sound drowned by the demon pressing against her ears and clutching at her throat until her breath came in gasps and she could find no breath at all.

Jonathan ran down the stairs to awake Mrs. Schuler, who called for a doctor. When he returned to the room he found her curled upon the bed and biting her thumb. She spoke little to Jonathan, who pleaded with her to describe her ailment.

The brusk Dr. Gerard at last arrived. Clearly arisen in the night, he wore a look of irritable skepticism.

"What ails the little lady?" the doctor said. Moving to the bed, he placed his hand upon Madeline's forehead and with the other checked her pulse. Madeline rose herself slightly when she saw him, a greater look of fear now welling in her eyes. The doctor turned and motioned Jonathan and Mrs. Schuler out of the room.

"Compose yourself, Madam," the doctor was saying to Madeline as Mrs. Schuler shut the door.

Jonathan paced the hallway. Mrs. Schuler in her dark dressing gown stood by.

"I don't believe it is serious," the woman said and returned to her room.

"Thank-you, I hope so," he whispered alone to the lantern sputtering a weak yellow light in the drafty hall. He was full of regrets. He loved Madeline after all, this he could not deny, and it pained him to see her suffering.

The door opened and the doctor came out. Jonathan began to enter, but the man closed the door and, taking him confidentially by the arm, ushered him down the stairway to the lobby floor.

"She will sleep. I gave her a mild opiate."

"What is the matter with her?"

The doctor paused at the entryway and surveyed him over the rims of his spectacles before he spoke.

"A touch of hysteria," the doctor said.

Jonathan knew not what to say and so the physician continued.

"Her affliction is hopefully slight. In worse cases it can destroy a marriage, render a woman an invalid for life."

"But," Jonathan said, "What are the symptoms?"

"Oh," the doctor said with what to Jonathan seemed a disturbing nonchalance, "Anything from headaches to dizziness, hysterical sobbing and seizures. You see sir, these women, these women hysterics, have no serious medical problems. No elevated pulse other than from fear. There really is very little one can do for them."

"That's impossible!" Jonathan said, "I cannot accept that."

The doctor was not a tall man, nor was he even stalwart, but his advanced years gave him a formidability that the younger man, ruled at this moment by passion and guilt, lacked.

"You will have to accept it," the doctor snapped. Seeing Jonathan's stricken face, the older man softened, looked at his watch, and motioned for him to follow him to the dining room where, apparently familiar with its furnishings, he opened the liquor cabinet and poured them shots of brandy into heavy crystal snifters.

"I do not know your wife," Dr. Gerard began, seating himself in a chair at the waxed oak table, "but there is something we refer to as the 'hysterical personality,' and if she fits that description, she might well be a burden to you, sir, for the rest of your married life."

This was horrific news, more than Jonathan could begin to fathom, and in response, he downed half the brandy in his first swallow.

"Sit down, man, sit down," the doctor ordered, "and I will tell you about women hysterics."

Jonathan seated himself reluctantly, as if joining in some conspiracy he wanted no part of.

"I can surmise your lady comes from a well-to-do family," Dr. Gerard said, removing a pipe from his pocket and filling it slowly with tobacco, "Perhaps petted and spoiled by her parents, waited upon hand and foot by household servants. Am I not right?"

Dr. Gerard lit the pipe with satisfaction, and before Jonathan could sputter a reply, continued.

"She has lived a self-indulgent life. She has never been taught to control her idle emotions and desires, and certainly has not been trained for her life's duties as a wife and mother. Having found herself suddenly confronted with the responsibilities of marriage, she has responded with an act of hysteria which she thinks will win her your sympathy."

"But of course she has my sympathy!" Jonathan exclaimed, "She is in pain."

"In her mind, that is," the doctor continued smoothly. "She is extremely willful, is she not?"

"Yes," Jonathan replied with reluctance.

"And manipulative, no doubt. Manipulative. By her distorted view. There is but one important personage in the universe, and that is herself. Am I not right?"

Jonathan took another drink of brandy and considered. It was as if the doctor were reading Madeline like a book, but one with missing chapters.

"Tell me," the doctor continued, not waiting for Jonathan's reply, "Is she frigid, your wife?"

"Pardon me, Sir?"

"You see, the hysterical personality – "

"I believe you have overstepped your bounds, Sir. "

"Hysterics are often asexual creatures, you see."

"You are speaking of my wife, Sir," Jonathan said, and to accent his displeasure, he stood, scrapping his chair upon the floor. He did not like this Dr. Gerard. He was too self-satisfied, too fond of his pipe.

"Calm down, son," the doctor said.

"This conversation is concluded," Jonathan said, "I will pay you for your services, doctor, but your opinion is no longer required."

"Very well."

Dr. Gerard calmly took a final draw on his pipe and stood. Desperate to see Madeline, Jonathan slammed his glass down upon the nearest table and ran up the stairs.

The hallway was as cold as when he had left it, but a dim blue light from the dawn seeped in through the beveled glass window. The door to their room stood silent and beckoning, and yet he approached it with the dread and fear of a man about to witness the finality of his future. Was she a madwoman? An hysteric? Would he have to lock her in an attic and spend the rest of his years hiding her from the world? Pausing, preparing himself, Jonathan at last opened the door and saw to his relief that Madeline was sleeping.

He approached the bed and stood silently watching her slow, even, peaceful breathing. The pendant rose and fell on her breast, glowing in moonlight. He understood that she must keep it now; it was hers after all. He had no business taking it. What harm could it do? It belonged to her and it made her happy, and there was nothing in the world he wouldn't do to assure her happiness. She was his princess, his beauty, his bright shining girl, and whether he be wise or foolish in his infatuation, he was with her for the duration.

Chapter 11

*M*adeline awoke to a view of a man's hand lying in gently curled repose upon a bent knee. Long and limbered, it had tapering fingertips that folded, palm upward, like a half-opened shell. It was a large hand, and Madeline stared at it for some time in dreamy, rising consciousness before becoming aware that the hand belonged to Jonathan, the man she had married.

Odd, that she would not have noticed the shape of his hands until now, and odder still that she would have married him without knowing his temperament, so evident last night in his shocking display of anger. And yet, as her gaze traveled from his gentle hand to his sleeping form slouched in the chair beside her, she could see that he was not a bad man and maybe even a good man. He had, after all, good hands.

His face seemed good as well. Lashes rested with benign innocence upon his smooth and tender cheeks; dark locks hung over brows that arched from the center of a straight, slightly pointed nose, imperfect and therefore comical, worthy of love. His lips, thin and wide, emitted a soft snore. With his head dropped in slumber, Madeline could not discern the shape of his jaw. Was it a "strong' jaw? A 'noble' jaw? She rose in bed to catch a better look, and in rustling the bed covers, woke him.

He turned to her instantly and, rising from his chair, took her hand in his.

"Madeline darling, I am terribly sorry I frightened you last night. Are you all right?"

"Yes, better thank-you," she replied.

She searched her memory for what had brought about her disturbance then remembered he had threatened to take back the pendant. He'd said that, as her husband, it belonged to him, as did all of her things, all of her life, belonged to him. She threw back the bed covers and rose.

Jonathan observed her with alarm, but she did not care. She recalled how she had unburdened her terrors to the doctor and how his eyes had been cold, colder than Dr. Thomas P. Wilson's. He had called her an hysteric then given her an injection which made her suddenly awash in good feeling. That was when she had loosened her grip on the heirloom and fallen asleep.

Awakening more fully now, she looked down at her nightgown lace encircling her throat and saw it there, the crystalline shape with the mirror-like shard inside. It was still hers.

He will try to smother me, she thought. No love is worth losing oneself.

"I see your pendant means a great deal to you," he said, "Therefore I promise I will not take it. I was angry with you for retrieving it without my permission, for you must know I have only your best interests at heart. I will tell you now how I heard many strange stories concerning your jewel piece and was troubled by them, although I doubt them to be true."

"Tell me the stories," she said.

He recounted what the antiquarian jeweler told him, and as he did so she worked to hear the truth behind his disparaging words, the truth obscured by his disbelief. She found herself despising his logic and certainty.

"There may be things in this universe, my dear husband," she said at last, "Of which you know nothing."

They stood a short distance apart, he in his robe, she in her sleeping gown, and glared at one another.

"Of that I concede," he said.

"That is noble of you," she replied.

It was an effort at reconciliation. She turned away from him and pinned up her hair, piece by piece, pin by pin, then poured water into the basin and washed her face. Her skin felt feverish. She strove to still her voice from screaming out the horrible truth that Jonathan, her new husband, had become her new jailer.

"I would be so very pleased to accompany you on your journey to the pueblo today," she continued, modulating her voice to project an air of serene, unquestionable confidence, "If you will not let me participate in your business purchases, you could at least grant me the pleasure of sightseeing."

"Very well, Madeline," he said, "You may accompany me to the pueblo."

She turned to him, her face washed, fresh and clean, and saw in his eyes that she appeared pretty, which was her goal. Speaking like the woman-child he expected her to be, she said, "Oh, thank-you! I promise I will be good!"

Married but a few scant days, and she had already learned one of the tricks of being a wife.

Chapter 12

*T*he desert was brighter, hotter, dustier and more wearisome than Madeline cared to admit, and worse yet, they rode in a carriage driven by an insufferably conceited man named Smithie, the trader, who had ordained himself an expert on all things New Mexican. This Smithie fellow treated her like an inconsequential shadow squeezed upon the carriage seat between them, and because she was nothing but a shadow, he spoke across her to Jonathan as though she weren't there, which of course she wasn't, being a shadow.

Soon shapes formed on the wavering horizon and sharpened into the red rock cliffs and rectangular dwellings of the pueblo, an entire civilization sprung up out of the earth, producing a living plateau with humans and animals and chimney tops spewing smoke in the still bright air.

Children flocked to their carriage. Smithie slowed it to a stop and brought out sugar candies, which the children accepted with shrieks of excited laughter. Tourists mingled near a set of adobe buildings where they bargained with Indian men over displays of earth-colored curios, baskets, blankets and rugs set upon woven mats.

Stepping down from the carriage, Madeline was assaulted by a sudden wind, her dress and shoes instantly coated with dust. Drums from a Pueblo dance rumbled the ground. Jonathan joined Smithie among the bargaining tourists while Madeline moved along the vendors in search of the animal miniatures her beloved suitor, now her less beloved husband, had given her on the day they met. She found instead a hanging display of whitened bones and feathers she recognized to be more deer head masks.

"Most anthropological," she muttered, and opened her parasol with a pop, brushing a display of hanging baskets and knocking them to the ground. A woman made scolding sounds in her native tongue.

"I am so sorry!" Madeline said. She dropped her parasol in the dust and bent to retrieve them. An elderly tourist and her companion tittered as the baskets tumbled and rolled. Jonathan noticed the ruckus, and to placate the angry pueblo woman, bought the entire lot.

"They're quite beautiful," Madeline said, and they were: Pale green and golden with tiny flecks of bird-like images in flight, and in many surprising and unusual shapes, some tall, others wider than serving platters. Jonathan barely gave them a glance. Madeline nevertheless deemed her clumsiness a triumph. He had bought them, had he not?

A sudden and powerful blast of hot wind blew up off the desert and persisted, unrelenting and harsh. The craftsmen scrambled to right their displays and blankets, and the baskets blew off suddenly toward the open desert, flying in every direction.

"Now see what you've done!" Jonathan scolded.

The baskets bounced and soared, landing on cactus and shrub, scattering across the sands. She ran to catch up, snatched them here and there, stacking one atop the other. Jonathan stomped upon one, crushing it, to stop it from rolling.

Madeline neared the brink of a chasm and heard the pounding of the drums growing distant, their vibration rising up through the soles of her feet. In her zeal to undo her wrong, she hurried in pursuit of the final runaway basket, but it flipped like tumbleweed and flew up off the ledge.

"Bullocks!" Jonathan cursed as the basket, truly the most exquisitely woven of them all, soared beyond reach. "That's money wasted."

I will show you my worth, thought Madeline, and stepped past Jonathan to snatch the basket from the air, for a moment triumphantly clutching its rim and simultaneously suspended in air. He made a grab for her skirt, but his fingers slipped past and soon she was falling, wind rushing through her hair, sun blinding her. She heard his wrenching cry.

She grappled for whatever her hands could find as she descended off the edge of the cliff, sliding past crumbling rock face and branches. The pain of the fall against rock and brush became a terrifying necessity. Solidity, a foothold, a branch, a sharp cactus or a jagged rock in hand meant survival.

Suddenly her downward fall halted. Breathing in air and dizzy with the effort, she was amazingly alive. She held onto a jutting piece of rock and pulled herself up onto a ledge. From overhead there came a horrible repeated howl she recognized as her name being called. Jonathan could not see that she was safe. Collecting her strength, she shouted back up to him, and heard in response a shriek of joy. Rocks and sand rolled past her, a blinding avalanche. She backed away from the onslaught.

Inside a cavity within the rock, there stood a woman.

White hair rose in wisps as thin and dry as the air, and bare feet planted at the base of a body that stood as firm as a pillar of ochre sandstone, her aged face a crevice of lines, dark and beautiful. The woman advanced and gently placed her claw-like hand upon the crystal pendant. Madeline remained still – her entire being warmed with the energy of heated earth.

Calmed to the very depths of her soul, she stopped seeing at all.

They brought her up the side of the cliff with a rope and the aid of the pueblo men and women who knew the cliffs and how to find their footholds and ancient hidden paths. People gathered around as they laid her down upon solid ground. Jonathan was but a shape, a shadow calling her name. She couldn't respond, couldn't even move her lips. Someone was giving her water to drink and someone was fanning her face with a wet cloth, but it was all hushed and distant, as though she were a spectator apart from the bustle around her.

Then the woman from the cliff parted the shadows. Her eyes sparked brilliant turquoise and when she spoke, her voice rumbled up out of the earth.

"Hold onto the amulet," the woman said, "Know who you are."

From far away Madeline heard her own voice. "Are you a Medicine Woman?"

"I am *la Que Sabe*, the One Who Knows."

"I have read in periodicals of the West about Medicine Men, but not of any Medicine Woman."

"That is because you are a white woman who is taught to know little."

It was horrible truth spoken clearly, and Madeline fervently wished to make it untrue. With a hand like the claw of a hawk, the woman grasped her chin and bestowed upon her a smile of infinite, tender compassion.

"You will change the ways of world when you know who you are."

A veil of clouds parted and the woman's white hair lifted. Her words faded into the wind. Soon Jonathan's face came into focus and then Smithie's behind him and then the others, the tourists and the Pueblo Indians who had brought her up from the cliff.

"Madeline, dear God," her husband said, "You are safe. I am with you."

And he was. She reached up to clasp his hand and he helped her rise from the makeshift stretcher. She searched the faces for the woman with the turquoise eyes, but she was gone.

"That woman," she began, "The One Who Knows — "

They gave her more water to drink. She heard the tourists speaking among themselves — *innocent bride, unbalanced, hysteric* — but she knew she was none of these things.

A crimson sunset sank into the Sangre de Cristo Mountains and dust devils rose up before the carriage as they sped back toward Santa Fe. Smithie was unusually silent and so was Jonathan. Madeline's body felt sorely bruised but a calm certainty burned within. Stretched beyond them stood a vista of rocks cast in orange light and purple shadow and what she saw in the crusted plateaus was a living earth, a voluptuous woman rolling over.

When she spoke of the woman named *La Que Sabe* the men silently exchanged glances and she understood that, to them, The One Who Knows was not real.

Chapter 13

They returned to New York with differing expectations, for rather than settling into her likely role as wife and mother, Madeline joined the Suffrage Movement, marched with shop and factory girls, and denounced the doctors who called her a hysteric. Jonathan joined her in solidarity and did not stop her from marching. He did not want to be counted among those who attempted to silence her. He dared not even try.

Still, he perceived the infernal trinket with its improbable history as an impediment to their perfect union. It had become her amulet and she wore it incessantly, even in the portrait he commissioned Mr. John Singer Sargent to paint of her.

And yet despite their disagreements they could not stop loving one another and children subsequently followed: Their first child was a daughter they named after Madeline who came to be known as Maddy, and their second was a son they named Stephen. With infant on hip and little Maddy clutching her skirt, Madeline became indispensable at the shop. She spoke of comb-back Winsors and Spinet desks, Duncan Phyfe reproductions and "authentic reproductions" by Stickley. She spoke of Bauhaus and how "utility is its own beauty," and she eradicated by example the notion that maternal love precluded any business acumen.

And so time proceeded into the first quarter of the new century.

Freud published "The Psychopathology of Everyday Life," Haley's comet was observed, Stravinsky's "Firebird" exploded upon the world's musical consciousness.

And Madeline became one of the first New Yorkers to drive a Model T. over the newly completed Manhattan Bridge.

Horace Gallacuty retired from his banking job and moved with the truculent Mrs. Gallacuty from Washington Square to a cottage on Rockaway Peninsula. It had been his dream to return to his boyhood seaside idyll in New Zealand, but when this wasn't feasible Madeline's ever optimistic and enterprising father made do with the seashore on a spit of land in the borough of Queens.

Then one day in March of 1911, a cigarette started a fire inside a bin of scraps inside the Triangle Shirtwaist Factory. Madeline heard the fire trucks, ran to the Factory and stood beside Hannah watching the smoke rise from the barred fire escapes while women and girls screamed from the windows and leapt to their deaths. The fire killed Hannah's daughter Simone and hundreds of other young woman. In the aftermath inhumane managers were blamed, including Ernest Wilkes who with the other male supervisors had inadvertently trapped the girls by locking the doors and windows.

Enraged at such injustice, Madeline joined in the fight to reform working conditions and hoped the new century would bring advancement for men and women alike. What it brought instead was war. Jonathan supported the War to End All Wars and Madeline joined the Women's Peace Party. Hannah's last living child Martin nearly died at the Front.

After the Armistice was signed there came the influenza epidemic. Feverish and dying, Paulette Rosario confessed to her daughter-in-law the many things she wished she had done if only her husband had allowed.

Soon after, Madeline's mother Adelaide's health declined and so too did her father's and the two passed on within weeks of each other. And in his final moments Horace Gallacutty looked upon his daughter with the same viridescent eyes as his sea captain father and proclaimed with all certainty that he would soon ride home to New Zealand on the back of his sister's whale.

And the century moved forward. Jonathan came to understand that, though he'd been forewarned by a Naples gypsy, the storm in his future turned out to be just that – a storm at sea that delayed his proposal but not his ultimate goal. After years of marriage and raising their son and daughter and oftentimes wondering if all would have been easier with a more pliant wife, he could not imagine a better life than the one he shared with his Madeline.

And Madeline went on working and loving her husband and children, discovering in time how her love for them unwittingly turned her into the domestic slave she once swore she would never be. Yet this did not trouble her for *finally,* the Nineteenth Amendment passed; *finally* women got the vote.

(*You will change the world, La Que Sabe* said.)

And as the Twenties began to roar and Madeline wondered at the faces inside the crystal who had come before, she thought of her own daughter Maddy, a bright light shining on the brink of the second quarter of the new century.

The Storm

Evening

The elevator lights blink back on and they lurch down one more floor until the doors finally open with a slow rattling creak. Five minutes inside a stuck elevator is an eternity to Maya, although her great grandmother is as unperturbed as only a 105 year old woman who's lived through two world wars can be.

Maya takes in a calming breath to stop her shaking and wheels Maddy and her walker out onto the lobby floor. She hears a nurse shouting into a cell about lost medical charts. Residents sit in wheelchairs, fretting, stupefied, as puddles of seawater rise up under their wheels.

A television blares news of the storm then briefly switches to a CNN story about a 14-year-old Pakistani girl shot in the head by Islamic radicals.

"Malala is one of us," Grandma Maddy says of the girl who has a fifty percent chance of surviving, "*She knows.*"

Maya tries to understand what her grandmother is talking about but it's hard to say, hard to know what she means, although she recalls she used to live in India. Now she stands before the television, fixated on news of the young education activist and the Taliban assassins who claim they feared the girl's "power of vision."

"Grams? We've got to go."

Outside, ambulance lights flash red onto droplets coursing down windowpanes. More paramedics have arrived. One of them is Joshua McFadden, his forearms a kaleidoscope of tattoos and his hair, almost as long as hers, brushing his shoulders.

"Hey," they say to each other in unison, then, "What're you doing here?" though it is obvious enough that she is with her grandmother and he is checking Mr. Buzzy's blood pressure.

"I'm taking my grandmother home to our house. If we can make it to the car."

"This white lady's your grandmother?"

"I'm Spanish!" Maddy protests.

Maya's cell is ringing from her jeans pocket but there is no way to answer with her hands holding the pillowcase satchel and her grandmother's arm and walker, and so with a flirty smile Joshua delicately plucks it out, the back of his hand brushing her hip.

"Hello Ma'am, hold on," he says and passes the phone to Maya's ear. Her breath falls on his nimble fingers and she nods her thanks, releases her grandmother, and takes the phone. He turns back to his patient. The squawking indistinct sounds she hears are her Grandmother Marjorie Berthe's strident voice shouting at her from the other end of the peninsula.

"COME —ET ME A— BREEZY POINT!"

"Where are you, Grandma?"

" – studio! –you get the – ?"

The phone goes dead and suddenly a piece of the Boardwalk slams into the seafront window. In one huge *whoosh* water and broken glass crash through the lobby and in a single quick impulsive movement Maya stashes the phone in her pocket, grabs hold of Maddy's arm and wheels her toward the exit.

"Maya!" Joshua slops toward her through the ankle-high water. "Where're you going?"

"I'm taking my grandmother home."

"There's flooding everywhere."

"She can't stay here! And I have four-wheel drive."

The head nurse is shouting orders for anyone who can walk to move up to the higher floors, but the elevator is out of order now so this means taking the stairs. Orderlies and volunteers begin wheeling the elderly up one stair at time. A woman is crying, her voice ragged with fear and dementia.

"Okay Maya, look," Joshua says. He rubs the top of his head and his hair stands up but he doesn't look comical; he looks capable, and she tries to not stare at his muscular arms. "I'm taking Mr. Buzzy to a shelter in Brooklyn if I can get across the Bridge. But I'll carry your grandma to the car, okay?"

"Thanks, Joshua, that's great, thanks so much."

She isn't going to cry although she feels something like the beginning of it swelling inside her chest. Her grandmother's eyes move from her and back to Joshua, then widen when he abruptly lifts her up with a *hang on, Ma'am.*

They are out the door in the pummeling wind and rain. A river of seawater runs under their feet on Rockaway Beach Boulevard. Maya flings open the Rover's passenger door and Joshua deposits her grandmother on the seat like a gunnysack of potatoes. *Whee,* she says as if she were riding a river raft. Maya sets the pillowcase satchel on the floor behind the driver's seat.

"Thanks Joshua," she says. Surging water pushes against her shins. She struggles to stand upright, grabs his forearm and notices one of the tattoos is in the shape of a vine encircling his wrist. She thinks of how he ought to be wearing a jacket in this cold.

"Hey, be careful," he says, "I mean it, don't do anything risky." He shouts to be heard over the wind and rain beating on the Rover's metal roof. An orange glow reflects off his face and when she turns around she sees that it comes from the sky.

"That's a fire," Joshua said.

"Where?"

"Breezy Point. Oh, man, looks like a big one."

Grandma Marjorie Berthe.

"I'd better get going," Maya says, and steps up into the driver's seat.

"Yeah, me too. You'll be okay. At least your house is the other direction. And a few blocks inland."

"See you," she says. She doesn't tell him she plans on driving toward the fire.

"Right. Hey, let's catch a movie or something when this is over."

He doesn't look at her but gives her shoulder a squeeze and then is gone, wading through the floodwater back toward Sea View to carry more elderly patients with his strong tattooed arms.

"Ready, Grandma?"

"Anytime."

She turns the ignition key, hopes the engine isn't flooded. It starts.

"We're making one more stop before home."

"My daughter Marjorie Berthe," Maddy said.

"Correct. We have to get her off Breezy Point."

"*Carpe diem,*"

"Seize the day. Right. We're going hurry and get her out of there."

Then Maddy Rosario says something else in Latin.

"*Tempus fugit.*"

"What's that mean, Grandma?"

"Time flies," says her 105-year-old grandmother.

Maya presses down on the accelerator and eases the Rover out into the seawater foaming over Rockaway Boulevard.

"*Tempus fugit,*" she repeats. "Well, you should know!"

"*They said I was the lost one,*" Great Grandma Maddy says, "*But I found her. I found myself.*"

1925
The "Lost Girl"

"We travel, some of us forever, to seek other states, other lives, other souls."

Anais Nin

Chapter 1

*T*he townhouse reeked of gin. Melting ice in the bathtub, the litter of glasses on the table and his desk and even downstairs in the lobby at the base of the staircase and on the mahogany banister, each held the remnants of some liquor, and now Martin Amberfitch stumbled downstairs to face his folly feeling as tired and used as an empty martini glass with lipstick stains on its rim.

The *bon voyage* party had started at Lou's Speakeasy and then moved on to the Cotton Club where they'd met up with the Huxley sisters and dear lovely infuriating Maddy Rosario, who had loved him since they were children and would not let him be. Martin went along because Fricky was a real cake eater with the girls and the ringleader in all the drinking. He knew every gin mill in town and wherever they went he had the waiters coming 'round every ten minutes, so the party went on and on, all the way back to Brooklyn.

And now, on the morning after a blotto party that left him with a nagging neck pain and pounding head, Martin stepped out into the wet spring morning knowing he must pack, say good-bye to Mother at Bellevue, and attend to his banking before setting sail for Paris.

Martin brought in the milk and *The World*. The headline – DARROW MERCILESSLY GRILLS BRYAN ON MIRACLES IN BIBLE – offered brief distraction. Bryan the fool. A noble fool perhaps but a fool nonetheless, and Darrow, "predator of the courtroom," had found Bryan's weakness. Martin agreed with *The World's* observation that Darrow was beyond proper etiquette in heckling Mr. Bryan, and yet Bryan's nobility was a fool's errand and no one knew it better than fellows like Martin and Fricky, which was why they drank and played at being merry last night until they stumbled back across the bridge.

Martin forgave Fricky the insanity and drinking just as Fricky forgave Martin his moods, for they had been brothers in arms in the allied offensive on the Marne outside Paris where among the shelled and battered farms they took shelter in pits and fought on the move without ever getting away from the smell of the unburied dead which stuck to their clothes and would remain in Martin's memory forever, his whole life forward, right down to his own dying day.

Fricky said the ticket to getting the smell out of your head was a bracing sea voyage to the City of Lights, which *was* a city of light now, no longer darkened by war but full of sparkle and jazz, beautiful women and art. Fricky's father was footing the bill and entrusting his son to be a reputable collector of the new modern art, and Martin had agreed to join his friend on board the *Aquitania* as companion and aide.

There was but one fly the ointment – well, their were many flies in the ointment – but the most predominant one was Maddy Rosario who had decided to impulsively invite herself along with her father's antiques buyer Mrs. Sullivan, and so they would be one big family: Maddy, Fritzy, Martin, and that fuzzy old dowager who was pushing forty at least.

Maddy was a sweet gal, a cute gal, the kind of gal any fellow would want, but she was a gal from a time before the war and Martin wasn't up for it. The boy she had known would never grow into the man he was supposed to have been, and every time he looked at her he could see she hadn't figured it out, would never figure it out, and he felt sad for it wasn't her fault but his that he was stuck with that smell from the Marne.

Washed and dressed in a dark linen suit, Martin cut a dashing figure as he walked toward the Avenue in Manhattan. Noise erupted all around and he tried to not flinch, for then people would see and know he'd been one of the doughboys.

How he hated the loudness of the city. It seemed New York was perpetually afflicted these days with the never-ending process of tearing down the charming and old and building the bigger and new, and the bigger the city grew, the uglier it became. He saw no point in staying other than to aid his mother who seemed nonetheless beyond his aid, caught up as she was in the sadness that had become their lives, with Simone gone and Martin himself a war casualty if not of body than spirit.

Ensnared in the day's rush, Martin pushed his way through the crowds, dust and smoke. Unlike his childhood friend Maddy, he bore no fondness for the unending and insufferable *New!*

Chapter 2

*M*addy was slim and strong and had the thick bourbon-and-red hair of her maternal great grandfather the sea captain. Though bobbed, her hair made her powerful according to some hocus-pocus her brother Stephen had read. She also had her father's dark Spanish eyes and her mother's porcelain skin and was given to outrage over injustices such as the subjugation of powerless women and children or the force-feeding of suffragists in her mother's time. Maddy was educated, and not from mere finishing schools. She read literature by Dreiser and Dos Passos and a new writer named Anais Nin and she wrote in a journal about fashion, music, and historical events in places as far away as Russia.

But what she wrote about most was love. Love, Martin, and erotic yearning; this covered the pages of her secret diary.

Maddy had watched Martin grow up six years ahead of her with all the fascination only a precocious little girl with a crush could have. She had studied his slim arched bare feet when they holidayed at her grandfather's cottage in Rockaway, had sneaked marshmallows into his hot chocolate when he wasn't looking. She had studied every aspect of his beauty, in and out: The way his face glowed and his long expressive fingers gestured in air, the way he sometimes looked at her, as if trying to unravel a puzzle. And she had held his hand after his sister died in the fire.

Now she was eighteen, dancing and drinking in speakeasies, and evading the Prohibition laws for which her mother's friends were to blame. As soon as they'd gotten the vote they went out and spoiled everyone's fun, only they didn't really, because there were now more speakeasies and secret places to dance and drink in New York than ever before.

Maddy believed life was for immoderate living, for exploring and loving as hard and furious as one could. While her mother believed in using one's intelligence for the service of others, Maddy did not. When it could all be taken away tomorrow by a useless and futile war, why live in service of others? Maddy's only service was her mission to heal Martin. She was certain that her love would return him to being the way he was before the war to end all wars, before the Great War became the eternal war inside his head. And so she was having loads of fun — determined fun, hysterical fun, fun tinged with a desperate sadness she aimed to ignore.

As far as Maddy could see it, her mother's generation was Victorian, Old Hat, passé. Her mother didn't understand how it felt to experience a grand passion such as the one she felt for Martin, nor did she comprehend the kind of blessed sweetness of infatuation that made you follow a man to the ends of the earth, or at least on a transatlantic crossing to Paris.

Madeline carried breakfast in to her daughter on a silver tray. She set it down upon the vanity and opened one of the curtains to allow the mid-morning light to hit the floor but not the bed where Maddy stirred. Maddy groaned and lifted her rumpled face from the pillow. Her mother poured but didn't pass her the cup. If her daughter wanted coffee she would have to rise to acquire it.

"Oh, I've such a head," Maddy said. Madeline made no reply.

"I visited at the Huxleys' house and then we went to Martin's for a little party, that's all, Mother, really."

"Was Fricky in your group?"

"Oh, Fricky's always around."

That was the giveaway, but what was a mother to do? Madeline wasn't one to lock her daughter up in her room. She would never subject her child to the incarceration she had endured, and so she simply had to accept the ways of the New Generation and hope they didn't kill themselves in their new motorcars.

"Alright, so I suppose I got a bit spifflicated last night. But you should have seen Martin, Mama, he was twice as ossified."

Maddy threw back the sheet and teetered in her wrinkled nightie over to the breakfast tray.

"I must look a horror," she said then smiled. "I'm leaving for Paris today!"

"With Mrs. Sullivan," her mother added.

"Mrs. Sullivan, of course," Maddy replied. She knew better than to sound ungrateful. It was an opportunity to travel to Paris, even if it meant being chaperoned by her father's most trusted antique buyer. Picking up the china cup, she took a careful sip of hot bitter coffee.

"I will be so happy to spend more time with Martin," she said, "He needs my help, you know."

"I know, dear," Madeline replied. She hoped Mrs. Sullivan would see to it that Maddy didn't spend all of her time with Martin. "But do know you can help boys like Martin in the future by speaking out in protest of all wars."

"Of course," Maddy said, then dutifully added, "I wish you could come to Paris too, Mama."

Madeline truly wanted to join her daughter and Mrs. Sullivan on their Paris buying trip, but their popular antiques business required the expertise of its owners and young Stephen demanded his mother's attentions and Jonathan needed her too, and so did the Women's Trade Union where she was treasurer.

And then there was her good friend Hannah. She most assuredly needed her.

Hannah blamed herself for failing to be in Simone's place on that day of the Triangle Fire, no matter that it was the fault of the factory owners for locking the exit doors and failing to clean the floors of hazardous scraps nor allowing the women any breaks from their machines. No, Simone's horrible death was not the fault of the mother who loved her. And now both mothers fretted for Martin who should never have gone to war. Madeline remembered him as a delicate boy and when she looked at him now she ached for what Hannah saw in the troubled soul of her only surviving child.

"Martin called me his little Sheba last night, Mother," Maddy said, "and I was so happy!"

"He's a fine young man," said Madeline. Seated at the vanity, she caught a glimpse of herself in the mirror and saw how her hair appeared burdensome and heavy. She looked like a Gibson Girl from the former century. It seemed only the young wore their hair in bobs, which was fine, but what she didn't understand was this generation's willful determination to perpetually party. She observed her daughter's fierce passion, her near psychotic intensity, and wanted the girl to seize such passion and channel it to good use. She hoped that life would be kind to Maddy and no disappointments would fall her way, that she would never be locked within the rules of convention like a canary in a covered cage – deprived of light, air and song. Her beautiful daughter was meant to sing, to soar, yet she feared Maddy's beauty would lead her to places in this modern world she couldn't begin to fathom.

And so Madeline felt a great hope that what she was about to give her daughter would protect and aid her on her first voyage into that wide and perilous world. She herself had no more need for it. She had gotten the vote and was a successful businesswoman now even though the slow forward process by which this had finally come to pass had taken a large portion of her youth. Time and aging invariably restricted everyone, but Madeline hoped the next generation, most notably her daughter, could make other good uses of the power the amulet had given her.

"I have something important for you, Maddy dearest."

She then lifted the chain up and over the mound of her Gibson Girl hair and held the gemstone pendant out in the palm of her hand to her daughter with the bob.

Maddy turned to her mother with a guarded expression, anticipating a lecture for last night's indulgences. But instead of a lecture her mother was giving her the strange pendant she had worn for years, ever since Maddy could remember. The jewel was as much a part of her mother as breathing. It had glinted above her in infancy when Mama came to kiss her goodnight, and was there when she cried on her mother's shoulder or snuggled beside her. It had rested upon her breast when she read aloud the inspirational passages from women authors of her day, and it was with her mother the day she'd cast her first vote for the presidency.

For her to be handing it over seemed as shocking and wrong as relinquishing a piece of her heart.

"You shouldn't, Mama, really. It is your prized possession."

"Which is why I am giving it to you."

Encircled by its ancient ornate filigree, the crystal glinted against the flesh of her mother's soft pink palm. A slash of blue silver ran through the stone, and for a brief instant Maddy saw movement – a woman's face? – inside its faceted world.

Maddy hesitated. In actuality, she did not want this heirloom she had heard so much about, with its old wives' tale history and magical mystery voodoo. But it meant a great deal to her mother, she could see, and so with reluctance Maddy politely, almost resentfully, accepted it. Though light of weight in her hand, it was a heavy burden.

In its own way, the heirloom itself was the ultimate lecture.

"Your grandfather's sister – "

"The Whale Rider, yes."

" – passed this down to me through my father. It will bring you a strength of spirit I promise you, that is, well, otherworldly."

Otherworldly. She had heard of how this gemstone of crystal and metal had come from a meteor and was once the possession of an ancient Iron Age queen. She had also seen how her father grew silent and watchful whenever his wife spoke of it, as though fearful of revealing any opposition.

"You will understand when you wear it," her mother said, "I know you will see."

But she would not see; willfully would not. The heirloom belonged to the world of women, not men, and Maddy aimed to be part of the world of men, not women. She was a man's girl, Martin's girl, not a girl's girl. She did not want to be in possession of an item that would estrange her from Martin. Martin was her reason for rising in the morning. Martin was the sun hidden by clouds, and like a nun she had made a vow of devotion to chase those clouds away.

"Thank-you, Mama."

Maddy did not put the pendant on but rather placed it in the glass ashtray among other trinkets she seldom wore. Madeline looked upon the gesture with disappointment.

"Let's pack for your voyage then," she said. In that decisive phrase there was a breath of resignation, but also hope, always hope.

Chapter 3

"All ashore that's going ashore," came the call over the loud-speakers

The *Aquitania* hummed and bobbed in the water, a giant ready and waiting. They stood at the railing – Maddy and the formidable Mrs. Sullivan, Martin and Fricky – alongside other cheering passengers waving white handkerchiefs in the traditional fashion, calling "bon voyage" to families and friends on shore. Burly Fricky made great happy sweeps of both hands to his father, Mr. Walter Fritz, the gentleman banker with the seemingly bottomless pockets of stock market riches that would presumably to make their lives merry for many years to come.

The gangplank pulled up and the ship moved away with a jolt, then with a low steady humming of its engines sailed further out until everyone on shore grew smaller and smaller, until all Maddy could see was her mother's pink kerchief and then nothing at all.

Soon New York's harbor lights receded from view. When they passed the twelve-mile limit, champagne corks began popping. They were now beyond the constraints of the Prohibition Act and the air crackled with laughter. Glasses of champagne were handed out by passing waiters and even the proper Mrs. Sullivan imbibed a sip or two.

"To us," Maddy said, tapping her champagne glass against Martin's.

"To us all," Fricky shouted, crashing his glass into hers.

Maddy thought of how intoxicating it was to be on holiday in a booming new world with champagne tickling their brains and the *Aquitania* slapping through the sea toward the City of Lights. One of the revelers shouted for more bourbon from the steward. Two ladies leaned over the railing until the garters holding their stockings showed. Mrs. Sullivan raised an eyebrow but was looking decidedly green, and as the ship rolled Fricky turned his small blue eyes upon Maddy and said, "Little Sister, you'd best see your chaperone to her room."

"In case your pickled brain has forgotten, the name is Maddy, not Little Sister."

Martin gave her a wink and Fricky honored her with a bright, white-toothed smile. He was right; it seemed the champagne had done Mrs. Sullivan no favors. The ship reeled and the ladies at the railing screamed. Fricky's solid chest bumped her shoulder and her champagne glass jolted loose from her hand, smashed onto the deck and shattered.

"Pardon me," said Fricky.

"Fricky's started early," Martin said, but his eyes sparkled now and the two men patted each others' shoulders in that awkwardly affectionate way of men.

"Rough seas!" someone shouted. Suddenly Mrs. Sullivan was at the rail retching.

"Passengers are please advised to leave the deck," the overhead loudspeakers repeated, "Passengers please be advised – "

"Come Mrs. Sullivan, let me take you to our stateroom," Maddy said. She took the woman's hand and together they slipped and slid their way toward the nearest door.

"We'll get us a real drink," Fricky said to Martin, "Not this silly bubbly."

Fricky had spoken exclusively to Martin, for that was how it was with them. When they'd shipped out to war, Fricky had been right beside him when Martin sealed Maddy's twelve year-old heart for good by telling her men fighting at the front were better off knowing they had "American beauties like you to come home to." Sitting at home being a beauty was not what Maddy considered contributing and her mother had protested the war, but she had always wanted to please Martin and so his praise made her happy.

"You boys go have fun in the bar," she said, "I'll take Mrs. Sullivan down and meet you later."

As she escorted Mrs. Sullivan back to their stateroom, Maddy saw how the voyage would be, that instead of romance and confidences alone with Martin, it would be overtaken by a long series of hard-drinking nights and days with Fricky.

But she was game; oh she was game.

"How can you eat?" Mrs. Sullivan said in their stateroom as the ship pitched and rolled. Maddy munched an apple from the welcome basket with no thought of her sea hardy stomach.

"You should eat too," Maddy said, and popped open the clasps on her steamer trunk. She didn't know where to begin with the unpacking, for there were travel suits and chiffon evening gowns and feathers and headbands. Plus there was the pouch of voyage letters, which were traditionally to be read each day on the crossing as through whoever packed them, in this case her mother, were right there, every day, dispensing advice and reprimands and so-called wisdom. Her precious heirloom was most likely somewhere in with the little parcels and letters her mother had so thoughtfully and maternally packed, but Maddy didn't want to think of it or even wear it. Wearing the pendant would only burden her with thoughts of what her mother wanted of her, which was to be more like her, she supposed, a woman of conscience and political action, when all Maddy wanted was to hold Martin in her arms, politics be damned. Politics had wounded him, wounded them all, and now it was time for the healing, or at least a little fun.

"Tea only," said Mrs. Sullivan. She didn't move from the small bed across from Maddy's upon which she'd collapsed. "I suppose it's just as well that you eat. You're awfully thin."

"It's fashionable to be thin."

"It's unhealthy. You must forget fashion."

"You like only one fashion, Mrs. Sullivan," Maddy laughed, "And that's old-fashioned!"

"I frankly don't understand your generation," Mrs. Sullivan pronounced, for she had caught a glimpse of Maddy bust flattener-brassiere, "First there is agitation for women's suffrage and now that we have the vote, you girls hide the fact that you are a woman at all!"

"It's merely the fashion."

"Fashion to look like a boy! I simply do not comprehend why you would want to reduce. In my day, big was better."

Maddy avoided a direct look at Mrs. Sullivan's copious bust and conceded that small breasts were once an indication of a woman's inferiority, but this notion was considered ridiculous and laughable now, or at least to everyone in the enlightened new generation, of which Maddy was decidedly a part. Making no comment on the woman's bigger-better challenge, Maddy paused in her unpacking to insert a cigarette into a long black holder and light it with a match from the Razzmatazz Club, all the while knowing full well the response her action would incite.

"Oh, now, look at you. *Now* you have gone *too* far!"

"It's nothing, really, just a bit of a puff," Maddy said, and took secret delight in watching Mrs. Sullivan observe her inhalation with dread fascination.

"You are ruining your beauty, Maddy dearest! Oh dear, I don't know what to do about you. I will report this to your parents. You appear like a bad sort, but you'll see soon enough when your future husband reprimands your disgraceful behavior."

"My future husband will not be the sort who reprimands. He will be my companion and lover."

"What a rude word."

"Lover? Lover, Mrs. Sullivan?"

Maddy inhaled again and fancied looking like one of those fabulously slinky Gordon Conway models.

"For shame, for shame," Mrs. Sullivan said. Then, switching tactics, asked her charge if she had unpacked the voyage letters from her mother.

"No, Mrs. Sullivan," Maddy said. She lowered her cigarette into a cloisonné ashtray, and said, "Did you know that Mary Garrett Hay predicts that sometime in the future married couples will share the burden of child raising, and that it will not fall on the woman alone? And there won't even be any separate men and women's political parties."

"I don't know why you talk this way," Mrs. Sullivan said, "None of this matters now. What do I care how strange the future will be? What matters is that you should be acting like a woman, instead of some young tart. I can see plain as day that your Martin is terribly disappointed in you."

"Not in the least," Maddy retorted, although she knew it was true. Martin in fact was very disappointed. Disappointed not just in her, but the world in general. Maddy crushed out her cigarette. "Let's not talk anymore of this."

"Very well. I'll order some tea. I cannot deny I'm a tad sea-sick."

Mrs. Sullivan rose unsteadily and teetered out into the corridor in search of a steward, leaving behind her heavy-powdered scent and the stale sensation of defeat in Maddy. The older woman had scored a victory, but the younger one nonetheless held fast to the notion that, being young, she was entitled to new ideas. She simply didn't quite know what her new ideas were, other than to rebel against the old.

Chapter 4

*D*inner was brought to their booth in the nightclub, and a good thing too as far as Martin was concerned, for the dining room had closed for the night, and he preferred the more casual ale and oysters besides. Maddy was a champ about it, not the sort of gal who would insist on things being fancy for no good reason. She wore a green wool tweed suit and a smart cloche hat and certainly appeared to belong among the journalists, sports writers and men's men. This was where people drank, argued politics and misbehaved, which was fine with her; she'd told him many times she found misbehavior interesting. Most of the ladies were in their staterooms for the night, but there were still some women around. It was hard to believe they were once excluded from bars. When it came to drinking, there was to be no more exclusion of women in *this* new decade.

The ship pitched more heavily now, and stewards were adjusting the catch strips on tables so as to prevent any sliding glasses or ashtrays from crashing to the floor. A jazz blues band was playing "Song of the Congo" and the room was lamp-lit and dark.

"Bryan got a skewering from Darrow," Maddy was saying, "Which he deserved, the pompous old fool."

"I'm sorry for the man," Martin said.

"Sorry!" Maddy and Fricky spoke together.

"He expressed his private religious beliefs."

"Which he expected to be taught to every school child in the country," Maddy said.

"The fool literally believes everything in the Bible," Fricky scoffed, "Jonah swallowed by a whale…"

"Eve made of Adam's rib," Maddy rejoined.

The two men looked at one another and smirked.

"Please don't make fun," Maddy said, "You know you don't believe it either."

"Adam's rib? Why of course not," Fricky said, "Otherwise you'd be a hunchback, wouldn't she, Martin?"

"Yes, her spine would curve like a rib."

"Much as I'm inclined to agree with Bryan on that point," Fricky teased, "Scientific logic of course disproves that theory."

"You two are intolerable." Maddy slurped another oyster, "I suppose you'll next say the War was a glorious fight for God and Country."

The men said nothing to this.

"I'm sorry." She had gone too far. "Of course neither of you would say that now."

"Unlike our man Dempsy," Fricky said, "You have a tendency to deliver below the belt."

"I didn't mean to put it that way." She gathered crumbs off the table with her moistened fingertips, "We all hated the war, and so we must now live for today."

"Those of us who *do* live," Martin said bitterly, and turned to search for the waiter.

"Three bourbons!" Fricky shouted, not asking Maddy if she wanted one. At this point she knew it was a matter of pride to keep up with the men. "Real bourbon," Fricky said to the steward, "You give the old girls the vote, and the first thing they do is cut off your drinking pleasures."

"Just my style," Maddy said, "I so disapprove of pleasure of any kind."

Maddy took a slim black cigarette case from her handbag and a cigarette from the case and fitted it into a long black cigarette holder and
held the polished holder between her lacquered fingernails and placed it
between her painted lips. Martin lighted it for her and she inhaled and
then she blew smoke into Fricky's face.

"Oh, excuse me," she said.

"Girls don't know how to smoke."

"Fricky, you're ossified. In more ways then one."

"Now hold on you two," Martin said, "Let's not start another war."

"Did you know the Paris Exposition will be showing the latest in
deco?" Maddy said to steer the conversation to safer ground, "Americans
are fascinated with it."

"Is that what fascinates them," Fricky said.

The young men tolerated Maddy's precocious attempt to convey
an aura of sophistication, what with her talk of French deco and her
bobbed hair. Martin missed her long girlish tresses although he hadn't
said so when she'd cut them, only remarked that it was stylish. Damned
stylish. She was a fine gal, a smart one too, but as far as Martin was concerned, she had lost her way among the Flapper set.

The jazz band started up again with "Swamp Blues." Maddy tapped
the table and swung her head from side to side.

"Now she wants to dance," said Fricky and promptly rested the
back of his head upon the booth and began to snore. Martin knew he
should ask her but couldn't bring himself. If he would dance with any-
body it would be Maddy of course, but his heart couldn't drive his body
to do it. Now she was looking at him in the way she did these days;
watchful, unwilling to ask what was wrong.

There was no denying the impact of the very *presence* of her: The
arch of her slim wrist as she gestured, the sheen of her skin, the glint
of red in her hair and the manner in which she tugged at the rim of her

hat or relished the oysters. Martin loved her appetite, her optimism, her knack for the more fantastical point of view, but she also drove him mad.

How to tell her he couldn't dance? What to say? The frivolity of modern life disgusted Martin but then, what else was there? Surely it was time to rebuild the world, not wallow in its distracting luxuries, but Martin wasn't up for it, not now, perhaps never. He had done his part, which was almost getting himself killed.

"Well, Martin, I believe I will turn in," she said.

"Yes, good."

She reached across for her little beaded purse, her face inches from his. The skin of her cheek was fine and lovely. He had seen all kinds of skin, skin turned to ash, skin gone pitch with flies and decay. He didn't mean to think of this, it just came to him. Her cheek turned to the side and in its place were her two dark beautiful eyes, watching, watching him, always watching.

"Goodnight Martin," she said.

Before he could stop her she kissed him on the lips and didn't pull away, taking from him her long drink of his mouth and he just waiting for her to stop, his heart hammering until he thought it would kill him.

Back in his stateroom, Martin made no choice. It was she who joined him, she who chose, and she chose him.

And so he made love to Maddy with the ocean rushing beneath them. He floated atop her surge, dove into the wake and slept in dreams that tossed him from wave to wave, her arms cool, her breath a breeze upon his cheek.

They slept like two continents separated by an ocean wall, the water a table of glass, the hum of the engines moving them along as if through a vacuum. He did not dream, but sank into a mindless darkness. When he awoke Maddy was gone, and as he lay there in the indeterminate hour of the morning he was sadly relieved by her absence.

But soon she was back after having seen to Mrs. Sullivan, who was too seasick to care about much of anything but her own discomfort. Maddy embraced him in the dark of his bed, her body curled around his back, and at some point before they fell back into the hum of the ship's lull and sleep overcame them he turned to kiss her and they made love again.

In the morning Maddy languished on the pillow beside him and petted his hair with short, gentle strokes. She casually remarked that he had talked of the war in his sleep.

"Oh? And what did I say?"

"Nothing discernible, really Martin," she said, "Your secrets are safe."

"They aren't secrets, Maddy. They simply are not what you would wish to know."

"You can tell me anything," she said. She turned on her side to seriously look at him. He believed her, but still he said nothing.

They breakfasted on scones, strawberries, cream and Turkish coffee. He poured the cream until his coffee turned the color of chocolate milk and spoke no more on a subject she could never truly understand.

She distracted him with her dressing and stood shamelessly before him, her slim body proudly naked and gleaming. To his conflicted regret and appreciation, she slipped her clothes upon her body. She strapped herself into a satin brassiere and then put on dark brown silk stockings that she fastened by suspenders dangling from an ivory girdle. A light slip trimmed in bands of ribbon and lace followed, then a matching skirt and simple green sweater and low-heeled mules. She looked like a girl, a fetching, outspoken, athletic, excitable girl, and nothing like the sort of women – well, woman – he had bedded in France during the war.

Through fashion Maddy aimed to be a woman of the world. He hoped that it would happen for her, the worldliness she craved, but for Martin, he was finished with that world and its bright promises. Her luminosity, her fierce clinging to happiness, her style and smarts and beauty, simply saddened him. What he wanted today was nothing more than an inebriated chat with Fricky. A dark bar would do him just fine.

Chapter 5

*H*e was her first, her first and forever.

Her pelvis ached. It was her red badge not of shame but triumph, to feel that itching heat between her legs. It was all for him, only him, so that he might drive into her and forget his past and pain. *Give me your pain, your war weary soul, I will soothe and comfort and love you forever, my first and forever.*

They would marry now, perhaps in some lovely chapel in Paris, and after Paris they would follow expatriates in the know to the Riviera, and then on to Venice. She'd heard that the time of the Flapper was finished, therefore she wanted to be ready for whatever came next. She and Martin would be like the Fitzgeralds or the Murphys; maybe they'd bring Fricky along to Madrid, and they would buy the paintings she fancied by that strange Spaniard, Dali.

But for now she returned to her stateroom and saw to Mrs. Sullivan. The woman appeared so utterly green and miserable Maddy regretted her own elation which really came at the convenient incapacitation of her chaperone who'd barely noticed her absence the night before and didn't even seem to care.

In the early afternoon she persuaded Mrs. Sullivan to come up onto the aft sun deck and sit in their reserved wooden fold-out chairs, but the fresh breezes offered no comfort and the swaying horizon was only more torment, and so she had to be escorted back down to their room.

Poor Mrs. Sullivan could do no more for the foreseeable future than consume tea and bits of toast, leaving Maddy to do as she pleased.

"Do go and enjoy the voyage, Maddy dear," Mrs. Sullivan said, and so Maddy did, although the remaining days at sea did not proceed as hoped.

Most mid-days they drank hot bouillon and admired the gusty blue ocean view. Fricky was always there, refreshing Martin's cup with dollops of brandy from his flask. They entered the ship's wager on their arrival time in Calais, partook in card games in the smoking room, had high tea in the music room's atrium of oriental carpets and tropical plants, and played laconic games of shuffleboard.

The pain in her pelvis subsided and she missed it. *Give me more of your pain* she wanted to say to Martin. He was kind to her and always saw to her comforts (a lap robe on the blustery deck? Another hot bouillon?), but expressed no interest in another tryst.

They ate every evening in the nightclub, and always there was more drinking, and the more the men drank the more muddled and depressed were their stories. Maddy was sorry they had suffered and seen so much suffering, but she wasn't the one who had insisted on their going to war, her mother in fact had fiercely protested the war, and now they were excluding her for not having suffered too. It was a men's club, this war business, and she wanted to be part of their club only without the part that entailed war, but the boys kept drinking and ignored her completely. She would return to her stateroom and the bed opposite the moaning Mrs. Sullivan and talk to her of how next time women voters wouldn't permit war to happen, their vote would count because it would stop all wars and put an end to the killing and the suffering.

"Vote to end all seasickness," said Mrs. Sullivan, and glumly sipped her tea.

On the night before their arrival in Calais, they attended the Captain's gala in the first class dining room, a monumentally proportioned room with two-story marble pillars, frescoes, and massive Lalique light towers. She hoped the event would distract Martin from his brooding, and with seduction in mind, she'd worn a dress she'd found in the *Tatler*, a backless white chiffon sheath. He had complimented her with cordiality in lieu of any real appreciation, however, and instead groused on the increasing affluence of a decadent world where the riches of the few were not shared by the many.

And yet Maddy's heart secretly thrilled at the dining room's pink marble pillars rising up to meet a massive ceiling dripping with chandeliers, at the brilliant, prism-reflected lights, at the men in evening dress and bejeweled ladies sipping cocktails and champagne. An orchestra played and exotic flowers bloomed like fireworks from giant deco vases. Banquet tables were bedecked to overflowing with braised meats, gleaming shellfish, glistening caviar and mounds of cheeses and brilliantly colored fruits. At the desert table, a spectacular cake shaped like the Eiffel Tower loomed over ice-sculptures molded into the boulevards and shops of Paris.

How silly of her to hope elegance and luxury would assuage Martin's mind; it produced only guilt. *This is all wrong,* he went on, gesturing to their tableware, that they would have this when so many had died futilely, not as heroes but as fodder buried in mud. Fricky agreed, but like Maddy he relished the turtle soup. Martin pushed it away. Maddy thought she was made for a moneyed life, but when she watched the movement of his beautiful hands and listened to his eloquent argument she knew she would give it all up in a heartbeat if only she could have him.

"But you must admit," said Maddy, "the decor is rather divine."

"If you don't mind I don't care to discuss the decor."

"I'm sorry Martin, I was only trying to distract you."

"Everything is a distraction these days, don't you see?"

"Yes. I do see. It really is deplorable, all the excess."

It was becoming increasingly obvious to her that to win Martin over she would have to see things not as herself but rather as Martin saw. She wanted to snap at him and say she was *not* Adam's rib, or Martin's rib either, but repressed the urge. She would see as he saw, think how he thought. She would do whatever it took to make love with him again even if she had to lie about the very person she was or provoke him to jealousy by dancing the Charleston, the Turkey Trot, and the Tango with a Mr. Debonair, a Mr. Footloose, and a Mr. Suave.

"You are one hotsy totsy Sheba," Mr. Suave said and pulled her into his Tango embrace.

"And you are a dashing Sheik," she replied, waiting for Martin to cut in.

"Perhaps we might tango onto the deck for a little harmless necking," Mr. Suave said. He swung her down within inches of the floor. Struggling to right herself, she clutched his shoulders, which he took as ascent.

"You are fabulous," Mr. Suave murmured hotly into her hair.

"Oh my, you've done me in, you Sheik you." She extricated herself, pleading fatigue. "I simply must have more bubbly."

"I'll bring relief," Mr. Suave said, and sauntered toward the bar. She seated herself on an empty loveseat within sight of Martin who was listening to a fellow who had given him a cigar. He was impossible. She couldn't make him jealous and she couldn't make him see how stunning she was in her silk dress spread around her like a fan. The only recourse was misbehavior. She accepted a glass of champagne from a passing steward and finally caught Martin's eye. Something smoldered the distance between them like a spark on a hot wire traveling toward detonation. He walked toward her.

"That is the one drink too many," he said.

"It's fabulous champagne," she said, "And besides, I have to uphold my frivolous image."

"You're spifflicated. I'm taking you back to your room."

"You gave me the high-hat, and so I'm finished with you ordering me about."

"OK then," Martin said. He sat beside her upon the loveseat, took her glass, and drained it in a single swallow.

"Hey!"

"I'll order more champagne in the room," he promised.

She insisted on going to his cabin, he insisted that she lie down. She agreed only if he would kiss her. When his kiss was merely brotherly she began to cry.

"This voyage was supposed to have been romantic," she said between sobs, "Haven't I after all this time earned your love?"

He thought this over, and the very fact of his not making a quick declaration made her cry all the more. All fight and determination had drained from her and now all she had was a yearning, pleading hope that he could love her.

He removed his jacket, loosened his tie, ran his fingers through his soft golden hair. It was a gesture she had long adored and in it she saw his confusion.

"Dear Maddy, I love you as my dear beautiful childhood friend," he said, "But I'm sorry to say I don't believe you will ever be the woman I want."

"I can be that person, Martin, just tell me who you want me to be."

She stood up and walked a few uncertain steps toward him, the white chiffon of her dress clinging against her torso and her legs moving against the current of his disapproval. He looked her over with eyes half-shuttered by what she hoped was desire. She laced her fingers behind his neck. He smiled sadly and sighed.

"You have grown into a woman, Maddy, that I can see."

His expression had an unbearable tinge of pity.

"You're smart and beautiful, a jewel, a high-cut diamond," he said, "When all I want is a simple stone. You are just too – " He searched for the word, " – Complicated."

"But I can't love anyone but you." She whispered and stroked the tension of his jaw, the tightness in his lips. "And that isn't complicated at all, that is so very, very simple."

What followed was inevitable. Their bodies had no other recourse, for despite the complications, they were made for releasing one another from their clothing, and then they fell back upon the bed.

Two hundred knots from the coast of France on the Atlantic ocean in the first class cabin of a luxury liner, two lovers wrangled over *le dife-rence* then eased together into a comfortable sleep, their bodies untangling. And yet, morning brought more uncertainty, for when Maddy awoke, Martin was gone.

She returned to Mrs. Sullivan who, now that the voyage was over, had at last gotten her sea legs. Together they prepared their luggage for arrival in Calais.

Chapter 6

*I*t was a different Paris, a harder brighter Paris.

The one-armed man on the Rue la Boetie had escaped the War to End All Wars with his life, and like many of the war veterans of France, he'd had more than half a decade to adjust to his new body. There was no time for pity. Like his fellow countrymen who had lived through the war he was simply getting on with it, arm or no arm.

The city had been transformed for the Exposition and the whole of its populace was eager to display its place as a leader in all things having to do with art and culture. The Eiffel Tower was decorated with silver and gold electric lights glittering the word, "Citroen," and sky signs spread along the wide bright boulevards toward the Arc de Triomphe.

Martin, Fricky, Maddy and Mrs. Sullivan were staying in a hotel on the busy Avenue des Champs Elysees although they gravitated nightly to Montparnasse. Fricky sought works of the modernists for his father's extensive collection and Mrs. Sullivan purchased items for the Rosario shop from the bohemian galleries. Released from her seasickness, the older woman was delighted with both *terra firma* and her new light-weight body after a week of inadvertent dieting on tea and toast. She made the obligatory objections to Maddy's nightly excursions with her male companions to the hot bodily heat of the infernal jazz clubs, but there was no restraining the girl from the music and dancing.

As it turned out, *la ville lumiere* would bring Maddy a *liaison* of an entirely different sort, one that in all her youthful expectation she never would have dreamed of, for Paris was *Paris, Paris, Paris*...Parisian women in particular held the secrets to fashion and allurement. They were chic, they possessed that *je ne sais quoi*, they wore the finest lingerie, the most individual perfumes, and the newest in deco jewelry. And the French had such style! A wine shop with basic bread and cheeses on display sent her into rhapsodies of praise. A manicure salon with perfume bottles decorating its window shelves provoked her to paroxysms of delight.

"Not all these perfumes come from roses off the Riviera," Mr. Sullivan said as they stood outside one of them, "I propose they're manufactured in suburban factories and contain nothing more than iodine and other crude chemicals"

"You can't ruin my illusion," Maddy said.

"I just wanted you to know," her chaperone petulantly replied, lifting her nose to breathe in a laundry exuding the smell of hot, freshly ironed cotton.

There was no doubting that Paris was a sensory experience, and while Maddy may have been lured by what the scent of perfume evoked, Mrs. Sullivan in her way was charmed by the industrious scent of fresh laundry.

They went to the Exposition des Arts Decoratifs, with its temporary modern structures housing furniture by the minimalist Le Cobusier, and Maddy fawned over it all – the pavilion, the displays, the obelisks at the ornate Porte d' Honneur entrance, the glass work by Lalique and the sculptures by Navarre. It was as if the entire universe was opening before her, and she was in awe of everything, the art, the fashion, the people and their expressions and language and foods.

And because Maddy was the only American woman in a red cloche hat on the Boulevard Montparnasse, Martin bought her a bouquet of peonies in a confetti confection of vanilla, pink and peach. She accepted them with a radiant smile that saddened him. He appreciated her zest for all things Paris, but it was never his intention to give her hope.

Chapter 7

On their third night in Paris Martin left the hotel for what he thought would be a brief walk to the nearest café, but after he passed the first one he continued walking, lured on by the next café, and the next, until he found himself following the Seine. It seemed the entire city followed the Seine, its mansions, bridges and barges, its trees billowing in the cool night air. It was well past midnight but the river paths were populated. People walked their dogs and lovers embraced near the balustrades. He headed toward the Left Bank, where the brightness of the avenues gave way to soft, shrouding, narrow pathways.

"Avance, avance, beau monsieur," came the low, caressing entreaty of a streetwalker, but he politely tipped his head and moved on, past the bookshops along the Rue de Passy and hidden artist studios on the Rue d' Abouhir.

Finally he arrived at Montmartre's old village square where the wartime Paris he once knew stood unaltered by modern times, its air thick with the scent of barrel wine. He saw a carriage driver putting his horses in for the night, a mother through an open window laying her children to bed. A violin drew the final notes to Mozart's tender "Divertimento" to a close. The violin too was retiring for the night.

He walked a dirt path beside rows of cabbages and drooping sunflowers until he found himself before the open second story windows of an old farmhouse. The violin player was closing the instrument in its case.

"Francesca," Martin called.

The violin player came to the window and looked out into the night. Raphaelite hair tumbled over her shoulders and swung across the windowsill. She wore a slip of a dress with a neckline that revealed her round breasts.

"*Que c'est? Que va?*" She queried in the low, calm voice he would forever remember. She had shut the life-lost eyes of soldiers, cleaned the amputated limbs left in the surgeons' wake and wrote the dictated letters of promise and farewell to families far away. She would never be a great beauty, but she was gentle and old-fashioned, and in her twenties still.

"*C'est* Martin," he replied, and stepped forward into her light.

"Martin?" her voice rang with warmth. Within seconds she had left the window and had burst out into the street, hair flying, her hands reaching for his.

"Martin, you are most *distinguer*," she said, viewing his face, keeping one hand on his arm as if unwilling to break contact.

"And you are as lovely as I remember," he said. He had much to remember: the first embrace on the Rue Laffitte, the cautious glances before, the meaningful stares, the final long sinking kiss and more under the ruins at Aisne-Marne. Surrounded by war and death, he had found life in the scent of her skin.

Now in a time of peace he sat at a wood table in her kitchen while she poured hot tea steeped from the mint in her garden. He looked at the hand-woven curtains and simple earthen pots and silently thanked her for remaining a nineteenth century woman in a twentieth century world. The violin, she explained, earned her basic livelihood. As part of a small orchestra comprised of accordion and guitar, she played in music halls, dining rooms, at weddings and wakes. She told him she loved her work and her life in all its basic, natural simplicity. He basked in the sound of her calm, contented voice while struggling to withhold his own litany of laments. Their eyes sometimes held then flickered away, hers to her chipped teacup, his to the dark night at the window. The tea was suddenly drunk, their silence heavy with the unspoken. He wanted to touch her again but not here, not alone in her rooms where he might forget himself. This wasn't wartime, he reminded himself. How he missed the war.

They went out for a cognac at Le Dome. It was of little or no surprise to either when they encountered Fricky happily in his cups at a table crowded with journalists.

"I knew you two lovebirds would find one another sooner or later," he said. He saw to their drinks and then to a second round. He hugged their shoulders, knocking heads together.

"Lovebirds," he said, cigar breath floating past their nostrils, "life is short, believe me."

The room swirled with smoke, voices, music and dancing, but none of it distracted Martin from the sight of Francesca. It was easier to love her in a crowded room, easier to flirt and touch like old friends.

"I'll tell you what we do," Fricky said in a conspiratorial whisper, pulling them both toward him in the crook of each arm.

"And what is that Fricky," Francesca said, indulgently leaning toward him as if she were about to hear a shattering secret. Martin laughed as he had not laughed in years.

"What're you laughing about, you knucklehead," growled his friend, "you don't even know what I'm about to propose."

"You're snockered."

"You see, I have a car, a Citroen, to be exact."

"And where are you going?"

"Spain, old bud. We're going to Pamplona. You, me and Francesca. To see the running of the bulls."

"*Espagne!*" Francesca exclaimed.

"And what of Maddy?"

Martin regretted the question the moment it left his lips.

"Little Sister stays with her chaperone in Paris," said Fricky, "She's a modern girl. She'll have a fine time without you in her favorite Paris."

The idea! Maddy enjoying Paris without him! Then he saw how it would be. She would miss him at first but then she would rally and Frenchmen would flirt with her and she would flirt back and in the end it would be better for them both, for no matter how hard she tried he knew they were wrong for each other. And so in yearning for the exquisitely right and lovely Francesca, Martin decided then and there to set Maddy free to be the independent woman he had never intended to wed.

Chapter 8

*H*er pride galvanized with the props of high fashion, she was ushered by Martin to a table where a dark-haired woman was seated with Fricky. Maddy wore an Henri couture straight gray skirt and white crepe-de-chine blouse with a button down collar and blue and gray checked necktie. The shop girl who had showed her how to do the knot said it made her look smart, but her version merely looked crooked. In fact her entire couture ensemble blended perfectly with the tastefully blue, gray and white dining room. So perfectly, she could have fitted into the wallpaper.

"Excellent! Excellent!" Martin was saying with more exuberance than the occasion required. She hadn't expected to see Fricky and his lady friend at breakfast, and wondered whether Martin had arranged it.

"Francesca Valois," Martin said, gesturing with his hand from one woman to the other, "Maddy Rosario."

Francesca Valois was older than she, older in manner, older in spirit. The woman had learned something early in her life and Maddy thought that if she could understand what that was, she would have the key to Martin. Francesca's dress was slightly worn but of good quality silk and of a soft ruby color that dipped gently along the line of her clavicles, exposing a flushed skin. Unlike Maddy, she did not blend into her surroundings but rather bloomed with all the brilliance of a fresh cut Bourbon rose.

"I am most happy to meet," she said holding out her long, slim hand.

"Likewise," Maddy said, feeling silly in her tie and not the least bit chic, dressing like a man. What had she been thinking?

Fricky appeared to be on unusually good behavior. He was wearing a jacket and wasn't drinking.

"Now we can tell Maddy our plan," Fricky said.

"What plan?" She inquired in as casual a tone as she could muster. Best to keep up appearances and project at least a semblance of confidence. Waiters hovered over the table offering fresh juice. Maddy nodded to the juice and accepted a butter dish with a croissant and small crock of jam.

"*Oeuf poche*," Martin said to the waiter, "and my friend will have the same."

"What plan?" Maddy repeated, and caught an expression of quiet pity on the face of the Frenchwoman.

"The running of the bulls," Fricky said.

"Bulls?" Maddy's smile moved frozen from Francesca, who was stirring the cream into her coffee, to Martin, who was passing Francesca the sugar bowl.

"Fricky and I are going to Spain," Martin said, "We'll rejoin you and Mrs. Sullivan later, Maddy."

Martin buttered his toast, searched for the jam, and swallowed his coffee without once glancing her way.

"You will stay here and help Mrs. Sullivan buy pieces for the Rosario shop."

"Oh, that *will* be fun," Maddy said, for she didn't know what to say.

"This is all my idea, Maddy," Fricky said, "I must confess I railroaded Martin when I ran into him at le Dome last night."

"He dragged me in," Martin explained.

"*S'il vous plait*," Fricky said to the waiter, "A champagne kir, kirs all around."

"No, please, Fricky," Francesca said.

Martin said, "We were never one to keep up with you, Fricky."

"Hell, it's ten o'clock, nearly lunch hour,"

"Fricky and I met Francesca at the field hospital," Martin explained as if the War happened just yesterday, "She was a nurse."

"Remember that deranged fellow," Fricky said, as though he were fondly recalling his college days, "Who lost his foot to a land mine?"

"*C'est terrible!*" Francesca said. The men stared at her with sobered expressions. Through her tears, Francesca lifted her face and bravely smiled. Maddy suddenly hated the woman. And yet she'd been a nurse. She had comforted hundreds of soldiers.

"Francesca was our saint," Fricky said.

"Not when you fed me bourbon," Francesca said, laughing, sneaking a coy look at Martin.

"Oh right," Martin smiled. He turned to Maddy, "Francesca couldn't handle her bourbon."

"Well, who can," Maddy said, because what could she say?

Her childhood friends had presented her with their plan to go to Spain as a *fait accompli* and she would have to concede without complaint or concern for the obvious, which was that she wasn't being invited to join them. She was Little Sister, but wasn't she also the Little Sister who had made love with Martin, her first and forever, onboard the *Aquitania*? Had he forgotten? Wasn't marriage what happened when girls made love with their first and forever?

It wasn't until Martin was loading the Citroen with his promptly packed luggage that, standing on the street and sending them off in as cheerful a manner as she could muster, Maddy spied the blue suitcase in the boot and realized it belonged to Francesca.

"Be good, Maddy dear," Martin said when he took her aside to embrace her beneath the portico.

"This is happening so suddenly," she said.

He stepped into the Citroen beside the driver, with Fricky and Francesca positioned in back. That was when Maddy remembered the way Martin had looked at Francesca in the dining room, the way he had poured her coffee and passed her the sugar, and it dawned on her as the car pulled away, as they all waved out the windows, as Maddy even blew a farewell kiss, that her very first and only lover in her young life was off on another love affair with a Frenchwoman and there was nothing, absolutely nothing, she could do to stop him.

Chapter 9

She retreated to the elevator and up to their floor. In the corridor she passed Mrs. Sullivan on her way to the Exposition. Refraining from any sign of heartbreak, she agreed to meet her later. She then entered the room and hurled herself onto her bed.

She cried and cried like a child, like the Little Sister they said she was. She had failed to grow-up. She had failed to capture Martin and make him love her. Most of all, she had failed at being the kind of woman he wanted. She was not French; she had not been a nurse in the War. She wondered if she was even a woman. But she was a woman. The ache in her groin and the blood she discharged from her body confirmed it. She was overcome with her own desire, this yearning, this insatiability, and she didn't know what she was to do with it, other than degrade herself by begging Martin to love her, but she had done that already.

It crept upon her unwittingly, the urge to confide in her old-fashioned Gibson Girl-haired mother. Her mother knew things; her mother was possessed of an iron will. This was what Maddy wanted to be, instead of a lovesick girl. Lovesick was what she was, sick with love.

With a jolt she remembered the ship's letters she was supposed to have read during the journey, still packed in the little cloth bag her mother had so lovingly assembled. Sniffling, wiping her eyes, Maddy slipped off the bed and went to the trunk and opened it. She found the soft canvas pouch sandwiched under a folded raincoat that was so sensible and American she knew she would never wear it. But the letters inside the pouch, these she withdrew. It would not be like having her mother with her, but it would be next best, and it was all she could hope for.

The letters were written on the softest of paper, and they were filled with motherly advice and wisdom of the kind Maddy had been listening to her whole life and for the most part been failing to follow: Make friends with the girls before you flirt with the boys. Know that your chaperone is also your companion and friend. Be aware that drinking can lead to unexpected consequences. Remember you are special. And above all: Make something of yourself.

It was from the final letter that Maddy let slip into her hand the object she suspected would be included. She unfolded the paper into which was written the simplest of words in her mother's hand:

Know who you are.

And from the folds of the paper in between these words glowed the otherworldly pendant, her heirloom, passed down from her grandfather's sister the Whale Rider to her mother, the Suffragist, and now to her. It caught the light and winked at her, and the question burst to the forefront of her mind:

But who am I?

This time she did not put the pendant into an ashtray and forget it, but rather held it dangling from its chain before the light. For an instant she saw inside it a movement, a miniscule silvery blue sea parting to reveal her mother's face. And then she saw the faces of other women superimposed over her mother's, unrecognizable faces flashing through time until her own face appeared and disappeared into the gemstone's glint of crystalline light.

It was magical; it would transform, soothe and comfort her like Mama. She slipped the chain over her head and let the pendant hang over the little necktie at her breasts. Her heart beat faster. A rush of poignancy passed through her, a sensation of purpose and physical well-being. It would happen now. She would come into herself. She need only wait and it will come.

But it did not come, this knowing who she was.

She left the Hotel Crillon and spent the afternoon walking among the people of the city. Grasping at identity, she told herself she was an American importer in search of French objects d' art, a person with a place in the world, but what she was in truth was a woman abandoned by her lover. She walked nonetheless with intention, down the Champs Elysees, walked and walked, away from Martin who had departed with that other woman, a Frenchwoman of sophistication with whom she couldn't possibly compete.

She became aware of being miserably hot. Her shoes were tight. She unbuttoned her jacket and held the pendant against her chest as she walked. She wondered if losing Martin was the price she would pay, the toll extracted in order to *know who you are.*

She strode toward the green expanse of gardens at Tuileries and then turned onto the walkway along the Seine. A breeze lifted up off the water, fluttering the leaves above. It was an ordinary day, this day so momentous to her. A vendor sold antiquarian books to a group of German tourists. A man pushing a cart of brightly colored vegetables called out *legumes, legumes* while further down river another vendor echoed *fraiche fleurs, fraiche fleurs.*

It was plain enough the world was indifferent to her dilemma.

A woman shouted a string of French words she didn't understand to a boy stomping along the muddy bank of the Seine. An unruly boy, a beautiful boy, like the boy Martin had been when they were children, now grown into a man, off with a woman who might bear him children. Martin, her beautiful Martin, whom she had always thought was meant for her. She could have bourn him beautiful children.

She walked past the church of Invalides which, being Baroque, Martin would have surely wanted to see. It looked dark and oppressive to Maddy, and the thought of visiting the tomb of Napoleon, that war-mongering madman, repelled her. And yet she would have been happy to tour Invalides if only Martin could have been with her. She would have held his hand, he would have discoursed on Napoleon's evil genius and the ravages of war, and they would be together, *together*. Not for a minute had Maddy considered that love-making would fail to make him hers. She had followed her passion but it proved to be her undoing. In love with being in love, she had failed to be the woman he wanted. Never mind her mother's admonition – *know who you are* – she regretted not being the woman he wanted with every ounce of her being.

And so in tandem with her regret she walked toward the specter of the Eiffel Tower until she drew close enough to find herself drawn under the shadow of its massive iron legs. Never had she seen anything so huge and strange and at once both ugly and beautiful. She gazed up through its metal lattice to the uppermost platform and recalled the story of a man who had jumped with a parachute. Had he lived? She couldn't remember. How would it feel to jump from such a height?

Propelled by an unfathomable yearning, she joined a group of people stepping onto the elevator. With a jolt and screech of metal, it began to climb. The occupants drew in their breaths. They were all traveling – an urbane man in spectacles, a trio of fashionably dressed women – up, up, up to where they could see all of sprawling Paris, but the ache inside her remained, exacerbated by the lifting sensation as they rose.

With a clang and a titillating jolt, the elevator came to a halt and the doors opened.

She stepped out onto the topmost platform of the Tower into the thin cool air above Paris. People were standing at the edge of the railing pointing out the distant fairy tale spires of Notre Dame. Suspended in sky, light-headed and dizzy, she was higher than she had ever been. The vast greenery of the Champ-de-Mars now looked like a tiny postage stamp and the faint mist rising from the river drifted over the thread-thin lines that were the bridges crossing the Seine.

She stood at the rail and watched a bird swoop by so close that if she'd tried she could have reached out and touched its wing. She wanted to fly with the bird. Or jump.

The world was sad and cruel. War destroyed hope, destroyed love, did it not? Life's sorrows would forever plague the world and its people, and what could she do to change it? She was merely eighteen, yet stretching before her she saw a loveless future in which she would become an aging flapper, a floozy, an unwanted woman with no purpose. Perhaps the heirloom had transformed her mother, but it had done nothing for her. What she felt instead was a terrible sorrow for the world, its forever and endless stories of loss.

The bird made a wide circle and came back to soar before her, it wings white and wide like a gull's. Lifted on a draft of air current above her head the bird appeared to taunt: *Look at me, I can do it, why don't you?*

Why not fly off the Eiffel Tower?

When it cawed and made another circle and came swooping directly toward her she realized it was drawn to the shiny crystal on her chest. She lifted the necklace up over her head and dangled it over all of Paris. If she gave it to the bird, would it lift her up and fly her away to a better world in the sky? Its talons swooped toward her. Her body tipped over the rail...

An arm encircled her waist and pulled her back.

"It is a long way down, no?"

She turned and looked into the face of a man with remarkably turquoise-blue eyes. His other hand quickly grasped the pendant.

"And why give so pretty an object to that bird?"

It was the man who had ridden up with her in the elevator. From behind his spectacles he observed her carefully. *He knows who I am,* she thought, and yet she never met the man in her life.

"I wasn't going to jump," she blurted.

"You were going to fly?"

"Well, no."

"We cannot fly like the birds. No matter what we wish. *Cela n'en vaut pas la peine.*"

"I'm sorry, I don't understand."

"It is – how do you say – not worthy of the trouble, this jumping, even if you do have *Weltschmerz.*"

"I'm sorry?"

"*Weltschmerz.* Pain for the world. *Welt,* world. *Schmerz,* pain. I am sorry to say the last elevator has gone. Your jewel, Mademoiselle."

The man draped the necklace back over her head and quickly withdrew his hands. It was an almost fatherly gesture, gentle and kind.

"Last elevator?"

"Unfortunate situation, yes."

An attendant in a blue uniform was speaking with the few people who remained. A thin haze surrounded them, and the air was getting cooler.

"*Il est fin,*" the attendant was saying, pointing to a thin, wobbly fire escape, "*Descendrez pied.*"

"*Mon dieu, no!*" The trio of fashionable ladies complained loudly. The attendant responded to them with indecipherable French, the gist of which indicated that it was not his fault and they were simply going to have to bear with the situation.

"What is the matter?"

"It has malfunctioned. The elevator," said the man with the turquoise eyes. He spoke English in a halting, careful manner, but he didn't appear to be French.

"But that's impossible!" Maddy blurted.

The man peered at her through his glasses.

"They will make the repairs tomorrow. For now there is but one way down."

He gestured toward the fire escape.

"A *fire escape*? Absolutely not. I'll slip and fall. I'd rather wait all night for the elevator."

"Come, you will be fine. It is too cold for you to stay here. And who is to say how long it will take to fix."

The fire escape was nothing more than a metal ladder leading down the side of the tower. The man shook his head at her and smiled. Standing together, they watched a group of young men start down it first. The fashionably dressed ladies followed, vehemently whimpering "*Je deteste.*"

She looked back at the man. He was polished, cultivated. Ever the gentleman, he indicated for her to go ahead.

She had no other recourse. The first step onto a rung built into the side of the structure was the hardest. It felt wobbly, insubstantial, and as slippery as the soles of her shoes. The entire ladder was unprotected and should she fall, it offered no backing to catch her. She was like a small bug crawling along the side of the Eiffel Tower. A breeze drifted through her fingers, drying the perspiration, but in her panic she produced more sweat. Images of her feet slipping, her hands losing their grip, locked her into a state of frozen terror. She paused, unable to move. The man above her halted as well.

"Do not think, mademoiselle, and do not look down."

He spoke calmly at a normal level yet his strong voice carried clearly over the rush and roar of wind and city.

"Breathe deeply and take one step and then another."

She did as she was told, and for a while she managed until she caught up to the French ladies below and heard their sobbing, hysterical phrases.

"*Nous allons mourir,*" one shouted, while the others punctuated her ranting with "*Mon Dieu.*" She stopped to allow the women to move on and once more found herself frozen. The man above her came on steadily until she had to shout out so he wouldn't step on her hand.

"Ah," the man said.

"I'm sorry, I'm sorry," she sobbed, "You have to pass over me, go on without me, you can pass."

"I will not pass, for you are in my way." The man's voice measured and logical.

"I'm sorry," she said again.

She gripped the rail, unable to take even a single step. If she moved she would fall and die, it was inevitable. She noticed the man's shoes on the rung at her eye level. They were of fine leather and well made. Brown.

"To think I contemplated jumping," she said.

"Why would a beautiful woman want to end her life," said the voice above the shoes, "When it is only beginning?"

"My life isn't beginning, it's ending."

"I am twice your age," the man said, "And *my* life isn't ending, so why is yours?"

"My life is over because the love of my life doesn't love me!"

It sounded absurdly melodramatic, but it was true.

"Then I would say the love of your life is a fool," the man said. Taking a different tactic, he added, "And now you must forget him, for here you are having a great Paris adventure with me and I can assure you I am much more handsome."

Maddy couldn't recall if the man was handsome. At the moment she could see no farther than the cuffs of his trousers. They were made of a fine fabric, linen perhaps. This calmed her for a moment until she noticed the open sky behind them, and below the tiny rooftops and cars and river.

"I'm not the suicidal type," she said, "I'm too afraid of dying."

The man laughed.

"You are funny," he said, "Now continue."

She took her next step on his command, and with the next step and then the next and the next, found that she could sustain the mindless rung-by-rung act of climbing down the face of the Tower. They paused to rest at the second platform then the final one before they resumed, and soon she got the hang of it, step by step, foot by foot, rung by rung, and the man kept saying, "Good. Now, another. Good. Now another. Good. Good." The ground came up slowly, closer and closer, until finally she was placing her shaking foot on solid pavement.

She sunk to her knees and put her face in her hands. She was giggling hysterically. She heard the French ladies caterwauling about their ordeal and suddenly they were embracing her, enveloping her in their thick matronly perfume. She was sighing and crying and they were laughing with her and crying too, then turning to the young men who had gone before them and scolding them for bragging to a riveted gathering of tourists.

Maddy looked up and waited for the bespectacled man as he descended. He was elegant, long-limbed and impeccably dressed, even with the soot from the Tower brushed against his clothing.

"We survived!" she said when his feet finally touched ground. He turned to her with an expression of utter confidence and pulled her into him with unexpected surety, holding her firmly against him until she grew aware of his warmly comforting body.

"Look!" she said, and stepped back to hold up her hands. They were covered with the black grimy soot from the ladder rails. He showed her his matching hands and they laughed, unable to stop. The fashionable ladies had turned away from berating the young men and were laughing too, shouting "*merde, merde.*"

"We must have a serious drink," the man said to her. "Yes!" she replied, and took his proffered arm. Her legs were shaking and she truly needed a drink. It turned out he was handsome, as he had joked, and indeed twice her age, yet younger than her father at least.

"A coffee and brandy *es appropriate, no*? I am Claus Diebkin."

"Maddy Rosario."

"Charming," said Claus, and patted her hand, wrapping it comfortably inside the crook of his arm.

Chapter 10

"Events in life can be symbolic as in a dream," Claus said, "If you pay attention, you will understand their importance."

He spoke with a melodious Viennese accent; a psychiatrist on holiday in Paris for the Exposition yet unable to leave his work behind. *I'm being shrunk,* thought Maddy, *my mind is shrinking down to its most essential thoughts.* They had found a café with a view of the Tower on the Rue St. Honore, washed in the *lavoir*, and sat at an outdoor table where they watched the sunset intensify into the same pale orange as the *Courvoisier* coursing through their bloodstreams.

"Freud and his male and female symbols," she said, "Why must the sky be exclusively male territory and women earthy? The Eiffel Tower might be one of those phallic dream symbols, but it's real, and I have the ach in my legs to prove it."

It was refreshing to argue without worry over consequences. With Martin, dear Martin, there had always been the consequence of his disapproval, but with Claus she could just be.

"Let us say," said the psychiatrist to whom she was becoming increasingly drawn with each sip of brandy and passing minute of sunset light, "That you and I were intended to meet. If you had chosen not to go to the Tower, if you had remained on solid ground rather than ascending into sky, our chance meeting would never have occurred."

He looked at her directly then. And waited for her response.

"You are saying I must rise to godly heights to meet you?"

148

"Ah, so you consider my observation, how do you say – "

"The word in English is patronizing," she said, surprised at finding the very word she was thinking.

"Yes, it is true. Men do tend to be patronizing toward women. I apologize for this but not for *le diference*. That is a wonderful thing, do you not think?"

"The difference between men and women? Wonderful so long as *le diference* isn't used to subjugate us in any way."

I am sounding like my mother and her suffragist friends she thought. But then why not? Something had changed. Perhaps it was the frightening experience they had shared or the way the world seemed to shine out from his eyes, or maybe it was simply the fact of his profession, but whatever it was, Maddy felt propelled to tell Claus everything even as she sensed he knew her in a way no one ever had before.

"You have my sincere understanding, Mademoiselle," said the psychiatrist, which was really all it took to open the floodgates. She remembered Martin's feverish love-making, and suddenly she was telling this man how they had been childhood friends, how she had loved him all through the War, how they had finally made love on board the Aquitania – *twice*. He listened to her with a psychiatrist's hypnotically dual expression of concern and fascination, as if she, teenage American girl Maddy Rosario, were the most interesting person he had ever encountered.

"I have powerful longings," she said, and grasped the pendant hanging by the chain from her neck, "I thought I'd love Martin and travel the world with him, but it seems that is not to be."

Something tickled her cheek. Claus reached up to smooth the tear away. It was a tender gesture, and it unleashed from her a sob. She took a gulp of brandy, sobbed again, and hiccupped.

"Don't be *triste*," Claus said, and patted her hand. "You will have many adventures in love ahead. Do you understand? Of course you don't understand, but you will, and I am here to help. Consider me your guide. If you are willing, I will introduce you to your life. You *do* want to understand your life, do you not? Here, this is for you."

Claus offered her the rose from the table. It was soothingly fragrant, and she took it and breathed in its scent.

"This – how do you say – is a propitious moment," he said.

"And how is that?"

"You are discovering that you are powerful. Here, now, as you are. With me now."

She watched Claus' gaze idly trickle, like warm water, down her neck and across her breasts and shoulders to the pendant at her breast and in that moment she understood that, yes, she had power. The power to entice. The power to be herself.

The sunset was over, and the lights on the Eiffel Tower twinkled. Twilight swept over the city. A waiter came around to light the candle on their table.

"Do you suppose," he said, "They have fixed the elevator?"

"I don't know," Madeline retorted, "Was it you who broke it?"

He smiled then did a simple thing that, in retrospect, she understand was all part of the art of seduction. He took the rose from her hand and slipped it into the buttonhole of her jacket, and in doing so the back of his hand lightly brushed her breast.

"You and the rose have much in common, Mademoiselle. You are both exquisite."

It so happened that Claus was also staying at the Crillon (it was, after all, reputedly one of the more "aristocratic" hotels in Paris), and so he suggested they dine together that evening. Back in her room, she informed the reluctant Mrs. Sullivan of Martin's treachery and her chaperone conceded that making new friends, even sophisticated foreign male ones, was better than pining over a boy who did not love her.

Dressed in a flesh-colored silk dress, her body spilling against the silk, Maddy emerged from the lobby elevator to Claus' gaze which, without once taking his eyes from hers, left no doubt she was to be the undivided center of his evening.

"I will take you to a little restaurant," he said, tucking her hand around his arm, "where you will dine on your every desire."

"You mustn't spoil me too much," she said.

"Don't be so American," he replied.

They took a taxi beyond the blazing lights of the Concorde to a darker area of the Montparnasse. The restaurant was in a low stone building off a narrow street that, had it not been for the round cream-colored moon beaming from the cloudless summer sky, would have been hidden in shadows.

"I came here in the years before the war," Claus said as they entered, his hand pressed lightly against her back. He had given her a soft-spoken summary of Vienna's hardships after the war: The fall of the Habsburg Empire, the food shortages, and finally the influenza epidemic that had taken his parents and many of his friends.

The dining area was small and simply decorated with a wrought iron chandelier and white linens and silver on the tables. From the humid air rushing from the swinging doors that led to the back kitchen she could smell meats and sauces and hear the low industrious hum of food preparation. The place had a quiet air of routine, one Maddy could well imagine Claus coming to year after year. The maitre guided them to a table near the window under the moonlight.

Dining with an older Viennese gentleman stirred Maddy's demur demeanor. She was quietly awed by the manner in which the waiters attended them, and by the graceful ease with which Claus selected the wine.

"I will order the pate and endive salad and I think the quail will be nice, if you like," Claus said. A waiter draped the white napkin into her lap and another poured ice water with lemon. Without pretense, Claus sniffed and tasted the cabernet and gave the waiter a courteous nod of approval.

"To your charm," Claus said with a casual lift of his glass. His eyes were filled with a watchful, fun curiosity, as if she were about to suddenly amuse him.

"And to your perseverance," she said, "I don't know how you tolerated me today."

"I was ready to boot you off the Tower and well out of my way."

"Instead, you psychoanalyzed me!" Maddy said with a laugh.

"Do not be afraid," he said, "of being a woman."

"That's all very well in theory," Maddy said, "but being a woman can be terribly restrictive, you know."

"Complete humbug. That is an old battle. You got your vote. You've shorn your hair and you undoubtedly smoke cigarettes, although I don't care to see you do it. Now get on with what you want."

"I'd like to believe you."

"Rebellion is very girlish. But you will progress from that. The world is filled with men who fear the sexuality of *des femmes*, but you have the power to change that."

She wanted ask how she might do that, what it was inside her that gave her that power. Perhaps it *was* the heirloom, this piece of transforming crystal, which would take her beyond her personal drama into what she could only think of as an opportunity to step into History. She wanted to ask him more, for he seemed to possess a wealth of knowledge of the world even while he hinted at answers rather than provided them, but their meal arrived, and so they spoke of other things: the Exposition, Le Corbusier, French fashion, food. She noticed that he did not have a voracious appetite but rather preferred to savor his food as if their flavors were telling him about something from long ago.

They were drinking brandies and coffees when Maddy blurted out the thought she had been nurturing all evening.

"I don't believe that *you* fear a woman's sexuality."

The mirth in his eyes confirmed it, and when he nodded his assent she added, "And when I'm with you I am not afraid of the sexuality in *me*."

He paused with the brandy halfway to his lips and studied her gravely.

"That is good," he said, as if making a clinical statement on her psychological condition. She wondered how blind he was without his glasses, how close she would have to be for him to see her without them. She then focused her attention on stirring her coffee with a tiny spoon.

They took a taxi to the flea market where, in their evening clothes, they sorted through dusty lamps and ashtrays and decorative objects in search of fanciful pieces of deco. Maddy bought five thin cigarette cases decorated in bold geometric colors, a blue Baccarat scent bottle, a round Lalique box and a handful of black enamel and rhinestone brooches. Claus showed her how cubes and geometric flowers were predominantly featured in French deco, then bought a green and silver scarf with the same patterns, a clock with Egyptian motifs, a lime green soup tureen, and a small wood bust sculpture of a nude wearing a bob cut not unlike Maddy's.

"She is like you," Claus said and raised the sculpture up to catch the moonlight. The figurine's shoulders were pronounced and bare, the breasts perfectly shaped, and as Claus made a bid to the shopkeeper, Maddy saw his thumb run along the curve of the miniature breast.

"I will take you to one more destination before we return to the hotel," he said, gathering their parcels together. She tried to remind herself that she was in love with Martin and couldn't possibly allow herself to be attracted to a man who had been on the other side in the war to end all wars, but failing at this, she allowed herself to be escorted into another taxi. Claus directed the driver to the Rue Dante. The taxi parked at the side of the road and waited. Suddenly the *train d' Arpajon* rumbled down the Boulevard Saint-Michel. Vendors approached the train to shout and haggle with the transporters. Bargains were made, and the wholesale produce was loaded in fresh, aromatic bunches onto carts and carriages.

"The *train d'Arpajon*," Claus said, "Arrives at precisely two o'clock in the early morning with fresh country food to feed the city for the day and flowers for you to purchase on the streets, you see?"

"I have never seen anything like it." Maddy saw it all as wonderfully French, the vivid colors and scent of earth, the bright vegetables and flowers.

A tiny bunch of stray violets fell from a passing cart. Claus picked it up, shook the flowers' bobbing faces clean and presented them to her.

"To a beautiful young woman on the brink of new adventures."

She accepted the violets, flung her arm around his neck and kissed him. He encircled her in his arms and held her in a way Martin never had. Approving shouts and whistles sounded miles away.

"I want to see your room," she said in the elevator back at the Crillon.

He took her hands in his and said, "This is not a tour, you understand. If you come to my room, you will not be coming out for some time."

"Exactly what I had in mind," she replied and thought, *does this mean I no longer love Martin?*

Claus' hands moved up from her waist, thumbs encircling the silk folds at her breast. The elevator continued its flight upward but the floor seemed to fall out from under her.

"My dear have you thought that I am returning to Vienna tomorrow and this will be our one night together?"

They had reached his door and entered the room's dimly lighted interior.

"No," she replied, "I haven't thought at all."

"That is good," he said.

He unhurriedly gazed at her standing before him. The crystalline jewel shined like a beacon lighting the way toward undiscovered country, and as he pulled the dress off her in a single swoop she realized that this, maybe this, this was a new way of discovering who she was.

It was an education of the kind she never would have expected. *Le diference* was what they were made for. Soaring to Eiffel heights of passion was not only *a propo*, but encouraged. This was nothing like Martin's rushed and guilty love-making but rather like the unfurling of musical notes that kept opening to reveal more layers, more notes, each touch upon her body accompanied by a cry from somewhere deep inside, rising up from her pelvis and out through her throat like jazz.

Early the next morning she sat cross-legged in his bed, a macaroon puff of tousled sheets and tangled hair. She watched him pack, absorbed in every part of him, his hands, his stiff bending at the waist, his careful attention to detail, his methodical control when he made his phone call to the steward and the calm manner in which he instructed the bellboy at the door to take the luggage.

He turned to her with fond regret. He sat upon the bed and cupped her face in his warm hands. His kiss upon her mouth lingered, his breath warm against her ear. He then receded from the pull of her desire.

He was leaving too soon, it was happening too fast. He had been her best lover ever, although she had had no other lover but Martin. Now he too was leaving.

He stroked her cheek and said, "You are a woman of rarest quality."

And then before he closed the door gently behind him she heard him say something else that, upon her recalling their day upon the Eiffel Tower, the first glimmer of sensual interest over their apertifs, the evening of moonlight and the gift of violets from the *train d'Arpajon,* she heard clearly, coming to her like an echo:

"Remember: *Know who you are.*"

Chapter 11

"I'm sorry, but I've decided and that's all there is to it," Maddy said and quaffed another slug of champagne.

"But to Pamplona and the running of the bulls!" Mrs. Sullivan said, "Running after Martin, more likely."

"I am *not* running after Martin. I'm tempted by Pamplona on its own. Why should I avoid Pamplona simply because he is there?"

"As your chaperone I say this is insanity!"

"You *are* aware," Maddy said, "That I am no longer a child in need of a chaperone."

In a single night something extraordinary had happened, and while Maddy knew it most certainly had to do with the gentleman with the turquoise eyes, she also suspected the heirloom had played a part.

"Tell Mama when you see her that I now know who I am," she said, "She'll know what I'm talking about."

"She will *not* know what you are talking about," said Mrs. Sullivan, "She most decidedly will not. You are supposed to return home to New York with me, not go gallivanting off to Spain like some poor lost soul."

Lost. Was she lost? She had not only *found* herself but had ordered a car and driver and room service breakfast and champagne. She had requested that the *concierge* send her steamer trunk to the dock for shipment home to New York, as she would be traveling lightly with sensible clothes like a lady journalist. A *free* soul not *lost* soul. She would make decisions on her own and she would no longer wait for others to make them or to tell her she was wrong.

Martin may have broken her heart but she had discovered in a single night a way to heal it.

From here on out Maddy would see things *not* as others said they were, but as the person she was. No more breast flatteners. And forget the frivolous gowns and furs and hats. She stuffed them into the steamer trunk and slammed shut the door, a Pandora's Box sealed tight. Someday, years from now, she would find these items and remember the strange day upon the Tower, and Claus, and the time when she had worn beaded dresses and smoked through long cigarette holders and danced the Charleston, but those trappings were needed no longer. Nor did she need the little perfume bottles and trinkets and deco treasures bought the night before. Here on out she would avoid impulsive purchases. She would budget and find a way to earn her own money among other expats who were saying the American dollar could go far.

From the buttonhole of her jacket she removed the rose Claus had given her and wrapped it into the soft folded paper upon which her mother had written *know who you are*. She considered the heirloom. It had served some purpose, strengthened and transformed her, just as Mama said it would. It truly was a family heirloom, too valuable to lose. She would send it home to New York where she would someday pass it on to her daughter. *If I have a daughter*, she thought. And so she lifted the pendant with its gold chain up from her neck and placed it in the center of the paper with the rose and folded both inside together.

"What am I to say to your mother?" Mrs. Sullivan was saying, "And what of your father? He will say I have failed in my obligation and dismiss me."

"Mama would never permit that."

Mrs. Sullivan considered her employer's final instructions, which were to invoke Maddy to be sensible but permit her a "long leash," and when all else failed, to ultimately set her free. Maddy was to be her own woman, Madeline had said, even if their own generation didn't understand.

"Champagne for breakfast, I see," Mrs. Sullivan said. Resigned, she reached for a *beignet*.

"Shall I pour you a glass?"

Mrs. Sullivan sighed.

"Oh, why not."

And there it was. Maddy and her former chaperone would drink the effervescence and the girl would declare her ambition expanding in proportion to the courage she claimed, and from within the skin of her newly found self and a bold certainty emanated from the depths of her person she would pursue life in the person of who she was. Claus was only the beginning. Through him she had discovered the language of passion, the seductive glance, the penetrating stare, and so she would allow her sensuality, her womanhood, to build and grow into a force. She would go to Pamplona and find Martin and see for herself if he loved her, and if all hope for his love was lost, she would accept what she could not change and partake in the luscious feast that lay ahead.

Chapter 12

She drove over the Roncesvalles Pass into Spain and as she descended into the arid Ebro Valley streaked with dusty olive trees and fields blazing before sunset, she thought of Martin and Francesca. She had to know for certain before she gave him up. The Citroen overheated again and again, forcing her to periodically stop. She looked again at the map and talked to other drivers along the way and soon the countryside turned to night.

When she arrived at midnight, the streets of Pamplona were filled with the feverish, hot-blooded excitement of the Fiesta. The night air was scented with sweat and wine and perfume. People shouted politics outside wine shops. Tourists who'd come to see the bullfights joined locals gathered in the cafes, and on the square men and women danced and drank streams of wine from leather *botas*.

Maddy parked the Citroen near the tiny hotel recommended by the concierge in Paris. No sooner than she was out of the car, she was approached by a stocky grey-haired man and his beautiful Spanish lady in a black lace *mantilla*. Gesturing and shouting, the Senora ordered her man to carry Maddy's light baggage, and with the woman's insistence he offered Maddy his wine *bota* and showed how to use it. Celebrants in the street cheered her on as she held the leather pouch up and poured the fountain of wine into her mouth, *rosa* dribbling down her neck, and with her head thrown back she saw standing on the balcony of the hotel what she had come to ascertain: Martin. Martin and Francesca in an embrace, firecrackers splitting the air around them. Music, dancing, singing and drinking wafted up from the noisy Plaza de la Constitution, but they were aware of nothing but each other. She stood unseen among the crowds beneath the man she would love forever, hidden among the exploding lights, her pain heightened by wine. She saw and knew it to be true: There could be no doubt that in the presence of Francesca, Martin was filled with happiness, and that Maddy must relinquish him so that she might find other lives, other souls, to love.

Chapter 13

A rocket explosion signaled the start of the running of the bulls, and while Francesca slept back in the room, Martin and Fricky were out in time to watch a band marching down the main street. Excited shouts erupted from the crowd. The earth was rumbling.

"*Aya estan!*"

Men and boys came running down the narrow street, and behind them came the bulls. It may be called the running of the bulls, Martin thought, but this is the running of grown adolescents running for their lives, running past him through the entryway that led into the ring. Hundreds more followed, running so hard they stumbled and fell against the fence. It was absurd, childish and pathetic, he thought, and it was just like Fricky to find this sort of thing entertaining.

They were soon situated in high up seats in time to watch the amateur fights down in the ring. Men and boys held scraps of cloth or their shirts, and only a few had a decent *muletta*. Martin wasn't up for seeing anyone, no matter how foolish, be gored to death.

A bull released from the pen circled at a frisky trot then raced toward a man's shirt, catching the cloth on its horn and flinging it into the air and trampling it under hoof. Another man sneaked out from the safety of the *barrera* and pulled the bull's tail. Martin felt sorry for the bull and so, apparently, did the crowd, which booed in disapproval.

"Enough amateur hour!" Fricky shouted, "Bring on the real *toreos!*"

In agreement, the crowd began stomping and chanting for the matador.

Suddenly a boy sprang down from the *barrera* and marched toward the animal. Barefooted, bare-chested, and in worn pants, the child held out a small red rag. The bull took one look at it and charged, but the boy stood his ground, and with the finesse of a true matador, executed a perfect *veronica*. Everyone cheered with hysterical relief.

"He's just a child," Martin said to Fricky.

The bull turned and charged again, its capped horns barely missing the boy's chest.

The *capeadores* were shouting, beckoning the boy to the safety of the *barrera*. But the boy attempted another *vernonica* and this time the bull knocked him down.

Suddenly there came a piercing shout from the part of the *barrera* nearest the bull. The shout came from a woman who was leaning over the protective fencing. She was holding out her red lace shawl, shaking it lightly, causing it to undulate and glimmer. The crowd shouted their encouragement. The woman had the bull's attention, affording the boy time to leap to his feet and limp away.

The bull ran to the red shawl and butted it against the *barrera,* its horns stabbing into the delicate crimson *ropa*. When the bull lifted his head, the lace caught in one of the horns. Martin watched in horror as the woman held onto the other end of the shawl, refusing to let go. There were gasps from the crowd, then laughter when it appeared as if the woman and bull were playing tug-o-war. It looked like the bull was winning, nearly pulling the woman into the ring, and finally she let the shawl go.

"Wait a minute," Martin said. There was something about this woman. She was too far on the other side of the *corrida* to see clearly but her shouting sounded like English.

"Where's those binoculars," he said. Fricky was grinning, binoculars limp in his hands. Martin snatched them away, put them up to his eyes and quickly adjusted them. And there she was, coming into focus, reddish tomboy bob framing her face.

"Maddy!" Martin shouted, although he knew she couldn't hear him. The bull trotted about the ring with the red lace hanging like a *mantilla* upon his horns. The spectators laughed and cheered. Through the binoculars Martin could see Maddy, his Little Maddy, turning to speak to a Spanish woman seated beside her. She accepted a drink from a *bota*, held it arms length above her head and squirted the wine into her mouth as if she'd been doing it since infancy.

"Where did she learn that?" Martin said, "Who is she with?"

"Maddy, oh Maddy," Fricky said.

"Damn you, Fricky, this was all your idea."

"And I didn't hear you object. How was I to know she would follow us? Here, have some wine."

"To hell with the wine. What are we going to do with our Little Sister?"

"She's not yours to do with, my friend, and she's not our Little Sister. Not anymore, it seems."

Martin looked through the binoculars again and watched Maddy return the *bota* to the Spaniards seated beside her.

A trilling fanfare of horns started up and a handsome matador in dazzling blue and gold stepped out from the gate. Standing erect then moving with all the grace of a dancer, the matador used his colorful *banderilla* to deftly lift the red lace shawl off the horns of the bull. Spectators cheered his chivalry, and as the bull was cajolled from the ring, the matador presented the torn shawl to Maddy.

From the other side of the ring Martin observed the way she leaned toward the matador, the way she seemed, even at this distance, to glow with sensual magnetism. He watched her stand and pluck her tattered shawl off the *banderilla* and nod her gratitude. He watched the matador make a deep courtly bow. He heard the spectators, caught up in the romantic theatrics, roar their approval.

Martin rose from his seat.

"Sit down, Martin," Fricky said, his face bright red from either the wine or sun or suppressed laughter.

Martin lowered the binoculars. He stared across the arena past men in ruffled shirts and ladies in boleros, past noisemakers and hawkers selling taffy, past the shouts and trumpets heralding the upcoming activity in the ring, past a man waving his black Basque cap in the air. The crowd screamed *Ole!* as if personally cheering her into the arms of the matador who would charm the spectators with his daring and woo Maddy into her first Spanish romance. She was lost to Martin, moving into her separate life, lost in the crowd of thousands.

Ole!

Ole!

Ole!

Chapter 14

The matador traveled with her to San Sebastian and then Bermeo and Cabo Machichaco and Santona and Punta del Pescador, where their days and nights were wine-filled feasts and they swam and fished and ate and drank and darkened under the Mediterranean sun. But when he brought her to his village and she saw how the women were made to be like servants to their men, she saw no future for herself in his world. She was the American daughter of a suffragist, she told him, and so having given the matador her love but no promises she left him to travel in the company of other American expatriates through the seaside towns of the Rivieras, from Cartagena to St. Tropez and Rapallo.

Sometimes she thought of Martin, but when such thoughts lingered too long she chased them away. He was lost to her as she was to him, and though he continued to visit her in dreams, she turned away from those dreams in her waking world. He became a vision arrested in amber, wrapped in longing.

News arrived from home, and it was through one of Mother's letters that she learned her steamer trunk had been lost, and with it their family heirloom. Mrs. Sullivan was distressed of course, as she had seen the trunk among their other luggage and boxes on the dock at the port in Calais, but it failed to arrive in New York harbor and no one knew where it was. It could be at any destination to which ships were leaving from the French port that year: Lisbon, Naples, Casablanca, Cairo, Beirut, Karachi, and the Oriental cities of Hong Kong and Shanghai. Mistaken for another tourist's baggage, the trunk and its otherworldly treasure could have been transported as far away as Singapore even, but no inquiries led to the discovery of its whereabouts.

Maddy blamed herself. If she had kept the pendant with her instead of shipping it home it never would have been lost, and she would have continued the tradition of passing the treasure on in the way her great aunt the Whale Rider had done. Now it was everywhere and nowhere, never to be seen again. She cared little about the trunk's flapper dresses and beads and the other small purchases she'd made in Paris, but the archaic jeweled amulet fashioned from the meteoric mysteries of the universe, found by a seaman in the buried remains of an Iron Age warrior queen, this she couldn't bear to lose.

She sailed home to her family and sought forgiveness from her mother. Together they shared their stories of transformation and speculated about the medicine woman *La Que Sabe* and the psychiatrist Claus Deibkin. With her faith in the unknowable trajectories of the universe, Madeline assured her daughter the heirloom would find its way back. Maddy couldn't imagine how, for to her the world was an immense reality, its forces chaotic.

When Maddy Rosario returned to Europe, she inquired about the lost trunk to ship captains and hoteliers, but they would shake their heads and say it was unfortunate, most unfortunate; such was the risk of travel, missing luggage. The greater her regret for its loss, the more crucial the heirloom grew in her mind until she perceived it as the answer to all the Weltschmerz that lingered within her.

A decade passed.

Between transatlantic crossings Maddy Rosario traveled light, carrying in her catchall bag simple clothes, clean hankies, and sugar in a jar. She took up residence in Paris, then Barcelona and Madrid, gravitating back to the native land of her father's father.

She had lovers and lived in numerous houses of love yet chose no home in any.

She became a connoisseur of the glance across a crowded room, the intimacy of a gesture, the ecstasy of touch. Sensual power emanated from her style, her walk, her thick reddish hair. The invincible health of her flesh and bones drew men to her, and this would have her live hard and wild and lead her to think of the passionate feminine and how it could alter the patriarchal war-driven world. She heard Martin had left Francesca to sail for Jamaica on a merchant ship reported lost at sea and she grieved for him, the boy of her youth hobbled by war.

Sadness for him and the many other victims of war solidified into the conviction that women must gain power to form a peaceful matriarchal world. She wrote and published her political and sensual views, and being paid for her voice gave her the means to empowerment, which she declared must be had by all women.

She joined the Spanish workers and *Mujeres Libres* who advocated for female liberation, women's literacy and education for their children. She wrote of how in the fight for workers solidarity women were also fighting for freedom. She wrote to develop political conscience among women and brought her ideas to rural collectives and traveling libraries so that women would gain the confidence to fight for themselves.

She did not believe in war but became a woman in war. When the Spanish Revolution struck she joined the republican loyalists in their fight against fascism and aided the evacuation of Basque children. Destiny drove her into the path of a man with the International Brigades, an artist named Max Hansman whose paintings had appeared alongside Picasso's *Guernica* at the International Exhibition in Paris after his work was banned in his own Germany. And so it was inevitable that the outspoken russet-haired Maddy Rosario of *Mujeres Libres* and the German Jewish expressionist would become lovers.

They traveled back to Berlin to recover a hidden cache of his work, but before they could find it he joined the Jewish resistance. He hid and fought in the Black Forest. She smuggled to him bullets and rifle parts inside the diapers of their infant daughter, Marjorie Berthe.

She did not believe in war but she was a woman of war: A girl in love with a doughboy of the Great War, a young woman embroiled in the cause of the Spanish Revolution, and now a mother with child in the middle of yet another war.

An uncensored letter from her mother miraculously arrived at American Express in Berlin. *Are you all right?* Madeline wanted to know, *isn't it time you came home?* The Rosarios' shop had been converted into a coffee house where German immigrants came and spoke of thousands of Jews deported to ghettos and camps. In the same letter her father warned that Europe was no place for a half-Jewish baby. They implored her to bring their infant granddaughter home, but she would first stand in solidarity beside the non-Jewish wives of Jewish men held prisoner in Rosenstrasse and saw what the voices of six thousand women could do. Fearing plummeting morale, *fearing the women,* Himmler released the men, many on their way to Auschwitz. They were saved by the rage and fury of women who stood out in the cold with their children and babies demanding their release, and Himmler backed down.

The reality of monsters that maimed and killed even children grew larger, beyond her ability to alter, no matter the temporary victory at Rosenstrasse, and she saw now that her dream of nations ruled by matriarchal influence was dying. Her child at risk, charged with the safety of one so helpless, she was a mother first and a woman second.

And so with Marjorie Berthe in her arms, Maddy Rosario would do what she most hated, which was run from a fight.

Maddy did not remember Max's final embrace nor the expression on his face, darkened by the soils of the forest where he lived among partisans and battled Nazis with the rifle bullets smuggled to him inside his infant daughter's diapers. She did not remember if he kissed little Marjorie Berthe good-bye or if their baby cried between them; nor did she see one last time his brilliant black eyes before he turned away from her and went back into the forest. What she remembered instead was the long terrifying train journey through German Nazi strongholds, the checkpoints and stops and requests for *papierre bitte,* the holding her breath and imagining themselves invisible, and then in London disappearing further still from the air raid bombings into shelters, holding hands with women and other strangers and comforting their children and wondering if it would ever end. This she remembered.

And then one night, after emancipating her generation with the vote and fiercely loving her beloved Jonathan and raising her children and hoping for her daughter's safe return from the war in Europe, Madeline Gallacuty Rosario tiredly went to bed, closed her eyes and never awoke. A week after burying his wife, Jonathan Rosario found himself standing in the freezing rain at Astor Place lost and confused. Struck down by pneumonia, his final words to his son Stephen were, "Ask Mama."

Maddy finally set sail for home with the child her parents would never see. Hitler had invaded Poland. Max had disappeared. On board the full-to-capacity Queen Mary, she joined thousands of emigrants leaving Europe. The staterooms were filled to bursting with multiple occupants and so she slept on a pool table and made do like everyone else who had left in haste and worry, leaving families, leaving homes and manuscripts and paintings, abandoning musical instruments and lives built for generations.

She carried with her the usual notebooks, simple clothes, clean hankies, and sugar in a jar, but she now had another piece of baggage who slept curled under her arm. Marjorie Berthe wore hankies instead of nappies, and the sugar in the jar was dissolved in water for her to drink with sips of dwindling milk from Maddy's breasts.

Maddy mourned her mother and remembered all Mama had given her: The love, the passion for independence, the encouragement to *know who you are.* She recalled how instead of bedtime stories Mama would read her Elizabeth Cady Stanton's *The Woman's Bible*, how she would repeat the words of the great Suffragist in everyday conversation so that Maddy could hear the words right down in her bones:

> *The best protection any woman can have is courage.*
> *Self-development is a higher duty than self-sacrifice.*
> *I shall not grow conservative with age.*

Having once thought of her mother as living in servitude to family and the Cause, she came to understand now that Mama had always been developing herself, refusing the conservative path for the more difficult courageous one. It seemed unfathomable that she and Papa were gone from this earth, that she would not find them there when she arrived home.

Maddy moved with her brother Stephen and his wife Annie to their grandfather Horace Gallacuty's cottage on the Point in Rockaway, Queens, and then into a grander house on the same peninsula overlooking the harbor. They joined the rest of the nation in the tidal wave that was the Second World War. Homes and businesses and streets and cities pulsed to the same beat that was war bonds, scrap drives, victory gardens, rationing.

They were fighting a common evil, fighting for the Four Freedoms: Freedom From Want, Freedom From Fear, Freedom of Speech, Freedom of Worship. Stephen left to fight in the Pacific. Maddy and Annie saved and separated their scrap and clothes and garbage: Steel in a shovel could make four grenades; girdles could be melted down into rubber.

She sent unanswered letters to an address in Berlin.

The war in Europe ended in May and by August an atomic bomb named Little Boy killed thousands of people and a few days later one named Fat Man killed thousands more. Hiroshima. Nagasaki. Then came the lists of names from Buchenwald. Dachau. Treblinka. Janowka. And finally Auschwitz-Birkenau, where the artist and partisan fighter Max Hansman, father of her child, had died.

Maddy thought of the women who protested outside in the cold at the prison in Rosenstrasse and how they had saved some men from the camps but not enough men. Nor women. Nor children. She thought *if only*. *If only* there had been more women to stand up to the Reich, *if only* more woman spoke out and gained power and knowledge and influence against war. *If only* men like her Max were still alive. They would paint artworks or build bridges or make love to their women and watch their children grow. They would plant food and teach in schools and listen to the women, women who could change the minds of even a Himmler. She looked back to that long-ago day in Paris in 1925 when, with one war over and another yet to begin, she experienced that sensation of potent influence the heirloom pendant evoked. And she recalled her mother's words on that thin slip of parchment paper and how the same words had been repeated by Claus, ingrained in her mind forever:

Know who you are.

 the celebrations and dancing in the streets, Maddy Rosario bought
a dark blue dress with shoulder pads and a pair of sensible leather shoes
with black wedge heels and told her brother Stephen she was returning
to Germany.

"I'm afraid for us all," she said, "The death of our souls. Murder,
horror, cruelty, we can't let this happen again. We have to change the
balance, because right now the scales are dipping toward evil, even if
we did win the war."

"You think you can tip the scales the other way?" Stephen wanted to
know, "Change the world?" He had always been an isolationist, though
he'd fought in the Pacific. He'd done his part and seen the horrors she
had spoken of, and now he wanted to raise a family and stay in Queens
the rest of his life.

"I have to try, Stephen. Women can change the world – this is how
we will stop people like Hitler."

"The allies stopped Hitler."

"Yes, but he never should have come to power in the first place.
How did it happen? Ignorance. That's how. Ignorant men and women,
powerless women. If women had power there wouldn't be war."

"You can't be serious, Maddy."

"Oh, I am. I am serious."

And she was.

She packed her small bag and spooned more sugar into that infernal
travel jar.

Stephen didn't approve, but then how does one approve something
so foolish and fanatical as returning to Europe in search of a family
heirloom deemed lost long before the war and certainly lost forever?

"It's more than that," Maddy had said to her brother and sister-in-
law, "There's Max's artwork to be considered, and his friends and the

ore than that," Maddy had said to her brother and sister-in-
law, "There's Max's artwork to be considered, and his friends and the

173

other partisans who might tell me what happened to him. And we must do everything we can to prevent another war. Finish what we started."

"*Mujeres Libres,*" Stephen said. It wasn't that he disapproved of her altruism, or her dedication to improving the lives of women and children in far-off reaches of the world, but why so far away? And what of Marjorie Berthe? He said as much.

"I can't sacrifice the woman I am to the mother," Maddy said, as if it were an edict written in stone, which in a way it was since it had been spoken by their own mother, although their mother had always been their mother first and a woman second.

In the case of Maddy Rosario, that apparently wasn't to be.

She had been a good mother, a loving mother for a time, but not for a lifetime. Speaking softly to little Marjorie as she drifted toward sleep, she explained why her aunt and uncle would make better parents, wonderful parents, and how she would be happy and secure in America where the vast Atlantic Ocean would separate her from the troubles of the wider world.

Little Marjorie Berthe was too young to understand what had happened to the father she couldn't remember.

And so burning with love and regret, she put Marjorie to bed, pressed her cheek against her soft head of dark curly hair and took in the spice and skin scent that was her daughter's alone, and with a gentle kiss promised she would be back.

But she did not come back. Not for a long time.

The Storm

Night

*M*arjorie Berthe Hansman thrusts her limbs through the powerful rush of water in her flooded cellar and reaches for the painting that started it all over half a century ago when she first came into her talent. "Body In Red" firmly in hand, she wants to save the other ones too, but with the water swirling up her shoulders and breathable air space rapidly diminishing, she will have to concede imminent destruction of decades of work.

On the other side of the peninsula her granddaughter Maya drives toward the fires lighting up the sky knowing that irretrievable time – *tempus fugit!* – is urging her to hurry toward the most dangerous place they could be.

Maya thinks of her mother's mother, how people say "*wow your grandmother is Marjorie Berthe Hansman?*" how she has always been the explosive type. When a person gets to be seventy she ought to calm down, but Grandma Marjorie Berthe is always driving the people around her insane. Like now, drawing Maya and Great Grandma Maddy into the maw of danger too.

"You okay, Grandma?"

Grandma Maddy sits in the passenger seat with eyes open so wide Maya thinks for a moment she is dead. But then the dry wrinkled lids blink slowly – like a lizard conserving energy.

"Yes, dear."

Three Generations of Family Die in Storm of the Century. She can see the local headlines now. Her poor Mom will be the last of them standing, still running her nonprofit, still holding down the fort and taking care of everyone while Dad is being a hero aiding Africans migrating to Europe, arranging their amnesty in the States and bringing them to the Gandela Center in Queens. Her parents are heroes. So what does that make her?

A daughter of heroes who is making a big mistake trying to be one herself.

And so with her cellphone battery spent down to dead and her ancient grandmother in the passenger seat, Maya keeps the heavy Rover plowing through water on a steady course on Rockaway Beach Boulevard. She stays on inland roads until the turnoff to Beach Channel Drive and wonders how long the seawater will keep rising and what she will do if the Rover stalls and how she will keep Great Grandma Maddy safe and if Joshua McFadden seriously asked her out or if he was just being nice so she could have something to look forward to before she died drowning.

Because Maya Jones doesn't look like a thin glamorous model she's decided she isn't pretty. Despite her parents' assurances otherwise, she's come to assume models in magazines are the kinds of girls guys like. Even though her mother is a feminist and her grandmother a famous rebel painter and great grandmother fought sexism in places all over the world, Maya is her own person. She frets about her college applications and global warming and saving people in need, and in between those bigger concerns she worries about what guys think of her.

Emergency vehicles flash by in the darkening gloom. She isn't the only car on the streets yet assumes the police cruisers hovering like sharks in the rain might stop her and order her home. If the flooding gets too high the Rover might take on water and simply roll over. It's a jeep, after all, not a boat; it won't float.

"Grandma," she says to Maddy in the passenger seat, "What we need is a boat!"

Her great grandmother nods.

"Okay," Maya says simply to hear what she hopes is her own decisive voice, "We're going to pick up Grandma Marjorie Berthe then we're all going back to the house where we're going to have a picnic with S'Mores. Remember how you always made me S'Mores?"

"S'Mores," her grandmother repeats, "Yes, I do."

A fire truck blocks the street so she takes a right onto Beach 142nd Street. She drives past clapboard houses shuttered tight and porches taking on waves of water. A burglar alarm blares from a house with nobody home, becoming louder and louder still. As they drive past the horrible shrieking her great grandmother suddenly releases an anguished, whimpering cry.

"*Get to the shelter!*"

Maya punches the automatic lock seconds before Maddy pulls at her door handle.

"We stay in the car, Grandma."

"*It's the warning!*"

The dementia triggered by sirens and alarms and fear for her daughter, as if Marjorie Berthe were a perpetually helpless infant instead of the stalwart queen of the modern art world she is today.

"It's not an air raid, Grandma, trust me."

"*Marjorie Berthe —*"

The house alarm continues to shriek, repeatedly, insanely, from the dark windows of the deserted house.

"We're going to get her, Grandma. We're in New York, not London and there's no war, the war is over. See? Raid's over." After they turn onto Beach Channel the alarm's wailing fades, replaced by distant sirens. Maddy calms and resumes her unblinking lizard gaze, staring beyond rivulets of water coursing across the windshield.

Wind hits harder on the right side of the Rover. Maya sees the Marine Bridge packed with hundreds of car lights and for a horrible moment imagines the entire bridge collapsing into the water with all those people in their cars. Her grandmother pats her hand on the gear-shift, as if she – Maya – is the one who needs reassuring, and in a way she does.

It's tempting to follow the mass exodus across the bridge, but she swings left onto Rockaway Point Boulevard, toward the crimson sky, past the shuttered houses in Roxbury and then the dark looming dunes of Fort Tilden, along where Rockaway Inlet is bleeding sea waves onto the road. *Keep moving* she admonishes, *keep moving or you'll die.* The engine of Dad's amazing Rover keeps roaring along like her big fearless Daddy is right there protecting them both. She thinks of her paternal Grandma Jana, safe indoors in the brownstone where Dad grew up in Jamaica, Queens, and of how she would say, *What you doin' saving two old ladies? They're old, you're young. You let them die, you hear?*

Sure, she thinks. A girl doesn't grow up the daughter of heroes to turn around and be a coward. No, she will *do something* not because she is a hero but because she wouldn't be able to live with herself if she didn't.

Fire trucks have stopped up ahead at Beach 201st Street as the floodwaters are too deep at Rockaway Point for even them to go on. She can see dozens of houses on fire, the flames flashing across the floodwaters, and the silhouettes of people leaving Breezy Point, abandoning their burning homes. Firemen wade through water toward the fires. Another fireman is waving an emergency torch at her, signaling for her to turn back. She stops, engine idling, and keeps gunning the accelerator with her foot, keeping it going.

"Back! Back!" the fireman shouts. He waves a group of people away from the houses. They cleave through waist-high water swirling insidiously around them, arms linked, six-seven people at least.

As they approach Maya sees the stocky woman in the middle, her arms hooked on both sides between two strong young guys and the guys in turn linking arms with two women in heavy jackets and then two bigger older men on the outside, their free hands holding up what looks like a huge door over their heads – a rectangular umbrella, but of course it isn't a door and it isn't an umbrella. It is a giant red-painted canvas.

And there she is, in the middle of the linked arms, broad of chest and breasts and shoulders, heavy thighs pushing along through the water, this formidable woman of part German Jewish stock, her indomitable grandmother, Marjorie Berthe Hansman.

And behind her, the sky is on fire.

Maya rolls down her window and shouts "*GRANDMA!*"

Wind punches through the Rover and flings her voice into the air. She calls out again until one of the men on the end hears her, and like a group playing the game "telephone," one leans into the other, shouting a message through the wind and rain down the line of people, until the eldest though not frailest but staunchest and stout-hearted woman in the middle sees Maya and shouts back:

"*What took you so long?*"

It seems as if everyone in the group is drunk and in fact they are, having left a house party that has suddenly, literally, caught fire. They are shouting frantically among themselves, to the firemen, to Maya too.

"I tried to stop it but the fire – "

"My dog is with my neighbor, I hope they – "

"My basement is flooded, all my work, everything," Marjorie Berthe shouts, "but I got 'Body In Red' out. It was my first major piece. More are at the Gagosian. Thank-god for the retrospective, or more would have been here."

Maya warns against opening the Rover doors that are already taking in water, and so Grandma Marjorie Berthe enters through the hatch-back, the big canvas pushed in with her through the rear, the front edge bouncing inches above Maya's head.

Great Grandma Maddy paws at her daughter's arm and cries *my baby Marjorie Berthe* but Grandma Marjorie Berthe ignores her.

"Excellent, thank-you, you are wonderful, thank-you," she says to one of the men in a show of gratitude Maya rarely hears from her grandmother.

"You take care, now, Ms. Hansman, keep safe," the man says, casting a look of concern inside the Rover at Great Grandma Maddy, whose mewling voice keeps repeating *Marjorie Berthe – Marjorie Berthe –*

"I'm here, Mother," snaps the grown daughter, "Take it easy."

"It's *Ground Zero* up there on the Point," someone says. A fireman is explaining the fire trucks can go no further through the flooded streets to the homes that are burning away.

Ground Zero. Maya was six when the Towers fell. She watched them fall in a continuous televised news loop she mistook for cities all over the world coming to ruin until her mother explained it was happening at one place in New York called "*Ground Zero.*"

"Where are you going?" Maya calls out as the group turns back toward the fire trucks.

"St. Frances Relief," shouts a woman from behind her slick rain hood.

"You can also go to my mom's Gandela Center," Maya calls, "At ninety-first – " but the woman has turned and disappeared with the others, arms linked, into the roaring wind.

A fireball erupts two blocks away and a plume of black and grey smoke billows up. Maya turns the Rover back toward the houses of Roxbury. She feels the vehicle straining against the water, like driving a motorboat on wheels, and hears a wail from Great Grandma Maddy who has turned around in her seat and is clutching her daughter's wrist.

"It's alright, Mother, I'm here," Grandma Marjorie says again, but Great Grandma Maddy cries softly, pitifully, and when Maya glances over she sees what it was that has so upset her great grandmother, more than the flames, more than smoke billowing toward them like the reaches of hell from a crematorium, for she is clutching her daughter's arm and staring in disbelief at the tiny numbers written across Marjorie's wrist, like a tattoo, like –

"What's that on your arm, Grandma?" Maya says, thinking, *those numbers look like* – She has seen the pictures in the history books.

"It's my social security number," Marjorie Berthe replies, "I wrote it with an indelible ink pen in case something happened to me in the floodwaters. For identification."

It is a morbid yet practical solution, but Great Grandma Maddy doesn't hear or understand. She continues her keening, presses her gnarled fingers across those tiny numbers.

"I won't let them take my baby girl."

Eyes widening with understanding, the famous artist says, "It's just my social security number, Mother, so I won't forget, like a string around your finger, in case I had to go the hospital. See, I'm fine, Mother. I'm here with you!"

Pushing the Rover back the way they came, Maya strains to see beyond the volley of water crawling over the windshield. It is almost too hard to bear, hearing the fear in her great grandmother's voice, saying *my baby* like it was just yesterday getting her half-Jewish infant daughter out of Nazi Germany.

"Listen up, Mother," Marjorie Berthe's voice soothes with begrudging compassion, "Look at me, will you? I'm not a baby. I'm an old woman, see? See how old I am? Look at my face, Mother. I grew up to be an old woman. I survived, Mother, I survived. I'm old — "

And then her final words are spoken in a whisper, almost as though their truth is too hard for the self-reliant Marjorie Berthe to say.

"Thanks to you, Mother, I lived."

1957
The "Woman Artist"

"I can see myself, and it has helped me to say what I want to
say in paint."

Georgia O'Keefe

Chapter 1

With her feet locked in cold metal stirrups and the doctor in the driver's seat, so to speak, of the steel instrument squeezing on her cervix, Marjorie Berthe recalled what she'd been told her whole seventeen years of life, which was to always, *always*, try and be nice. This being her first gynecological exam, she was discombobulated and embarrassed yet determined. She would leave with a prescription for that new miracle of science called The Pill. For that she would be nice, nice enough to even listen to the doctor emulate the recently deceased (and good riddance!) Joe McCarthy, gritting her teeth through every word.

"Subversive influence is everywhere," the doctor was saying, "Movies. Books."

"Art. Don't forget art," she said, and winced. As a student at the New School in the Village she wanted to shake the very tenants of hypocrisy and conservatism, but all she'd managed to do so far was paint pretty gardens.

"Art, sure," the doc said, "I'd say Hollywood's to blame. Relax."

Out came the speculum. In went the rubberized fingers that probed and pushed.

Maybe he'll find something subversive in there, she thought.

"Good girl."

How she hated being a "good girl." Every woman in America was expected to be a "good girl," and if you didn't behave, dress, talk and conduct your life in a certain way federal agents would come knocking on your door asking questions. Good girls didn't take birth control, good girls didn't paint subversive art, and good girls certainly weren't like her Aunt Maddy.

Not only was Aunt Maddy most likely a Marxist traveling somewhere on the wrong side of the Iron Curtain, she wasn't even her aunt. She was her mother.

"How old are you, Marjie?" Dr. Anderson asked over her kneecaps.

"I'm eighteen," Marjorie Berthe said, though she wasn't quite.

"Eighteen," Dr. Anderson absently repeated, "Well, that wasn't so bad now, was it? Just a little cramping."

The doctor stretched off his rubber gloves. He was gray at the temples, golf-tanned.

"But doctor, my periods," she said, "The cramps are unbearable and the blood flow is, well, scary."

She lifted her feet out of the stirrups. The nurse nodded from her position near the door where she'd been placed to insure no hanky-panky. Everyone spied on everyone these days, even in gynecologist's offices.

"You're a perfectly normal girl," said the doctor, "No doubt things will settle in the next few years when you marry and have children."

She had no intention of marrying or having children, but what she said was, "Yes, I hope so. Still I was wondering if you might prescribe me that new kind of menstrual control I've heard about that comes in a pill?"

The doctor's face visibly blanched and the nurse frowned.

"Are you planning on getting married?" He spoke slowly now, with none of the buoyant enthusiasm of his earlier pro-McCarthy talk.

What would she say? Would she tell the truth, which was that she hated pretending to care about her virginity, which she couldn't wait for the opportunity to finally discard? Would she say she was spending more time in the Village and going to the clubs and meeting beatniks, artists, and musicians, and since one thing leads to another, she'd decided the best thing to do before having sex would be to see that she didn't get pregnant? Why should boys have all the fun?

No, she would not say this.

"My fiancé is very concerned," she lied, "My periods have been excruciating and quite frankly I've considered breaking our engagement if I can't find relief. I'd heard the new pill was ideal for regulating the menstrual cycle, doctor. That is, until we can start a family. I'd love to have a big family," she added, turning to the nurse and making her eyes sparkle with happiness at the abhorrent image of a house filled with hideously screaming children; not unlike the house she lived in now with her young cousins.

"So you have no intention," said Dr. Anderson who clearly thrilled in his role as head inquisitor, "No intention of ever using the pill for birth control?"

"Oh, heavens no!" she said, "All I want is for the cramps to go away, and to marry my fiancé and have a family!"

She thought she'd overdone it, but the nurse clapped her hands and the doctor smiled with his whitened teeth.

Outside it was a warm, summer day. She walked up Main Street in her checkered gingham dress she couldn't wait to change out of, past the "Pretty You" beauty parlor. Inside, women sat in rollers under giant dryers. The place reeked of permanent wave and the smell of heated hair wafted out onto the street. A picture out of *Vogue* plastered onto the window promoted the sleek new "perma flex" hairstyle. "It's polished," the ad said, "Shaped to the head and molded. It doesn't flow unrestrainedly. The smart hair-do is trained to look exceedingly well-groomed and well-behaved."

Who wants to be exceedingly well-behaved?

"Marjorie, here we are!"

Aunt Annie was standing outside the "Starlight" movie theater with Susan and Stephen Junior, who were shooting streams of pop drink at one another through their straws under the marquee, "Invasion of the Body Snatchers."

"You're becoming such a young lady," the aunt who used to be her mother said, "I hardly recognized you!"

Aunt Annie had a bachelor's degree in home economics from Smith and ran her home with precision and dedication, but in Marjorie's view she appeared depleted and small now, as if the blue airmail letter that arrived last week with all its truths had shrunk and robbed her of any authority, which in fact it had. Aunt Annie really had been a kind and good mother before becoming distracted by the birth of her real children. Marjorie was nine when Susan was born and she had loved her little sister (who was really her cousin) like a dolly. But what could Annie and Stephen have said when they first brought Susan home from the hospital? ("This is our real child, not you.") And when Aunt Maddy came and left again for her itinerate life in Europe, what would they have said then? ("She's your real mother, but she doesn't love you enough to stay.") The truth was too complicated for a child to understand, they now told her, and so they delayed, and the unfortunate side effect of the delay was that Marjorie felt betrayed by everyone.

There was no going back, no returning to the nice normal girl she thought she had been.

"What did the doctor say?" Aunt Annie asked, her voice soft and concerned.

"It was just a check up, *Aunt Annie*," she said, placing emphasis with the implication *you're not my mother.*

"Did I tell you Dr. Anderson delivered both Junior and Susan?"

"Yes, you did."

"Maybe someday, when you find the right boy and marry, he will deliver *your* children."

"Maybe someday, sure," Marjorie said, although she couldn't think of anything more repugnant than remaining in Rockaway, having a family, and being ordinary. She was studying to be a painter yet suspected that she too was ordinary. With each passing year mediocrity was creeping into her soul and soon she would end up married to some dullard like her uncle, whose job at Drexel Furniture made him even more ordinary, which she supposed was the point, why her mother had left her with Uncle Stephen. He and Annie were stable people who had kindly fed, clothed and sheltered her. Unlike her real mother, who thought only of herself.

"I found a new recipe in *Good Housekeeping*," Aunt Annie said, "That I'm just dying to try. Junior, get away from that car! Susan, if you're going to play yo-yo, do it properly!"

Susan and Junior stopped spinning their yo-yos like boomerangs at someone's Pontiac and swung their yo-yos at Marjorie's head instead.

"Stop it," Marjorie hissed at the monsters, and followed her former mother into the store. The children skulked behind. Susan stuck out her tongue, and Junior appeared to be in some world of his own, flailing and grasping at items along aisles as if his sole purpose in life was to create mayhem and chaos. Resignation weighed on Marjorie as she pushed the shopping cart into which Aunt Annie placed half a dozen cans of frozen orange juice, two boxes of Betty Crocker cake mix, a stack of Libby's cling peaches, several containers of Pillsbury hot roll mix and a box of Minute Rice.

They drove home in the family's steel green Oldsmobile to their neighborhood of nicely cut lawns and picket fences. Uncle Stephen's fruit trees were already lush with leaves and the beginnings of summer fruit. He had cleaned the Weber grill and said they were going to invite the Johnsons and other neighbors over for a cookout. Aunt Annie unpacked the groceries and asked her to hang the laundry, which was fine, because Marjorie was screaming inside, screaming *get me out of here*. The house was stuffy with the smells of fried eggs and toast and her uncle's shaving cream and that starch smell from the shirts Aunt Annie ironed for her husband.

Marjorie pulled the damp sheets out of the washer and took them outside in the basket. All the housewives on the block had their laundry hanging, so of course her aunt would have her do it too, because that was how it was, everyone doing the same thing, at the same time, on schedule. She flung the sheets over the line without bothering to untangle them, and as she was furiously slapping on clothespins she heard the slam of a car door and looked across the street toward the sound.

It was that man, their neighbor Roger Johnson's brother, who'd come to live with Mr. Johnson and his family after fighting in Korea. The man walked in his dark grey suit from his blue Pontiac convertible toward his brother's house. He looked over at her and nodded hello. She realized suddenly that he'd been watching her and had seen her slam the basket down and hurl the sheets in a wringed-out mess over the line. He smiled and kept walking with his briefcase in hand, a tall boney man with fine blond hair. He paused at the front door to unlock it, and entered his brother's house.

Spies, she thought, spies everywhere.

She thought of the prescription for The Pill and smiled. She had fooled Dr. Anderson, convinced him she was in anguish when in fact she barely paid attention to her monthly menses. She would take The Pill and discard all the pretence. Her innocence was gone, why not her virginity too? She would reject the trappings of children and home economics and stop painting flowery gardens on tidy *well-groomed* canvases. She would become the artist her father had been.

Max Hansman was a specter carried along in her very blood. She had seen his works in catalogues along with the sepia toned photograph of the face of the man she had never known, a face very much like hers: The deep-set eyes and mass of dark hair, the large mouth so perfectly shaped; all that was Max Hansman, gone in flash of fire.

She was the last Hansman standing.

Chapter 2

kay, so he had been watching her. She was so watchable, he could watch her watch paint dry. She was half his age, a teenager, but he watched her. She was untouched by experience. This made her a blank slate and for that reason he wanted to just look at her; that blank slate with all that fresh promise. She didn't know what she had.

She wasn't a pretty girl; she was a beautiful one. Beautiful girls were often acutely aware of their imperfections yet unaware those imperfections were in some cases the very thing that made them beautiful. She moved with a coiled fury, jerky and assertive, and the gingham dress she wore, cinched tight at her waist and flared below her knees, looked all wrong on her thin-hipped, leggy body. If he were an ad man he'd have her barefoot modeling Levis, but he wasn't an ad man, he was a stock clerk at a furniture showroom with its living spaces of fake windows and plastic flower arrangements and bleached wood sofas.

When he drove home from work in the evenings in his blue Pontiac Bonneville convertible, he tried to think of the good life ahead, of the road trips he would take and the places he would see in this great wide and free country – the Grand Canyon, the Painted Desert, California. But what he saw on the drive back to his brother's house in Rockport was billboards advertising Coca Cola and Metropolitan Life and U.S. Rubber and Life Savers and Maxwell House Coffee, and the more billboards he passed the duller he felt. They were signposts leading him back into that dead-end feeling of meaningless commercialism when

194

what he really wanted after Korea was to leave it all behind, every last inch of it. Still, he had a sneaking suspicion he just couldn't get out of second gear.

He was supposed to want to start a family just like any other family in the houses he passed, with their water sprinklers showering the lawns and children hollering on bikes and the silvery light of brand new televisions dancing behind windows. It was a strange new time, but if living thorough war had taught him anything, it was that new times changed into old times.

As he arrived home to his brother's place and parked his car in the driveway and heard the shouts of neighborhood children he realized that, in many ways, this teenage neighbor girl, throwing laundry despondently on the line, was in the same predicament. Like Drexel's living spaces of unread books and phony rooms, he was living in an in-between place, not looking for wife or housewife and or "wife-servant" so much as a life-mate with whom he could escape. All he thought of was escape.

Chapter 3

After returning from the gynecologist with her prescription for The Pill and catching Mr. Johnson's brother staring at her as she hung the laundry, the postman delivered to Marjorie another letter. The letter was identical to the first one with its light blue paper and *par avion* stamped above her mother's delicate scrawl, the one that had told her about her father dying in the holocaust, the one that ended with *all my love*, which was a lie, for if Marjorie was in possession of *all her love*, her mother never would have been abandoned her in Queens, never would have allowed her to believe her aunt and uncle were her parents. And she never would have disappeared in Europe and Asia and wherever else her mother had been.

And so when she looked at this second blue envelope with its flamboyant handwriting and patriotic red and blue airmail border and felt her heart freeze and her fingers too as she held it in hand, she thought, *what now,* what new life-changing bombs will Aunt Maddy-Mother drop today.

She cut the top of her mother's letter with the scalpel she used for scraping paint off canvases, and took satisfaction in seeing the blue smeared with a slash of cadmium red. She unfolded the thin lightweight paper.

> *My dearest Marjorie Berthe,*
> *I have news that will change your life!*

The strings of Mantovani played in the living room where after a Saturday working sales at Drexel, Stephen Rosario relaxed in an oasis of quality furniture inherited from his parents. Here was the velvet sofa from his mother's house and the Chippendale breakfront and his leather armchair with the cherry wood trim, plus the Chinese urns they had saved from the shop, their only concession to modernity being the peanut-shaped coffee table and, on it, a ceramic peanut-shaped ashtray. Annie had filled the ashtray with white breath mints, and next to it she had placed a tray with a pitcher of martini mix, martini glasses and olives. Stephen plopped two olives into the glasses and poured the mix over them, then sat down in his leather chair with a groan of satisfaction.

His wife was in the bedroom getting dressed for the Johnsons' party and the children were running into the kitchen from the backyard and out again. He heard something crash, but it didn't sound breakable, so he stayed where he was.

And now he looked up to see Marjorie Berthe walking into the peaceful atmosphere of his Montovani moment. She was wearing Levis and a kerchief around her hair, and was holding another one of those damnable letters from his sister who had just last week turned their household upside down with her unspeakable yet necessary truths.

"She wrote me another letter," Marjorie said. She waved the sheet of paper with her mother's scrawl of loops and curlicues (even her handwriting was erotic!), then flopped down upon the couch and stared at the writing, as if by gazing at it she might conjure up the exotic woman who confounded even her own brother.

In recent days Stephen had spent much time trying to explain to his hurt and confused niece the reason for her mother's extended absences behind the Iron Curtain. Having fought with *Mujeres Libres* in Spain and written books of shocking erotica which could never have been published in the U.S., Maddy had traveled to cities as remote as Moscow,

Beijing and Singapore, making her "Un-American" by some standards. But all Marjorie Berthe wanted to know why he'd lied to her, why he'd led her to believe he and Annie were her parents, even though he suspected she'd always known. (She'd had faint memories of a woman holding and kissing her whom she identified as "Aunt Maddy," memories she said she'd mistaken for dreams.) What could he say but that he wanted her to feel loved and safe, that they had done what they thought was right?

Stephen and Annie knew Marjorie's father had died at Auschwitz yet they were astounded by the letter from his sister finally telling their adopted daughter the truth. If only Maddy had told Marjorie in person, but that was Maddy for you. She drops a bomb then isn't around to deal with the fallout. They were.

And now here was another letter, and Stephen braced for what it contained.

"Aunt Maddy – oh, sorry, *Mother* – says that somewhere in the city there's an old steamer trunk with a family heirloom inside, and she wants me to have it."

Marjorie made her voice sound disinterested, tossed the letter onto the coffee table, and grabbed a handful of mints.

"Do you know what it is?" she said, "This heirloom pendant thing?"

Stephen looked down at his hands and glanced down the hallway where his wife was finishing dressing. As Marjorie Berthe waited for her uncle to speak she thought of how often she waited for him to speak, how many long waits she'd endured, and when he did speak he rarely said much of anything important, at least to her. *All that waiting for nothing,* she thought.

"Why don't you get ready for the party," he said.

"I *am* ready. Are you going to answer my question *Uncle Stephen*?"

"My mother wore a pendant," he said, "My sister, I have no idea, but my mother, yes. Mother said it healed her in some way when she was a

young woman, and my father, he – didn't much care for the whole idea,
to him it was a bunch of silly nonsense."

"But is it valuable? I mean, could I sell it?"

"An heirloom shouldn't be sold, no matter how ridiculous."

"So you think it's ridiculous? Why?"

Suddenly this pendant heirloom thing had more import. If it was
tied to everything that fell into the category of his disapproval it was
worth reconsidering.

"No reason, really," he said, although he suspected this so-called
amulet was associated with his sister's long absences and before that his
mother's emancipation. A good thing, women's emancipation, but not
without conflict. When faced with conflict Stephen's impulse was to
retreat from the action. He worked hard, and he worked on Saturdays,
and now he was trying to relax before the Johnsons' party, but instead
his daughter Marjie or rather his niece Marjorie Berthe needed to bat
him around some. Some women were like that. His sister was like that
and now his daughter *Marjorie Hansman* was growing up to be like that,
though through no fault of his own. Stephen saw in his adopted daughter's growing face not merely a resemblance to his wild lost sister, but
also the temperament of a stranger, an exacting and explosive personality he couldn't control; he wouldn't even dare try.

Stephen sipped his cold wet martini (*ah!*) and thought of Annie changing in the next room. She would brush out her soft, shining curls and
outline her lips with a thin brush painted with a bright crimson color
from the lipstick tube. She would put on a strapless brassiere and a
crisp, calf-length petticoat that rustled. She would then slip on that
navy dress from Lord and Taylor.

Thank god his wife wasn't anything like his sister. Or this one.

"Marjie, don't make everything so hard on yourself," he said, "Why
don't you change into something pretty and come to the party. I'll drive

you into the city tomorrow, and we can find the trunk at the storage facility. Then we'll see if we can locate your heirloom."

"I don't want to go to the party. The Johnsons make me hang out with the kids. Why am I the designated baby-sitter? They act like I'm happy to play with their stinky baby just because I'm a girl."

"Just put in an appearance," he said, "That's all I'm asking."

"Does the whole neighborhood know I'm not your daughter?"

"Nobody knows. And you *are* my daughter, Marjie."

"Please don't call me Marjie. Marjie was your daughter. I'm Marjorie Berthe Hansman now, the little orphan."

That hurt, but it was her intention to hurt. *How sharper than a serpent's tooth.*

"You're not an orphan. You're my daughter and always will be, and we both love you. I just want what's right for you, Marji – Marjorie. I want you to be happy."

"Why should I be happy? My real father was murdered because he was a Jew and I'm half-Jewish. What's there to be happy about? I'll never be happy. Happy is bullshit."

"Would you like your mouth washed with soap, young lady?"

"No," Marjorie whispered, and glared down at her mother's letter. They endured a mutually discomfited silence punctuated by the melodramatic strings of Mantovani.

"Okay," she said, "I'll put on something pretty and then I'll flirt with Mr. Johnson's brother."

"Now you're trying to upset me."

"Hey, let's make a deal, Dad! I'll go to the party if you give me the key to the storage facility with the trunk containing my *inheritance*." She said this last part sarcastically, but what he heard most was "*Dad.*" It was her gift, a concession.

"Okay, it's a deal if — " Stephen swilled the last of his martini and stood. "If you change out of those dungarees."

"They're Levis."

For a moment he saw the fanciful child she had been when she was the only one in their household, and so he went to the drawer of his impeccably organized desk, opened it, found the box with the bits of this and that from his parent's former home, and located among the pens and rubber bands the old Schlage key tied to a red string. He fingered the key with trepidation. He had never cared for the Myth of the Heirloom, but his mother had felt strongly about it, and now it was Marjorie's turn. Like his sister and mother and the great aunt who was known as the Whale Rider she was on her way now into the tumultuous sea of womanhood and there would be no stopping her.

"I'll drive you to the Village tomorrow. It's on Bleecker. Morty's Storage. We can make it a family field trip."

"*Great,*" Marjorie Berthe said. She was suddenly buoyant, having won her victory. He raised the key up and paused.

"You'll go to the party?"

"Yes, Dad."

"Fine."

He slapped the key into the palm of her open hand.

"Now change out of those Levis and into something more feminine, young lady."

Chapter 4

*S*he arrived in Levis and a strapless electric blue tube top that clung to her breasts like paint. Her parents hovered on either side of her as if trying to hide her from view, but there was no hiding her, she was meant to be seen, an aloof and arrogant package all rolled into one shining young woman.

"What's your poison?"

His brother Roger was rubbing his hands together at the chrome-trimmed bar decked out with ice buckets, cocktail shakers and just about every kind of liquor, and a fancy assortment of condiments too.

"I'll have a martini," Annie said.

"The same," said Stephen.

"You folks agree on just about everything, don't you?" Roger said, "Dry? Up? Rocks? Sweet?"

"Me too," chimed the girl, "Up. Dry."

Roger's eyes flickered over to the father.

"I can have a martini," she said, "I'm eighteen!"

"Well, aren't you grown up."

After a nod from the father Roger poured extra gin into the shaker.

"Have you met my brother, Aaron?" Roger said, jerking his head in his direction, "Stephen, Annie and Marjorie Rosario."

Aaron Johnson was slouched comfortably against the bar, a service-able scotch before him. Marjorie Rosario turned her dark suspicious eyes briefly on him and said nothing. It was a pleasant shock to be this close to her; he hadn't been pleasantly shocked in a while. A long while.

"Nice to finally meet you all," Aaron said, looking at the daughter.

"Yes, hello, nice to meet you too," Stephen said, and shook his hand. The house was full already with guests holding some drink or other, as if the highballs and martini glasses were required accessories for them to remain there. Conversation interwove under the soothing tones of Sinatra's "In the Cool Cool of the Evening." Someone was saying his son had hit a homerun at Little League and someone else was talking about his Ford dealership in Newark, but the new topic of conversation was a little known country called Vietnam. "*Our next Korea,*" a neighbor said, "*The communists are spoiling for a fight, and we'll give them one.*"

To Aaron Johnson, they sounded like boys brandishing squirt guns. He sipped his scotch and said nothing. His pregnant sister-in-law Page Johnson breezed up to the bar with vodka and tonic in one hand and baby in the other, orange lipstick smeared. She tossed a strip of hair from her face, which the baby delighted in pulling back, and without looking at Roger, held out her glass. He assessed her condition, and poured in a small dollop of vodka.

"You must be so excited," Annie enthused, "With another one on the way."

"Married with babies," Page said, "Who would have thought that a Phi Beta Kappa MIT mathematics major would end up married-with-babies to a shoe salesman. And lookie here at little Marjie, all grown!"

"Really?" Marjorie said, "You went to MIT?"

"You sound surprised," Page said, "Where are you going to school?"

"I'm studying art in the Village."

"Art in the Village," Page repeated. The baby flailed her spitty fist in her face.

They were like night and day: Marjorie young and sleek in her Levis and tight electric blue top, and Page in a pink pregnancy dress with puffy sleeves, bouncing her baby daughter. Roger handed Marjorie the martini while Page observed her husband admiring the young woman, his eyes trailing from her firm round breasts down to red painted toes wedged between inelegant thong sandals.

"You should visit me at the shoe store," Roger said, "I'll show you some pumps that'll dress those pretty tootsies."

"That's a nice offer, Mr. Johnson," she replied. Aaron could bet that pumps were the last thing this girl would be wanting to wear.

"You could model shoes," his brother persisted, "Hell, you could model, period. Has anyone ever told you that?"

"Of course they have, Roger. Little Marjie's all grown!" Page announced as if she hadn't said it already.

Aaron watched the young woman take one delicate sip of her martini and, after carefully assessing his drunk sister-in-law, say:

"It's Marjorie."

"Well, all grown up Marjorie, hold little Katie for me, will you?" She thrust the child toward her, bumped the martini glass from Marjorie's hand and sent it tumbling toward the floor. In the same instant she released the infant and the weight of the baby descended.

"Eeek!" said Heather Sutter, moving her foot. The martini glass plopped onto the carpet unbroken and Marjorie caught Katie before she hit the floor, but Katie began to cry – a low, confused whine that abruptly increased in volume, becoming piercing and hysterical.

"Katie, it's okay, I caught you didn't I?" Marjorie said, but the baby squirmed and screamed in her arms. Aaron ducked away from the infant's ear-spitting screams.

"My pooooor baby," Page cooed. She reached out and ordered, "*Give* her to me!"

A hush descended on the room, then murmurs of consternation. Page snatched Katie, sobbing, back into her arms.

"What happened?" Roger said in mid-pour from the bar.

"Marjorie dropped Katie!" Page giggled. "Maybe she isn't so grown-up after all. Two sips of gin and she's dropping babies!"

"Butter fingers!" Heather Sutter said, and picked up the martini glass. Relieved laughter trickled through the room.

"That isn't exactly what happened – " Marjorie began.

"Don't worry about it," Roger interrupted, "No harm."

"And she spilled gin all over Katie!" Page elaborated.

"You bumped me," Marjorie said.

Aaron watched the father, Stephen, walk over and touch his daughter's arm. It was a signal, urging her to back off. She wouldn't.

"Do you know what I think, Mrs. Johnson?" The young woman said. For a moment, Page looked frightened. "I think you need a cup of coffee."

Harriet Sutter gave a little gasp. Then Annie was there, taking the sobbing hiccupping baby from Page, whispering something into her ear. Page followed Annie to the kitchen and party conversation resumed. Roger returned to making cocktails and Stephen Rosario turned away from his daughter to listen to someone talk about how he would hypothetically stock a bomb shelter. As if she herself were radioactive, Marjorie stood alone, abandoned and furious. Aaron snatched up a replacement martini, offered it to her, and touched the warm – *hot!* – soft skin of her beautiful bare back.

"I saw it all," he said, "You didn't drop Katie. She did."

"Thanks." She knocked back half the drink as if it were Pepsi. "Why didn't you say something?"

"Hey, I don't mess with my sis-in-law, she's the boss around here."

"You must be suffocating to death."

"Yep. Like you."

Someone was passing a dish of pickles and cheese chunks speared together. Aaron turned his back to the party and in so doing shielded the feminine object of his interest with his broad back, useful for blocking unwanted conversation about pickled delights and pigs-in-a-blanket.

She really looked at him now, pierced him with those angry girl eyes.

"You were in Korea," she said.

"I was in Korea."

She didn't dredge up the usual platitudes (*What was that like? Must have been hell. Are you a war hero? How many of the enemy did you kill?*).

"Oh," she said, and that was all. She was probably feeling the gin too. He could soak her up, just standing there, every fresh clean inch of blushing skin and corpuscle. She didn't need to say a thing, but she did.

"I was wondering," she said, "If you'd like to take a drive into the city."

He drank down the last of his scotch and when he took his time answering her, she didn't squirm or look away. There was something steely about this girl.

"Into Manhattan? Tonight?"

"Not tonight!" she said, having the decency to look aghast, "Tomorrow. In the morning."

He'd let it linger, the mystery surrounding whatever reason she had for wanting him to drive her into the city. It was nice to think she wanted his company.

"Sure, Marjorie," he said.

He waited for her to say *don't tell my parents*, but she didn't.

Chapter 5

The next morning, Sunday, Marjorie woke up sickened by the smell of barbecue lighter fluid, cut lawns, and fertilizer. She was mad as she rose from bed, mad as she showered, and mad when she wondered if that man Aaron Johnson would remember about driving her to the Village. *Maybe he's just toying with me*, she thought, and that also made her mad. She thought she might start screaming and never stop, but then it occurred to her that maybe this was her version of a hangover. She'd never drunk a whole martini before.

The birth control pills Dr. Anderson had prescribed for her yesterday were still in her bag. A month's supply for starters. She took the packet out, punched the tiny pill through the foil, and stared at it. *This* was what was going to change her life!

She made coffee in the drip percolator intent on drinking it quietly before anyone one else in the house woke up, and was stirring the milk in with three tablespoons of sugar when she heard a car pull up. Through Annie's perky yellow curtains she saw that it was Mr. Johnson's brother. Aaron. She gulped down The Pill with half the coffee, grabbed her bag with the storage key and quickly wrote a note – *I got a ride into the city, be back tonight* – and slipped out the door.

His Pontiac Bonneville convertible idled at the curb. The top was down, and he didn't get out to open the door for her, which was a relief, since this was a getaway, not a date as far as she was concerned. She was dressed for the Village in tight black t-shirt and the Levis and boots. With the short strap of her bag hanging on the crook of her arm she'd tied a blue and green printed silk scarf around her neck the way she'd seen Audrey Hepburn do in "Roman Holiday."

He looked her over when she stepped into the car.

"Good morning," he said.

"Thanks for the ride."

He pulled away from the curb and accelerated through the quiet Sunday morning neighborhood with newspapers waiting on identical front doorsteps and no one even out for church yet. She'd never been in a convertible before, and since her hair began blowing about and would soon turn into a tangled mess, she unknotted the scarf from her neck and tied it around her head instead. She'd seen Grace Kelly do that in some picture.

As they drove away from the house she'd lived in for most of her life she wondered suddenly if this was a bad idea. In the note she had deliberately avoided saying who was giving her a ride. Looking over at him, this Aaron Johnson, she noticed how his hair was longer than Uncle Stephen's or any of the men in Rockaway. It waved down along the back of his neck and gave her a sudden thrill.

"So, where to?" he said.

He was driving her where she wanted to go, and she liked that. This older man, her driver, must be almost thirty.

"It's a storage warehouse in the Village on Bleecker called "Morty's," she said. The coffee made her feel jumpy and she'd taken The Pill too, and so she distracted herself by telling him everything: Her mother leaving her, her father the artist Max Hansman dying at Auschwitz. And now this heirloom, Heirloom with a capital "H," really, at least from the way her mother referred to it, that was supposed to change her life. Marjorie didn't believe in magic, she said, but she could use a little right now.

He drove and listened, and as it poured out of her she heard and hated every inch of herself: her voice, her effort to appear fashionable, her ungainly breasts and hot skin. She could hear herself with his ears.

"You've had a lot to contend with," he said.

"What an understatement!"

She didn't want to be grateful for his sympathy — was it sympathy? — she didn't want to be grateful to anyone. She wanted autonomy, independence, confidence, but instead she sat in a man's car as he drove them along the turnpike, and between them there was the weight, the burden of her sexuality. He was giving her a ride toward her fantasy salvation because he found her attractive, and how wrong was that? It was all wrong wrong wrong.

"Tell me about Korea," she said.

"Why don't you tell me about what you paint," he replied.

Like most adults she knew, he dictated the terms of the conversation.

"I'd rather you told me about Korea."

"I prefer to hear about your art," he said, then: "Your father was a great painter. I'm familiar with his work."

Suddenly this man Aaron rose in her estimation, not that she didn't already prefer his company to most people.

"If you know about Max Hansman, what are you doing in Rockaway?"

He laughed at that, laughed too much, she thought. *He's weird*, she decided, *but then, I'm weird.*

"What did I say?" she asked, "What's so funny?"

"I'm considering your question and have no answer other than that I don't care about much of anything at the moment, but your point is well taken."

He'd answered her question, whether he knew it or not, and so she proceeded to grill him into fessing up: On his upbringing off Gramercy Park in Manhattan; on how his brother was classified 4-F due to his partial deafness which was why he'd ended up selling shoes; on how everything changed for the brothers when their parents died together in a shooting in Rome that may have been politically motivated, since the parents were Stalin supporters for a while. Aaron Johnson knew about artists such as her father Max Hansman because he'd grown up in a household that knew about artists.

"And so you see, Marjorie *Hansman*," he concluded, and how she liked that *Hansman* without her even having to ask, "There's more to people living in places like Rockaway than you think."

"I see." She said, and she did, even though it was almost a lecture, but that was all right for the time being.

"So why don't you tell me about what you paint."

"You know what I paint."

"How could I know?"

"I paint pretty pictures," she said, wretchedly.

"Well, you'll have to change that, if it makes you unhappy."

"I don't care about being happy."

"Then I suppose you have the soul of an artist."

They drove into the pulsating city, and the closer she got to her destination, the more rejuvenated she felt. Her anger dissolved, and in its place Marjorie experienced an anxious worrisome hope.

Chapter 6

When they arrived in Greenwich Village they drove around Washington Square until he decided to park near the Arch. He put the top back up on the Bonneville. Clouds hovered motionless in the sky and the air was breeze-less and humid. A vendor rolled by selling sooty blue cotton candy. Marjorie felt herself teetering at a crossroads that was no more than an intersection really. She remembered that her grandparents once lived near here somewhere off the Square in a house she'd never seen.

They crossed the street into the park and walked past the fountain where old men played checkers and Sunday strollers walked their dogs. NYU students had staked out spots on the lawn to study, and a man was playing an upright piano in the middle of all the action – Mozart's *Divertimento*, Aaron said.

The music tailed them, growing more distant as they headed down to Bleecker where they found the storage house. The lettering, "M—TY's," had faded into bricks washed nearly white with age. The building occupied half a block but had an open courtyard area lined with large metal numbered doors. The metal fob attached to the key Uncle Stephen had given her had a number engraved in the steel, directing her to one of the doors. Number 27. Aaron stood beside her as she slipped the key into the lock and pushed it open. He helped her push, as the door was heavy.

"It's like a bomb shelter," she said, although she had no idea what a bomb shelter was like.

She found the switch and turned on the lights. Covered like sleeping ghosts under sheets were the objects from nearly fifty years of her family's life. She picked her way among giant urns, luminous wood furniture, gilded mirrors and silver tea sets. A stack of linens carelessly heaped onto a rocker included an infant Victorian sleeping gown. The tiny white dress had yellowed some, but it was pristinely ironed and folded, with a loop-stitch embroidery upon the hem and tiny silken blue rosebuds at the neck. It had about it the scent of attic dust and a type of talcum powder that was like none sold today, a scent that, like her grandparents, was gone with the ages.

A large chandelier, dripping with prisms and cobwebs, reflected shards of light upon the walls, and as she wandered the cavernous space her body seemed to vibrate like a magnet honing in on its attraction. She didn't know if the objective of that attraction was the heirloom calling to her or the presence of this strange man Aaron.

"Do you see some old steamer trunk?"

She spoke to him with what she hoped was authority, hiding any impression of being intimidated or drawn. He was tall, strong-boned and rangy. She was soft and fleshy. It irritated her, to be soft and fleshy. The Pill, she thought. Could my body already be reacting to the chemicals?

"We'll find it," he said, pausing before a bookshelf with glass panels covering travel books and old board games.

"Someone had a fascination for New Zealand seafaring," Aaron said, bending to read the titles.

On the exposed top shelf, next to a Pueblo Indian basket was a hardcover book with a peeling spine titled *The Twentieth Century Book for Everywoman*. She lifted it up and swept off a thick layer of dust.

"What a joke," she said, turning the pages, "Look at this!"

2

2

One of the chapters was titled, "The Girl's Treasure" and was, she gathered, about saving one's virginity for marriage.

"This is the world my mother grew up in," she said, "Can you believe it?"

Aaron looked over her shoulder at the pictures of nubile girls dressed in tunics and flowers.

"Oh yeah, these are my kind of girls," Aaron said.

"Oh, bull. This is the kind of book that says – look here – that masturbation is bad for you."

"Isn't it?"

He looked at her. She flushed. He was joking, of course. But why did she have to say the word, alone with him here? She plopped the book back down into its bed of dust and turned away.

It was as though they were encased in a time capsule cocoon. Particles swirled inside a beam of sunlight shooting through a filthy window, and there was a certain smell in the air of age and old skin, as if time had grown weary and decided to stop for a breather.

She found the stand-up trunk behind a bookcase under a grimy window. It stood dark and ominous, and was almost as tall as she. It was relatively dust free, having been deposited at the storage facility within recent weeks, and bore several stickers, notably a black and white stamped drawing of a ship with the lettering *Aquitania* beneath. It had to be the ship her mother had taken to Paris in 1925.

"Here it is," she said, unable to mask the awe in her voice.

Aaron came over and wedged the bookcase out of the way. She pulled at the trunk's rusted clamps. They popped loose with a creak. She pulled the lid to the side, swinging it open like a door, and breathed in the stale perfumed air. Had it been over thirty years since her mother had sealed it? A luscious mass of elegant eveningwear slid out and glittered through her hands. As she pulled out a silk beaded dress and a long white fur, she experienced a sudden apprehension, as if her mother at that moment was once again slipping through her fingers, on her way to the glamorous life. Of course it had been ages ago, the Roaring Twenties, before she was born. Whose idea was it to call it the Roaring Twenties, anyway?

"Some stash," Aaron said.

"I bet it's in here somewhere."

Like the flapper beads running through her hands, the answers to the questions that had been building and eluding her ever since the first letter arrived seemed tantalizingly within her grasp. Who had her mother been back then, between the wars, she of the so-called Lost Generation? What kind of mother deserts her only child? How could she leave her to grow up in Rockaway while she heads off to consort among communists or whatever it was she did? *And who does she think she is, offering as recompense a trinket she claims has the magical capacity to alter my life?* Marjorie conceded her life needed altering, no doubt about that, but she doubted her mother's consolation prize would perform the trick.

But still. She was curious.

And so she dug further into Pandora's Box and tossed aside her mother's silly Isadora Duncan scarves and wraps until she came upon a stack of small drawers at the back of the trunk.

Here, she thought, trying to suppress her excitement. She opened the top drawer, and something rattled inside. Perfume bottles with deco designs on their lids and a compact in a similar geometric black-and-white design. Beautiful, but not what she was seeking. She sensed Aaron standing back, intrigued, as she opened the second drawer.

Just handkerchiefs, she thought, but her fingers sifted through the drawer anyway on the off chance.

She felt it first and then drew it out, the soft sheet of paper wrapped around a hard object. The paper unfolded in her hand like a flower opening. Nestled inside was a dried rose, its scarlet petals faded and fragile, and beside the rose a spark of chiseled crystal with a silver chain. The Heirloom.

"You found it," Aaron said.

"Guess so."

Clasping the pendant in her palm, feeling its solid weight, she untangled the chain and dangled it before her. Dust-infused light from the window pierced and refracted through the crystal, and inside she saw a darker reflective metal and inside that a passing movement, a face fierce and bold, then another, faces dissolving in and out of each other until she realized the face she was seeing was her own.

This is me. I see myself now.

It wasn't a thought so much as a sensation: *Of course. Me there. Hello, Me.* Then her face faded into the crystal as if stamped into the memory of the mineral within.

Without thinking one way or the other about the significance of her choice, she slipped the chain over her head and let the pendant dangle between her breasts. Aaron stood back.

"Well," he said.

There was a tone in his voice of — trepidation? Uncertainty? Maybe even fear? *He doesn't fear me,* she thought, *he desires me.* It was just a fact, nothing to ponder or worry over. She fingered the dried rose petal in her palm and noticed a thin scrawl on the paper:

Know who you are.

And she did know; knew with a sudden clarity that was not so much a revelation than crystallization — an overpowering sensation of *being.*

I am I am I am, she thought and laughed, because she thought of Popeye and his "I yam what I yam."

"What is it," said Aaron. She shook her head and felt the smile of Mona Lisa upon her lips.

"What does the note say?"

She passed it to him and he read it.

"You already know who you are," he said. He handed back the soft slip of aged paper. "I could have told you that."

The gentle weight of the pendant pulled pleasantly on the chain around her neck. It was her possession now, hers, passed down from Grandma Madeline to her mother Maddy and now to her, Marjorie Berthe.

"So are you feeling the magic or something?" She heard caution in his voice.

"What I'm feeling is hungry," she said, "Thirsty too."

"I've got just the cure for both," he replied.

She folded the scarves and dresses back into the trunk and decided to leave behind the deco perfume bottles too. They were her mother's after all. Everything was her mother's, except for the heirloom. The crystal with its strange reflections of her face passing inside was hers and her alone. Contrary to her expectation, it was more than a trinket.

And she loved it.

Chapter 7

She locked the door to the storage space and they walked down Bleecker. As they walked she saw him look at the pendant or rather, her breasts, and knew it wasn't the pendant he'd been admiring.

Clouds hung thick overhead and soon they were walking by a building where a group of people stood hunched under a stripped awning. Suddenly a burst of rain followed by an explosive crack of thunder and a bellowing gust of wind tore loose the awning. The crowd shouted excitedly, and a rush of sudden hard-driving rain propelled them forward, and suddenly they were moving with everyone else into the shelter of a gallery.

"Excuse me, please excuse me," Marjorie was saying, but they were going with the flow of bodies, jostled through the entrance. Voices echoed from the interior and they found themselves crammed into an eclectic crowd of people drinking and gesticulating, pronouncing opinions about the surrounding art that literally dripped from giant canvases. A slim boyish man in a black knit cap said, "I dig that crystal, lady," and pushed two wine goblets, the size of a cereal bowls, into their hands. They were thrust toward one another with only the bowls of wine separating them.

"Well, I guess we're drinking this," Marjorie said.

"I guess we are."

He looked down into her face and realized with a shock that he was going to seduce this impossibly beautiful young woman and they would even run away together. This he understood as if he'd been given an assignment, a life's path, which was fine with him. For too long he had been in an in-between place and now he wasn't, now he was the man with Marjorie Hansman, the daughter of the artist Max Hansman, a force in her own right. He could feel it coming, her force, it was coming right at him – Wow! Pow! – like the femme fatale in a Lichtenstein.

There was no space for maneuvering in the crowded room, and she inadvertently backed into a woman in a black dress and dark sunglasses.

"Excuse me," Marjorie said.

"You, darling, are excused from anything and everything," the woman said.

"Well, that's good to know," Marjorie replied.

More art viewers had squeezed in through the front entrance to escape the rain. Sweet-smelling smoke permeating the room, and the red wine was dry and peppery.

"It's rioja," the woman said, assessing them both from behind her the dark glasses. Her silver hair was pulled back from her pale lined face and she wore the frank, bemused smirk of one who enjoyed adventure, the city-kind of adventure full of late night hours and people who misbehaved.

"The Village muse," someone said. Aaron recognized the woman, if only from the society pages: an heiress with unconventional ideas and patron of the new American School of Art. He figured her for the sort of woman one took at face value, pedigree be-damned. Folks in Rockaway referred to the Village as "the psychotic community," but he'd always felt at ease among the psychos.

"What do you think?" the woman said, pointing with her nose to the paintings.

The crowd obstructed full views of the large canvases, but the partial glimpses nonetheless offered glimpses of the intoxicating, shimmering paint: There were bold red gashes and delicate purple lines, there were bright white and dense black dribbles and drips, random yellows, explosive bruising blues and reds. Marjorie stared at the paintings, her eyes wide open and her mouth open too as if she were not only seeing the paintings, but ingesting them too.

"I think," Marjorie said slowly, "That I just awoke from a long hibernation."

"Well, happy awakenings then," the woman said, "These are Janet Sobel's, and I swear by her."

"Not Jackson Pollock?" Marjorie asked.

"Think again. Think of a woman doing these paintings," said the woman in black. Her voice was hypnotic, fused with certainty, "Don't you see it? Can't you imagine a woman painting these? Don't you see the embryonic release of blood flowing uncontrollably, the one who sees the void, the unconscious?"

Marjorie gazed intently, her neck straining up to see and take it all in.

"Yes." The singular syllable was saturated with transformative nuance and color.

"Janet is the woman who dripped paint before Jackson," the heiress said, "And he'd admit it too if he wasn't dead from that horrid crash. Janet's paintings flow from her unconscious feminine space. Jackson saw that and used his male authority to usurp her vision, but she was the first Outsider primitivist."

Marjorie tore here eyes away from the paintings to stare intently at the woman.

"*Who are you?*"

The woman smiled and said, "I'm Lula Brightenson. I am also your guide. Come."

Lula toured them through the packed gallery. Art patrons in black and berets, in kaftans and silk sheaths and business suits nodded and whispered as Lula parted bodies and moved front and center to each work and showed Marjorie how to look at the paintings, how to really see them. Aficionados leaned in, pricked ears, as she spoke of how the artist named Janet would tack her unstretched canvases on the floor and dive fearlessly in, letting both the paint and the motion of her own body take over and her instincts be both controllable and uncontrollable as the colors of the paint flew into creation and the paintings took on lives all their own.

And then like a witch imparting some devilish incantation, Lula stood before a painting with faces in lines of black and indigo and purple oozing through space and said:

"*Know who you are.*"

"I'm sorry, what did you say?"

Chapter 8

The heiress Lula Brightenson insisted on taking them to the Cedar Tavern. The rain had abated into a gentle mist which made it almost impossible to light the rolled cigarette she produced from one of many mysterious pockets in her multi-layered black outfit, but she flicked her silver lighter many times and light it she did, inhaling deeply before quickly passing it to Marjorie.

Instructed to hold in the smoke, Marjorie did as she was told. Lula and Aaron watched her, bemused, like parents observing a child walking for the first time. Of course she coughed and coughed. She had never even smoked a cigarette before, but this wasn't a cigarette, it was a "joint," Aaron explained, and she retorted "I know, I wasn't born tomorrow, I mean yesterday," and then they all laughed, laughed a lot, it was hysterically funny, her mistake, *born tomorrow*.

"Welcome to Cannabis," Lula said, as if she were talking about the Land of Oz, which in a way she was. The Village had sprung into living color, and the street signs and walkways and even the mist vibrated with vitality.

Outside the entrance to the Cedar tavern, two grown men were gleefully stomping through puddles in the pouring rain.

"Hey man, don't mind us," one remarked.

"And they're not even drunk," Aaron said as they swung through the door.

"It's a brave new world," said Lula.

And how! The bar was black velvet dark and glittered with gleaming mirrors and glasses of booze. There was no seeing through the smoke and bodies at first, but soon they settled at the end of a long wood bar, she and Lula, their heads bowed into one another, nearly tipping off the end of their tilting bar stools. Aaron leaned across them to order their drinks and Lula oh so gently, with her beautifully stark face close to hers, took up the dangling pendant and lowered her black sunglasses to study the crystal. Marjorie saw the woman's eyes for the first time. They flashed turquoise, turquoise and red, shuttered into slits, stoned eyes, eyes like the earth and all its blue seas, eyes that sparked like star storms in space.

"Remember: Know who you are," Lula said. It wasn't a coincidence. She'd said it before.

"What? *Who are you?*"

Lula flipped her silver hair and laughed, an unleashed gleeful sound.

"Consider me your spirit guide, though I'd say you're well on your way."

"Way to what?" Marjorie Berthe wanted to know.

"Only you know where the path of your life goes and what you have to say about it."

Aaron returned with their drinks, his large hands holding all three glasses. Scotch for him, brandy for Lula, and something he'd brought for her, something sweet and tasty he called a Sidecar that she gulped like liquid candy until he said, "Whoa, slow down girl." She liked his big hands and she liked the blue veins at his wrist. She thought of how they would make a painting. She also liked the flesh of his fingertips and thought of another painting that would explore the feelings inside her body bursting to get out. Ideas were suddenly crystallizing in her mind yet coming from a place bigger than her mind. The universe was unfurling, pulsating before her, and all she could do for the time being was watch. She figured she was stoned.

The Cedar Tavern was a rowdy riotous place, an insane place. Lula drifted off to other friends and acolytes. A man with a balding pate at the other end of the bar unzipped his fly and was about to do more before someone persuaded him not to. Jazz musicians were blasting sweet cool notes on trumpet, alto sax, bass and drums, and it was all lifting her up into the air, the golden light refracting off the bar and the tinkling of ice in Aaron's glass. He drank in a calm quiet way, not like how others drank; to them alcohol was a toy, a raucous diversion, but Aaron took his time.

She swung the crystal pendant in little circles from its chain around her neck. He took her hand and interlaced her fingers between his. People were shouting for drinks and the artist named Kline was sitting cross-legged on the bar, holding court, it appeared, before a clutch of people. It was chaos inside the Cedar Tavern, but she was high and clear. She stood up off the bar stool and pulled Aaron toward the back door.

Wild cats scattered in the alleyway and the sweet smell of fruity garbage rose up. She shoved him against a wall and kissed him, and what she liked was that he didn't touch her, didn't kiss her back. *He's too surprised,* she thought, but finally he responded, his large hands covering her ears, filtering the rising call of the sax that even she recognized as "You Go To My Head." He pulled her into an alcove behind the alleyway and onto a stone bench in a back garden with orange Chinese lanterns. *I'm going to fuck you, Sweetheart* he said and unzipped her Levis.

She vomited afterwards because she was dizzy and drunk, but not because she didn't like it.

This was it. This was the beginning. She wasn't going to paint pretty gardens anymore.

Chapter 9

*H*er first abstract painting was titled "Body In Red" because that was what she was: Red. Raging red, blood red, red-blooded female.

Her methods became legendary, but with "Body In Red," it began like this:

> First, she hung the giant unstretched canvas on the wall of her studio.

> Next, she stood naked on the other side of the room.

> Then, she brushed one side of her naked body in cadmium red. Half her hair, one shoulder, one breast, down her armpit, across her arm and hand, along her side, across her pubic hairs, along her hip, thigh, leg, and ending with the underside of her right foot.

> Finally, before the paint dried she ran toward the wall and hurled herself against the canvas, reaching, grasping, clutching, flying, falling.

There was more to it. There was the moment before she ran when she took stock of her mind-body-spirit and what it was telling her. There was the instant of painful impact then standing back to view the outcome and what she saw, which in the case of "Body In Red" was a whisk of bloodied flying hair over the stain of a woman: Her breast, arm, pubis and mad arching foot and hand clawing toward the top of the canvas. And then there was the refining of the red stain; the careful outlining of the shapes in black, the painting of dense fleshy background that breathed like skin.

Her professors didn't know what to make of her, but when they discovered who she was they altered their tune. The daughter of Max Hansman can paint! The daughter of Max Hansman emerges from the obscurity of Rockaway into the pulsating beat of the Village!

She became Marjorie Hansman, but not without a fight from her adoptive parents certainly, and also from the experts who questioned the validity of her paternal parentage, especially since her mother had once again disappeared off the face of the earth, or at least wandered into East Germany. There was no denying however that her facial features were those of the German Expressionist killed in the holocaust and that the art she produced was good enough to evoke speculation she'd conjured his spirit.

When she announced she was moving to the East Village with Aaron Johnson, Uncle Stephen protested loudly. But he knew she would leave as soon as the heirloom came into her possession and now he had no choice but to let her go. Their argument over her decision left Marjorie bruised and wriggling on the hook of an uneasy triumph.

"I'm half-Jewish, not wasp like you," she'd said, to which he'd replied, "For your information young lady I'm half Spanish Catholic, which makes you one-quarter Spanish, half Jewish and one-quarter white Anglo Saxon. Whether you care or not, you have my Spanish blood, little Marjie, and I will always love you."

She cried but she left home nonetheless. She had once been his little girl: Riding on his shoulders through the waves at Breezy Point Beach, following his trail through a snowy wood, holding his hand at her first birthday party.

They'd dressed her in pink, but red was her color.

He hadn't wanted to think of it, he couldn't bring himself to question or hear. It was too strange, too otherworldly, this jewel of hers, and Uncle Stephen was not the sort of man who believed in the otherworldly.

And yet there were stories, family stories, Uncle Stephen said, that warned the heirloom was dangerous: Of his mother falling from a cliff and nearly dying but for the ministrations of a mysterious Medicine Woman; of her great great Maori aunt, last seen riding the back of a whale; of a warrior queen waging war against her husband's tribe. And finally of his sister Maddy, lost in her travels and returning home only to abandon her own daughter for other worldly passions.

"I just want you to stay home and be safe," he said in one last feeble attempt to keep her.

"Women who stay home safe don't change the world," she replied, and in that moment Stephen heard the voice of his sister. She would take up the banner of rage on behalf of her murdered Jewish father and never let them forget.

Chapter 10

She was his satin doll, his prize, his tempestuous and beautiful problem. And when they made love to the street music drifting through the open window in the summer cool cool cool of the evening he was a rocket ship blasting into space, a shower of sparks penetrating her perfectly round, promising moon.

He'd found them an East Village loft and turned half of it over to her studio space. He brought home the paychecks from Drexel while she was being creative. For the first time in years he had a goal, which was to support his artistic queen. His brother Roger laughed at the notion of him shedding his grey flannel suit. The salesmen at Drexel talked about how he'd stolen Stephen's daughter but no one picked a fight, least of all Stephen, because Aaron wasn't the sort of man one picked fights with. Just looking at him you knew he could go the distance because he had nothing to lose, nothing to lose, that is, until Marjorie, and he wasn't about to lose her.

"You're too old for her," her uncle said to him in the Drexel showroom as other employees watched from a safe distance.

"Maybe, but she's an old soul," Aaron replied.

"You'll regret you helped her recover that heirloom. It caused my mother and sister to become – restless."

Restless was a word nice men like Stephen used when they meant *shrewish* or *hysterical*. Aaron thought of how all the women ended up with the spark in that family, which was why his future uncle-in-law had married a woman like Annie, nice like him and not at all *restless*.

"Maybe so, but she's inherited a heap of talent and a big legacy," Aaron said, avoiding mention of the biological father by name. He didn't want to offend this man who was not much older than he.

"Well, she's yours now," said Stephen Rosario with a bitterness that dripped from each word as he turned to the display case window.

"I don't think she's anyone's," Aaron said, and bent to adjust the carpet edge under the display couch, a gesture that said *we're coworkers, let's get along.*

And they did. Over time they shared a common concern over Marjorie's anguish and fury, just as they shared a vague paternity with the missing father. Plus Aaron came to understand what Stephen meant about the heirloom. She wore it all the time. It shined against her breasts when she paced the studio before one of her works, although she always took it off before she flung herself onto the canvases, not wanting to damage the crystal but doing a fine job of jarring her own bones.

When she painted this way it seemed to him that she was in the company of her father. She'd grown up in the suburbs but she didn't come from innocence but rather from war, genocide and displacement, and when she painted he could see this was what it meant for her to know herself. But he also wondered how far it would take her. Over a cliff? To the other side of Germany's Iron Curtain?

"My job is to keep her happy," was all he'd said to Stephen.

"Good luck with that," her uncle replied.

The Village muse held a show of Marjorie's Red paintings and they were snatched up by the cognoscenti. There were critics who said to create art after Auschwitz was "barbaric," but then her art was barbaric, that was her point; prettiness no longer mattered.

"I don't do pretty," she said, looking not at all pretty, dripping in cadmium red dark. She was beautiful instead. Labeled a "nihilistic humanitarian," she kept painting, and her paintings were bought and sold, and the prices kept going up and he figured that too was because she was *restless*.

He quit his job at Drexel with her full approval, and when people asked what he did for employment he laughed and said, "My job is keeping her happy."

No small feat!

She switched to blue and its many shades – cerulean, ultramarine, cobalt, Prussian – and instead of the bruising leaps she swam naked across canvas laid on the floor, as though she were drowning in slow motion. This method became a sensation as well, and there was speculation as to its roots. She didn't say. She rarely explained her work to the clients who bought her paintings, which was part of her mystery, another thing the art world talked about. *How could one so young...?*

She's an old soul, he would say, never revealing the impact of the heirloom, for what could he say? She was bewitched? The so-called witch hunters would really be on their trail if that was the case, but it seemed the only hunter who worried her was her mother.

Maddy Rosario's slim blue airmail letters with their spidery scrawl came with postmarks and exotic stamps from cities all over the world: Berlin. Copenhagen. Moscow. Istanbul. Beijing. New Delhi. And then back to Berlin. She wrote her daughter long ramblings on her travels and thoughts, insights into other cultures, notably on the oppression of women. *Women can change the world*, she wrote, *if only they can see who they are, fight for who they are.* And always the letters came with the question: *Did you find the amulet? Is it in your possession?*

Marjorie did not write back, not even to the home address in Berlin. "How can I?" she said, "She's everywhere!"

But of course there was more to it than that. She didn't want her mother to know.

"It's mine," she told him, "The woman wants it back. She had her chance and lost it, so it's mine now."

Marjorie Berthe was afraid that she couldn't paint without it.

If her mother came to claim it, the woman would steal *who she is.*

Perhaps it was the blue letters, but her Blue period didn't last. She complained the colors of the city were wrong, that it was the fault of Manhattan, the superficial influence of the city was wrong. She had to escape the city, both its good and bad. What she was really saying was that she was a sitting duck; Maddy Rosario would someday come for the pendant.

Maybe the West will make her happy, he thought.

"You could paint some place new," he said, "California, even."

"California!"

It was as if he'd said, "Jupiter."

Jupiter would do.

They would undergo a metamorphosis, the kind that would release them from conventional trappings. And they would make themselves near impossible to find, for no one was going to stop her from painting, not even "Aunt Maddy."

After they'd spent the night packing to Charlie Parker on the Hi-Fi, after they'd smoked a joint lit with a matchbook from the "Five Spot," a reminder of what they'd be giving up, they heard the slap of the newspaper and clatter of a milk truck signaling the start of the day. The air held a hint of a nip of cold when he stepped out for the paper, but they would be leaving winter behind for the Golden State, that state of mind, where their lives could be as infinite as their dreams.

She kissed him hard and long on their Village street, her tongue a hot serpent, her paints and canvases already in his Pontiac Bonneville convertible, and then she said, like a parody of a book he'd been reading, like a heroine in her own inflamed story:

"Let's blow this crazy scene."

Chapter 11

They drove west through Midwestern farm towns, past silos and windmills and cornfields baked by the sun. The car radio played "Ragg Mopp" and "A Bushel and a Peck." They roared on through the hot, bright Southwest on Route 66, past the steep crumbling cliff where her grandmother had been saved by a medicine woman, the pueblo replaced by a gas station with a giant plaster dinosaur.

They reached California at last: Its surfers and strange little buildings shaped like donuts and derbies, fresh fruits and vegetables amazingly ripe in mid-autumn, the Venice boardwalk with its Muscle Beach and shops filled with Far East paraphernalia and different beatniks with longer hair who talked about ending war as through it were a novel concept conceived by them alone.

They drove south and settled finally in a remote community in the Sonoran Desert, where she could paint and he would run the household, making trips to the nearby town of Julian for supplies. They tuned in, took daily hits of crumbly blond hash from a cloisonné wine-filled bong; they drank gallons of cheap white California wine.

The pendant was her beacon and guide, its faces like figurines on the prow of the ship at her breast. She called her new abstract canvases self-portraits of what she sensed in her body. She added new shapes, dripped new colors, and always she thought of who she was, which was the daughter of an artist destroyed by Fascism, now newly reborn in her own right, she who would not be silenced.

She received through the galleries fan letters from woman all over the world who felt struck by a deep unconscious chord in their psyches, women who said *your paintings changed my life*. And in the flood of these letters came other voices, new voices they were calling The Women's Movement. Women were breaking out of domesticity and coming to understand both their sexuality and power, which had never before been considered to be coexistent.

When she began painting the flesh tones of embryos suspended in red, he knew.

Mary Jane Johnson was born.

Marjorie Berthe Hansman and Aaron Johnson got married at a tiny courthouse near the sea during an idyllic time, for she was still selling her work and he wasn't drinking to excess. They bought a nearly all-glass house in the desert in a style that would later be called mid-century modern. They made new friends who were hippies, bikers and desert rats, and between hits on the bong on those desultory desert evenings they took to calling their daughter MJ.

And so the name stuck.

Chapter 12

*M*addy Rosario didn't stop in the small town of Julian, but continued on, taking the curving mountain highway, slowly dropping down to the Borrego Badlands of sand and rock and rolling light and shadow. She hadn't seen a soul in what seemed like hours, not a car or roadside store or gas station. The road stretched before her to unknown territory, but extreme travel to remote parts of the world was familiar to her. She considered Marjorie Berthe's decision to live far from the beaten path a smart one if not for her also suspecting that her daughter was hiding. From her.

Wind whipped the air when she stopped to read from the map. The heat of the day was gone, and with it came the increasing chill of early evening and an urgency to arrive at her destination before dark.

She pushed onward down the sandy road, the engine of the rental Ford Fairlane station wagon straining, wheels churning underneath, and with each forward motion, each fishtailing slide and lurch, her trepidation increased. It would be their first visit since she was "Aunt Maddy," and given what she had come to do, there was bound to be trouble.

Marjorie Berthe had not sounded happy to hear from her.

Looming ahead was a road sign in dark yellow, diamond-shaped, fixed atop a post in the dry river wash of a road that read:

END

And just beyond the sign, up against a massive shelf of a mountain shaped like an Indian head, was her daughter's silent, coldly modern, and nearly all glass house. *People in glass houses* — but she couldn't continue the thought, couldn't remember it. She was exhausted and shaking after the drive. Her feet crunched across rocky sand in the still desert air. Maddy felt her breath tightening in her chest and her body temperature rising. Another hot flash.

She approached the heavy door and rang the bell. So civilized, this house, here in the middle of nowhere, and impressive, she couldn't help but be impressed, although vaguely disapproving. She had seen a great deal of poverty in the world: Women who carried precious water on their heads, girls who had no schoolbooks, mothers struggling to feed their starving infants. And then there were people like her daughter, so young and not yet a quarter century old, who earned her wealth with the aid of good fortune, talent, and drive. And something else.

The door opened finally and there she was, holding the chubby baby who must be Mary Jane. For a second the adult Marjorie Berthe took her breath away. She had that dark wild-eyed look of Max, the same wiry hair and moody expression, and yet the infant in her arms with that soft blond peach fuzz of hair framed a face that more likely resembled the father, Aaron, whom she had yet to meet. Mary Jane picked up on her mother's mercurial nature and stared at her with wide brown suspicious eyes.

"Hello, Aunt Maddy," said her daughter.

So that was how it was going to be.

Chapter 13

When the woman who was her mother looked at the pendant first, then into her eyes, Marjorie Berthe instantly knew, if she hadn't suspected before, why she had come so far to see her.

"You found it," her mother said, gesturing to the gemstone hanging between her milk-filled breasts. As if aware of the adults' interest, little MJ reached up to pull at the bright plaything.

"You said it was in the steamer trunk, and it was. Come in."

Marjorie tried to imagine this fashionable European woman, so petite and perfectly coifed, as her mother, but it was as impossible as allowing a stranger access to her bank account. Odd, having that thought, but there was something predatory about the woman as she entered the house and immediately began looking around.

"That was quite a drive. You really are out in the middle of nowhere." Marjorie heard the subtext: *As if you were hiding.*

"We like it this way. I'll show you my studio later if you care to see it." *If you care at all about me.*

"I'd love to see your studio, I've heard so much about your work, your success. I've seen it in magazines in Berlin but never in person. And now marriage and a child! My! And where is your husband?"

"Aaron is getting supplies in Julian, but you'll see him tomorrow."

The older woman leaned in toward the baby and touched her soft little arm. "And how are you, MJ?" By way of greeting MJ thumped her fists in the air and blew spit through her lips.

"I think she just pooped," Marjorie said, and lifted MJ to sniff. MJ kicked the air happily, and let out a triumphant fart. They both laughed, and to her credit, there was no discomfort her mother's laughter. They hadn't hugged however, with the child performing the deliberate role on Marjorie's part of barrier between them.

"I knew you'd found it," her mother said, "As soon as I heard you were making a name for as an artist. Good for you, Marjorie Berthe, I'm so proud of you, and your house is beautiful. You've done well."

Marjorie made no reply to this. As far as she saw it, "Aunt Maddy" was attempting to lay claim to a mother's pride, but this woman with the smart white blouse and elegant khaki pants had never been her mother, and so she had no right to that pride.

"Coffee's percolating," she said, "Would you like some?"

"A café would be lovely, thank-you."

A café. The foreigner who was her mother followed her through the sparsely furnished living room, past the heavy oak dining table and into the kitchen. Her leather heels clicked on the hard wood floors. MJ tilted her head to follow and comprehend this new sound. In stark contrast to her sophisticated guest, Marjorie wore pedal pushers and blue Keds; she felt like an elfin teenager.

"I'll get you settled in our guest room," she said, "but first things first, isn't that right, MJ?"

She plopped her infant daughter onto the kitchen counter and as she began removing the used diaper MJ emitted a loud happy screech.

"I swear she's a caca machine," she continued, wiping the baby's bottom with a Kleenex and rolling it with the soiled diaper into a plastic diaper bag. "She gets the runs, and this yellow goo seeps out. How do you like your coffee?"

"Black, thank-you." Maddy said, and seated herself on a tall stool at the Formica bar separating dining area from kitchen. Marjorie was disappointed when her mother didn't appear the least bit ruffled by the poopy diaper change. She'd hoped she would display signs of disgust or squeamishness, which would then confirm what a cold, unfeeling mother she'd been, but Maddy sat and smiled, glowed even, as she watched her robust granddaughter.

"How old is she exactly?"

"Eleven months."

She speared a safety pin into the corner of MJ's fresh diaper. MJ kicked and giggled.

"Ow! Hold still!"

When Marjorie was done changing the diaper she lifted MJ off the counter. MJ squealed. She kissed her stomach. MJ squealed again. *This is how a real mother acts.*

"Can I hold her?" Maddy asked.

"You want to hold her? Really?"

"She's my granddaughter!"

She passed the infant, hoping MJ would scream in protest. With surprising dexterity the woman took little MJ in her arms.

"She's a big girl," Maddy said. With the baby in her lap, she seated herself at the dining table and turned MJ around to face her. Her granddaughter stared up at her with curious round eyes. "She's adorable. And talkative, like you were. Girls are early communicators. They build relationships from the start, unlike boys, who tend to play at war then grow up to make real wars."

There was sadness in her tone, not what Marjorie had expected to hear. She poured the coffee into a white ceramic mug with indelible paint smears along the handle and tried not to stare at her, this Maddy Rosario, in the flesh, fashionably clothed yet visibly hurting with something she could only discern as a sort of world-weariness. She'd spoken of war, war hung in the air between them, but Marjorie reminded herself that it was more than the worldly kind that preoccupied them both, but rather the domestic. *The personal is political,* Marjorie thought, *but don't forget, this is personal.* She wasn't about to let her mother take her off-game, no matter how big a worldly burden she bore.

Marjorie sat the mug of coffee onto the table well clear of MJ's flailing arms and watched as her mother bounced the delighted infant on her lap. The woman looked as though she might weep. *You should weep* thought Marjorie. Did her mother even once look at her this way when *she* was a baby, before she gave her away? Did she love her the way she herself loved MJ, or had she been too inconvenient, discardable? Maddy took hold of her granddaughter's tiny hands. The little fingers gripped hers.

"They're so cute when they're babies," she said.

"Until they get to be around five," Marjorie said, "and they apparently become unlovable."

"If you're referring to yourself, you were never unlovable. You were heartbreaking. I wanted to bring you with me, but East Germany was a terrible place at the end of the war."

"And then what? And then you just got busy? Enjoyed your independence a little too much?"

"When I came back, I saw how happy you were with your new family."

"Sure. I was a cheerful little girl."

"You were!"

"And then you sent me the letter. Wow! What a kick in the head that was!"

"I had to tell you, but I felt it best that I wait until you were old enough. I'm sorry it happened that way. I couldn't think of any other way. War changes how people live, the choices they make. War does that. War and – "

"Genocide?"

"Yes," she said, and ducked her head down to gaze into little MJ's face, as if by absorbing the simple innocence and beauty of the child she could repel the crimes of the past. *Maybe she once looked at me like that,* Marjorie thought, but disregarded the notion. Marjorie Berthe wasn't one to dilute strong emotions with complicated thought; she stuck to the emotion, emotion propelled her forward, enabled her to create. Creation, her art, her child, yes, that too – and protecting her home, this was what mattered, not trying to understand this woman who'd stopped being her mother.

"Aunt Maddy – "

"Please just call me Maddy."

At least she didn't ask to be called Mother.

"Alright. Maddy. Why are you here? It's been years since we last met at Uncle Stephen's. When I was fourteen, I think. You went your separate way years ago."

Her mother – Maddy – looked at her with those painfully large dark eyes. They were the eyes of those big-eyed girls in those sentimental paintings and Marjorie was in no mood for sentimentality, it didn't fit into the picture of her personal narrative. Seeming to sense her daughter's discomfort, the woman pulled her gaze back to the infant in her arms, enabling Marjorie to study her profile without eyes boring into her, and she saw how she must have been a striking woman in her day, still was really. Her jawline had softened but she had taken care of her skin in the way of some European women. She wondered how Maddy made a living these days, wondered if she was even a spy or some sort of subversive revolutionary or if she still supported herself through writing. There had been the erotica novels that weren't sold in the U.S., but perhaps sold well enough in Europe. Her mother in any case looked like a survivor: weary yet poised, vulnerable yet steely.

"I've brought you something," Maddy said, and with one hand over MJ's fuzzy golden head, gestured with the other to the large open leather bag she'd set upon the floor. A smart-looking jacket spilled out from the top alongside the edge of a battered old notebook with rusted spiral. The notebook was the only thing about her person that didn't look groomed, tidy and new.

"I finally located an old friend of your father's," she said, "He gave me this."

She pulled the notebook out and extended it to her. Taking it, Marjorie understood it was heavier than it looked, heavy because she knew with a sudden jolt what it was. She opened it carefully, and when she did she smelled the pines of a forest where the pages had once been filled. On the first page there was a sketch in charcoal of a man's face, or the representation of a face, gnarled within the trunk of a representational tree near a representational gun resting against the tree, and all of it – gun, tree and trunk, were molded into the face of the man. The man in the sketch was her father, Max Hansman. It was his Expressionist self-portrait, done in the final weeks of his life.

"He was with a partisan force before the Gestapo captured him," Maddy said, "but he kept this notebook and sketched when he wasn't fighting. He met you when you were a baby. When I smuggled in ammunition. Here, turn to the middle pages."

"You smuggled ammunition to the partisans?" Her mother nodded, her interest focused on turning pages to the middle of the book with MJ's little hands reaching out from her lap to grasp them too. She turned the sheets past Max Hansman's final days, his visions of nature and war, beauty and brutality. And then there it was, the sketch of a tiny infant surrounded by intricate flora and fauna and, like a love poem, a few small words.

For Marjorie Berthe, wherever I may find her.

It hit her like a freight train with a million doomed passengers and she emitted a dry wrenching cry. Marjorie rarely cried, that was just how she was, but she cried now, and her mother reached out and placed her hand gently on her shoulder, and the together they bent their heads in a way that said they were of the same blood, though the other half of Marjorie Berthe's blood had been murdered.

MJ squirmed in Maddy's lap. Finally Marjorie pulled back and said, "I can't accept this."

"But it's for you," her mother said, "He wanted you to have this, he made it for you. Marjorie Berthe, it says here, for Marjorie Berthe. Berthe was his mother's name."

"I can't accept it."

"Why, Marjorie? I don't understand."

"Because you want something in return."

Maddy Rosario's silence confirmed it, but more than silence her eyes inadvertently looked down to the pendant on her chest. She couldn't hide the longing in her face, like a burglar coveting glittering jewels on the neck of a lady.

"No," Marjorie said, and stood, scraping the chair on the floor.

"My dear, it will go to MJ when she is ready, just as it was passed to us when we were ready, but other women need it too, don't you think? I will never let it out of my sight, I promise, but I'm convinced its power will be useful to others. Too many women give up their power by thinking they don't have any, but this pendant, it causes us to see the power we've always had."

"I need it now," Marjorie Berthe said, her voice rising, "You have no idea. You don't know how it is to be a female artist and have your work ignored or demeaned as second rate simply because you're a woman."

MJ fussed, her baby voice whining and soft. Her mother and grandmother were facing off, their bodies tensing.

"But you're an accomplished artist now and will continue to be! You have the power and it can't be taken. Trust me."

"Why should I trust you? You took me away from my father — "

"The Nazis took your father! He wanted you to be safe, we couldn't let them know you were – "

"Half-Jew?"

"You were safe as long as no one knew. He told me to bring you to America because this was where you could be safe. Not with me, I couldn't keep you safe."

"Why not, Mother?"

Maddy hesitated, and then spoke so softly her daughter could barely hear her reply, "I'm not like you, Marjorie Berthe."

There was a world in that answer, one of growing up between two world wars and losing a boy to one war and gaining a man only to lose him to another war, but this was not the kind of answer Marjorie Berthe Hansman would hear. There was no comprehending what had happened in her mother's four decades of life. Suddenly little MJ began to wail, loud and fierce, and the only sound in the house was the infant girl's furious cries.

"Give her to me," Marjorie Berthe ordered, but Maddy held the child in her grip and tried to comfort her like the grandmother she wanted to be. "I'm sorry, Little MJ," she cooed. The baby girl squirmed in her arms, crying louder, and so she rose her voice above the scream-ing to say, "Look, look, I have something for you too!"

Holding the child closer, she extracted from her bag a children's book she'd bought in Paris. It was titled *Goodnight Moon*, and was beau-tifully illustrated in bright colors. MJ turned her head away and wailed. Undeterred, Maddy opened the small book to the title page and showed it to her squalling granddaughter.

"You see here? It's for you. I wrote your name in the book."

To Mary Jane
From your Grandmother Maddy
August 4, 1959

But MJ was on a crying jag now. She screamed louder and pushed the book away.

"She doesn't want your book," Marjorie said, taking her crying daughter in her arms. "Don't think you can exchange the pendant for a children's book. The heirloom will go to her, *from me,* her mother."

"Of course it will go to her. I'm sorry I've upset you Marjorie, and MJ too. Truly I am."

Maddy put the children's book back in her bag but she left the Max Hansman sketchbook on the table. Marjorie didn't refuse her father's work again even if it threatened to come with an unacceptable price.

Later, when Marjorie was putting MJ down into her crib, she heard her mother creeping up. The baby's room was peaceful and quiet. There was a red toy telephone near the bassinet, and a Buckaroos hobbyhorse riding stick leaned against the tiny table with a tea set. There were musical tinkle bells extended over the white wood crib with its Disney cartoon decals of Donald Duck and Minnie Mouse, and a Bakelite rattle nestled into the pretty patchwork quilt. Marjorie had filled every corner with any toy a child born in the booming years could want yet Maddy's presence seemed to judge it somehow. It was too American, too full of privilege.

MJ drifted off to sleep under the crib exerciser with the baby blue rings and a cat face smiling down.

"Marjorie Berthe, you're right," said her mother. She spoke quietly so as not to awaken MJ, who had turned her soft baby face into a field of pink and blue flannel stars. "The heirloom is yours. Yours to have and pass on to MJ."

"Thank-you," Marjorie said. They stood side-by-side with their hands on the edge of the crib looking down at the sleeping infant.

"I was so terribly afraid for you during the war, Marjorie Berthe. I didn't know who to trust, and many knew that Max Hansman – a

Jew – had been my lover, so when the Nazis saw me with you, I was afraid for you. I have seen such sadness and horror, my dear, and I never wanted you to be a part of that. Please know I have loved you. From afar perhaps, but loved you, and I am sorry, so terribly sorry, that I was unable to be a proper mother to you."

What could she do but accept the apology from the mother who not only took her from her father at his behest, but brought her to America? Her mother may have lost the Heirloom, but she'd found it too and seen that it was passed it on to her despite the turmoil and chaos of a world gone mad with war. Marjorie Berthe had acquired the crystal at the very moment in her young life when she was ready to give herself over to the transformative force of who was, and with that power she conjured the quintessence that had been her father in every painting. To create art after a holocaust *was* abominable, but it was all they had.

And so in the spirit of revealing herself to the woman she had never truly known but to whom she so desperately wanted to say *see me, see who I am*, Marjorie Berthe brought her mother to the sanctum where she created her work.

Her daughter's studio was a large space in the rear of the sprawling one-story house. On one side there loomed tall glass windows such as one would see in a church, and on the other a long smooth wall set into the side of the mountain. As it was night and no natural light permeated the studio, Marjorie turned on switches and bright focused light bulbs illuminated the massive painted canvases.

"Did he last long after the Gestapo took him?" Marjorie wanted to know.

"Not long, but then how is one to say."

"So he was tortured."

"He was strong. Like you."

As she positioned a light here, another one there, to focus on one painting or other, she said to her mother that her art was a repeated representation of her father's life. And his death.

"And your life too?"

"His is my story."

"I understand," said Maddy Rosaio, "believe me, I do."

And she did, only too well, for in that moment she was standing not in her daughter's studio but rather at the Paris International Exhibition, where she had first seen Max's paintings and the work of his friend, Picasso's *Guernica* and its powerful protest against the wrongness of war and the bombings of that Spanish town and its innocents. Then she was transported to Spain and its civil war, with Max by her side, and once more, as if she could never forget it, she saw the children they evacuated, and along with it the suffering and misery and chaos and fear.

Marjorie Berthe's work was viscerally like her father's, a testament she had subconsciously passed on to the world when he was no longer alive and able to do so, and whether her daughter conceded or not, Maddy Rosario knew what she must do and would do.

They ate dinner together on the patio where the temperature had cooled to the low eighties. Reserved and cordial, they sipped white wine and pointed out the stars. She listened to her mother's stories of how her father had single-handedly carried four children in his arms through knee-deep tides to the evacuation boats, of how he continued to draw even when his hands shook from hunger.

Her mother spoke of the world's disempowered women: the ones who were stoned to death for unsanctioned love, the ones who bore children who grew up to join in the detritus war and its reminders of loss. She spoke of how in her search for Max's past she found the remnants of others lost to war, even a perfectly preserved pair of socks in the rich soil of a battlefield turned back to farm.

246

Someday there will be a new kind of war, her mother said, not the phony claim to end all war, but one that would begin with women knowing the power they had. They would return the world to a matriarchal society, she said, and it would start with empowering women and their vision.

She told her how much she was her father's daughter.

At the guest room door before retiring for the night, they gave each other a tentative feminine kiss on both cheeks.

"Sleep well," Marjorie said, "You'll probably hear coyotes."

"Oh, I hope so," her mother said, and then they parted.

Sometime in the early morning hours, when the sky was barely turning to blue dawn, Marjorie heard a car door slam and the sound of an engine, and then tires on gravel. In half-sleep she assumed it was Aaron home early from Julian with the supplies, but as she rose to consciousness she realized the sounds were reversed.

The car was driving away.

Suddenly she was fully awake, and as she rose she reached for what she always reached for first thing in the morning, hanging from the lampshade, but it wasn't there. Her amulet, beacon, creative light, key to her father and message from the otherworld. And then she realized that everything her mother had said that night, all she had spoken of concerning war and women and empowerment and art, all was intended to explain what she had already decided to do.

It was gone, stolen by her mother, burglar, jewel thief, soul thief, and that was when she screamed, screamed with such fury and rage, her glass house nearly shattered in pieces.

The Storm

Midnight

"**W**hat do you mean, you *don't have it?*"

Grandma Marjorie Berthe's hot breath bursts from the back seat, her face thrust toward Maya. She may be in her seventies but with that booming alto one wouldn't know it. She has nearly drowned in her basement while saving from flood and flames the only piece of artwork she can't live without, she has marshaled an entire house party of neighbors into escaping the encroaching fire, and she has walked through chest-high water to the main road, yet Maya's maternal grandmother still has all the drive of a Mack truck.

"I couldn't find it Grandma, I'm sorry."

They reach the harrowing stretch along Beach Channel Drive. Maya guns the accelerator, punishing the Rover, keeping to the right of the road away from the Bay side with its roiling waves, hugging the edge of dark Jacob Riis Park. And now they pass the exit to the bridge that would take them to Manhattan, which is where they should be instead of remaining on their drowning peninsula simply because it is home.

"I don't know why your mother didn't keep the heirloom to begin with because Mother hides everything, don't you, Mother? Money, jewelry, gumdrops, hairpins, no one can find anything!"

"Gumdrops, yes indeed," Great Grandma Maddy says, and pats the paint-spattered hand that grips the back of her seat.

"Try to remember, Mother, what you did with it," Marjorie Berthe says now, but Great Grandma Maddy sits silent in the passenger seat, seeming not to hear or understand.

"*You can't remember, can you?* You always had to have your way! You can't remember where you put it, but you remember how you *stole* it from me, don't you, Mother. You remember that!"

"Wait, hold it," Maya intervenes, "Don't talk to her like that or I'm dumping you out on the street right now! Look out the window, Grandma. Don't you see what's happening?" Maya pushes the Rover through a new stream of seawater gushing across the road. "Let's just concentrate on getting through this."

It is as real as a living nightmare: Two blocks down on the Atlantic side waves larger than houses crash down on rooftops. She sees the cresting foam in the dark, like some giant tsunami monster, and hopes the people have evacuated. She wishes *they* had evacuated.

Grandma Marjorie Berthe thrust herself back into her seat with a huff and fumes. Maya hears her shifting, fussing, and then her speaking into her cellphone. Her muttering soon turns into shouting.

"*Well then, MOVE the collection to the upper floor! I WON'T HAVE MY WORK DESTROYED IN SOHO TOO!*"

With her life's work facing total ruin at not only her studio on Breezy Point but at the flooded gallery in Soho where her retrospective is supposed to happen, Marjorie Berthe will retaliate for Mother Nature's vengeance by releasing her own brand of vengeance upon everyone in range, including her own mother, who must be on overload as events from the past keep repeating and distorting: A house alarm in Rockaway becomes the air raid sirens of the London Blitz, smoke from the burning houses on Breezy Point curl from the crematoriums of Auschwitz. And now Marjorie Berthe pragmatically, morbidly, has marked her tiny social security numbers on her arm with indelible ink as if she were purposely doing it to torment the mother who saved her from Nazi Germany's grinding death machine.

"*I have 'Body In Red' and that's ALL I HAVE!*" Grandma Marjorie Berthe shouts into her phone, "*Move the rest NOW or I will sue you all for the millions they're worth, I don't care if you're afraid of the flooding, DO IT!*"

"I'm sorry your retrospective is in trouble, Grandma," Maya says when Marjorie Berthe disconnects, "But please be civil to Great Grandma Maddy."

"It will all be ruined, ruined. All my work."

"You don't know that yet," Maya replies then turns and speaks soothingly to her great grandmother. "Your daughter's just upset. When we get you home we're going to make chocolate S'Mores. What do you say? *Grandma Maddy?*"

How long has it been since her great grandmother said anything?

"MOTHER?"

From the tiny wrinkled body in the passenger seat there comes a small mouse of a sound that is part squeak part clearing of an old used crackling throat.

"I like chocolate."

"HA! Let her eat chocolate!" Marjorie Berthe roars, "The world's coming to end but let her eat chocolate."

A giant blast of wind rocks the Rover and Maya is certain the wipers will be ripped clear off the windshield. She clutches the steering wheel and pushes the accelerator to the floor, hoping by sheer speed to part the waters under the tires. She may have gotten both her grandmothers into the Rover, yet one might end up killing the other if they aren't drowned in the storm first.

Skidding, screeching, she turns off Rockaway Beach Boulevard onto one of the Beach streets. They head inland now away from the Atlantic side of the peninsula where the sea roars toward them in one giant mass, and as they pass the street that would take them back to the nursing home Maya wonders if Joshua is still carrying more old people up to the higher floors or if he has driven some to the shelter in Brooklyn.

"Stop at Sea View," Marjorie Berthe says. "We need the heirloom."

"We aren't stopping there. It's too dangerous. We're going home. Besides, the heirloom is just a thing."

"You don't know how valuable *this* thing can be in a woman's fight for equality."

"Feminism, yeah, okay," Maya says. What she knows of feminism comes from listening to her mother and her mother's friends talk of how they are now *equal but sexless*, how with so many career *and* family responsibilities they have no time for romance. *If that's feminism*, thinks Maya, *count me out*.

Up ahead an ambulance tears down a side street, its flashing lights circling over the water, and she again thinks of Joshua and how kind he is. He carried Great Grandma Maddy to the Rover, and right now he is probably still taking care of the old people at Sea View. Why had the mayor instructed nursing staff not to evacuate the elderly before the storm? Was it because the mayor thought old people didn't matter? *Old people matter*, she wants to scream at the mayor, *my grandmothers matter*. If *she* were mayor she wouldn't build giant skyscrapers with international money and throw lavish parties with Republican cronies. She would protect the old people, disadvantaged people, *your tired, your poor*. Maya has learned firsthand about that from her parents' Gandela Center where immigrant families from all over the world – *your huddled masses yearning to breathe free* – seek aid, sustenance, advice.

"*Someday*," her mother MJ has said, quoting Gloria Steinem, "*An army of grey-haired women will quietly take over the world.*" But what Maya wants to do right now is berate the mayor for failing to order the evacuation of nursing homes.

"Without the heirloom I'm concerned for you Maya. You – "
Marjorie Berthe pauses, and Maya waits for her pronouncement, "You
could become ordinary."

"I may be ordinary," Maya says, "But someday I'm going to be mayor."

She turns left into their dark flooded neighborhood and suddenly
the Rover dies, right in the middle of their street, as if her Dad's trusty
vehicle, shocked by her pronouncement, has decided to give up the
ghost. They have made it to the street where she lives. Without the
engine running on high and the wipers clicking as they sped against the
water engulfing and swooshing around them, it is suddenly, stunningly
silent.

"Mayor!" comes Great Grandma Maddy's delayed reaction, "Try
topping that, Marjorie Berthe!"

They are smack dab in the middle of a slow moving river. Up ahead
is a half submerged stop sign. Maya turns the ignition, hoping to restart
the vehicle or at least activate the electronic windows, but the Rover is
dead, dead in the water, a hundred feet from their house. Close but not
close enough.

"Don't open the doors," Maya says.

Great Grandma Maddy's door is child proofed locked, but Maya
worries Grandma Marjorie Berthe will open hers just to be contrary.
She doesn't. If she does, water will rush in at their feet and fill the
Rover. Since the engine can't restart the automatic windows can't be
rolled down. Not good if the windows become the only means of escape
through rising water.

"Okay, this is what we're going to do," Maya says to her grandmothers. "Grandma Marjorie, you're going to crawl out the back through the
open hatchback and then we're going to follow you."

"Yes," Marjorie Berthe amazingly agrees.

Is it her imagination, or is the Rover suddenly rocking in the slow
torrent of water?

"Push 'Red Body' out ahead of you, Grandma," Maya adds, since the painting needs to be moved out of their way if they expect to get Great Grandma Maddy out through the back.

"Body In Red,'" Marjorie Berthe corrects, but she does as directed, wedging the canvas out first then inching her way toward the back. A full-bodied woman, she grunts with the awkward effort of hunching over in a crawl. The Rover rocks again when she reaches the back and finally steps out into the river.

"It's strong, the current," Marjorie Berthe shouts back. Maya hears fear in her voice.

"We're coming out," Maya calls. She climbs from the driver's side over the console onto the back seats. Great Grandma Maddy faces forward, waiting. Maya taps her boney shoulder and grasps the old woman's upper arm.

"Come on, Grandma, we're going out this way."

"Oh?" It is part question, part exclamation.

"Easy peasy," Maya says. The Rover tilts to the right. "We got ourselves a boat, Grandma! Turn this way, this way."

She shifts her weight away from the sinking side, and gently pulls at Maddy's right sleeve until the old woman shifts in her seat to face her. She keeps pulling – *this way, come on, Grandma, follow me.* She hears Marjorie Berthe shouting from outside.

The Rover is moving in the current.

"Okay, now we're going to hurry," she adds. Praying she won't tear the old woman's ligaments like a roasted turkey wing, she clutches both of her great grandmother's arms and drags her toward the back of the Rover.

"*Oww,*" Great Grandma Maddy says, but her complaint is followed by a good natured chuckle, and she's moving on her own, crawling toward the open hatchback.

They will either get out of the Land Rover or drown inside it; it is that simple. She feels Marjorie Berthe's hand clutching her ankle.

"Get out! Get out!" her grandmother shouts. They scramble backward through water rising fast, and just as fast she feels the vehicle coming unmoored from the ground and lifting up. Can water be so forceful as to set an SUV afloat? Maya steps out onto the road that is a river now and struggles to stand upright as the cold water tugs at her thighs. Her great grandmother chirps *I'm coming* as if she's spent too long powering her nose. Marjorie Berthe stands waiting, a colossus in water, one hand gripping the edge of her "Body In Red," the other reaching for her mother crawling backward.

"She won't be able to stand in this," Maya says.

Marjorie Berthe's obstinate face makes a grimace of resignation. She then yanks the canvas of her famous painting, her seminal work, the one some art critics say rivaled the genius of Jackson Pollock, and lays it face-up flat on the water in front of her mother.

"She saved me at the beginning of my life," she says, "I can save her at the end of hers."

"Here we go," Maya says.

Together they reach for Great Grandma Maddy, Maya holding her under her shoulders, Marjorie Berthe grasping her calves, and lift her off the back of the hatchback and onto the floating "Body In Red."

"Whee!" The old woman says. Maya knows it is her way of being a sport, but her joints have to be aching and the water lapping around the canvas is certainly seeping into her frail old bones.

"Lie still, Mother," Marjorie Berthe barks, "Try not to tear my million dollar masterpiece, will you?"

They wade away from the vehicle, holding onto the canvas like a surfboard with Great Grandma Maddy floating on it between them.

Her silvery hair glints under the crackling power lines. The current is chest high, moving in the direction of Maya's house.

Their block is dark and silent. No electricity. Sirens cry steadily in the distance. Candlelight glimmers faintly inside houses, but it's as if the whole neighborhood has slipped into a dormant sleep; no blue tinted television light, no music drifting from windows. Water laps against porches and up steps and topples picket fences. Cars rest silent in the stream.

"Ho! That you, Maya?"

She hears a screen door slam. Their neighbor Herbie Weiss comes down his front porch and wades toward them, arms up, in a bright yellow rain slicker.

"Your mom's been calling from the Center, worried sick and now my cell's out of juice. Hello there, lookie here."

In his fifties, sinewy strong, Herbie is just the man for the job of carrying Great Grandma Maddy up the porch stairs.

"Here, I gotcha, let's get you inside," Herbie says, and in one sudden heave the good man lifts Great Grandma Maddy up in his arms off the canvas and they are sloshing up the steps. Grandma Marjorie Berthe pulls along her "Body In Red" and pauses on the porch to assess the bowed yet intact canvas.

Maya reaches into her deep rain slicked pocket for the house keys she slipped in there hours ago, unlocks the front door, and fumbles for the flashlight they keep near the entryway. Everyone marches into the damp cool house.

She is done, exhausted, finished. She can't even think of how long it had been, or what time it is. What she wants to do is collapse into her own warm bed and sleep, but first she will see to her grandmothers and finish what she has set out to do, which is to bring them home safe and put them into warm beds in the downstairs guest room.

It is only later, after she has called her mother from Marjorie Berthe's cellphone and settled both her grandmothers into the guestroom's twin beds, after she has thanked her neighbor Herbie Weiss and is nestled into her own bed listening to the wind and smattering of rain against the window glass, after she glances at the clock that says it is past midnight and wonders at all the siren sounds and people struggling through the storm in the night, that she remembers the portrait painting of her great great grandmother Madeline wrapped inside a saturated blanket in the back of the Rover, drowning in seawater.

Just stuff, she thinks, *not lives.*

And then Maya remembers what her pragmatic mother said when she told her their family heirloom was lost:

"Don't fret, Maya dear. Objects are never lost to themselves, only to the people who seek them."

1975
The "Women's Libber"

"A feminist is anyone who recognizes the equality and full humanity of women and men."

Gloria Steinem

Chapter 1

*K*hujaraho was not the ideal place to approach a girl he didn't know. The town was out in the middle of the arid, dusty flatlands of India's northern Madhya Pradesh. No mountains, no beaches. Cow dung littered the dirt streets. Vendors hawked batik bedspreads, saris, bells and bronze Shivas, hookah pipes and *paen*, a mixture of tobacco and opium, the scent of which brought to him a welling of self-disgust.

The stand where the bus was to stop was on the quieter eastern side of town where the women did their washing in the Khodar River and their children came by to stare. Marcus Jones waited under a six-inch spot of shade beside a vendor selling Campa Cola and postcards of the temples. The heat was nearly unbearable, and so was the smell of the opium from the *paen*. He thought about how he could use the money the woman had given him to buy some of the *paen*. Instead he bought a cola from the vendor who smiled and nodded nervously at him, the tall Black American with the red bandana encircling his Afro.

"Jimi Hendrix!" the vendor said, pointing to his long wild man hair.

"Right," Marcus said, "May the man rest in peace."

He drank the cola, which was lukewarm but wet at least.

Just hours ago, an older white woman in a colorful sari had stepped up to his table at a local café and inexplicably entrusted him to pass a blue letter on to her granddaughter who would be arriving that afternoon on the bus from Agra. She had paid him a handful of rupees for this amateur bit of messenger service, giving no indication as to why she couldn't – or wouldn't – meet the girl herself. Then after making her strange proposal, the woman had walked out to an awaiting Citroen and driven away to parts unknown.

You're an American she had said, *I have a good feeling about you.*

Marcus didn't agree. He had not been good, not to himself nor to his poor mother, who wanted him home in Jamaica (Queens, that is). His mother didn't understand why he said he couldn't go back, not yet, maybe never.

He could blame it on the sixties or the war, but the truth was that he'd joined the Air Force for opportunity and advancement. Fresh out of high school, he'd fallen for the recruitment ads, imagining himself a hero flying choppers and rescuing Marines for God and country, but what he'd done was kill people, plain and simple. There was no turning back the clock, no rewind of his personal documentary to the instant he pushed the button that dropped the bombs that made him a "baby killer." It was this stark unforgiveable truth that drove him after his discharge back to Southeast Asia in search of other gods that turned out to be nothing more than the opium dens of Thailand and Malaysia.

When he flew for the drug trade all he wanted was the sweet smoke in his lungs, the ritual of sticky opiate on his fingers, until one night a beautiful Malaysian woman led him back to her apartment, stripped off her clothes and lay fetchingly upon the bed. That was when he knew the opium had become his lover. She escorted him to the door with pity in her eyes. Stung with the memory of the hooker's unwanted body, he threw his packet of drugs, all two hundred American dollars worth, into the sea.

And now here he was, his journey of self-discovery leading nowhere but to dusty Khujaraho, taking petty cash from a well-heeled white lady and waiting for the bus from Agra and a girl he didn't know, free of opium but not demons and sweltering in his own version of well-deserved hell, which was India in April.

And how apropos, he thought, that the granddaughter, an undoubt-edly naive American teenager who went by the stoner name "MJ" of all things, was coming from a "goddess cult" in Bathinda.

Chapter 2

*P*icking the window seat was a mixed bag since she got some air circulation but with it dust from the road. Travel in India had a way of challenging every decision one made, especially when the person you've come to visit fails to be there, leaving behind a mysterious blue letter, just like the first blue letter, and now another one urging her to come to Khujaraho.

MJ Johnson suspected – no, she knew – she was being manipulated. Her mother wasn't on speaking terms with her grandmother, for starters, so she was stuck in the middle, a familiar place, as she had also grown up in the middle of her parents' failing marriage.

Her father had warned her about the "culture shock" she would have. She had it the moment she got off the plane and walked into New Dehli airport and saw children begging and teenage girls younger than she carrying babies with hungry eyes. *It is a different culture* said a Frenchwoman on the bus to the ashram. *Sure,* she thought, *if you consider starvation, ignorance and sexism culture.*

And a week at the goddess ashram seemed like a mind-blowing eternity. She'd joined in the archeological digs in search of goddess artifacts in the soils outside Bathinda. She'd listened to women of all nationalities speak of matriarchal societies. She'd met women who were goddesses in their own right, who raised children on nothing but love, who scrapped for water and sustenance out of the thin air of their

Untouchable status. Some knew her grandmother, and the few who spoke English assured her that Maddy Rosario was near, would see her soon, it was fated, etc. etc. Karma. Fate. Destiny. MJ tried to wrap her mind around these words.

MJ shifted in her seat and raised her nose to a whiff of warm air. Dust coated her sweaty skin. The bus rumbled and lurched at a promising forty mph. Rudyard slept on a small indentation at the top of her backpack squeezed into the space next to her feet, his tail curled over his nose. Carefully so as not to wake him, she reached into the side pocket and pulled out the first blue letter, the one that had slipped through the mail slot of their bungalow in Venice Beach.

She'd found it before her mother could snatch it up and say it wasn't for her. It had been the day before spring break of her senior year and MJ was already taking college classes in linguistic feminist theory. She'd been in limbo between Venice High and Berkeley and in a big hurry to leave home, but she'd known the letter was from Mad Grandma Maddy. Mother had thrown away the postcards and letters that had come from places all over the world: Germany, Russia, Afghanistan, Iran, and now from a place called Tamil Nadu in India.

This one had been addressed to her, and so she had a right to read it and did:

> *My dear Mary Jane,*
>
> *You don't know me but I am your Grandmother Maddy Rosario, your mother's mother. She would tell you I have not properly served the function of motherhood in her life, and she would be right, but it is my hope to rectify my transgression by inviting you to visit me here in India where I have made my home. I wish to pass on to you your inheritance, a jeweled*

*pendant known in our family as the heirloom of which I sus-
pect your mother has spoken.*

*It is your time to know who you are and make a difference
in the world.*

With love, your grandmother,

Maddy Rosario.

The letter included an airline ticket to New Dehli, travelers checks in
her name, and the address of the reclusive "goddess cult" outside a town
called Bethinda where Grandma Maddy proposed to meet her.

When MJ read the letter aloud, her mother predictably said, "I forbid you to go. You're too young."

MJ nearly laughed.

She was not too young to be her mother's confidant and listen to
the details of her parents' disintegrating marriage or to be her mother's
shrink and even financial advisor, but she was too young to visit her
grandmother.

MJ nearly laughed but didn't laugh, because no one laughed at
Marjorie Berthe.

"I'll bring this pendant heirloom home," was what she said, "and
give it to you."

Gratitude, let alone hope, was not in her mother's repertoire of
emotions. Her thirty-eight year-old face permanently etched with lines
of bitter disappointment, she said, "You would do that for me?"

It was not a question but a challenge, and so MJ rose to it. It was
what she always did, because teenagers of thin-skinned parents develop
thick skins.

"Mom, consider me a spy in the house of your mother's delusional
games."

"Did her letter say something like, 'you can make your own reality?'"

MJ skimmed through the letter again and passed it to her mother.

"No, but sort of."

"It's the mantra of the con artist, you know."

To Marjorie Berthe, child of a parent lost in the holocaust, no one makes her own reality. Reality instead kicks the shit out of you, your family, your dreams, your art, and finally your life, and all you can do is keep getting up for the next blow until it is finally over.

"The pendant will be yours someday too," her mother said, which was nice of her.

MJ had heard of the heirloom's fantastical properties – how it was made of crystal and a piece of meteorite that millenniums ago crashed into the bogs of northern England, how it had been fashioned into a jewel for a warrior queen. The meteoric crystal had at one time given Marjorie Berthe Hansman a creative surge, turning her within months into an overnight art world sensation. This was why she put so much stock in believing the heirloom was magical.

But unlike the women in her family who came before her, MJ Johnson was a realist. As far as she saw it, the pendant had no real influence other than psychological on her mother's ability to paint.

And yet here she was, engaged in her own psychic archeological dig, about to unearth her ever-elusive Grandma Maddy, her only living grandmother and a woman she didn't know, a woman who had reached out across continents and nations to tell her she was special.

It is your time to know who you are, her blue letter said, *and make a difference in the world.*

Her grandmother was a con artist of course. Con artists manipulate people, pure and simple, and Mad Grandma Maddy certainly fit the bill. Why else would she fail to show at the goddess cult in Bathinda where she'd said she would meet her? And now, after a week at the ashram, MJ had received another blue letter that had her on a bus packed tight with ripe bodies that smelled like everything from spices to feces, beckoning her to yet another destination. Since it was in Khujaraho, famous for its graphic statues carved into its temples, MJ could only assume it was related in some way to one of her grandmother's erotica novels.

At the ashram MJ had found a published novella Grandma Maddy had left behind in her room titled, "An Erotic Adventure Unfinished," but after reading the first page, had put it aside. It was embarrassing, having a grandmother who wrote about sex. How could a woman as old as her grandmother be thinking such things? Wasn't she supposed to be crocheting doilies or canning pickles? And the picture on the back cover: A dark-eyed woman with multi-colored strands of fiery red and golden bourbon bobbed hair. It looked like it had been taken decades ago. So Roaring Twenties. So Mary Quant. Really pretty far-out. But still, the bright red hair contributed to that impression of a woman not to be trusted.

Prepare to be disenchanted, her mother had said, *your grandmother thinks only of herself.*

Many times, while her mother was having her ubiquitous glass of wine and cigarette, or while she was furiously splashing paint on bigger and bigger canvases, she'd tell MJ the story: How Mad Grandma Maddy was the Bad Mother who'd abandoned her; how when MJ was just a baby her grandmother had dropped by their former home in the Anza Borrego desert and taken her rightful inheritance away. How after its theft her career as an artist plummeted and she was passed over by an art world which turned to worshipping male artists who'd usurped her feminine unconscious, claiming it in their own work. Labeled a "woman artist" and featured only in shows with other "women artists," she'd worked various jobs from waitress to window cleaner to support the family while her husband joined the peace movement and got repeatedly arrested at marches where he wasn't – or frequently was – drunk.

"She wants *you* to have the heirloom," Marjorie Berthe said, "Not me. Your young and I'm old. My life is over."

"You're not old and your life isn't over," MJ said, but her mother continued speaking as if she hadn't heard her, MJ being that tree falling alone in the forest, the sound of her voice unheard.

"I'll just wait another forty years," her mother said, referring to the art dealers who said her mother's standing would "pick up" after she turned eighty.

"Why wait forty years for your chance?" MJ said, "Let me go to India and get it for you now, Mom. If you believe it will make a difference, let's do it now."

In a way it was her challenge: *Stop blaming everyone and get on with making your life work.* If a crystal amulet does the trick, then MJ was willing – eager – to recapture the meteoric alchemy that had once made her mother a star.

"You would do that for me?"

This time it *was* a question, and inside the question she heard the soft tinge of hope in her mother's voice.

"Of course I would do that for you," she said, then dared to hug her mother's strong resistant shoulders.

And so it was decided.

MJ would go to India and accept the heirloom as her graduation gift then bring the magic home to her mother. And in doing so she would leave behind the wreckage of her mother's disappointments and move on into her own life, knowing she had done everything she could to make amends for having been born.

Mad Grandma Maddy needn't know she would be passing it back a generation.

Chapter 3

*M*arcus spotted the bus, or the dust whirling from the wheels of the bus. As it drew nearer, he leaned against the shade of the building and tried to not think about how he would approach the girl without frightening her. It was too hot to think. He drank his cola. Charged by the caffeine, his pulse picked up speed but the bus did not. It moved slowly, like everything in India. He stayed in the shade of the building and remained there when the bus stopped, its engine coughing and spewing, rattling to a consumptive end.

The bus was painted in a multitude of chipped colors, and tobacco smoke poured from its open windows. Vendors ran up to sell tea in thin terra cotta cups, baskets of *samosas*, bottled mango juices and colas. Passengers stepped down, and as they did, the tourists among them were confronted with insistent offers of maps, postcards, and hotel transportation.

He didn't know why, but a tightness rose in his throat. He observed each passenger: The dark-faced man in the limp white shirt and business pants, the woman in the blue sari with the baby and goat, the three hippy chicks in varying degrees of undress, one in short cut-offs and tube top, another in a transparent kaftan. The third hippie wore bell-bottom jeans that clung to her hips like unwashed skin and a dirty t-shirt with bold lettering that read, "WOMEN UNITE." A tiny monkey clutched her head from its perch atop her backpack. Then there was a woman in a khaki safari shirt and pants but she was older and traveling with a man carrying an array of camera cases.

Marcus tried to remember the picture the older woman had showed him and understandably refused to part with. She'd explained the photo was of her daughter and not her granddaughter, of whom she had no pictures other than one in infancy. She assumed her granddaughter would at least look a little like the woman in the picture, taken from an art magazine some years ago: Dark-haired, serious and ample-breasted, with full lips and deep-set eyes. The woman artist was standing next to a giant splashy painting; or it appeared splashy. The photograph was in black and white.

How was he to find this chick, based on a black-and-white picture in an art magazine of the girl's mother?

More passengers emerged: Sooty children in oversized cotton clothes, a man carrying an elderly woman, three slim youths with slick black hair who helped the driver pull down bundles of clothes and baskets of sand-coated fruit from the roof of the bus.

No one resembled the dark-eyed artist.

It was to be expected that he would miss her. She could have changed her plans and decided not to meet her grandmother in Khujaraho. What teenager today cares a hoot about an old woman anyway? As logical as this sounded, it did not ease the crushing sensation in his chest. He'd been entrusted to do a simple job and as usual, he was blowing it. He didn't want to disappoint the old white woman, who must have been seventy at least.

"Is that for me?"

One of the hippie girls from the bus, the one with the "WOMEN UNITE" t-shirt and the monkey on her backpack, was standing in front of him. She wore pink sunglasses and a red head kerchief and was pointing at the blue envelope he'd taken from his pocket.

"She's done it again, hasn't she?"

"Are you Mary Jane Johnson?"

She nodded and so he handed over the blue envelope and she ripped it open and read it right in front of him, her brow wrinkling and mouth turning downward.

"Jesus Christ, not again," she said, "I can't keep chasing this woman all over India." The monkey glowered at him, as though he was responsible for her heavy sigh, her sag of disappointment. Then she looked at him. "What's your part in this?"

He threw up his hands.

"Don't kill me, I'm only the messenger. I got no part in whatever you folks got happening."

She was tall for her age, nearly his height, and didn't look at all like the picture of the mother. More like a suburban white girl from California, he thought, although he knew nothing about suburban white girls from California, except that they apparently wore t-shirts without bras bearing feminist slogans.

She caught him looking her over and blushed from chin to hairline.

"Well, I've done my part," he said and shrugged and turned away. "Good luck."

"Wait!"

He turned back. Of course he turned back. The monkey chattered at him from his perch on her backpack, peeking like some interloper over her head.

"Her letter says you are to be my – can you believe it? – 'Escort.'"

Looking at her, tan and strong and apparently fairly independent for her age, one might say she needed no escort.

"Well, I don't know nothing about that."

"Did she give you any clue as to what she's up to? Are you her spy or something?"

They stood in the road, two American tourists having a nonsensical discussion. From the corner of his eye he could see children watching them as if they were a larger-than-life couple on a movie screen.

"Why would I be her spy? I met the woman for the first time today and she told me to deliver this letter and that was *it*."

"It's just that she writes these blue letters and talks in riddles and keeps disappearing on me!"

Incited by her tone, the monkey bared its tiny teeth at him, jumped from her shoulder to the backpack, and shrieked in his face.

"Jesus, what is that?"

"It's a Ceylonese monkey."

The monkey grimaced at him. *You fool,* it seemed to be saying, *you silly fool.* Tired of his efforts at chivalry, Marcus turned away, but the girl reached out to stop him and when he turned sharply back the creature emitted a shrill shriek and landed, like a giant spider, on top of his head. He felt tiny claws digging into his head and was consumed by sheer terror. *I'm being scalped by a Ceylonese monkey,* he thought.

"Rudyard, stop! Stop!" she shouted, and pulled the monkey off.

He reached up into his hair and felt something wet, brought his hand down and looked in his palm. It wasn't blood, but confirmation of this brought no relief. It was soft muddy yellow feces instead.

"Oh, lord," he said.

He heard laughter. The children from the Kodar were laughing and pointing at the big American with the monkey.

Her sunglasses had fallen off and he could see her eyes and the concern in them, but she was laughing too, pulling off her kerchief, using it to reach up and wipe the shit from his hair. The monkey Rudyard was still shrieking, doing a little squatting dance on his shoe.

"You frightened him," she said.

"*I* frightened *him?*"

He wanted to kick the little monster, but this was taboo: *Don't kick the monkey,* he thought, *or this beautiful girl will walk away without even pity.* With monkey shit in his hair however he at least had her attention.

"Let's get you to a bathroom, wash your hair and see if you have any scratches," she said. "Did you get a tetanus shot?"

"I don't recall."

"Where are you staying?"

He gestured back toward town. Disoriented by panic, he nevertheless insisted on taking her backpack though the creature danced around it.

"You take Rudyard," he said, quickly pulling away, afraid the little monster would bite his hand.

She lifted the tiny creature onto her shoulder and turned to walk ahead of him in the direction of town. The monkey climbed higher and did an about-face from his perch on her head to stare back at him, like a child facing through a car's rear window. She had a firm assertive stride, yet he saw by the way she'd smiled when he said the monkey's name that he'd scored a point with this smart angry girl.

Chapter 4

"This is not my problem," said the manager at the Hotel Sunset View, "This is for you to remedy."

"You don't understand. I want my own room, please."

"That is a sorry thing, but we have no extra room because you are not happy."

"He thinks we're together," Marcus said. He turned to the manager. "Look, we don't know each other!"

She peeled a $20 traveler's check from the pouch under her t-shirt and slapped it on the counter. Money talks, she thought, but the manager merely glanced over it, his eyes turning to potential customers from the bus, richer customers, like the couple with the camera equipment who were entering his stark little lobby.

"Yes, you are a woman's libber," he said to her, and tilted his head in that infuriating way, "but that is for you to remedy."

"What's that got to do with anything!"

She had shouted, and so she lowered her voice and muttered, "I can't believe this!"

The manager's expression turned to one of professional empathy, like a shrink or marriage counselor, and looking up at them both, from the tall black American man to the white blond woman, and said, "I do not understand the caste ways in your country but it is different than our untouchables here."

Untouchable! She was suddenly embarrassed and wanted to say, "Hey, just 'cause I don't want to share a room with you doesn't mean I'm racist." And besides, there was nothing untouchable about him. From the first second she'd laid eyes on him stepping out from the shadow of the building, before she saw the blue letter in his hand, she thought he was the most desirable man she'd ever seen.

"We are not a couple!" she said. The photographers approached the counter and the manager turned toward them.

"Look, I've got to wash this crap out of my hair," he said. "You can stay in my room if you want, just keep that monkey away from me."

"Thanks, but I should probably look elsewhere," she said, although she'd heard the whole town was filling up for some festival.

"Okay," he said.

"But wait."

He looked back at her, patiently, tiredly.

"Maybe I should have a look at your head first?"

He studied her, and she saw in his expression a mild tolerance with the whole business: His kindness, her rejection – although she hadn't really rejected him.

"I've got First Aid stuff," she offered, "Not much but you know, mycitracin and scissors."

"If I need mycitracin I'm in big trouble, and so is your monkey."

The room was surprisingly nice, nicer certainly than the room she'd shared at the ashram with the two German women who had taken a vow of silence. She tried not to look longingly into the bathroom. It had a tiny tub on claw feet under a window with a view into a courtyard with palms and birdsong. The room had one bed and a mat on the floor where his backpack and clean jeans had been neatly folded. She thought of asking him if he did his own laundry, but that seemed too personal, although their situation was already turning somewhat personal.

He told her his name was Marcus Jones.

"And you already know mine," she said.

"MJ Hansman."

"Johnson, actually," she said.

She was loyal to her father, even if he was a drunk, and so she would keep his name. Not her mother's. Not her grandmother's. When she had joined her father in Golden Gate Park to protest the bombing of Cambodia, she'd seen that he practically lived there, but she was still his daughter.

She washed Marco's hair at the sink (him bending his lanky body to dip his head under the gushing faucet) and now he sat on a low stool with his head bowed, anxiously awaiting her verdict as she searched for monkey scratches on his scalp. She'd never washed a man's hair before, and his Afro was thick and super absorbent, a big black sponge.

"You have beautiful hair," she said, because she had to say something. And actually it was beautiful. Soft like a bird's nest of Spanish moss. He made no reply. He was worried, and with good reason. Rabies shots were no picnic; the needles were long, and the vaccine was injected into the stomach.

Rudyard watched from a corner looking sufficiently contrite, and when she finally pronounced the scalp free of any injury he seemed to heave a tiny sigh.

"You're off the hook, Rudyard," she said, and he blinked up at her with those little button eyes.

"How'd you happen to buy a monkey?" Marcus said from his squat little stool.

"I didn't buy him." Sensing his fate under scrutiny, Rudyard climbed up into her arms with a pitiful look. "A man I met on the train to Bethinda gave him to me."

"I'd say he spotted you for a soft-hearted sucker."

He said it gently, but she resented being called a sucker. Rudyard was her little friend, sometimes even her confidant. He made travel less lonely and appreciated her off-tune singing.

"We'd better be going," she said. Rudyard took his cue and wrapped his infant arms around her neck.

Marcus studied them.

"You really can stay here," he said, "No strings. Both of you."

It took all her willpower not to look again into the full bathroom with running water and its tiny tub. She could hear water trickling from the courtyard fountain and the trill of an expressive, improvisational bird. It was a relief to be away from the constant crowds of people. It was a relief to Rudyard too who, having sensed a change in atmosphere, was drowsily nudging his head under her chin. A bath, after a week of sponging over a basin in a communal toilet, would be heaven. And the room had a ceiling fan that moved the warm air around and made a soft tick-tick sound.

She pulled Maddy's letter from her pocket, the one he'd given her only moments ago, and read it carefully this time:

> *My dear MJ,*
> *I know you must think me batty —*

That isn't the half of it!

> *— but I must return to my home in Tamil Nadu to deal with an emergency at the school.*

What school? Was Mad Grandma Maddy running a school now?

> *I hope that you can join me there at first opportunity, but until then, I have left the heirloom in the trust of a dear friend*

with the understanding that she is to pass the pendant on into your possession.

Why couldn't she have just waited and given it to me? MJ wondered. She skipped town just hours before I arrived!

Before you can meet my friend —

And who is this friend and does she have a name?

— you must first meet with Mr. Todi
— .

Another instruction! Another hoop for her to jump through!

You will locate Mr. Todi at the Temples tomorrow morning at 9.

What Temples?

Simply inform him you wish to go to the Kali Shrine, and he will be happy to accommodate you.

"Happy to accommodate me," thought MJ. How suspicious!

Everything happens for a reason, my dear —

Especially when you're dealing with a con artist.

and I know you are prepared to face every challenge that comes your way.

Do I have a choice?

> *My thoughts remain with you,*
> *Your Grandmother Maddy*

At the last part, MJ could only shake her head:

> *P.S. I believe you can trust the young man who handed you*
> *this letter. He would make an excellent escort and is a good*
> *American.*

What does it mean to be a "good American," anyway? She looked up at Marcus as he rose to his full impressive height from the low stool and gathered his folded laundry from the mat.

"Do you do your own laundry?" she asked.

"Sure," he replied, "There's a machine down the hall on the second floor."

Marcus went out to get food while MJ eased her grimy limbs into the claw-foot bathtub's warm encompassing water. Rudyard sat on the edge of the tub watching her worriedly, but soon curled up asleep inside a nest he had made from the dirty laundry piled beside her backpack, his thin long tail tucked under his nose.

She was finished with her bath and wearing a clean t-shirt that said "WOMEN ARE NOT CHICKS" and a pair of wrinkled khaki shorts by the time Marcus returned with tea and a basket of potato cakes, curry puffs and mangoes. She was bra-less, the shape of her nipples showed through the fabric of her tee, but she wasn't about to wear a dirty bra. He kept looking away, focusing his attention on the spicy eggplant and fried *pooris* bread. *Why should I wear a dirty bra just to spare him embarrassment?* she thought, *It's the seventies, and we've come a long way, baby.*

They ate on the mat with Rudyard accepting the occasional piece of mango. Soon they were talking about their digestive systems, an unavoidable subject for most travelers in Asia. His stomach was toughened by experience, but hers was not. She confessed she'd had a humbling bout of "Delhi belly" when she was in Bathinda, her meditation exercises with other cult members interrupted by constant trips to the outhouse.

"I don't know," she said, "It seems like this search for enlightenment is little more than inglorious time spent squatting over a hole in the floor."

He laughed loud and long at this, laughed so hard that he was crying, and every so often, even as it was getting darker and he was cleaning up the food, he'd start up laughing again.

"You got a funny Grandmammy, inviting you to a goddess ashram."

"Yeah, and then not showing up."

Again she wondered if he'd been hired to be some kind of spy or maybe her baby-sitter, but she didn't ask. Nor did she inquire about his story. She wondered what he was doing in India and figured he was escaping something back in the States.

He gathered the food remnants and took the garbage out. She feigned near-sleep when he returned, lying sideways on the mat with her money pack and passport under her nightshirt, Rudyard curled against her lower back. It wasn't that she didn't trust him; she just hadn't decided to trust him.

And then her mind dropped like a smooth stone into a sudden encompassing sleep.

She heard Rudyard's chatter, then a "shhh." Now she was fully awake. She opened her eyes and peered at her roommates.

Rudyard was seated on Marcus' wide shoulder accepting pieces of mango. He would cut a sliver and hold it up for the monkey to take, and then he would cut another piece and eat it himself. One for Marcus. One for Rudyard. Both appeared quietly content with the arrangement. Rudyard saw MJ stir and, uttering a little squeal of delight, jumped off his shoulder onto the floor mat.

"We've made you breakfast," Marcus said.

"We?"

"Rudyard and I."

Rudyard shrieked his agreement.

"So you've made up and become friends, I see."

It touched her in one respect, but she didn't want to get too friendly with this man. He seemed rootless to her, and sad. She had known plenty of guys at Venice Beach who were lost and sad. Some were vets from the war, old already in their twenties. Even in high school she knew she wasn't the solution to their problems, even if they wore their hair long and looked cute and had Thai sticks and hash and stronger stuff too. Sometimes she and her friends would smoke the Thai, even the hash, but the other stuff she avoided.

He set a flat basket of toast and fruit next to the mat.

She stared at it for a moment, her stomach rumbling. Which was it going to be today, she wondered. Hunger or the other?

"Excuse me," she said, and dashed for the bathroom.

He would hear it all, the whole exploding gushing stream and shit, but *fuck it,* she thought, this was India not the Ritz.

When she emerged he quietly poured mint tea and said nothing.

"Thank-you," she said.

"Try the toast."

"Does it have butter on it?"

"No."

She ate the toast, first in small bites, then with more relish and increasing hunger. She was strong. She'd get through this and return home with stomach intact.

"You've been really nice," she said, "I really appreciate you letting us stay here."

"Sure, well. You're a good hair washer."

"Due to our fault. Well, his." She nodded to Rudyard, who seemed perfectly content nibbling his piece of mango from his station on the big hard shoulder of this guy whose biceps bulged under the cut-off sleeves of his "peace" symbol t-shirt.

"You remind me of my dad," she said.

"I bet a look a lot different from your dad."

"Not much different. Well, a bit."

They laughed.

"I'm going to go see this guy at the Temples today," she said, "I guess he'll give me some directions to this Kali shrine where my grandmother's friend is. It's all pretty weird."

"Do you know where the Temples are?"

"No, but I'll just follow the tourists with the big cameras, I guess."

"Well, I'll take you there, if you want. I'm not doing anything today."

"What *are* you doing? I mean, in general?"

He considered her question for only a second before answering, but that second had hundreds of images in his head.

"I guess you could say I'm escaping the war."

"So you *are* a lot like my dad."

"Your dad was in 'Nam?"

"Korea."

"Another war," he said, "meant to hold back the commies."

She sipped her tea and waited for him to say more, but he didn't and so she didn't. She wasn't going to ask what he was running from but based on the sarcasm in his voice she had an idea. Her father had told her the soldiers he'd killed in Korea were human beings, not "commies." As if she needed to be told, but her dad told her so she would know *he knew* whom he had killed. Human beings.

Marcus stood, an indication this aspect to their conversation – her interrogation – was over. She passed a piece of toast to Rudyard. He studied it thoughtfully, turning it over in his tiny monkey hand.

She looked out the window at the increasingly brighter hotter day and who-knows-what awaiting her, and hoped her stomach was up to the task.

"Well, if you don't have anything special to do," she said, "I'd appreciate it if you'd show us the way to the Temples."

"Sure, no problem," he said, and placed the basket of nearly finished breakfast on the clean surface of a dresser then carefully covered it with a thin cloth.

"Waste not want not," she said, tucking her money belt and passport under her waistband.

"You got that right," he replied, "Especially when people are starving every where you look."

She washed her face in the sink as he stood behind her to look in the mirror and adjust his headband, this guy Marcus, the man her grandmother had described in her letter as "a good American."

Chapter 5

The Kandarya Mahadeva Temple rose up like a giant penis, its façade of intricately carved men, women, gods and goddesses dancing and cavorting high above the flocks of tourists who had come to see it. Although she had read about it in the *Lonely Planet* guidebook MJ wasn't prepared for the temple's blatant celebration of lusty, unbridled joyful sexuality.

She was not a prude and no virgin either, but still she was shocked to the core. Nothing like this existed in America except maybe in cruder form in bathroom stalls. Here they stood out in broad sunlight, statuettes copulating in every position of the Kama Sutra: Voluptuous thighs and stomachs grinding against one another, arms and legs embracing, muscular buttocks tightened in copulatory thrust. Marcus gave off a low, reverential whistle.

"Is it beautiful or is it obscene?" she said.

"Beautiful *and* obscene," he replied.

From his perch on Marcus' shoulder, Rudyard pounded his chest.

Suddenly a slim young Indian man in a white business shirt with rolled-up sleeves was standing beside her.

"A mighty aphrodisiac, no?" he said, wiggling his eyebrows suggestively. MJ made no reply. She didn't want to encourage this man, clearly a guide trying to solicit a tour. She had come to the Kandarya Mahadeva Temple not to sightsee but to locate, per her grandmother's instruction, the man called Mr. Todi. The guide turned to Marcus.

ystdemetಠ

"What say you, Sir?"

Marcus gazed in silence at the statuary. Coolly removed, he might appear intimidating if not for the monkey curled upon his shoulder.

"Tantric ecstasy," the guide continued, undaunted, "Necessary for life." The guide went on to explain that for "a very worthy" eight rupees, he would help them better understand the *Kama Kala*, or erotic sculpture.

"You see, the union of the male and female is the greatest joy in nature," he said, gesturing with his delicate hands at the undulating bodies, "This you must understand. Do not be uncomfortable. All is well. I am Mr. Todi. At your service."

"*You* are Mr. Todi?"

MJ didn't know what she had expected. Someone elderly, scholarly, in a frumpy tweed jacket perhaps and bifocals. Mr. Todi acted like a flirtatious teenager.

"My grandmother Maddy Rosario said I'd find you here."

Mr. Todi gazed at her for a moment then his face blossomed into a genuine smile.

"Ah! Madame Rosario, the great writer of tantric sex!"

Marcus turned to her, eyebrows raised.

"Yeah," she said, "that's my grandmother."

Was this why her grandmother had her come to the erotic temples of Khujaraho? It was too gross to fathom. Marcus reached up to hold the hand of the monkey on his shoulder then walked a short distance toward a group of tourists.

"The books for the girls are in the rickshaw," Mr. Todi said.

"I don't understand."

"She wishes me to transport them to the school, yes?"

"I don't know about any books. Or school." she said and wondered, *what else has Mad Grandma Maddy gotten me into?* "I'm to go to the Kali

Shrine and find a woman there – a friend of hers who – has something for me."

Best not mention the Heirloom, she thought, although she wasn't sure why.

"Yes, yes," Mr. Todi replied, and whistled loudly to a man with a rickshaw from a large grouping of them, a bicycle version of a waiting cabbie line.

"The Living Shakti lives a short distance from town, but I cannot say if she will be there."

"I'm not sure about any shakti," she said, doubtfully. Grandma Maddy's letter had said nothing about a Living Shakti, unless that was the woman she was to meet at the Kali Shrine. A Living Shakti was a living goddess, she'd been told at the cult, one who returned from the brink of death. The idea of some living goddess in possession of the Heirloom was of course another inexplicable turn of events in this mad obstacle course her grandmother had devised.

"We will transport you with the books," Mr. Todi said, "as Madame Rosario requested. Are you ready?"

The rickshaw was suddenly beside them. Mr. Todi whistled for a second one.

Suddenly a tourist – a blond woman standing near them – emitted a shriek of laughter. A man peered up through binoculars. People were pointing to a spot high on one of the temples and, following their line of sight MJ glimpsed a faint movement, as if one of the carved figures had come to life. Then she saw Marcus standing at the base of the temple, looking up, shouting and cajoling.

"Oh no," she said.

Rudyard was on a high ledge beneath a pair of entwined stone lovers. Inspired perhaps by their passionate stand-up intercourse, the tiny monkey was embracing the lower shin of the woman and doing a little dance. Not a dance. He was *humping* the woman's ankle, humping like a dog!

"Rudyard!" MJ shouted, but the tiny primate continued unperturbed.

"I couldn't stop him," Marcus said, "He jumped off my shoulder and before I could grab him, he climbed up. He's a fast little guy," he concluded proudly, as though he were talking about a son in Little League.

"The *mithunas'* spirit has moved him," Todi said, arms folded, calmly watching.

"Go, monkey, go!" someone shouted.

A cheer rose up from a group of hippies. One of them performed some bumps and grinds. A portable tape deck blasted out the Stones' *(I Can't Get No) Satisfaction*.

"Rudyard!" She shouted again, but Rudyard pumped on, ignoring her.

"It's only natural," the blond woman said.

"How could you let him get away?"

"He just jumped off me. He's an animal, not a human baby."

"Animals are beautiful," the blond said.

I can't get no girlie action, Mick Jagger sang. The hippie gyrated past.

"I'm going with Mr. Todi to the Kali Shrine," she said, "I'm sorry, but can you stay here until Rudyard comes down?"

"She is two, three kilometers away," Mr. Todi said, "And I must warn you this shakti is a powerful woman."

"I'll come with you," Marcus said.

"Can't you stay with Rudyard? And make him come down, please?"

Everything was going wrong. This Mr. Todi wanting to talk about some living goddess and this other thing with the books, and now Rudyard climbing the shrine. *I never should have let Marcus baby-sit my monkey*, she thought, *Rudyard is my responsibility*. Why was everything so hard?

"He just leaped out of my arms," Marcus said again, then added, "I guess I'm a bad Dad." He hung his head in a mock-chastised pose.

"Yes you are," she said, "And that makes me Bad Mom."

They contemplated one another and then Marcus smiled. He had a beautiful smile because it was so unexpected. She'd gotten the impression he didn't smile much these days, and yet he appeared to be the sort of person who took private pleasure in helping others, this man her grandmother had called a "good American," so maybe he could help her by staying with Rudyard.

The monkey had climbed even higher and was now sitting on the head of a goddess with large melon breasts.

"I'm going now, Rudyard," she shouted up.

"Don't worry," Marcus said, "I'll get him down."

"I really appreciate it," she said.

Mr. Todi was calling out instructions to the two rickshaw drivers. They were moving two large boxes from a beat-up VW bug into the rickety vehicles. She noticed there were stacks of books inside the boxes, and one, *Goodnight Moon,* gleamed its bright green and blue children's book cover from the top.

"Well," she said to Marcus, "I'll see you later."

"Don't be gone long," he replied, and she could see from his expression that it was hard for him to let her go, that he was worried for her, and as she stepped into the rickshaw holding the boxes of books she wondered again if he was her grandmother's spy.

Chapter 6

$\mathscr{S}$he rode in the back of the bicycle rickshaw like some elite colonial figure in the time of the Raj while the driver sweated and pedaled in front. The boxes of books at her feet undoubtedly made the rickshaw even heavier and harder to pull. They pedaled through the narrow streets of mud and stone houses, back toward the old town section of Khujaraho, past the women and children washing in the Khodar River. The sun bore down and she chanted inwardly to the rhythmic squeaking of the wheels: *"Mad-dogs-and-Englishmen, Mad dogs and Englishmen -- go out in the noonday sun - "*

It seemed her grandmother was giving her a tour of India, abandoning her to travel alone while at the same time arranging friends, acquaintances, and strangers to hover nearby: There had been the women at the Goddess Cult in Bathinda, and then Marcus in Khujaraho, and now Mr. Todi and apparently another person at this Kali Shrine in the middle of nowhere.

Soon they rode beyond the outskirts of town. No streets, no road signs, no hawkers. The trail grew rockier. The hard-breathing drivers pedaled over patches of shrub and grasslands, past a lone man walking. (Where is he coming from, she thought, why is he out here?) Grasslands gave way to a desert plain. The drivers' backs were slick with sweat.

MJ had never been away from her mother except when being shuttled to see her father in San Francisco, and so the further she traveled from Khujaraho, the more apprehensive she felt. India was her first experience as a solitary traveler. What she saw by observing the country through her own eyes was girls laboring with their mothers to wash and feed younger children, and men and boys scrambling to make a few rupees driving rickshaws for fat tourists riding in the back.

Since childhood she had listened to her mother lamenting on how women artists had been screwed, but here so many were screwed and in the most basic ways. Without her mother's presence, her voice in her ear, her artworks and artistic process and forceful personality dominating the house, MJ wondered how one measured such inequality: The rage of a snubbed western world artist versus the anguish of daily seeking food and shelter. Was this visit to India a ploy on the part of Mad Grandma Maddy to make her see her side?

Shapes took form on the shimmering horizon. As they drew closer, she saw a series of long concrete buildings and dark silhouettes running toward them. Girls. Dozens. Girls in saris, girls in blue jeans and shorts, waving and shouting excitedly. Bright faced girls, aggressive girls, shy girls, girls with long black hair and girls with shorn bangs and plastic headbands, girls with smart crackling eyes and girls who laughed and girls who giggled, silent girls and curious girls. Walking slowly behind them was an erect woman in a silken sari.

The girls amassed around the rickshaws as they came to a stop. Mr. Todi stepped off and bowed reverently to the woman in the sari then raised his hands in mock surrender to the girls. He shouted greetings and instructions, but there was no controlling them. They leaped into the rickshaws and reached in and passed around from hand-to-hand what they came for:

The books. Books that disappeared in a flash into a circle of hands: A spelling primer, E. B. White's *Charlotte's Web,* a Dorothy Parker book of poetry, *Call Of the Wild,* picture books and dictionaries.

The woman turned her sharp gaze upon MJ, observing her with an intensity she was unaccustomed to.

"I am Elakshi," the woman said.

"This is the granddaughter of Madam Rosario," Mr. Todi said to the woman as the children screamed and fluttered in and around them.

Because the woman had an unquestionable regality about her, MJ inclined her head with her hands together, a gesture of *Namaste*. The woman smiled with eyes that seemed to spark like turquoise stars in the noonday sun.

"Mary Jane Johnson," MJ said.

The box of books was emptying fast, and so was the second box in the back of the other rickshaw. A group of teenage girls not much younger than herself pulled out a copy of *Our Bodies, Ourselves* and a trio of pre-adolescents passed around *2001: A Space Odyssey*. There were some Hindu/English dictionaries and a stack of *Supergirl* comic books. Elakshi issued an order in Hindi to the girls and with a chatter of excitement and curious glances at MJ they ran off with their books, back toward the school building, bright butterflies on a desert terrain.

One crying child stayed behind; the tiniest of them all.

"What have we here?" MJ said. The girl was not much older than five and light as a twig when she picked her up. The girl automatically wrapped her bare legs around her waist and sobbed wet tears onto into her shoulder, a string of injustices issuing from her lips in indecipherable Hindi.

"She has no book of her own," Elakshi said. She shook her head with a gentle accepting kindness that took in the sight of MJ holding the crying girl.

"We can fix that," MJ said, "There must be a book somewhere here for you."

And there was, one overlooked on the floor of the rickshaw.

Goodnight Moon. Fallen off the top in the confusion.

Carrying the little girl on her hip, MJ picked up the book.

"Here," she said, handing it to her, "This is *your* book."

The girl grasped it with a small intake of breath and looked up at her with awe-struck brown eyes. MJ set her back down on the ground and said, "Here, you should write your name in the book, since it is your book."

She opened *Goodnight Moon* to the title page and saw that there was already something written on the inside cover:

> *To Mary Jane*
> *From your Grandmother Maddy*
> *August 4, 1959*

It was unfathomable, here in the middle of India's northern Madhya Pradesh, and yet there it was, written in that undeniable hand, undoubtedly from her grandmother's library, a book saved over the years.

"This was my book," MJ blurted. "Or it was meant for me once."

She had never received it; she would have remembered such an inscription. And now here it was, meant for her those many years ago.

Had it been placed at the top of the box for her to see? And what was the likelihood of her opening it to the title page and seeing Grandma Maddy's handwriting?

The little girl looked at her, startled.

"It's yours now," MJ said, and handed it to her. "Here, write your name in it right next to mine."

MJ extracted a stubby pencil from her knap sack and handed to the little girl who took it, cautiously.

"You can write your name, no?" said Elakshi, and the little girl did so proudly, slowly, pressing the pencil stub down as MJ held the book open, on the top of the first title page: ANUJA.

When the girl had run back to the school and her older sisters, the woman Elakshi said:

"You ask the universe a question, and you receive an answer if you are willing to hear it."

MJ wasn't sure what her question was exactly, but she nodded anyway.

"You have come to receive your family heirloom from our Goddess Kali?"

"The Kali Shrine," MJ replied, "Yes, I have."

Elaskshi observed her with care, seemed to look *into her*, then finally gestured for her to follow her to a small hut with an open archway over which hung strings of bright stone shards. The woman parted the dangling shards and motioned for her to enter.

The dark interior was punctuated by a stream of light shining down through a high, circular window that, catching dust particles in its beam, cast a spotlight upon a life-sized figure of the Kali goddess enshrined against the wall. Carved of deep red stone, she was beautiful, strong, naked, proud. And terrifying. Legs bent, her tongue dangled lasciviously. She had stepped into the lair of a she-demon and was far from help, far from Marcus, whom she desperately wished was with her now.

"Here is Kali," Mr. Todi spoke softly beside her and dropped to his knees.

MJ backed away. As if alive, Kali's eyes followed her. The woman Elakshi took her hand and guided her toward the statue. As they drew closer MJ finally saw it, hanging on the red stone neck of Kali. A crystal pendant. It sparked white and black in the hazy light. The Heirloom. What she had come for.

"You must first," said Elakshi, "Make a gift to Kali."

"A sacrifice," Mr. Todi said from his position of servitude. He had reached into his pants pocket and pulled out a small switchblade.

"I beg your pardon?"

"It is not difficult."

"What are you doing?"

"Come, see, you will understand," Mr. Todi said.

"I'm sorry," MJ replied, "But actually, I don't understand."

Was this what her psychic archeological dig into her subconscious had brought her to? A goddess at her most blood-thirsty and terrifying, with four arms and disheveled hair?

"You cannot take the Heirloom from the goddess Kali," said Elakshi, "Without giving in return."

"It is not a problem," said Mr. Todi. Exposing the blade, he made a tiny cut across the base of his thumb.

"I can't believe you're doing this!"

"Do not be afraid," Elakshi said. She felt the woman's grip on elbow.

The cut Mr. Todi made was as thin as paper. He squeezed the skin around the slice in his skin until a few small droplets of blood formed, then he dropped them, one, two, three, into a stone bowl set before the naked feet of the red stone goddess.

"You see?" he said, "You must appease the goddess. Or she will be angry."

"She's already angry. Look at her."

"This is not a laughing matter."

"Do I look like I'm laughing?"

Mr. Todi closed the switchblade, and set it down before MJ. Heart beating wildly, she raised her eyes to Kali. The goddess's eyes took on a liquid life. The statue was alive!

"Think of the Heirloom," the woman prompted, her voice a whisper of wind at her ear, "And of why you have come."

MJ reached out and touched the pendant, the tips of her fingers trembling against it with her own rush of fear and daring, and lifted the crystal up, its chain dangling from the neck of the goddess. This object of her mother's bedtime tales of longing was a rough, multi-faceted prism, fashioned centuries ago into a rugged piece of jewelry.

Drawing it closer, she peered into the crystal and glimpsed a shard of what appeared to be a mirror, and as she turned it in her hand saw her own startled face replaced by her mother's face and then another face, a bobbed flapper and then another woman, her soft Gibson Girl hair wavering in the milky interior universe until she transformed into the dark-skinned face of another woman and then she too was gone. She dropped the pendant back upon the red stone breast.

This is about blood, she thought, *the blood of women.*

MJ swung her small knap sack around off her back, dug inside, pulled out her Swiss Army knife, opened it to the sharpest, smallest blade and, without giving herself a second to hesitate, swiped it across the center of her thumb. It began to pour blood. Feeling vaguely nauseous, she held her aching pounding wound over the sacrificial bowl. For a second she thought would faint.

"That is what is called overkill," Mr. Todi said as the blood from her self-inflicted sacrifice continued to flow freely into the bowl and MJ felt the pendant being gently hung, like a benediction, around her neck.

Chapter 7

*M*arcus was waiting for them at the Temples when they returned, Rudyard perched on his shoulder, tail draped around his neck like a thin fur wrap. Hard body in loose camo-pants and ragged T, Marcus affected a posture of indifference. By contrast, having descended at last from his antics among the Temple lovers, Rudyard did a little dance of greeting.

"Here's your damn monkey," Marcus said.

"Looks more like *your* monkey."

"No way," he replied.

With a screech of approval, Rudyard settled onto her shoulder and pulled the bright crystal pendant up from its chain into his tiny leathery hands.

"So you found it," Marcus said. He thrust his hands into his pockets and stood back, aloof but not.

"It was at a shrine to Kali, also a girl's school," MJ said, "Just another surprise from Grandma Maddy."

Marcus licked his thumb and ran it down the side of her dust-coated cheek. He then saw sock turned pink with blood wrapped around her thumb.

"What happened?"

When he took up her wrist, she winced.

"Grandma Maddy has founded several girls' schools in Pakistan and India that are like little libraries with teachers, and she sends them books. She has a school in Tamil Nadu where she lives."

"What happened to your thumb? Marcus asked again.

"A sacrifice," MJ replied.

"Perhaps more sacrifice than necessary," Mr. Todi apologized.

"A *sacrifice*?"

"I cut my thumb. It was supposed to be a nick, but – "

"We have to bandage that right," Marcus said, "Not with some dirty old sock."

"It isn't dirty," MJ said, "I'm not a complete fool, you know."

"Please," Mr. Todi intervened, "Allow me to escort you to a First Aid. It will be all right."

First Aid was inside a small concrete hut, impeccably clean and ordered inside, with a receptionist handling the steady stream of patients and two nurses attending to the sick and injured. Most complaints among the tourists were intestinal, and there was a discussion in one corner between German tourists on how best to treat the problem. MJ was called and seated in a plastic chair before a small table where a nurse carefully inspected, cleaned, stitched and bandaged her thumb.

"I did not foresee," Todi said, and paused, searching for the word, " – her *enthusiasm* for the Kali. She acquired the pendant with the blessings of the Living Shakti. It is divine will."

"Divine will, huh?" Marcus didn't sound convinced.

It was decided after leaving First Aid that they would go to "Raja's Café." Mr. Todi spotted a table on the terrace and as they followed him MJ looked over at Marcus and gave him a smile that grew in radiance. He returned her smile with caution.

She sat at the table beside Marcus and across from Mr. Todi and took in the pulsating lives of those in the restaurant and beyond, the fortunate and not, the rich and poor, American and Bangladeshi, fat and the hungry, and understood from here on out that she would adhere to a social contract drawn from the empathy in her heart. No longer did it seem insurmountable and hopeless, no longer were her dreams too big and confidence too small. Now she dared to think it, dared to believe it: One betters the lives of others by knowing oneself. She *would* change the world, one girl, one school, one sentence, one book at a time.

I must make him understand, she thought of Marcus. But what? *Understand what?* What had happened at the shrine?

Perhaps it *was* the power of the shakti, or female energy, as Elakshi had said. She told MJ that, centuries ago, before the Aryan invasion introduced India to patriarchal gods, there were matriarchal tribes who worshipped Kali.

"Kali represents the female principle," Elakshi said.

She was tied to the Great Mother Goddess and equated with the transcendent power of time. *She is more than the goddess of destruction,* Elakshi said. Kali destroys to *recreate*. She destroys sin and ignorance. *She can even destroy war.*

"Does it hurt?" Marcus asked her.

"Not really," she said, "Well it throbs a little."

"Here is good medicine for a sore thumb!" Mr. Todi said when the waiter brought their Bombay tonics.

The café swam in an atmosphere of festive sensuality. The heat of the day was cooling and a breeze came off the plains where the temples rose in the slanted, late afternoon light. Rudyard sat on MJ's shoulder and tenderly stroked her hair with his tiny hands.

"Kali is one of the fierce Mahavidyas," Mr. Todi said in the voice of the professional tour guide, "She was pleased with your sacrifice. The Mahavidyas arise, you see, when a goddess expresses independence from her husband."

"Even the gods can't make their wives subservient," Marcus said.

"Hush," MJ ordered. He felt something bumping his shin. It was her sandaled foot.

"Once, when Shiva saw Sati's fury," Todi continued, "He closed his eyes."

"Excellent avoidance technique," Marcus said.

"And when Shiva opened them," Todi said, "a fearsome female stood before him."

"I'm familiar with that transformation," Marcus said, "You should see my mama when she's mad."

"Shiva looked at her," Todi continued, "and the woman became very old. She grew four arms, her complexion became fiery and her hair disheveled, and her tongue lolled out and began to wave from side to side."

"Some hot chick," Marcus said.

"Hey!" MJ gave him another gentle kick and pointed to her t-shirt: "WOMEN ARE NOT CHICKS."

"Oh, yeah, sorry," Marcus said. He tore his gaze away from her breasts and handed Rudyard a lime.

"Shiva was afraid and tried to flee," Todi continued, "but the terrible goddess filled the directions around him with ten different forms, which were the Mahavidyas, and one of them was Kali, the one who makes trouble."

"There's always one who makes trouble," Marcus said.

"Trouble may be one interpretation," MJ said.

"Kali brings spiritual liberation to Shiva," Todi said, "because he sometimes needs to be overpowered by the feminine shakti. It is Tantric."

"Oh yes. Tantric. Tantric sex," Marcus said, and swilled the rest of his gin and tonic. MJ concentrated her attention on Todi, but her foot, having shed her sandal, remained on Marcus' leg.

"Tantric sex is the union of opposites and is necessary," Todi said, looking from MJ to Marcus, "for the world to endure."

Suddenly Mr. Todi stood, his lecture abruptly over.

"You're going?" MJ asked.

"I too seek Tantric union," he said. "At home with my wife."

Todi turned to Marcus and winked.

"It is a good night," he said, "For liberation of the *jiva*."

"Sure," Marcus gamely replied. Although he did not know what *jiva* was, he had an idea.

"I wish you much luck in your spiritual search," Todi said to MJ after she paid him double his original price, twenty rupees, for his long day of service. He then bowed politely and was gone.

"That was some story," Marcus said, "I'm not sure I got it."

"You will," MJ said, and when she looked boldly into his eyes he thought about how blond, brown-eyed girls were fine.

"So who's this Living Shakti?" he asked, "What's with the blood sacrifice?"

Her story was riddled with a lack of logic, but he could hear the truth in it, or at least the emotional truth. She told him that after she had made the required sacrifice to Kali ("and believe me, it was stupid how I overdid it, they were shocked, and so was I"), the woman whom Todi calls the Living Shakti simply gave her the heirloom. She then showed her the school and explained how many years ago, when she was a young woman, she had through quirk of fate and wind currents survived the flames of her husband's cremation after she'd been ordered to burn with his body. Smoke served as a screen, blinding the mourners and enabling her to run away. She returned years later to learn she had become a legend. By surviving the flames, she was made a living goddess.

"Imagine a widow being expected in those days to throw herself on her husband's funeral pyre," MJ said, "Burned alive. Like Joan of Arc. Talk about sexism and witch trials!"

"You wouldn't see that happening in the States," Marcus agreed.

"No, the Puritans just drowned their witches."

303

"So this Living Shakti," Marcus said, "Is a woman who made her own choice to live instead of follow some crazy tradition that expects her to burn with the body of her dead husband."

"You got that right Charlie."

"The name is Marcus."

"I know," she said, and there it was again, that smile, just for him, her bare foot on his and her toes curling under his bare arch. The lyrics to a Clapton piece bloomed inside his head. *In the sunshine of your love.*

"Damn, woman, what're you doing to my foot?"

"You don't like it?"

He looked at her lips. Then he kissed them. The kiss was quick. A test. When he began to pull back she reached out and pulled him back for another, longer kiss.

Rudyard picked up a wedge of lime, sucked on it loudly, and made a wide grimace that could easily be mistaken for a leer.

"I don't know what you got planned," she said. Leaning down to rummage in her knap sack, she produced a familiar blue letter.

"Another one?"

"Would you like to come with me to Calcutta? Grandma Maddy has a girls' school there. She'll reputedly be there, but you know how that goes."

He studied her in close up. No make-up, and those dark eyes of hers; *maybe the blond part is fake*, he thought, but didn't look it. Brown-eyed blond. So fine. Too good to be true.

"I'm not the guy you think I am."

"What guy is that?"

"A good guy."

"Oh, yeah? What are you then, some serial killer?"

He winced at the word – *killer.*

"Sort of."

"Uh-huh. I thought so."

She watched his face turn rigid. She knew that face.

"What do you '*think so*,'" he said. His voice turned hard. It was sad, after his kiss, to feel that warmth disappear and be left out in the cold. She knew that too.

"My dad – like I said, you're a lot like him."

"Was he a baby killer too?"

It was like he'd thrown the ice from his drink in her face.

"Did you kill babies?"

"Yes. Yes I did. I killed babies."

"Were you at Mai Lai?

"No."

"Then how? How did you kill babies?"

"I dropped bombs on them."

"You were a pilot?"

"That be me, 'hon."

"And you looked down from your plane and said, 'Hey, I see a baby down there,' I'm gonna drop a bomb on her."

Marcus glared at her and said nothing.

"Is that how you killed babies?"

"What do you think?"

"I think you faced an angry nation when you got back from the war. You'd served your country. You were a soldier who followed orders."

"So were the Nazis."

"So now you're a baby killer *and* a fascist."

"I enlisted in a bogus war. It was wrong."

"So what are you going to do? Be that person the rest of your life? The war's almost over, you know. It should be for you too."

"You don't know how it is."

"I'm just saying you're more than some myopic peacenik's definition of you. I've been to the demonstrations. With my dad. I know what they're like. Yeah, let's end the war, but spitting on G.I,'s coming home? Calling them Baby Killers?"

"Maybe I was. I didn't see it, but the bombs I dropped killed somebody."

"Then maybe you make up for it by deciding to change things. In places like this, you know?"

She picked up the lime Rudyard had eaten and sucked on it.

"That lime," he said, and pointed to the big-toothed, grinning monkey.

"What?"

"Never mind."

Marcus stared off at the Temples where a group of children had begged him for change. He'd given them American dimes jangling from the deep pockets of his cargoes and they had boisterously joined him in cajoling Rudyard down from the Temple. He had noticed then how the dancing goddesses looked nothing like the children's mothers bearing water and fuel on their backs.

How was it that in a country of so many gods and goddesses the mothers looked like grandmothers?

"You know we could do something," she said, "Change just even one girl's life, and that would change another girl's life, and another, and the lives of that woman's children. I say someone should *do* something, so why not me? Why not us?"

With her uninjured hand MJ reached across the table and laced her fingers through his. Her hand was cold from the icy drink. He warmed her fingers. She cooled his hot palm. When he spoke his voice was soft.

"You recruiting me to your cult of optimism?"

"Of all those words," she said, "I'd say optimism is the only one I agree with."

Down at the temples, a guitar joined the percussion instruments. Its play worked its way into the heads and shoulders of the café customers and they bobbed and rolled their heads and bodies to the music. Sunset light bathed her face and hair and it was, she was, beautiful.

But he'd be lying if he told her he was an optimist. He didn't owe her anything but the truth.

"Sorry, Sweetheart, I'm not your man."

"Sure, I get it," she whispered, accepting his rejection. "The last thing you need is another recruitment office."

She pulled her hand away, but he seized it mid-retreat.

"Hold on," he said, "I'm thinking."

Her fingers were long and tapered, and her nails were blunt cut, economical, not clean exactly, traveler's hands. He could imagine these hands anywhere, and not just on him: On the shoulders of children and women, hefting a backpack, serving a meal, turning the pages of a book before a circle of listeners.

He looked down at the pendant hanging over the words on her t-shirt – WOMEN ARE NOT CHICKS. With his other hand he reached out and, careful not to brush a nipple pushing against the thin cotton cloth, picked up the chain and turned the crystal over in his fingers.

"What do you say, Rudyard," he said to the tiny monkey crouched at his elbow, "Is it magic? Has this thing turned MJ into a one-woman goddess cult?"

Brow furrowed, appearing to be more scientist than primate, Rudyard inspected the glowing shard. It captured the mauve and magenta sunset blazing across the western sky.

The rhythmic beating from the temples was reaching a feverish pitch. There was something in the air, an electrified excitement, like simmering water preparing for a roiling boil.

Marcus imagined himself on the precipice of a life-long journey with this woman, but if he let go of her hand, if he said no, the journey wouldn't happen. People were getting up from the tables and following the beat of the *tablas* down to the temples.

"Marcus?"

"You've got me," he said. He released the pendant, but not her hand.
"What?"
"Let's dance," he said.
She had him, now and forever.

In the warm night air they joined the dancing procession down to the copulating figures lit by floodlights on the temple facades. They swirled and boogied, sinuous shadows over the sand. Dancers in saris, dancers in bell bottoms – Germans, Indians, Americans, French, Norwegian, Spanish – they swirled and pivoted, an international language of friendship and seduction. MJ wore Rudyard like an exotic turban, a monkey-hat upon her head. She was a goddess with multiple arms, a woman among women of color and women in barely anything at all. And as they danced, these taunting women, these sisters to the temple beauties, he pulled her into his arms and with her body and the beat of the music caressing him with joy and desire, he began the release of the jiva.

Chapter 8

*T*he next morning, they took the bus to the junction where they were to catch the train on to Calcutta. The bus was filled to capacity and already warming with the upcoming heat of the day. Rudyard chirped with disappointment – *not this again* – as they boarded. A little girl in the seat across the aisle stared at him, eyes filled with love, but like a celebrity used to a fawning public, Rudyard looked away.

The railway junction was a mass of bureaucratic confusion, food smells, body odors, smoke, and noise. They stood in lines for their tickets, shared a guava juice, fed Rudyard a mango. Child beggars tugged at their sleeves, railway dwellers slept on their *charpoys*. Women cooked stews in pots set upon the floor while their children brought them water from the toilet marked THIRD CLASS.

"Why should people," MJ said, nodding toward the women cooking on the floor, "Have to live like this?"

"I hear you, sister," Marcus said.

"You want hashish? One kilo twenty dollar."

A boy with a milky eye followed them back toward the boarding lines.

"You want LSD?"

"You have LSD?" Marcus said to the boy.

"I have pot. I have LSD."

"No. Thank-you, no," Marcus said, flicking Rudyard's tail from his face, taking MJ's hand. He was now the family man. The reformed addict.

Western travelers were milling about reading papers, listening to radios, huddled in animated, argumentative groups.

"The sky is falling," someone said in English, but then they heard more clearly.

"Saigon is falling."

At the area marked FIRST CLASS somber Americans huddled over a short wave radio. The voice of the newscaster sputtered in and out: -- *South Vietnamese storming the U.S. Embassy -- final helicopter evacuations -- President Minh's speech declaring the Saigon government completely dissolved.*

"You Americans made a big mistake," snarled a Scandinavian hippie, "You didn't know your enemy."

"Nobody is askin' your opinion," said a woman in a syrupy southern accent.

"And your President is corrupt," the Scandinavian added. Hunched beneath his backpack, he ducked back into his *Asia for the Hitchhiker*.

"Everybody's gotta have an opinion," the southern woman snorted. She wore a beaded necklace and jean jacket, and stood beside a man carrying a large camera. Two Samsonite suitcases, a suit carrier and a camera case were piled beside them.

"If women ruled," MJ said, "We'd have no more war."

Marcus noticed that she was wearing another one of her ubiquitous t-shirts – WOMAN POWER this one said. *"-- Ho Chi Minh City --"* The short wave sputtered. A group of European and American youths cheered, arms raised in the two-fingered "peace" salute.

"Pardon me, Sir," said the man with the camera, and nodded to the monkey on Marcus' shoulder, "Is that your son?"

MJ turned and looked at the couple, sizing them up as Americans but not fellow Americans.

"Sure," MJ interjected, "This is our boy Rudyard,"

"He's starting kindergarten this fall," Marcus rejoined.

The woman's mouth dropped, and then from it came a titter of nervous giggles. Rudyard blinked back, unimpressed with the woman's mirth. Marcus and MJ matched his deadpan expression.

"What do you find so amusing?" MJ asked, a cool blond when necessary. Tall and chilly.

The woman's giggles petered to silence.

The chain barrier had been removed and an official was taking tickets and directing travelers toward the train. MJ swung her backpack up onto her shoulders, eager to escape the couple that was so cruelly amused by their little family.

"I want to take yawl's picture," the man demanded, seizing MJ's arm. Marcus bumped the man's hand off.

"Excuse me," Marcus said, his voice low and deep and with something else in it.

The line was moving now, and people were crowding in, hurrying to get to the train.

The man was raising his camera to take the shot, but they turned away and moved fast through the crowds, dodging a luggage rack, swerving around a vendor selling tea. They walked fast together with Rudyard bouncing and chattering on Marcus' shoulder and MJ's backpack slamming against her, and when she turned around for one last look she saw the man futilely raising his camera to snap a picture, the woman angrily shouting at him, slowed to a halt in the stream of people by their cumbersome suitcases. And in the flash of the camera suddenly blinding passersby, the couple's suitcases were gone, robbed in an instant. Now the woman was really screaming, hurling racial invectives against the entire Indian race and all races.

Joining the population of brown and black and yellow faces, the railway dwellers and passengers and conductors and train whistle calling all aboard and the voice of bigotry drowned in a hiss of engine steam rising up off the tracks, MJ laughed grimly at the woman's blinding stupidity, for if the fall of Saigon was any sign, their world would soon be changing.

Chapter 9

"Quick, here," Marcus said, checking their tickets.

He ushered her up the iron steps into their sleeper car. Characters in their own thriller, they barreled down the narrow corridor, backpacks crashing against the walls and window, Rudyard shrieking with the thrill of the chase.

"In here." He pushed her into their compartment and slid shut the door with a slam.

Rudyard leaped off his shoulder and swung up onto the luggage rack and across the upper bed then back to the rack, his tail tip curling around the bars, arms swinging and flailing.

"Our son," Marcus said, throwing off his pack and gesturing to the monkey, "better not swing on the ceiling in kindergarten class."

Rudyard dropped a tiny yellow turd. It landed with a splat on his Birkenstock.

"Damn!"

"How can he go to kindergarten," MJ said, "When he isn't even potty trained!"

The train lurched and Marcus fell into the chair beneath the window and flung off his sandal.

"Eww!" MJ shrieked, dodging the sandal. It flipped against the wall behind her, staining it with yellow goo. "Someone stole their suitcases! Did you see?"

They were laughing now, unable to stop, she was almost breathless from the running and the excitement of seeing the couple getting their luggage stolen right under them.

"How do you stand it," she said.

"Stand what?" he replied.

So that was how they would treat it.

Their room was tiny but comfortable, with a lower sofa chair that turned into a bed and a chair on the other side of the window under which stood a drop leaf table with a small lotus flower in a squat, glass vase. Marcus cleaned his sandal and the wall with a tissue.

"Nothing so exhilarating like running from southern bigots," he said.

"Close the curtains!"

A man passed by their window, but it wasn't the southerner. Marcus drew the dusty curtain shut.

"I don't feel the least bit sorry for them," MJ said. Then added, "I suppose that's wrong."

"They'll be on this train."

"We've got to avoid them."

"You're the one who started the conversation by talking about woman power."

He reached for a small pillow and propped it behind his head then, thinking better of his remark, added, "Which I wholeheartedly approve of, by the way."

"I don't care if you approve."

"You don't?"

Pushing the envelope of their newfound love affair she said, "A woman without a man is like a fish without a bicycle."

"Say what?"

"I said – "

"Do you have that on one of your t-shirts too?"

"Yeah, I do," she replied, "It's here somewhere," and she began pulling clothes, all dirty, from her backpack.

"That's okay, I believe you."

The train hissed, then lurched, then lurched again, and spewing steam, whistle blowing, trundled out of the station.

With the outside station dwellers and food vendors whisking by and the train rocking over the tracks beneath them she thought, *Marcus is my lover and he is also a black man.*

The train gathered momentum, passed buildings and warehouses, clattered across the rail bridge over the Ganges River. They passed the Raj Ghat, one of many ancient stairways leading down into the river, and its lingam, a phallic symbol of the god Shiva. Along the banks stood a group of women bathing discreetly in their saris, and an old man praying.

Further up the holy river they could see smoke coming from the funeral pyres. They rode past a procession of villagers carrying their dead, swathed in white, on a bamboo stretcher. Sheltered behind their window, lulled by the rocking car, the scenes appeared serenely benign in the softening light. An Indian businessman on the bus from Agra had told her about a slab of stone in the Ganges bearing footprints left by the god Vishnu. In India, she thought, the gods are so real they even leave footprints.

The train was really moving now, rocking from side to side, the Ganges receding behind them alongside squalid shantytowns and the crumbling monuments standing beside dwellings patched with rubber tires and scraps of plastic. She thought of the women who lived in the tiny rubber tire dwellings and the children they struggled to feed and shelter. Who had time for books and reading? Apparently her Mad Grandma Maddy had decided they did. Or must.

She looked across at Marcus riding backwards to their destination in the seat opposite her. He stared moodily out at the shantytowns, a half-lidded, thoughtful expression on his handsome face.

"The Vietnam War is over."

It had to be said, her declarative, final pronouncement, no matter how obvious. He gave her a sharp look and again she thought of her father. When it came to the subject of war Marcus and her father were identical twins.

"Time to rebuild until the next war," he said.

Rudyard had fallen asleep on a folded blanket on the upper luggage rack. The close compartment air was cooling slightly.

"It's strange to say this to you," she said, "I mean, I barely know you. But I can imagine us aging together and creating an enduring love together. Not just romance, not the fun, easy stuff, but the growing old and facing death together stuff."

He didn't say anything, and just when she decided she'd gone too far and made a fool of herself, he spoke.

"That," he said, "Is the most romantic thing anyone has ever said to me."

She rose and kicked the heap of dirty laundry out of the way, straddled his lap, and gently kissed his neck and lips, the scent of curry and cinnamon emanating from their skin.

Chapter 10

$\mathcal{S}$he awoke to the startling dead silence of the motionless train. Marcus slept on oblivious as she rose halfway up from the narrow bed the porter had pulled from the wall only hours ago.

The train had stopped in the dark of what was to her a nameless town. She peered out at the innocuous cement station building and, above it, the dark blue hint of morning in the sky. Shapes with bundles came and went from station to train and back. The occasional spark from someone lighting a cigarette or a rare set of headlights illuminated the face of a traveler or vendor moving along the platform. It had been hours since she had last eaten, and she was suddenly hungry. She saw a man selling *samosas* from a basket and another vendor passing a cup of steaming tea. Dare she get off the train for only a second?

A large baggage cart trundled to another area of the platform, exposing a slim older woman in a purple and green sari.

A woman with bobbed fiery red hair streaked bourbon gold.

Marcus groaned, turned over and continued to sleep. In the dark MJ groped for her jeans and found her sandals. She kept her eyes on the woman. She was watching the porter wheel along her luggage: A large leather valise and two sealed boxes. MJ wondered if the boxes contained books.

She unlocked the door of their cabin and stepped carefully by the sleeping forms of mothers and children, saris protectively blanketing their faces. As if in a dream she jumped down from the train and floated

317

through the blue-dark morning air. The red-haired woman stood with her back to her, her posture erect, the light hem of her sari wavering gently in the steamy exhaust.

"Grandma Maddy?"

The woman turned.

"Mary Jane!" her grandmother Maddy Rosario said. She didn't appear in the least surprised to see her, and this alone made her suspect. MJ had traveled through all of India looking for her, and now that she had found her, it seemed almost by sheer coincidence. Was the woman skipping town again? And what town was she skipping? Where were they?

"What are you doing here?"

"I'm catching the train," this calm, nicely coifed woman in the sari replied, "So as to join you at the school in Calcutta."

"But —" MJ looked around at the middle-of-nowhere station. "What are you doing *here*?"

"Oh, I travel to many places."

The red-haired woman didn't look like a grandmother. She looked like an author who wrote shocking books about love, passion and sex. Bands of gold bracelets encircled her elegant wrists. Her skin was darkly tanned and she wore black kohl around her deep-set dark brown eyes. And now those eyes gazed at the pendant against MJ's chest.

"I am so pleased to see you have the Heirloom at last, for it will make all the difference in your life to come, you will see."

Sure, and I only had to travel to the other side of the world to get it, MJ thought.

"I've promised to bring it back to Mother."

"MJ dear," said her grandmother, "You do not owe your mother the Heirloom. Your mother must make her own life."

After all this time, after all her mother's stories about Mad Grandma Maddy, MJ struggled to quell her distrust.

"Mother said you abandoned her."

"Oh dear," said the woman who at least had the decency to look ashamed, or abashed, or saddened, and now MJ couldn't figure out what the woman was up to, only that she was another sort of person altogether, the sort of person she had never known and the sort of person she now wanted to know, even if she disapproved. "You have been sorely brainwashed, but she is right in a way. How is your mother?"

"Fine, struggling to be the artist she was meant to be," MJ said. She couldn't avoid her accusatory tone. "I didn't know about your girls' schools."

"I will show you the one in Calcutta and then we can travel on to my home in Tamil Nadu. When are you due back at university, dear?"

"I haven't started university."

"Yes, but you are starting somewhere aren't you?"

"Berkeley," MJ said doubtfully, "Women's studies."

"Well, that's fabulous!" This woman who was her lost grandmother replied.

Were they really standing on a train platform in the middle of nowhere in the heart of India talking about Women's Studies? She heard the sound of a train whistle, but it was far away. No one seemed in a hurry, and the porter was standing nearby, talking to a conductor, the boxes and luggage on the platform beside him. Then she heard voices shouting, the hiss of steam, the whistle again, only louder, furiously loud, like a scream, or was it a voice that was screaming?

"We must get on," said her grandmother, "and we'd better hurry." She turned and walked abruptly toward the train. Metal wheels screeched against the rails. The train began to move.

"MJ!" It was Marcus's voice, frantic, distant.

Suddenly and without hesitating, her grandmother took two firm strides toward the moving train and held up her hand toward the porter who lifted her elderly body up into the moving car like another piece of luggage. She turned around to MJ still on the platform.

"Mary Jane! Hurry!"

Her grandmother was rolling away, shouting in Hindu to the porter, but the man shrugged and shook his head and the train continued moving.

"MJ, come on!" Marcus was standing on the lower step of the vestibule of the second car coming her way. He held onto the handrail and reached out his hand.

"Jump up!" he shouted above the shrill of the whistle.

At first she was able to keep pace without running, but the train was moving faster and now she was running toward Marcus, he was moving away from her, and she had nothing, no money, no identification, just the jeans on her body and her WOMAN POWER t-shirt and the heirloom.

"Hustle, baby, come on, do it!" Marcus yelled.

She ran as fast as she could and jumped up onto the step and in the same instant Marcus was pulling her to safety, enveloping her into his wide strong chest.

"You're okay," he said, "I gotcha."

"I don't think it applies to me," she said, gulping in breaths, heart racing against his.

"What doesn't?"

"A woman without a man is like a fish without a bicycle."

"Mary Jane, thank all goddesses, you made it!"

This woman who was grandmother stood firm in the rollicking passageway in her sari and scuffed hurachi sandals.

"Marcus Jones," he said, and shook her little hand, "We've met."

"The good American," she replied. He never looked so big as he did now beside her elegant little grandmother. "We must have tea and samosas in my compartment."

MJ grasped the Heirloom on its chain and said, "You want it back, don't you?"

Her grandmother's regretfully firm expression said it all.

"But it's mine now."

"It doesn't belong to anyone."

"Yes, it does. It's an *heirloom*. It was my great grandmother's and her aunt's, and it was meant to be passed down, and my mother was supposed to give it to me, but you stole it from her."

The outburst was more than she expected to unleash, but it was the truth and it had to be said.

"I am sorry for that," her grandmother said. She *did* look sorry, sorry yet unbending. "But there have always been greater things at stake than Marjorie Berthe's artistic fame."

MJ looked to Marcus, but he held up his hands, palms out, as in *keep me out of this.*

"So you've brought me to India," she said, "And had me go through this obstacle course of tests where I even sacrificed my *blood*, and now you want the Heirloom back?"

Feet set wide for balance on the floor of the lurching train, Maddy Rosario crossed her arms and studied her granddaughter carefully.

"No, my dear. That is for you to decide."

And for the first time since they met, her grandmother stepped forward and gently hugged her, and when she hugged her grandmother back she felt how the woman was fine-boned yet steely.

Fulfill a promise to my mother, MJ thought, *or keep it for myself. Or give it back.*

"You will know what to do," Maddy Rosario said, "Come have breakfast in my car, you poor dears must both be hungry. I have enough to feed the whole train. And I will, you know."

"Thank-you ma'am, I appreciate that," Marcus said.

"It's 'Maddy,' please," she replied.

"What about Rudyard?"

"I'll go get him," MJ said.

"Rudyard?"

"Our son," Marcus said, and winked.

MJ struggled for balance, stepping gingerly, as the train clattered over the tracks, careful not to wake the figures along the passageway. Some were already awakening under glare of the desert sunrise seeping through the sooty windows. Others lay still under piles of clothing and tightly strapped bags.

A trio of somber-faced little girls played a hushed cat's cradle with a piece of string. She pictured them reading books, if they had them, and she remembered the little girl back at the Kali Shrine with *Goodnight Moon,* the book that her grandmother had for some reason never given her. MJ had grown up with *Goodnight Moon,* another copy of it anyway; she remembered her father reading it to her. And now her grandmother had finally, nearly two decades later, passed the timeless book to another child.

The cat's cradle girls turned to look at her in passing, their eyes large and curious. *What would their futures hold,* she wondered, *who will they become?*

Suddenly Mary Jane Johnson understood why her grandmother had brought her to India. She also understood why the book once meant for her had been passed into the hands of another little girl. Ultimately there was no determining the fate of the heirloom. The mysterious jewel crafted in prehistory from a meteoric piece of the universe had a secret history – and fate – all its own.

"*You ask the universe a question,*" the Living Shakti had said, "*and you receive an answer.*"

It was because of the girls. This was why MJ no longer needed the amulet.

Because they did.

Chapter 11

*I*n Sanskrit the name "Elakshi" means "woman with bright eyes," and that was what The Living Shakti's were: Electric, tumbling kaleidoscopic turquoise, indigo and jade, bright as sea glass.

Elakshi's appearance at the Calcutta girls' school came with much speculation and excitement. Who is the Living Shakti, the girls wanted to know. How does a woman emerge from the burning pyre of society's constraints and not only cheat death, but become a living goddess? Elaskshi was everything her name promised to be, and with words of candor and insight, she urged the schoolgirls to open their eyes and ears and hearts to what they were about to encounter. They would soon see, hear and feel something that would change their lives.

With such a fanfare, the American visitors arrived with books and food. Among them was a tall brown-eyed blond woman with a monkey on her shoulder. The woman wore dangling from a chain on her neck a glimmering object. Then in a wistful manner she lifted the object up over her head and passed it to a girl. The object was then passed from one girl to the next, each receiving it with expressions of puzzlement and awe.

Within each infinitesimal moment, as the jewel with its enigmatic meteoric shard gleamed upon the person of its wearer, figures were seen passing within: A tribal queen of northern Britain who battled those who'd enslaved her people; a Maori girl who threw off her Victorian stays to ride a whale into the sea; a suffragist who burst from her room to join friends in their fight for the vote. Women warriors and mothers and stateswomen; poets and dreamers; seekers and speakers; they were now an alliance of women empowered: A doctor who returned to her childhood slum in Calcutta with new medicines and birth control; an Iranian poet who challenged the religious authorities on the practice of stoning women; a lawyer who fought human rights abuses.

And there would be more in the future: Indian women, Afghani women, African women, Amazonian women; women in burkas and women in bikinis. They would meet the teachers of their time with names like Medicine Woman, Elakshi, Claus, and Lula, and they would all come with the same message: *Know who you are.*

Before returning with Marcus Jones to the United States where they would attend college and become human rights lawyers and found a nonprofit organization for disadvantaged immigrant women and finally marry, MJ Johnson entrusted the heirloom to her grand-mother. Maddy Rosario in turn kept the crystal pendant under the custody of the Living Shakti at the girls' school in Calcutta, but she promised that it would someday be passed on to MJ's daughter, if she had a daughter. Until then, the transformative piece of ancient jewelry would serve as an amulet for other girls and women of the world.

MJ couldn't say for certain the pendant held magical properties nor claim that it had changed her life, but she understood after having pos-sessed it that she *knew herself* in a way she hadn't before. Had the time been ripe? Or had the universe answered? To MJ, the *why* it had hap-pened wasn't as crucial as *what* had happened.

One thing was certain, and that was that before she and Marcus said goodbye to little Rudyard, who would stay in his native land to be fed kumquats from Maddy's orchard in Tamil Nadu, MJ learned of her grandmother's regret over failing to be a mother to the only child she bore. *"You make a better grandmother,"* was MJ's response, and Mad Grandma Maddy was unable to turn away in time to hide the tears.

Back home, MJ was met with a firestorm of blame and recrimination when she informed her mother she had left the heirloom in India, but the brilliant painter restricted by the label "woman artist" could no longer instill guilt in her daughter, and MJ could only say, *"I can't live your life for you, Mother, you have to live your own."*

MJ and Marcus settled in Far Rockaway, Queens in the house left to the family by MJ's great uncle Stephen, not far from Marcus' mother, Jana Jones. And because they lived close, their children Johan and Maya grew up knowing and loving their paternal "Nana Jana" while MJ would return to India over time to visit her "Mad Grandma Maddy," who turned out to not be so mad after all.

Then one day in the fall of 2002, when Marcus and MJ Johnson-Jones' nonprofit Gandela Center was undergoing a peak crisis of critical need, MJ received a garbled cellphone call from India - *"Your grandmother... lost... wandering... dehydration... fever..."*

MJ boarded the next flight out of JFK bound for New Dehli, and within 48 hours 94 year old Maddy Rosario lay across three tourist class seats on a flight headed for home, her tiny feet resting on her granddaughter's lap.

Like a beacon the crystal pendant upon the old woman's chest drew her through early passageways, from the speakeasies where she'd drunk bootleggers gin and danced the Charleston to Martin returning home from the Great War. In her fever she wondered how different her life would have been had she opened her mother's letters on board the *Aquitania*. Would Martin have chosen to love her and would she have been guided toward another future with other children and who would those children have been? Would she have become someone other than the Lost Girl? If she had worn the amulet on the *Aquitania* would Martin? Martin? Martin...?

MJ heard the rattled breathing of the iron-willed old woman and the fevered first syllable — *Mar* — unaware her grandmother was speaking of a man who had died over half a century ago.

"A beautiful baby you were," said Grandma Maddy, "I would have loved to have spoiled you like a proper grandmother."

MJ heard the regret for all that her grandmother had chosen: Leaving Marjorie Berthe, taking the amulet to India, alienating a daughter who punished her by refusing her access to her only grandchild.

"Well now you're coming home to meet your great grandchildren!"

"More grandchildren?"

The old woman sounded alarmed. Exhausted, too.

"You'll give Maya the heirloom someday," MJ said, "Remember what Elaskshi said? 'The teacher comes when the soul is ready.'"

Grandma Maddy made a long breath of an exhale. The plane buffeted in the dark over the Atlantic. MJ listened for another breath. She didn't want her grandmother dying on her lap on a transatlantic flight from New Dehli to JFK. She didn't want her grandmother dying, period.

"Maya," the old woman said, fingering the pendant at her chest. "I will pass the heirloom to her. And then she will *know* — " and now her grandmother spoke forcefully, rallying, "*Who she is.*"

Contrary to all appearances, Maddy Rosario wasn't yet done with living.

The Storm

Morning

Maya woke early on the morning after Hurricane Sandy and looked out her window. It was barely light; no one was up. The rain and wind had stopped and the floodwaters of the Atlantic and Jamaica Bay had receded from her street, leaving behind carpets of sand, trashed cars, torn tree branches, and junk. Lots and lots of waterlogged, twisted, ruined junk.

Their family heirloom would also be junk if she didn't return to her great grandmother's room at Sea View and find it.

She dressed in jeans, sweater, jacket and knit cap. *Forget the shower.* There was no hot water anyway. There was also no electricity.

Slipping quietly down the first floor hallway, she passed both of her grandmothers snoring in their beds. Marjorie Berthe's famous "Body In Red" painting was propped against a wall, and it didn't look too bad, almost okay, given that Great Grandma Maddy had floated on it the night before. It had representational splashes of red and black paint of a woman jumping up, as if clawing toward something in the sky, and was pretty amazing really. Maya figured her grandmother would milk it for all it was worth, the story of how she saved her mother using the canvas as a floating device. The painting might even be worth more now.

She had left her beach cruiser on the porch and it was amazingly intact, pushed up on its side against the house, covered in sand and debris. She carried the bike down the squishy wood steps, mounted it, and pedaled down the street toward where she saw the Rover.

Her dad's car had ended up in someone's front lawn, like she'd parked it there drunk. She was afraid to look, but she peered inside, and there it was, the waterlogged bundle in the back. She opened the back door and water poured out. She half expected to see fish flopping about, but no, just sand.

She picked up the saturated bundle and unwrapped the blanket, dropping it on the back seat. Her grandmother's toothbrush fell out along with some of the framed pictures she'd grabbed in haste: A beautiful dark-skinned woman in a lacy Victorian blouse, and a picture of a young man in what looked to be a World War I uniform. The water had seeped through the frames to the edges of the photographs, but they weren't ruined. Neither was the portrait painting of her great great grandmother Madeline. It was damp but the painted image of Madeline's beautiful face and celadon eyes and honey colored hair was solidly there along with the representational pendant hanging from her neck.

The heirloom. In the painting, but not in the flesh.

She was back on her beach cruiser after plopping Great Grandma Maddy's toothbrush into the cup in the downstairs bathroom and leaving the pictures to dry on the breakfast table.

Rockaway was beginning to wake up. There was a kind of glutted shock in the air. People moved slowly as if underwater, assimilating all the destruction nature had wrought. As there was no electricity she saw some folks firing up barbecues from propane tanks to make breakfast.

She could hear the ocean roaring still, but it had retreated from the streets, leaving behind the strangest sights:

A VW atop a fire hydrant.

Giant tree roots hanging on telephone wires.

Lawns turned into beaches with seashells, sea foam and sand.

Emergency vehicles cruised the streets, checking downed power lines, hauling away sand and garbage, clearing the gutters of debris. Lots of debris. Soggy books, old video tapes, clothing, broken chairs, stuffed toys and pillows and soaked cardboard boxes and matted papers. It was as if the whole peninsula had thrown some insane party with people deciding to toss out everything they owned.

The Sea View Nursing Home was nearly unrecognizable. The front porch steps were ripped in half, the Stars-and-Stripes long-gone, and there was no furniture outside for the old people to sit in. Maya leaned her bike against a rotten board and climbed over the broken floorboards through the front door. The lobby was desolate, the elevator still out of service. *Where was everybody?*

She heard the din of clamoring voices and the steady sounds of purposeful movement on the floor above.

She emerged from the stairwell to elderly people in wheelchairs lining the second floor hall, some with heads bowed, silent, waiting, others staring off, confused, uncertain. An old man lay sleeping on a cot, another old women struggled to eat without her dentures. Exhausted and harried staff tried to feed and reassure, but Maya could see right away that it was overwhelming. There were too many old and helpless and not enough able-bodied.

She spotted the blind Mrs. Espinoza sitting outside her door, head cocked, listening patiently as a meal cart rolled past.

"Hey, Mrs. Espinoza, how're you doing," Maya said, and grasped her hand. It was cold and soft, and it crushed Maya's fingers in its grip.

"Hello?" said the old woman. She was dark as mahogany and just as strong too, and when she turned her puzzled expression up to her, Maya remembered she had dementia.

"You're okay, Mrs. Espinoza, the storm's gone and we're bringing you breakfast."

The heirloom was maybe floating among debris somewhere upstairs on the third floor in Great Grandma Maddy's room, but Maya wasn't going to let go of Mrs. Espinoza's hand. Not for a thing.

The heirloom would have to wait.

Later that evening, after she had spent the day bringing food and touching and comforting frightened elderly people, Maya returned to Great Grandma Maddy's uninhabitable room on the third floor of Sea View.

The air was chilled by an Atlantic breeze blasting through a broken window and the bed was soaked. Perfume bottles floated in salty puddles beside mottled headscarves and old lady knitting projects, tangled and coated in sand. The elegant vanity had floated to the middle of room, and when she opened the tiny drawer she found beneath the handkerchiefs a plastic sandwich bag containing an envelope.

This is it, she thought, her chest pounding with an unexpected anticipatory beating of her heart, but when she opened the envelope she found only a piece of paper with a thin old-fashioned scrawl:

Know who you are.

No pendant. No heirloom.

She looked inside the other drawers, but they were filled with the wet items she'd expected to see: Hairpins and old lady underwear and silk stockings and garters and handkerchiefs and glittery old beaded purses. She searched the rest of the room too and, recalling Marjorie Berthe's comment about her mother's penchant for hiding things, looked inside the cut glass jars and bottles that had fallen on the floor and hadn't broken. She found handfuls of foreign coins, soaked candies, paperclips and perfume residue and pieces of broken flapper beads. But nothing that resembled the pendant in the painting.

It was gone. Lost from their lives, this amulet that would presumably alter the course of her young life as it had done for her brilliant and successful grandmothers and her phenomenal mother too. And since Maya was turning eighteen and had decided to major in political science at New York City College which *wasn't Harvard, wasn't Brown*, she saw her inferior life stretching before her and figured she would become ordinary, just like Grandma Marjorie Berthe said she would be. She would fail to arrive at her transcendental destiny.

I will never know who I am, she thought.

"Everything's fucked," Maya said to her mother as they dragged wet and ruined bedding up the stairs from their flooded basement that evening. She had shown her the note and given it back to Great Grandma Maddy, who'd awakened after sleeping all day. It had been a grueling evening for the old woman and Maya suspected more thoughts and words and memories would be slipping beyond her 105-year-old mind. At her age, she had every right not to remember.

"Everything's fucked for me," Maya repeated, "I'm fucked."

"Everything is not fucked," her mother said.

MJ had carried boxes of soaked and ruined books and pictures from her basement floor up to be collected by the dump trucks that would be circling the 'hood in the ensuing weeks and months, and she would be back at Gandela Center the next day to help Dad register the women and children refugees he'd brought back from Italy. Her mother never seemed fazed by the heaps of responsibilities and things she had to do, only by what others failed to do, such as help people in need.

Maya saw her mother as one of those boomers who worked and played hard and whose only complaint was that she needed more time to work and play harder.

"Let me tell you something about that note – " her mother began.

"Don't tell me I'm young. Being young doesn't make it better you know. In fact it makes it worse."

"I wasn't going to accuse you of being young," said MJ, "Heaven forbid!"

They tugged and pulled the soaked and filthy mattress down the porch steps and dumped it at the curb next to the boxes of waterlogged books. When they were done MJ stretched her back and adjusted her headband. She was still blondish, and she rarely wore make-up. Her skin was flushed pink and about as different from Maya's as could be. Maya looked more like her dad and people sometimes thought she was adopted, which never failed to irritate MJ, and sometimes when she'd had too much wine she'd shout *my daughter looks plenty like me,* and Dad would laugh and say, *sure, MJ, she's got your eyes,* which was true, since MJ's were brown too. Score one for Mom.

"I was just going to repeat," her mother said, "What the note said. '*Know who you are.*' And assure you that you have always known who you are. From the moment you were born."

MJ then drew Maya into the crook of her arm and kissed the top of her hair that sprung up wild in the damp and was extra curly now.

With or without the heirloom, Maya and the girls of her generation would speak up, stand up, and move on with a magic all their own.

The next day, when Maya was volunteering with the Rockaway Youth Task Force bringing food and supplies to the elderly in high-rises without power, she encountered Joshua MacFadden coming halfway up a seventh floor emergency stairwell. He was administering flu shots to people who couldn't leave their homes, he said. She was bringing hot Meals-on-Wheels, she said.

"When this war is over – " he said, and laughed, and when she didn't understand what he was talking about he had to explain that was what the soldier says in an old war movie before he gets killed, and so she laughed too, now that she got it, although she didn't like to think of anyone getting killed, not after hearing how many had died in the storm, but she hoped Joshua McFadden would think she had a sense of humor.

"Okay, not so funny," said Joshua, "But what I mean is, when this is over, do you still want to go see movie?"

"Sure," she said, "As long as it's not a war movie."

"Or about hurricanes."

"Or vampires."

"You don't like vampire movies?"

"I hate vampire movies," she said with a vengeance, "but I like the old Boris Karloff ones," she added, which was probably why he set down the med bag and kissed her.

Marjorie Berthe returned to what she thought would be the burnt remains of her Breezy Point studio and found it, amazingly, standing, a lone house surrounded by the ashes of her neighbors' homes. It was an unfamiliar sensation, not being a victim. She almost felt victimized, knowing she would have to acknowledge the misfortune of others.

She also had to thank her ex-husband Aaron for gallantly rescuing her work from the flooded gallery in Soho. He'd stopped drinking at last, being almost eighty and no longer capable of imbibing an entire bottle of bourbon in a single sitting without it threatening to eventually kill him. He was the same handsome man she remembered, the tall

Korean War vet who drove her to the Village on the night that changed her life.

She'd always claimed it was the heirloom that transformed her, but perhaps it was other things too: Learning that same week that she was the daughter of Maddy Rosario and Max Hansman, then understanding in a flash of art, marijuana and lost virginity the rebel painter inside her.

And Aaron, loving Aaron. That had to account for something.

At 105-years-of-age, Maddy Rosario was learning Latin. Not the conjugation of verbs or the painstaking accumulation of a vocabulary into her sieve of a brain, but rather phrases — Maddy perceived them as messages — handed down through the millenniums:

> *Carpe diem.* Seize the day.
> *Tempus fugit.* Time flies.
> And another floating around in the zeitgeist:
> *Idem amor initium.* The origin of our identity is love.

The meaning of the words floated beyond her grasp, but it was their *feeling* that remained with her. What she did these days, sleeping and waking, nodding off in the guest room of her granddaughter's house, MJ's fine husband Marcus sometimes popping his handsome head in, was mull over the *feeling* of words.

> *Idem amor initium.* The origin of our identity is love.

Love. She had loved many and she had loved forcefully. It filled her up. She was filled with love. She slept with it, she dreamed of it. Love was in the voices of family in the hallway and in the faces she met on the other side. While the voices of her family slowly faded, the faces on the other side grew more distinct and suddenly, rushing before her, she saw Max, the father of her child taken in his prime, and she saw Martin, the boy damaged from the Great War. And all she felt was love.

The heirloom floats out of Jamaica Bay inside a stoppered deco perfume bottle bought at a Paris flea market in 1925.

It drifts along in a mass of objects and joins the Gulf Stream currents of the North Atlantic, swirling in the wreckage of houses and their contents: Antlers of a stuffed deer's head from Maine, a Sponge Bob from a Universal Studios tour, a lace bridal veil from Red Hook. It moves en mass to the blue calm of the Sargasso Sea, devoid of current, destination, human manufacture or want, a sea where ships have been lost, their contents never excavated or found, gold amulets and wine casks never traded.

But the amulet is another story. It came from a meteorite fashioned into an ornament worn by an Iron Age queen buried in a Viking ship found by an English seaman passed to a Whale Rider. Lost and found, it adorned generations of women. And now, floating inside its glass coffin, the pendant works its mysterious ways. Faces flicker like lightning in a bottle, causing the tiny vessel to lean toward a faint draft and skip upon the water.

The bottle escapes the doldrums of the Sargasso Sea and its cargo, never lost to itself, continues its voyage.

The Next Girl

*"The greatest threat to extremism isn't drones firing missiles,
but girls reading books."*

Nicholas Kristof

The girl is an infrared heartbeat viewed from a satellite in space, a pixilated image running. The black burka they made her wear flaps like wings unfurling. She sheds the burka but not her wings.

She has lived in forced captivity under the demonic Boko Haram. They have bombed churches and markets, subjugated her sisters and mothers, beaten and burned her and worked her bones and raped her flesh.

But tonight the storm is her mother-in-arms. Mother pounds the earth and fells giant trees and turns the demon fighters into little men huddled in shelters.

And so she runs. She runs with the wild animals because she has discovered power in her willingness to die.

The girl is more than an infrared heartbeat viewed from a satellite in space, a pixilated image running.

For days and nights she runs and hides, and now she leaps from the cliffs, flying for but an instant before hurling herself into the sea. Wings become fins and they propel her through sea currents unknown in her inland village. No longer chattel — never again, she would rather die – she swims to the boat and is pulled up by fellow migrants sailing for the coast of Sicily.

It is a long voyage and some nearly die but they are rescued.

She sends word back to her family that she is safe, safe for now, until chance or fate decides what will happen. She joins other girls at the camp and steers clear of the boys and men who notice her beauty for she has known the brutality of men who say she has no right to think or be educated. She washes dishes in the cafeteria and stands in the food line. Time creeps by. She is neither patient nor wise, but has learned that it is smart to appear to be so.

She files applications for immigrant status and hopes for a small break in the impasse, a promise of change, a glimpse of a new future in a country the demons claim is evil but which to her is a haven called freedom.

She is more than an infrared heartbeat view from a satellite in space, more than a pixilated image.

On the day she isn't washing dishes at the camp cafeteria or standing in the food line or waiting to hear on her immigrant status she rides the bus down to the seashore. The beach is a rare solitary place where she finds the occasional sand dollar or scalloped seashell.

Or a perfume bottle with a cork stopper.

She nudges the bottle with her sandaled toe. Unknown objects in bottles are known to explode, but not this one. The bottle is old, its glassine surface etched in square-shaped designs unfamiliar to her. She bends to pick it up. The cork stopper holds tight and there is no leakage, preserving the object inside. She pries the cork loose and when she upends the bottle a chain with a crystal falls like a burst of shooting star into her palm. She has never seen anything so beautiful and there is no doubt about it:

It is hers.

She slips the chain over her head and holds it up between her fingers to study it closely. And that is when she sees her. A face. Then another face, and another, girls and women through the ages until she sees her own face fading into the silvery interior and she is just here, standing on a beach.

It is valuable, this treasure she's found, and so she tucks her secret knowledge inside her blouse against her skin.

Back at the camp she joins the others. She shows them the empty bottle but says nothing of what she found inside. For now she is cautious, for now she will wait and see.

A lawyer with immigration services has arrived at the camp. He is a tall Black American and he has her name on a list. When he speaks with her she blurts out that she will someday be mayor of her town and he doesn't laugh at her like the others, nor does he pat her on the head or tell her to be quiet. He says he can take her to the city of New York in America where she can learn English and go to school and meet other American girls. He says he has a daughter her age.

Her limbs have loosened; she feels a different step in her walk. No longer will she crouch, frightened, hurt, damaged, shrouded and defeated in black. She strides.

We have no jihad on the menu today.

She hears from the camp radio a song she forgot in her months of captivity, one she once listened to with her sisters as they washed and danced by the river. The words are about being held down and having had enough and getting back up like a champion and dancing through fire and telling the world *you're gonna hear me roar.*

She presses her secret multifaceted gemstone against her thundering heart and sees:

> An ancient warrior queen battling for the freedom of her people.
> A Whale Rider.
> A women marching with sisters.
> A writer seeing the world.
> An artist painting in red.
> A traveler finding her soul mate.
> A girl braving a storm.

She will speak, she will howl, she will run with the tigers, the sisters, the army of women.

She knows who she is.

Idem amor initium

Acknowledgements

This novel began years ago in a writing workshop referred to by some as "the woman's group," and like the women in the group *The Heirloom Girls* has been through many transformations. I'd like to thank them – Jane Alcala, Miriam Sidanius, Rebecca Carpenter and Rachel Canon – for their early encouragement. And a thank-you in memoriam to my early mentor and teacher, Brian Moore, who urged his students to include a fundamental aspect to every character, which is how she earns a living!

I also want to thank Johnye Culler for reading aloud every word of an early draft to my father, and Ellen Glasgow for that Thanksgiving we will always remember.

Many others read and offered invaluable insights on early versions, including fellow film industry story analysts Geoffrey Grode, Chris Bomba and Julie Robitaille. Dear friends Doug Schneider, Paul Ilmer, Carrie Zivetz, Allan Leavitt, Maddy Talbot and my sister Cynthia Culler also offered their views on early drafts. Thank you to all of you for taking the time to slog through those early explorations.

And thank you most of all to my husband, Doug Vaughan, who read, edited and endured all the many permutations of the manuscript (including "the one hundred year marriage!") leading to this one.

Plenty of books helped me time travel through this last past century, notably George and Pearl Adam's *A Book About Paris*, Robin Tolmach Lakoff's *Language and Woman's Place*, Barbara Ehrenreich and Deidre

English's *For Her Own Good*, Kate Walbert's *A Short History of Women,* and Michael Kimmel's *Manhood In America.* Finally, Clarissa Pinkola Estes' *Women Who Run With the Wolves* introduced me to La Que Sabe, The One Who Knows "the personal past and the ancient past for she has survived generation after generation... an archivist of feminine intuition."

54104280R00215

Made in the USA
Charleston, SC
23 March 2016